# Apitcote
# The Conjurer – Book Three

Wings Press, Inc.

## Peggy P. Parsons

# Apitcote, Book 3 – The Visionary

When VJ opened her eyes, she felt as though she had slept for hours and hours. But she was utterly disoriented.

Where was she? Not in the bed where she had gone to sleep. Not in the mansion either. But she was with Holt. On a single bed, snuggled close. Both were fully dressed. Except for their feet. She heaved a quiet sigh, not knowing whether to be relieved or disappointed.

As she lay there trying to figure out how she had ended up in bed with Holt, she had a vague sensation of being inside a ski-like cage plunging at warp speed down a deep, dark shaft. Her heartbeat sped up and her pulse raced.

She hadn't caught her breath when Holt said, "Good morning."

"Where are we?"

Holt looked around, his expression amused. "In my cottage."

"In Apricot?"

"Yeah."

She had foreseen the future. She hadn't seen this. "We can't be."

"Where do you think we are?"

Miffed by his calm, she tried to leap off the bed. But her wrist was tied to Holt's and he didn't budge. She glared at the yellow ribbon. "What is this bloody thing?" She jerked his hand with hers.

"Looks like a ribbon."

"Why is it tied around our wrists?"

# What They Are Saying About Apitcote – Book 3

"WOW! Peggy Parsons' third book in the Apitcote series is the best! You will love getting to know the new characters and how they save their alternate universe. I loved the mixture of a love story and suspense in this book!"

—Kathy Villa
Sun City Poms Marching Director

# Apitcote

# The Conjurer – Book Three

Peggy P. Parsons

**A Wings ePress, Inc.**

Romantic Fantasy Novel

# Wings ePress, Inc.

Edited by: Jeanne Smith
Copy Edited by: Christie Kraemer
Executive Editor: Jeanne Smith
Cover Artist: Trisha FitzGerald-Jung

*All rights reserved*



Wings ePress Books
www.wingsepress.com



Published In the United States Of America

Wings ePress, Inc.
3000 N. Rock Road
Newton, KS 67114

# Dedication

To my sisters and brothers: Kathy, Lorraine, Jim, Dan, and to my beloved husband, Bill, who helped make my writing possible. Also to my special editor, Jeanne Smith, whose suggestions and patience are very much appreciated.

Every step we take on earth
brings us to a new world.
—*Garcia Lorca*

# *Prologue*

Holt's pulse raced when he read the atext from Mist.

*All kew mates requested to stay after tonight's kew meeting and sleep in the dream chamber. Purpose: decide best way to help newest denizens acclimate to living here.*

He had a hunch his kew mates would ask him to find Verity Jane, the doctor he loved, and convince her to return and work with Minalu's sept, a group of a hundred and forty-three people, mostly women, who had accepted the kew's invitation to leave their cave dwelling and live with them and Apitcote's other denizens.

Sitting down, Holt willed his pulse to calm. A moment later, his heart thumped as he recalled the wonderful days he had spent with Verity Jane on the surface and here in Apitcote.

"My homeland is a special realm beneath the surface of the earth with its own sun, moon and stars, where magic is common and illness is rare, as are some of our words," he explained after she agreed to visit.

"Such as?" she had asked, smiling and caressing his cheek as they sat in her mum's London flat.

"We use enquay for entries and exits to Apitcote. Atext for text messages. Afone instead of smart phone. Apad for tablets and iPads. Trax for train systems to and from the surface. Mater for mother. Pater for father. Our neighborhoods are klusters, and we eat in dining halls called constats."

Verity Jane grinned. "Brits have their way of using language. We often omit vowels and we say in hospital, not in the hospital, in car park, not in the parking lot, and we say goose pimples, not goose bumps."

Holt's afone beeped, rudely interrupting his reminiscing. He glanced at the atext. A new photo of Harmony, the little girl who now owned his heart. She lived on the surface with her mater and grandmater. Someday Harmony would return to Apitcote and he would share more of her life.

~ * ~

Holt arrived at the chateau fifteen minutes early. His eight kew mates were already there. Five, two of whom were twins, shared the same June birthdate. The other four shared the same August birthdate. Six mates had been born in Apitcote. The other three had come from the surface.

Rene was tied to Drew, who came from the surface.

Tess was tied to Dane, Rene's twin.

Mist was tied to Jordan, who came with Drew from the surface.

Monteith was both tied and married to Juhree, who came from the surface.

Holt was the only single kew mate, as well as the newest.

The kew governed Apitcote and had assumed leadership last year when the eight leaders who named Apitcote during civil war times all passed away on the same day. Holt had joined the kew three months ago and been gifted with the ability to levitate shortly thereafter.

~ * ~

Holt awakened at the same time as his mates. Looking at each one before she spoke, Rene said, "We all had the same dream."

"The same idea," her twin, Dane, added.

"And we came to the same conclusion," Mist said.

"Right," Monteith agreed. "Are you willing to accept the task, Holt?"

"Do I have a choice?"

"Always," Tess said, "but you're our best hope."

"Minalu's sept needs more than a tutelary. They need a doctor with Verity Jane's skill and expertise," Rene said. "And I sense Apitcote needs her visions."

# One

*September 2020*

"Hello, Verity Jane."

VJ's heart ground to a halt. Holt! The man she loved but hadn't seen for three years. What brought him to the surface? How had he found her? And why was he dressed in scrubs, masquerading as a hospital employee?

She opened her mouth to ask. Staggered backwards instead as blades whirled between them like an electric fan gone haywire. She closed her eyes. The speed of the fan increased. Spinning blades backed away. Moved closer. Dizziness threatened. She started to fall, but Holt caught her. She inhaled a whiff of his piney scent before the fan exploded and a vision claimed her.

When she opened her eyes, she lay on a hospital trolley. Holt stood at her side, along with her boss, Flint, who had ignored her request for advancement last month and hired a bloke for the physician's assistant position she coveted still.

"Are you ill?" Flint asked, clearly annoyed.

VJ gathered her composure like an invisible cloak. Never before had she fainted or had spinning sensations precede a vision. Seeing Holt had put her in a bloody dither.

"I'm perfectly fine," she said and began to sit up.

But Flint locked his gloved hands on her shoulders. "Be still. Your vitals haven't been taken."

"I'm not ill. I just had a bit of a shock."

"I'm the reason she fainted," Holt said. "She thought I was dead."

His fib knocked her emotions further off kilter. She inhaled quickly, swallowed a dram of saliva and coughed to relieve raw discomfort.

Holt's eyes filled with concern. "Are you okay?"

"Yes."

"I apologize. I should have given you some kind of warning, Verity Jane."

Flint hiked his bushy eyebrows. "Verity Jane?"

"I've known her for years," Holt explained, "and I don't use her initials." Keeping his gaze trained on her, he added, "I understand you're about to leave for lunch. May I join you?"

"Yes." Dislodging Flint's restraining hands, she swung her feet over the hospital trolley.

Flint seized her chin and raised it until she met his gaze. "Are you pregnant?"

"No."

"Are you sure?"

She tamped her temper down by sheer force of will. "Yes. I am not pregnant."

"Isn't that a discriminatory question?" Holt asked.

Clearly shocked at being questioned, Flint blinked—twice.

Beyond him, Barden, the guy who had landed the coveted position, rushed close. "Vicki paged me. Said there's an emergency. What happened? Why is VJ on a gurney?" He stepped back, his eyes filled with fear. "Do you have Covid?"

"No. I'm quite well, thank you very much."

The pandemic required everyone in hospital to wear masks, but hers had been removed. Holt extended a new yellow one. After VJ put it on, he cupped her elbow and kept her steady while she slid her feet to the floor. His touch sent quivers to her heart. She managed not to gasp, but her insides were quivering, her brain scrambling to believe this was real–that Holt was truly there.

"Should we eat in the cafeteria?" he asked in the husky voice that still haunted her dreams. "Or do you prefer somewhere else?"

"The cafeteria." VJ had the satisfaction of seeing blighter Flint scrunch his forehead into a scowl as Holt escorted her through the double doors and down the hall to the elevator.

~ * ~

Still flummoxed after Holt insisted on paying for her lunch, VJ struggled to keep her wits about her as he carried their food trays. Without his support, she wobbled like a drunken sailor as she followed him to a table in a remote alcove. He set the trays on the table, slid a chair out, and waited for her to sit before he sat across from her.

Her keen sense of smell drew in the lemony scent of recently sanitized tables, chairs, and floors. Moving beyond the pleasant aroma, she inhaled Holt's essence again—his piney cologne and the minty crispness of his breath when he removed his mask. Was she dreaming? Or was he truly sitting across from her looking so hot she wanted to take hold and never let go?

While he unloaded their food, she studied his smoothly shaven cheeks, clear eyes, wavy hair. Heat flushed through her when he caught her staring.

"Would it be inappropriate to ask if you fainted because you had a vision?" he asked quietly.

Setting her napkin across her lap, she picked up her fork and toyed with her salad, waiting for her embarrassment to subside before she answered. "Not inappropriate, although you might consider it mundane."

"Try me."

He was the only man who knew she had visions—the only man who had ever listened, understood, and helped her reach conclusions, make decisions.

"My best friend is married and preggers. She's had one miscarriage and she'll have another. She wants a baby, but her husband is having an affair. Their marriage isn't going to last."

"Sorry to hear that. Is Madeline still your best friend?"

"Yes. She'll feel terrible when she gets divorced, although she has several paths to the future."

"Does one path include a second husband and children?"

"Yes. How did you know?"

"I didn't. That's why I asked."

VJ knew Holt couldn't 'read' her because she was 'bloxed.' Although her memories of his homeland had faded considerably, she remembered he had asked Rene, a kew member, to 'blox' her so no one could 'read' her because he thought humans owned the right to conceal their private thoughts.

"What are Madeline's other options?" he asked, pulling her thoughts back to the present.

"She could remain single and dedicate her life to her career. Work at a hospital. Be a high school teacher. Join a university faculty. Return to England and live near her mum. Or..."

Holt hiked his eyebrows. "Or?"

"I cannot explain that option. What I saw has to do with magic in a place where magic is considered 'the norm'."

"Sounds like any path Madeline chooses could lead to a satisfactory life."

VJ didn't mention the obvious—Holt believed in magic. He was an Arcane—whatever that meant. "All options are viable if she lets go of the past and embraces the future."

"Are you going to tell her about your vision?"

"I haven't decided."

"Where is she?"

"She lives in Texas, but she's here in Colorado at the moment visiting her husband's grandparents. I'm planning to see her before she leaves."

"Whatever decision you make, I'm sure it will be the right one." Picking up a shrimp, Holt dipped it in red cocktail sauce, took a bite and chewed before he asked, "How have you been?"

His hushed tone still had the capacity to melt her insides. "Perfectly adequate. How about you?"

"Not as good as you, apparently. Have you ever had a vision about your own future? Or mine?"

"No. However, I had one about your homeland a few months ago."

She saw no surprise in his steady gaze.

"And?" He leaned closer. His masculine scent threatened to undo her. Had he spent all morning handling freshly cut Christmas trees? The question was beyond ridiculous because he lived far away in a place she barely remembered. Besides, it was September—too early for him to visit a Christmas tree lot.

"Someone will spread a rumor about a fountain of youth and a secret place beneath the surface of the earth where people live to advanced ages. Gobs of publicity will inspire a crush of humanity to scour Tennessee, Kentucky and Kansas, searching caves and caverns. Social media will describe the activity as tantamount to the California and Alaskan gold rushes back in the nineteenth century."

Holt looked concerned, and not smug. "Our enquays are secure. Unscrupulous strangers are rarely allowed to enter and never in groups."

"Cameras on satellites see through water, all the way to ocean floors. They show every formation, every living creature. Such cameras could reveal the tunnel that leads to your birthplace."

"My homeland cannot be seen from above. Mater Nature provides an invisible shield, and our security system keeps most undesirables from entering."

VJ frowned. "Don't blame me if you are proven wrong."

"Never crossed my mind, but I appreciate the information. I'll tell our governing kew. They'll decide if security should be increased." Raising his glass, he swallowed a slug of water. "Do you know when it will happen?"

"Before Christmas."

"This year?"

"Yes."

"The world is in the middle of the novel coronavirus pandemic. People are still isolating. Social distancing. Staying home."

"That hasn't stopped some from rioting, destroying other people's property, or looting, shooting, stealing, setting off explosives."

His nod indicated he agreed and was contemplating her vision, deciding how to handle it. No wonder she confided in him. He always took what she said seriously.

"Why are you here?" she blurted.

"To extend an offer."

"What kind?"

"Api needs someone with research, health care, and medical skills. Wondered if you might be interested."

"I wasn't born below." The inane reminder made her feel like a ninny. Still, she added, "I was born on the surface, in England, as you bloody well know. And I'm only a nurse."

"I suspect you're working as one because men are intimidated by your knowledge and expertise and won't hire you as a doctor because you know more than they ever will."

"I didn't complete my residency."

"You graduated from medical school and worked as a resident for a full year. You left because your mater needed help after her accident. You are exactly what Api needs. I don't know what you want long-term—but if you agree to help us, every denizen in Api will do their best to see that you get it."

Tiny thrills shot through her, along with the deep-seated yearning she had denied three years ago. "Everyone? Including you?"

"Especially me."

"That's quite an offer. However, I'm turning it down."

"Why?"

"My life is here, on the surface. I went with you once. I'm not willing to go there again."

"I'm not asking you to return for me. I'm asking for people in my homeland who need a tutelary."

"I have no skills that could possibly qualify me to work as a protector or guardian."

"You are an excellent candidate for the position."

She blushed at his compliment, unnerved by his confidence. For a few moments, they stared without speaking. Finally, she said, "I can't go with you, Holt."

"Can't or won't?"

"Both." Despite her determination to remain aloof, she explained something she hadn't meant to share. "I applied for a promotion which I didn't get. If I quit, I'll look like a sore loser."

"If you resign, you won't have a pompous boss. This hospital doesn't deserve you."

Her reply came out before she could stop it. "Someday, I'd like to be an established doctor with female patients."

"You're already an OB/GYN, and in Api most of your patients will be women. You'll start at the top of your profession. A few ladies are expecting babies. You would help them deliver." He spoke quietly yet forcefully. "In addition, six new medics who will graduate in December want a leader to guide them through research projects. You'll also confer with our doctors and medics and consult in areas that concern the kew who now govern my homeland."

When she didn't comment, he added, "I don't expect an answer today. Take your time. Think it over."

Picking up his knife and fork, he tucked into the steamed vegetables swimming in butter. Well one thing hadn't changed—he still selected seafood if it was available, and veggies, but the addition of butter was new.

VJ removed her mask and started to eat. Neither spoke again until she gave in to her curiosity. "How long do I have to think about your offer?"

"Until the end of the week. I'm heading home Saturday."

"Are you here alone?" She loathed herself for asking, for giving in to the need to know.

"No. Mater and Pater are with me."

Relieved he hadn't brought a lady friend or a wife, she asked, "How are your parents?"

"I keep wondering that myself."

Her stomach gave an odd lurch. "Is something wrong with them?"

"My sister died seven months ago. Their energy died with her. I'm worried about them."

Dismay swished through VJ. She adored Shelan and Kirt, even though she despised her own father. "I'm sorry. Is there anything I can do?"

"I doubt it." Holt's dour expression softened. "But thanks for asking." Setting his knife and fork politely across his plate, he leaned closer. "One of the things our kew would like you and your team to research is departed human spirits. Think that fits in with scientific research?"

"I think that subject is rubbish and falls under the category of witchcraft and sorcery."

"Will you think about our offer, anyway?"

She blinked. She had expected a snide rejoinder. But Holt didn't make snide remarks. Not his style. Pap and Freddie, the man responsible for her breakup with Holt, had skewed her opinions of men. Both were cruel, mean blighters. Holt wasn't. She had almost forgotten he was gentle, thoughtful, considerate. And the man she loved. Had loved.

"You didn't answer my question." His husky voice brought back memories that had lain dormant for so many months she had almost convinced herself they weren't real.

Stalling for time, she took a sip of tea, and then another. If she said 'no' she might never see him again. "I'll think about it." Leading him on was reprehensible, but she wasn't ready to send him away. Yet.

"Good." His gaze searched hers.

Her heartbeat sped up. Seeing him again before they went their separate ways put her in a dither that expanded when he added, "You knew as a child you would leave England because your destiny lay elsewhere, Verity Jane. You are more gifted than you realize."

She did not like to think about her youth. "You can't know that," she sputtered. "You didn't know me when I was a child."

"True—however, I read your thoughts before I asked Rene to blox you years ago."

~ * ~

VJ paced the floor of her flat—a very small floor compared to Vincent's huge home in Boston. If she still lived in Massachusetts, she would have a three-story, ten-bedroom mansion to pace. But Vincent was dead, and Freddie had set her up to look like his murderer.

With an internal shudder, her thoughts reverted to Holt. She had always wondered how she would feel if she ever saw him again. And now she knew. Excited. Nervous. Alive. Miserable.

Her mantra slid through her. *Muddle through. Make do.* A slew of questions intruded. Would Freddie, the scrummy bloke who had framed her, discover where she was? Would he blackmail her if he did? Or turn her over to the police? And why had Holt come to Denver? Did he know her problems? Or had he come to plumb her mind?

To clamp the fear that never left her, she gave herself a mental shake. She had to stop thinking about Holt. She could not love him. That possibility had died when they split. She should not have allowed herself to fall for him in the first place. Doing so was another mistake, and she had made more than her share.

Snatching her remote from the end table, she turned the TV to her favorite music channel. Classical music curled around her but it failed to erase her reaction when Holt had helped her slide off the gurney and held her elbow while he guided her to the lift. The memories sent tingles cascading through her, warming her as she hadn't been warmed since she left his birthplace—a realm so different she hadn't even remembered the name until he said 'Api.'

Now, they returned like a tidal wave. A sudden flash reminded her that he had said her memories of Apitcote would evaporate if she left. But she hadn't had a choice. Freddie had threatened to harm Madeline, Mum and both sisters if she ignored his summons.

With another determined shake of her head, VJ used the remote to change channels. As she listened to local news, she tried to force her thoughts off Holt. Off his offer. Off his homeland. Off his touch. Off the intensity of his magnetic gaze.

Part of her still wanted the hospital position she had been denied. Another part yearned to be a practicing physician who delivered babies and dealt with women's health issues. A third part wanted to leave the hospital and never return. If she didn't see gaffer Flint and his superior-than-thou attitude ever again, she might be able to smile.

But she couldn't go with Holt. Couldn't entangle his life with her problems. Couldn't escape them either. Would she ever find peace?

~ * ~

When VJ arrived at hospital for her next shift, Holt was standing in the parking lot. He met her as she climbed out of her Prius. Not having expected to see him so soon, she sputtered, "Wh—what are you doing here?"

"I've been wondering if you thought about my offer. Thought I'd stop by and ask."

"Thought about it, yes. Changed my mind, no."

"The request is important, Verity Jane." Leaning close, he used his persuasive husky tone. "What can I do or say to convince you to leave the surface and make your home in Api?"

She was tempted. Just being near him was reason enough, not even considering the marvelous place where he lived. "If I accept, and I'm not saying I will, what would our relationship be?"

"What would you like it to be?"

"That isn't an answer."

He shrugged his shoulders—shoulders she ached to lean against as she had before their break-up. "Strictly professional, if that's what you want."

What I want, she was tempted to say, is to be your cherished partner. Secure in your love. Free from worry. Safe from Freddie. And murder accusations.

But that was impossible. Holt had already proven he didn't love her. Even if by some miracle he did, she had no intention of burdening him with her problems. "You said I have until Friday. Today's only Monday."

"You do have until the end of the week." He stepped back, eyes calm. "If you accept, how much notice will you need to give the hospital?"

"I didn't say I'm going to accept."

"Does your resistance have anything to do with us?"

"No," she fibbed.

Holt frowned. "Too bad. I hoped you might still fancy me."

"I never fancied you." She crossed her fingers behind her back to negate the lie, feeling like a silly school girl.

His frown faded. He looked grim. But not devastated. "Well, just so you know, I may go to my grave wanting you."

She was too startled to comment. He didn't give her a chance. He had already turned and strode away.

Like a besotted twit, she tagged after him, snagging at the meager crumbs his words had left behind. "What did you mean?"

He stopped and turned. "Think about it, Verity. You're as lovely as an English rose. Not just smart—you're brilliant. Compassionate. Considerate. Beautiful. Pleasant to be near."

Thrown off balance by his unexpected compliments, she felt like she was being seduced in broad daylight, right there in the hospital parking lot, and he hadn't even touched her. Her heart pounded. Her flesh tingled. And she found it impossible to tear her gaze from his. She had forgotten how strong his magnetic pull was.

"All the men who've had you probably still want you," he continued. "What I said wasn't an attempt to get you in bed. To me want and pant have vastly different meanings."

VJ's heart lurched in dismay. *He thinks I've been intimate with other men.* Not willing to correct him or discuss Vincent or the other patient she had lived with after Holt brought her back to the surface, she cleared her throat. "Will I hear from you again?"

"Do you want to?"

"I need a few days before I make up my mind." Another fib. She could not, would not, go with him. She hated her deception. Hated the thought of never seeing him again even more.

"Good," he said, tone crisp. "I'll call Friday or Saturday morning if either day works for you."

"Both are good. Do you need my phone number?"

"No."

"My number is new and ex-directory."

"I know." With a wink, he reverted to the intriguing man she loved. Had loved. "I'm nosy, remember? And thorough."

"How thorough?" she asked to prolong his departure.

"Thorough enough to know you not only changed Verity Jane to VJ, you use Hummel as your last name instead of Bagner, and you stopped using doctor as your title."

Her heart stumbled over its next few beats. She had been very careful to cover her tracks when she left Boston. But apparently not careful enough. Holt had found her. Would Freddie find her, too? Surely, he knew his Uncle Vincent had deeded his mansion to her and he would be furious. Bonkers. Bent on revenge.

"When you search for something, you collect all the details."

"But not all of the elements."

Not having a clue what that meant, she frowned. "I need to get to work."

"I know. I'll be in touch." Once again, he strode away.

She heard a car engine rev. Looked up. Saw a black van screech around parked cars and speed toward Holt. She screamed a warning. Too late. The van hit him. Hard. His body shot straight up in the air. The van sped toward the exit as Holt floated back to earth.

To her amazement, he landed on his feet.

She ran to him. His mask was askew, but he looked calm and unharmed.

A bystander dashed close. "I videoed what happened. Made sure I got the license plate." He waved his phone as a small crowd began to gather.

"We should go inside," VJ said, forcing a calm she didn't feel. He voice quivering. "And have you examined. Make sure you're okay."

"I'm uninjured." Holt straightened his black mask. "I jumped before the van touched me."

"Some jump," the bystander gushed. "Are you an acrobat?"

"No. However, I am trained to sense danger and react accordingly."

"Please come inside," VJ pleaded, fearing the bloody hit-and-run driver had been there because of her.

Holt placed one hand on her shoulder. Her quivers stopped, as though by magic. "I have never lied to you, and I don't intend to start now. If I were injured, I would do as you suggest." He lowered his hand and cupped her elbow. "I'll walk you to the entrance and make sure you get there safely."

She inhaled a deep breath, using her unique ability to confirm he had no internal injuries. "Thank you."

"You are quite welcome, Dr. Hummel."

After they watched a bystander's video, VJ memorized the green and white Colorado license plate while Holt called the police and reported the incident.

~ * ~

When not consumed with patient care, VJ pondered what Holt had said. He wanted her, but he didn't pant for her. What did that mean? And how much did he know about her reason for changing her name?

Assuming a new identity and moving across the country had made her feel safe. When she fled Boston, she had spent a full week riding different Greyhound coaches from one state to another, trying to decide where to go, and finally concluded one place Freddie and the law might not find her was where she had once considered completing her residency. But now she felt vulnerable. And frightened.

During her lunch break, Holt showed up at the cafeteria and explained. "The black van was a rental, reported stolen last week and found today, abandoned near Cherry Creek dam, southeast of Denver, all fingerprints wiped clean."

"I think the driver deliberately tried to hit you," she said. "Do you have any enemies in Colorado?"

"Not that I am aware of. Do you?"

"I certainly hope not." VJ looked away, averting his gaze. "I appreciate you letting me know."

"You are welcome, Verity Jane."

Thankful he had followed through, she worried through the remainder of her shift. Why did someone want to harm him? Did the reason have anything to do with her?

<h1 style="text-align:center">Two</h1>

Holt stared at his parents who were seated on a loveseat in the two-story mansion owned by one of his kew sister's parents. Both Shelan and Kirt looked unhealthy. Mater looked the worst—pale and exhausted as though she were fading and had lost the will to live.

Had his sister's spirit zapped their energy before the kew managed to expunge it?

He had hoped bringing them above again would stimulate their appetites and fire their desire to live. So far it had done neither. "How are you feeling?" he asked for the umpteenth time.

"Fair," Mater said.

"Middling," Pater added.

"What sounds good for the evening meal?"

"Nothing," Mater answered.

"Soup," Pater suggested.

"Would you like to have Chinese? Indian? Seafood? Mexican?"

"Rather have soup."

"Martha made soup last night," Holt reminded, grateful for the kind housekeeper and her husband, who took care of the mansion. "Martha and Blaine are minding their grandchildren tonight, but I'll order soup and have it door dashed."

Pater looked up, his eyes haunted. "Is Jilly's spirit truly gone?"

"Yes. She can't hurt you or command you now."

"Are you sure?"

"Yes."

Mater glanced around the spacious room. "Did her spirit follow us here?"

Once more, Holt explained. "Before she was outed from the mortal world, Jilly's spirit attached to you, her ashes, her afone, and other items. But those have been destroyed, and her spirit is gone."

"We still fear she's going to pounce any minute and take control," Pater mumbled.

"She won't. She can't."

"We want to believe that. Wonder if we ever will."

Leaning forward, Mater whispered, "Jilly's spirit made us miserable for such a long time."

Holt resisted the urge to curse his sister. All her life she had demanded attention and devotion from their parents and in death she had damaged them—two of the many people he loved.

He released a grateful sigh. Jilly hadn't had a chance to hurt Verity Jane. Or Harmony and Hanna, who he planned to visit before he left the surface. When Jilly returned to Apitcote after a prolonged absence, Harmony and Hanna had left so Hanna could take care of her invalid mater in Philadelphia.

Holt refocused his thoughts, settled them on Verity. Three years ago, he had been shocked speechless when she insisted on leaving Apitcote. In retrospect, her decision had been wise. Jilly hadn't met her. Hadn't had a chance to use or harm her. But now she was in some kind of trouble. He doubted she would tell him what. Inviting her to return to Api and offering the position was his way of keeping her safe. His kew members all agreed, and he had money to make the offer more lucrative.

If he weren't so concerned, he would ask someone else to convince her she belonged below. But his concern was too keen. When he and his kew mates had slept in the chateau's dream chamber, they all had the same dream. Verity Jane was being stalked by a man with a gun. Although kew mates possessed magic, none of them knew why. Their attempts to 'read' the guy failed because he was so high on crack his thoughts were jumbled and unintelligible.

In addition to the shared dream, Rene reported having performed a 'deep delve' into her ancestor's bequeathed memories and found a disturbing fact: Apitcote was in danger of being invaded by an unknown source. Kew mates needed to devise a plan to prevent that. Although Rene possessed the ability to 'see' future events, she was convinced Apitcote needed Verity Jane's visionary expertise as well.

Last year, Verity Jane had virtually disappeared. But Holt's Arcane magic allowed him to zero in to her location and discern she now lived alone. After leaving him, she had lived with one man for four months. Another for twenty. Holt hadn't allowed himself to discover if she was stringing another guy along.

How many men had held her in their arms? Caressed her silken skin? Fingered her long gleaming black hair? Kissed her seductive lips? Made love to her?

Jerking his thoughts from questions he didn't want answered, he confirmed his decision not to give her another chance. A second split-up would not just wound, it would devastate. Still, he wanted her back in Apitcote, as did his kew mates.

To protect her, he had disabled her follower's gun and reduced the bullets to cardboard, but using more magic wasn't how Holt perceived he should deal with the dude. And if he employed force to take Verity back, she would never forgive him. Returning should be her choice. Not his. Or his kew's. He had hired a detective to tail her and keep her safe, hoping she would eventually agree to leave Denver and return to Api.

~ * ~

Chills crawled up VJ's spine as she entered the parking lot after work. Was she being followed? She glanced around. Didn't see anyone except other hospital employees.

More chills scooted down her back as she drove away and a green van pulled behind her. Had Freddie hired someone to find her? Was the driver the same chap who had driven the black van yesterday and attempted to run Holt down?

Flipping her left indicator, she turned at the corner. The van stayed behind her. If she had anywhere else to go, she wouldn't go home. But she didn't. After leaving Boston, she had severed contact with practically everyone she knew.

She sped through an intersection with a yellow light. The van driver ran the red light and kept behind her.

At the apartment complex, she parked under her assigned carport and dashed to her flat. Still spooked by yesterday's van incident and wondering if Freddie had sent someone to harm her, she unlocked her front door, rushed inside, and slammed it shut. She didn't stop shaking until she relocked and reset her security system.

Cold dread ramped up her heartbeat. Who had followed her? Freddie? Someone he hired? She dashed those possibilities away. Tried to rationalize. If Freddie knew where she was, he would make more demands. Or worse, sic the law on her.

Her hands trembled as she heated a pot of water. While tea steeped, she reminisced. Shortly after she and Madeline had moved to the U.S., they met Freddie. At first, they believed he was their friend. He had drawn VJ into his web by wining and dining her, treating her as though she were the most wonderful girl he ever met. When he proposed, she turned him down, explained she wanted to be a doctor and planned to apply for student loans. Freddie had taken her refusal in stride and convinced both her and Madeline to borrow money from him to attend university. VJ was deep in his debt before she discovered he was a manipulator who issued commands as though she were his indentured slave.

He treated Madeline fine. Never asked her to do anything ugly or vile. But after VJ's second refusal to marry him, he treated her abominably—as though he wanted her to suffer. Because she said she didn't love him?

Pulling her thoughts from the past, she carried her tea tray to the living room and sat on the settee, wishing Holt would call just so she could hear his voice. Why had he said he might go to his grave wanting her? The man was a paradox. Warm and gentle one minute. Calm and remote the next. Teasing one moment. Solemn seconds later.

Plucking the cozy from her teapot, she filled her cup. Her fingers shook as she raised the delicate saucer. She inhaled slowly to stop the tremors before she sipped. The tea tasted wonderful, and she relished the warmth as much as the familiar creamed flavor.

Having lived in England for the first sixteen years of her life and never trusting Pap, she was wary of manipulation and propositions, even more so after her experiences with Freddie. Holt was the exception. She didn't have a single doubt that his offer was on the up and up.

Why couldn't she purge him from her thoughts? Only he and Vincent had ever touched her heart. Other men had disappointed or hurt her, contributing to her distrust of the opposite sex. After Vincent died, she had sworn not to get involved with another man ever again. But now Holt was back in her life. In some ways, she felt as though he had never left. Except she hadn't seen him smile. And that saddened her.

~ * ~

As Holt and his parents finished breakfast in the mansion's dining room, Pater said, "Shelan and I feel a bit under today. Think we'll go upstairs and rest."

"Good plan," Holt approved. Rene and Drew, two kew mates who possessed healing magic, had examined his parents. Apitcote's medics and doctors had checked them as well. But no one knew how to heal the lethargy and melancholy Jilly's spirit had inflicted.

Not having talked to his kew since he left home, Holt checked his awatch. Knowing his mates were scattered throughout Apitcote's klusters, he used his afone to synk with all eight.

"Have you seen Verity Jane?" Rene asked.

"Yes."

"Did she accept our offer?" her mate, Drew, queried.

"No. However, I'm hoping to change her mind." To satisfy his own curiosity, he asked, "How are Minalu and her sept getting along?"

"Fine," Tess said. "But they need someone dedicated to spending hours, not just minutes, with them each day."

"Right," her mate, Dane, agreed. "We're all so busy, our schedules don't allow much time."

"The dwellers also need better nourishment," Mist reminded.

"For sure," her mate, Jordan, agreed. "Their diet at the dwelling was limited and we're reluctant to offer menus without expert advice, which reinforces our need to hire Verity Jane asap."

"I know," Holt agreed, and changed the subject. "Have you finished the contract we discussed before I left?"

"Yes," Monteith said. "We'll atext it today."

"Feel free to use the printer in Dad's study to make copies," said Juhree, whose parents owned the mansion Holt and his parents were staying in.

"How are your parents?" Juhree asked.

"About the same."

As Holt ended the call, Pater dashed into the den. "Shelan's having trouble breathing."

Holt charged up the stairs. As soon as he saw his mater, he lifted her off the bed and levitated down the curved staircase. Out in the triple car garage, he buckled her in his rental, backed up and sped away, grateful he knew how to maneuver Denver's streets.

~ * ~

Strolling through the ER on her way back to the lift after lunch, VJ didn't see Holt until he seized her arm and all but dragged her across the lobby.

"Let go," she hissed, not wanting to make a spectacle.

"The ER nurses are busy. Mater's having trouble breathing. Take a look. See if you know what's wrong."

VJ stifled a gasp as her training kicked in gear. Shelan was struggling to breathe and her skin was an unhealthy pallor.

"Oxygen," VJ shouted, drawing attention from everyone in the ER, including the two nurses flirting with new patients. "STAT."

Placing her hands on Shelan's arms, VJ lowered her voice and murmured soothing words.

Moments later, Shelan lay on a trolley, breathing with the aid of oxygen, and attached to an EKG monitoring her heart. Both nurses had abandoned check-in stations and were fussing over her, vying for Holt's attention. VJ knew he wasn't impressed.

She felt the change in Shelan moments before her skin lost its bluish tint. It wasn't the first time VJ had felt an inner connection with a patient.

When she was satisfied Shelan was in stable condition, VJ inhaled slowly. She could smell disease. Shelan was not diseased. And the EKG indicated she had no heart problems. Inhaling again, she sensed Shelan was already on the mend. Whatever ailed her was being defeated. Confident Shelan's condition was improving, VJ excused herself and returned to her own floor.

After her shift, she went to check on Holt's mum. Shelan was in a private room, sleeping, breathing peacefully, still hooked up to oxygen. She looked haggard. Nothing like the pretty, vivacious woman VJ had met three years before.

Holt was not there, but his father, Kirt, dressed in brown hospital scrubs and a yellow mask, sat beside Shelan's bed. Looking up, he said, "Verity Jane. Nice to see you. How have you been?"

"Good. And you?" She remembered Shelan and Kirt as one of the happiest couples she had ever met, but his drooped shoulders indicated he had seen better days.

"We've had a bit of trouble."

"What kind?"

Kirt motioned her to a chair. "Will you sit for a spell?"

"Sure." Goose pimples crept up her arms. Some people in Api could cast spells. Was Kirt one of them? She thought Holt was, although he hadn't admitted it and she hadn't asked.

Because the Covid-19 pandemic outlawed visitors, she closed the door, hoping they wouldn't be discovered and booted out. "Would you like to discuss your problems?"

"Do you have time to spare?"

"Yes. My shift is over."

Kirt didn't waste a moment. "Something strange happened after a friend brought Jilly's ashes home last February. Her spirit descended on me and Shelan and fed on us. We couldn't leave our cottage. Didn't work or venture out for days. We had no strength to resist Jilly's orders."

The fine hair on VJ's arms stood on end. "What did she order?"

"Told us not to spread her ashes. Convinced us she would return if we obeyed. Took a while to realize we didn't want her there. She controlled us. Demanded. Zapped our strength. It was very unpleasant."

In spite of her disbelief that deceased spirits haunted humans, VJ swept her gaze around the room. "Is Jilly's spirit still bothering you?"

"Holt said she was ousted from the mortal world. But she drew strength from us before they expunged her—before they forced her to move on to the spirit world, if there is such a place. She may be gone, but we're not relieved of the burden. Shelan's ill health is due to a wicked spell Jilly's spirit cast."

VJ scrubbed the goose pimples on her arms, wondering if Jilly was the reason Holt had mentioned researching departed human spirits. She felt small and mean for not giving his words more credence. Rather than her flippant reply—spirits are rubbish—she should have asked some questions. Any decent researcher would have.

She bit her bottom lip to stop the tremor. Holt loved his parents. If only he felt a small portion of love for her. She chastised herself for the selfish thought. For three years, she hadn't allowed herself to dwell on how much she missed Holt— how wonderful she felt when they were together, how complete when he held her close. Now she ached for the comfort his arms alone could provide.

Disgusted with her self-centered thoughts, she chastised herself again. "Shelan is recovering. She should be well enough to leave hospital tomorrow."

"I appreciate the information." Kirt's worried frown eased. "We missed you after you left our homeland."

"I didn't think Holt wanted me there."

"Told you that, did he?"

"No. But he didn't ask me to stay."

"Maybe he didn't know he needed to."

Before she could respond, the door opened and Holt walked in. The intense blue of his eyes made her wonder if he was 'reading' her. But Rene had bloxed her and she knew she had not been unbloxed.

"Pater needs to eat," he said. "Will you join us in the cafeteria?"

Prudence dictated she should say 'no,' but she felt like she was in the middle of an unfinished puzzle, and wanted to find the missing pieces. "Yes. Thank you."

Like his father, Holt wore brown scrubs so they both looked like hospital staff. With the pandemic still a grave concern, she suspected they had used magic to obtain identical lanyards with name tags and employee ID to clear security.

In the cafeteria, Holt insisted on paying for her food again. They sat in the same secluded alcove. He didn't ask if she had given any more thought to his offer, but it hovered between them like a ghost swinging on a string.

Lowering her gaze from his neatly trimmed hair, she flicked a glance at his bare arms. A deep-seated yearning pummeled her as memories intruded. In Apitcote, they had spent hours at the lake, in the water and on the beach. Seeing Holt suntanned with windblown hair was one of her favorite memories. Regret sloshed through her as she recalled they had planned a camp-out in the woods, but she had left before they took it.

Holt gave her an intense stare. Unable to tear her eyes from his, she felt connected as they had in the past. Suddenly, she felt discombobulated--so nervous her stomach tied itself in knots. She told herself she could handle this. All she had to do was muddle through. *Make do.* It had worked in the past. It would work now.

Kirt broke the tense silence. "Why didn't you two stay together?"

"I've wondered about that, too." VJ baited Holt before he could comment. She knew full well she was responsible for their break-up.

"Verity wanted to live on the surface. I didn't. End of story."

Part of VJ wanted to snark, "What does the unperturbable Holt want?"

But he had never been snarky with her. He had always been kind. Open. Clear minded. Fair. Except with her heart. He had broken that in pieces when he brought her back without uttering a single word. Without even saying goodbye. He had left abruptly—as though he couldn't get away fast enough. She had glued her heart back together. But sometimes the cracks still hurt.

Once again, she chastised herself. It had taken less than a day to regret the secrets she had kept from him. The blame was hers, not his. But if he had given any indication that he wanted to share the future, she would have had something to look forward to. And her life might have been very different.

Big Boss Flint snagged her attention when he entered the cafeteria with the two ER nurses, so busy chin-wagging they didn't see VJ. Didn't even glance at the alcove. Her shoulders suddenly felt weighed down by another heavy load. She would pay a price for taking charge in the ER. For interfering in a department where she didn't work. Would she lose her job for helping Shelan?

She didn't blame Holt for nabbing her. Shelan had needed immediate attention. Had fate intervened to push her into accepting Holt's offer? She told herself she was asking the question because she had the freedom to waver. What a lie. She had signed her future away years ago.

~ * ~

When VJ entered the hospital for her next shift, she had a sick feeling in the pit of her stomach. Gaffer Flint must know she had assisted in the ER. He would be livid. And she would pay the price.

As anticipated, he stood in the hall when the lift opened on her floor. "Follow me," he growled, drumming his fingers on his crossed arms. "I have disciplinary action to enforce."

To her astonishment, Holt stepped out of the other lift and followed them. Flint started to shut his office door, but Holt forged in, his expression unfazed. "I came to explain what happened in the ER yesterday."

"I don't know where you work," Flint said, "but you have nothing to do with what transpires in nursing."

"If disciplinary action is required, do it where it belongs—with the nurses who failed to do their job. I snagged Dr. Hummel because I know she's capable of handling life threatening emergencies. My mother was gasping for every breath and both nurses ignored her."

"I have what happened in writing, and I intend to follow hospital procedure," Flint snorted, attempting to look down his nose at Holt, but failing because Holt was taller.

"If you don't want a lawsuit, I suggest you pay attention to what I said." Holt's tone and gaze remained calm. What VJ could see of Flint's masked face flamed red. "I do not intend to repeat myself."

"You have no proof," Flint stammered. "It's your word against the two nurses who filed the complaint."

"They filed it to save their own useless behinds." Holt raised his afone. "I videoed the event. My recommendation, although you might not be smart enough to take it, is to discipline the inept nurses and praise Dr. Hummel for her dedication to the medical profession. If not for her expertise and quick reaction, my mother might not be alive. Dr. Hummel's talent is wasted working with idiots like you."

He glanced at VJ. "Have I made myself clear? Do you think this half-wit understood what I said?"

VJ nodded. She had just seen a side of Holt she hadn't seen before. He wasn't angry. Hadn't even raised his voice. He was stupendous. He had exposed blighter Flint to fear—the first fear she'd ever seen him display.

"Let me know if the guy gives you any problems," Holt said. "I'll text my number."

~ * ~

*Muddle through. Make do.* VJ's mantra repeated itself when the hospital administrator had her paged and summoned to his office a few hours later.

She arrived, worried that Flint had complained and she was about to get axed. She was more than a bit stunned when Dr. Wagner smiled and waved her to a seat.

"I'd like to extend my appreciation for your quick action in the ER yesterday. Holt Mackay showed me a video of the incident." Dr. Wagner glanced at his computer screen. "I've read your personnel records and I'm impressed. Mr. Mackay also confirmed your credentials that state you are an obstetrician-gynecologist."

"I am."

"Why are you working as a nurse?"

She gave the only answer she could think of at the moment. "Nurses were in demand when I moved here."

"The hospital has openings occasionally. Would you like to be notified if a position becomes available?"

"Yes. Please." She already regretted her reply. Not only had she not completed her residency, if the police were looking for her, they would likely be searching for a doctor, not a nurse.

Peering over the rim of his bifocals, Dr. Wagner smiled again. "I've released an article praising you that will be published in the online staff news this afternoon."

"Please don't," VJ pleaded, not wanting anything about her posted online.

"Too late. The article has already been uploaded."

VJ returned to her floor in a haze of worry. Even though she had changed her name, she feared Freddie or someone he knew might find her and notify law authorities.

During the remainder of her shift, big boss Flint left her alone, but she couldn't stop worrying about Freddie, the police and her predicament.

~ * ~

Knowing Thursday should have been Verity's day off but she had switched with another nurse in order to have Friday and Saturday off, Holt used his Arcane magic to watch her drive to work. She was followed by the green van that had followed her from work. Behind the van was a white sedan, driven by his hired detective. They arrived thirty minutes before her shift began.

Sensing she intended to visit his mother, he watched Verity enter the hospital and walk to Mater's room. After smiling and greeting his parents, she studied the up-to-date wallboard Holt had already read. Shelan had slept peacefully with twelve hours breathing on her own, and she was much improved. Using his enhanced Arcane hearing, he listened to their conversation.

"I'm leaving today," Mater said with a rare smile.

"An aide is bringing a wheelchair," Pater added. "Holt went to get the rental car and will meet us at the entrance."

The aide arrived and looked at Kirt who wore brown hospital scrubs and a yellow mask. "Are you here to wheel our patient down to the lobby?"

"Patient is our friend," Verity said. "We both want to ensure she connects with her proper ride."

Holt was parked near the door when Verity pushed the wheelchair through with Pater behind them. After his parents were seated in the back with seatbelts fastened, Holt stared at Verity across the hood. "Thanks for your help."

"You're welcome. You're also good at manipulation."

"Mater's life is important."

"I agree."

"As is the offer I extended."

"Explain it again. Please. I'd like to know more."

Pleased with her curiosity, Holt said, "We have a new group of denizens, mostly women and children, who need help adjusting to living in Api. Their diets were limited, and they need someone to teach them the value of good nutrition."

"If there are children, there must be men. Where are they?"

"Living by themselves in another part of Api, under primitive conditions."

"Is that why the women left them?"

"You will learn their reasons if you accept the position."

"How many people are there?"

"A hundred and forty-three left the dwelling. Twenty elders live in a kluster with denizens near their ages. The remaining hundred and twenty-three include forty children, seventy-five women, and eight men. Five women are expecting babies. You would be their attending physician."

"Sounds like a dream job. But I haven't completed my residency."

"You're a better doctor than many who have." Hoping he had said enough to whet her curiosity, Holt raised his hand and waved. "Cheerio, Dr. Hummel."

Confident his hired detective could and would protect Verity, he left.

Would the salary his kew mates had agreed to pay convince Verity to return to Api? After they split-up, he had learned money was very important to women on the surface. Only one lady, Hanna, cared more about people than she did about wealth. Her decision to become a single mater had forever changed his life. Her daughter, Harmony, was one of the greatest joys in Holt's life, and he looked forward to seeing them. A visit with Harmony would cheer his parents. It always did because they loved her, too.

~ * ~

VJ was surprised to see Holt in his gray car following her home behind the green van. Knowing he was there made the drive less frightening than yesterday's—until the van slowed and Holt slowed as well. She glanced in her rear-view mirror. Saw Holt swerve to avoid hitting the van when it slammed to a stop in the middle of their lane. She breathed a bit easier when Holt pulled behind her and followed her the rest of the way home.

In her flat, she sat on the settee and waited for Holt to ring the doorbell. After ten minutes, she realized he wasn't going to. Shoving her disappointment aside, she decided to call Madeline and confirm tomorrow's plans. When she left Boston, she had changed both her phone number and provider and purchased a prepaid cell phone that she used to call Madeline.

"Hi Madd. How are you feeling?"

"Good, except for wretched morning sickness."

"Are you up to seeing me tomorrow?"

"Of course. Dwayne's parents left this morning, so I'm still planning to ride to Denver with you. I've decided to hire a car and drive myself home after we spend a whole day together."

"Galveston is a long way from Denver."

"True. But I'll take my time. A few days alone will give me time to do some serious thinking about my marriage. I was over the moon when I discovered I'm preggers, but Dwayne didn't exude a smidgeon of joy. I'm glad he went home before we got here. Glad I've had a whole week away from him. But I don't want to dwell on Dwayne. I'm so looking forward to our gabfest."

"I am, too. We haven't had a long face-to-face chinwag for months."

"Two nights and an entire day together will be smashing."

"Spot on," VJ agreed, then added, "I've seen Holt."

"Have you talked to him?"

"Yes. Every day since Sunday."

"How did he find you?"

"I don't know, and that worries me, because Freddie might also find me."

"Let's hope not. What was it like to see Holt after all this time?"

"Wonderful. Marvelous. Devastating, because we have no future."

"Did he say why he's in Colorado?"

"He offered me a job in his homeland."

"Are you going to take it?"

"You know I can't."

"I don't know any such thing."

"I won't drag Holt into my problems."

"If you went with him, you might not have any."

"They will be with me wherever I go, unless I find a way to resolve them."

"You don't have to do that alone, Ver."

"Yes, I do. In any event, we can talk about everything when we're together."

"Righto."

After the call ended, VJ pondered her recent vision. Would telling Madeline her marriage was on the rocks help her get through the divorce more easily?

VJ didn't always share her visions. Didn't like to interfere in people's lives. But sometimes she didn't feel she had a choice. Was this one of those times?

# *Three*

Using withheld information as an excuse to talk to Verity Jane, Holt called her in the evening.

"Holt here. Thought I should mention there's a stipulation to our offer."

"What?

"The governing kew wants you to sign a five-year contract."

"Five years is a bloody long time."

"If five isn't agreeable, we'll settle for three. We prefer to have you in Api permanently, but we'll understand if you don't want to commit. If you sign our contract, we'll pay you twice as much as you would make as a doctor on the surface."

"Unbelievable," she gasped. "I had no idea your homeland could be so generous."

"We have ample financial reserves. You won't have many expenses. Your cottage and food will be provided, except when you eat out. You could wind up bagging a substantial sum, Verity."

"I'm flattered by the offer." She didn't sound flattered; she sounded dumbfounded.

"Think about it," Holt suggested, hoping he had made progress. "Let me know if you have questions. You have my number."

Ending the call, he lowered the back of the bedroom recliner and clicked the TV remote to unmute the sound. The newscaster spouted Covid-19 statistics and predicted the dire expectation that the virus would worsen now that winter and the flu season were approaching.

Turning the TV off a few hours later, he admitted his desire for Verity Jane's safety wasn't the only reason he wanted her back in Api. He still wanted to tie with her. But that was a lost dream. After Verity left, he had committed his future to Hanna and Harmony.

He and Hanna had worked together at NASA and resigned on the same day. A month later, Harmony was born in Apitcote. When Harmony was five months old, Hanna returned to the surface to care for her mother who had stage four lung cancer and hip problems that kept her in a wheelchair. Holt had suggested moving Aleece to Apitcote, but she refused to leave her home and lifelong friends.

His afone beeped. Checking his atexts, he grinned when he saw a new photo of Harmony.

He atexted back, thanking Hanna for the photo and asking how her mother was. Within seconds, Hanna called. "Hi, Holt. Do you have a few minutes to talk?"

"Sure." He glanced at his awatch. Midnight in Denver. Two hours later in Pennsylvania. "What are you doing up in the middle of the night?"

"I haven't been to bed yet. This is the only time I get to myself."

"How is your mater?"

"Better. She actually feels good. A dear friend visited yesterday. Mom got dressed in new clothes I ordered online."

"Is she still having chemo?"

"Radiation now. Once a month. The reason I called is to tell you that her friend offered to stay with her so Harmony and I can visit you in Api."

"That's great. When?"

"Will early next month work for you?"

"Sure."

"I'll call or text dates after I make airline reservations."

"How long can you stay?"

"A week. Maybe two. I don't want to be away from Mother too long."

"I'll meet you at the airport."

"Thanks. There's another reason I called."

"What?"

"The answer to your question is yes. I'd like to tie when Harmony and I move back to Api permanently."

After the call, Holt planted his elbows on his knees and plunked his head in his hands. Hanna had said 'yes.' She had waited so long to reply he thought she had forgotten his question. She wanted to tie with him. Live together. He should have been relieved, but regret burned through him. Hot and scalding. A future with Verity Jane was impossible.

~ * ~

Staggered by the amount of money Holt had offered, VJ contemplated all the things she could do if she accepted the job. Pay off her debt to Freddie. Hire a lawyer to clear her of the murder charge. Reimburse Mum for the money she had borrowed to help her and Madeline emigrate to the U.S. Help Madeline when she got divorced.

If she paid off Freddie's loans, she would never be beholden to anyone again. But she didn't want to sign a contract. Signing

Freddie's to get through university and medical school had been huge mistakes. Determined not to make more, she squashed the tempting kernel before it could grow.

Having worked five twelve-hour shifts in a row—two more than her usual schedule—VJ felt bone tired. She undressed, donned a silk nightdress, and climbed in bed.

As she did every night, she snuggled her handbag close as though it were a beloved pet. Her handbag contained the deed to Vincent's mansion, and she kept it with her all the time—except when working. Then she locked it securely inside her locker at the hospital.

Holt's offer snuck back inside her head. Half tempted to take the leap and return to Api, she argued with herself. If she didn't accept, she might regret it for the rest of her life. But not only did she not want to sign a contract, she didn't want to jeopardize Holt's life or any of the denizens who lived below.

An inner voice tried to convince her she wouldn't jeopardize anyone's life, and Freddie would never find her there. But if she left, what would she do about the mansion? She had already ignored last year's property taxes. If they went unpaid, she could lose the property—and Vincent's Boston home held some of her dearest memories.

What a conundrum. She needed to ensure taxes were paid. If she inquired, would Freddie be able to locate her? Trace her? Turn her whereabouts over to the law?

There were so many things she didn't know about owning property in the U.S. She knew the mansion and land were owned freehold, not leasehold as many properties were in the U.K.

Having focused on her medical education and studying to become an American citizen, she didn't know the proper words to use to search online. Using her prepaid phone, she googled property in Massachusetts. Then she started over, typed in property taxes. After that, she searched for back taxes. Finally, she typed the address of the Boston mansion. By the time she finished reading about liens and unpaid taxes, her thoughts brimmed with questions that kept her awake most of the night.

~ * ~

Early the next morning, VJ spent more than an hour talking to Massachusetts state employees before she satisfied herself that the mansion's taxes were not in arrears, and the deed was still in her name—Verity Jane Bagner.

By the time Holt called, she had begun to fear he wouldn't call at all. That he might have changed his mind and left.

"Hello, Verity Jane. How are you?"

"Busy," she said, trying not to sound relieved.

"Too busy to talk right now?"

"No."

"Have you made up your mind?"

Was that panic in his voice? "I'm not going with you."

"What would convince you to leave Denver? More money? Fame? Name it."

She wanted to blurt, 'Are you willing to help me figure out how to prove my innocence?' But she didn't. Although they had been close once, he had never mentioned the future. The love they shared was behind, not in front of them.

"Your offer is incredibly generous, Holt, but I can't accept it."

"I think you can." He sounded calm.

She felt more nervous. "I'm not moving to your homeland."

"Sorry to hear that." Instead of coaxing as she anticipated, he said, "I'll let you go. You must have things to do on your day off."

Disappointment gushed through her. He had gone to the trouble of discovering she wasn't working today, but he hadn't tried to change her mind. She told herself she hadn't expected him to. But part of her wished he had.

She stared at the closed curtains she had never opened. Her social orbit was so small she could count the people she kept in touch with on one hand. Hiding had kept her from cultivating new friends or contacting old ones. Rarely did she make plans for her days off. Sometimes she thought she might as well be in jail. Living alone, social distancing before it was necessary, not going out, avoiding people, made an extremely lonely life.

In Boston, she had communicated with Mum and sisters often via telephone, email, and texts. During the past year, she had sent cards and letters, but she hadn't mailed them from Denver. She sent them to Madeline who reposted them from Texas. Would she ever see her family again?

Swiping her fingers through her hair, she reminded herself that feeling sorry for herself wouldn't change a bloody thing. And today she had plans to see Madeline.

Just as her mood perked up, her prepaid phone beeped. She checked the message from Madeline. *What time are you leaving Denver?*

She texted back. *Still in my nightdress. Plan to leave around ten.*

As she finished texting, her old phone with a new number rang. Holt. Her heart lurched and she had to clear her throat before she could speak. "Hello."

"Hello again. How are you now?"

His second call reminded her of the fun they had shared when they first met, often texting mere moments after they parted, sometimes when they were only a few meters apart and could still wink and grin at each other. "I'm uncommonly good. How are you?"

"Better than you probably remember."

"That's a weird thing to say."

Instead of commenting, he said, "I haven't accepted your 'no' yet. I'd like to drop by, and let you take a look at the contract."

VJ's heart rate spiked. She had a chance to see him again before he left. What could she say? "Will your parents be with you?"

"Yeah. They need an outing. We're taking a drive up the mountains. The aspens have turned. Mater and Pater want to see them. You're welcome to go with us."

"Do you have a destination in mind?"

"Thought we'd make a loop. Take I-70 west to Frisco, south through Breckenridge and Fairplay and return via Colorado Springs. Want to go with us?"

"I'll think about it."

But she didn't have to think. She was already going. Might as well be with them. And Madeline would enjoy seeing Holt again.

Heart pounding, she texted Madeline as soon as Holt's call ended. *Would you mind terribly if Holt and his parents accompany me today?*

*Not a smidge,* Madeline texted back. *I'd adore seeing Holt. And Dwayne's grandparents always enjoy meeting new people.*

*I'll call when we reach Placer Valley.*

*Jolly good!*

~ * ~

Emotions gyrated inside Holt like rocks inside a cement pitcarn. Verity had not accepted the offer. What could he do to incentivize her? He had made sure she wouldn't face disciplinary action for what she'd done in the ER. She liked her job. He doubted she liked her boss, though. Why hadn't she followed her plan to be a doctor? She was smart, gifted, dedicated.

"Have regrets, do you, son?"

Sometimes, Kirt was too alert. And tuned in. Even though Holt kept himself permanently bloxed, Pater often sensed his thoughts. "Doesn't everyone?" he countered.

"Regrets. Yes. I've had a few. A daughter for one."

"You are an excellent parent."

"Good of you to say. You are an outstanding son, but Jilly wasn't an ideal daughter. She had too many flaws to be happy."

"We can't change the past."

Kirt's sad gaze made Holt's gut clench. "Right. The present, perhaps. The future, maybe. But not the past."

Pulling a mug of hot chocolate from the microwave, Holt carried it to Pater, who was seated on a high-backed stool at the mansion's long kitchen counter. "How is Mater this morning?"

"Serene. Thoughtful. Quiet."

"Are the two of you up for more time on the surface?"

"For what reason?"

"I need more time to convince Verity Jane to return to Api."

"She might return to be with you. She loves you."

"No, she doesn't. I doubt she ever did."

Pater flexed his brows. "Asked her, have you?"

Holt shook his head. "She removed that question when she insisted I bring her back to the surface."

"Perhaps she's had a change of heart." Pater patted Holt's arm. "If you don't ask, the question will remain."

*I'm not free to ask.*

"I'd be pleased just to have Verity back in our homeland." Holt still didn't have a clue who he and his hired detective were protecting her from. Or why.

"Are we planning to stop in Philadelphia to see Hanna and Harmony on our way home?" Pater asked.

"Probably not, if I convince Verity to return with us. But Hanna is planning to visit us next month."

Kirt grinned. "Best news I've heard in a long time." While he sipped more hot chocolate Mater entered the kitchen.

"You look well rested," Holt observed.

"I am, and I'm looking forward to our outing."

"Holt said Harmony and Hanna will visit Api in October," Kirt announced.

Shelan smiled. "That's marvelous."

Holt gave her a gentle hug. She looked better than she had for months, but not entirely like her old self. Hopefully the outing would be good for her and Pater. He was sure it would be if he convinced Verity Jane to join them. Looking forward to a visit from Harmony and Hanna had cheered them for sure.

Martha, the housekeeper, bustled into the sunny kitchen.

"I'm pleased you have made yourselves at home. However, I enjoy cooking. Tell me what you want for breakfast, and then go seat yourselves in the dining room."

Holt's afone trilled. He pulled it off his belt hook. Juhree—his closest kew sister.

She said, "I called because our kew mates want to know if you had any problem printing the contract for Verity."

"I didn't. Tell them I plan to have her read it today."

"I assume that means you're not coming home soon."

"Even if I convince Verity to return with us, she'll need to give some kind of notice."

"That brings me to the other reason for my call. Doctors and medics have suggested closing all enquays. The coronavirus is spreading on the surface again. No one wants Covid to travel here."

"Closing enquays is a good precaution. Will you keep me informed?"

"Sure. And Mist will send atexts when or if there's more to share."

"Thanks. I'm driving Mater and Pater up to the mountains today. I've invited Verity to go with us. That will give me more time to convince her. If I fail, I might hire another detective for double protection, and we'll come back without her."

After disconnecting the call, Holt considered calling Hanna to tell her about the potential enquay closing.

But she called first.

"I have to put my plans on hold. Mom's visitor yesterday just called to tell us she was exposed to Covid-19. We have to isolate for ten days. If we all remain healthy, I'll make reservations to visit later in October."

"There might be a problem on my end," he said. "Our doctors and medics have advised closing all enquays to keep Covid out of Api."

"Can't say I blame them. Keep me posted."

"Will do. I miss Harmony. She's growing so fast."

"She's also talking early. And more every day. Her phrases sound like gibberish to Mom, but I understand what she says. Should we face chat?"

"Sure." Holt saw and heard Hanna coaching Harmony, telling her what to say.

"Ha-wo, Miz-ter Holt."

His throat choked up before he managed to say, "Hello, little Harmony."

She repeated, "Ha-wo wid-o Arm-man-ee."

He was so pleased to see and hear her he still felt choked up when Hanna spoke again. "I need to go. Mom's ringing her bell. I'll take a video of Harmony and forward it."

"Thanks."

"Good news or bad?" Kirt asked, his brow furrowed.

"Not good. Hanna and Harmony and Aleece might have been exposed to Covid so the early October visit will be delayed."

"Let's hope they don't get the virus."

"We've only seen Harmony once since she started chattering," Shelan said. "Last time, we weren't good company. The spell we were under kept us quiet."

"Harmony probably doesn't even remember who we are," Pater grumbled.

"Hanna shows her photos of us every day, tells her who we are, and has her repeat our names."

Kirt grinned. "That's great."

"Do you expect Hanna to keep her promise to bring Harmony back to live in Api when she turns five?" Shelan asked.

Holt nodded, reluctant to share his news—that Hanna had agreed to tie.

"How long do you think Aleece will live?"

"Her cancer doctor said two to five years."

"Hanna and Harmony left Api eight months ago," Mater recalled. "I have a feeling Aleece won't survive much longer."

"That's a gloomy prediction," Pater said.

"Aleece might not think so," Mater disagreed. "I suspect she is exhausted by cancer treatments and tired of living in a wheelchair."

With a nod, Pater looked at Holt. "Are you going to tell Verity Jane about Harmony?"

"I have no reason to. I doubt she'd interested in knowing anyway."

"Be that as it may, we are proud of you for agreeing to help Hanna raise Harmony. Watching her grow gives us great pleasure."

"I feel the same, although I'm not looking forward to disciplining her when she needs it."

Mater smiled. "You'll do fine. You love her. That's more important than anything else."

Pater cleared his throat. "Back to Verity. If she moves to Api, she will hear about Hanna and your agreement. You should tell her."

"I won't cross that walkway unless I have to." Holt knew telling her sooner was better than later. But when he had agreed to be the father figure in Harmony's life, he hadn't expected to see Verity Jane again. And after suggesting tying with Hanna more than once, he hadn't expected her to ever say yes.

~ * ~

At Verity's apartment, she opened the door with the first warm smile Holt had seen all week. "Please come through."

The threesome trooped inside. "You look lovely," Shelan complimented. "Your blouse is the color of spring buttercups. It matches Holt's shirt."

Verity's cheeks turned a becoming shade of pink as Kirt asked, "Do you have a favorite color, Dr. Verity?"

"Yellow," she said. "Same as the aspens you're going to see."

Holt extended a stapled document. "Here's the contract I mentioned."

Verity scanned each page before she said, "I don't sign contracts. They have consequences."

"No problem. We could agree by shaking hands. We'll still pay twice what you could earn as a doctor here."

Her jaw dropped, but she recovered quickly. "I'm not making a verbal or written commitment."

Holt extended his hand anyway. "Let's call a truce for the day. Come with us to see the aspens. I promise not to mention my offer again. Deal?"

"Deal."

Holt almost grinned. But her refusal to accept his offer choked the impulse. Taking her free hand in his, he shook it. "Jolly good."

Verity set the contract on a table. "I have a request."

Holt released her hand. "What?"

"Madeline is near Alma, visiting her husband's grandparents in Placer Valley and I promised to see her today. If I go with you, will that interfere with your plans?"

"Not at all. I'd enjoy seeing Madeline again."

"She said the same about you. I also agreed to drive her back to Denver. Is there room for her in your car?"

"Of course."

"She'll have luggage. Is the boot full?"

"No. The trunk's empty."

She gave him a steady, considering look. "You're very accommodating."

He returned her scrutinizing stare. "Was there a time when I wasn't?"

"No. I thought perhaps you had changed."

"I have."

"In what ways?"

"I'm dedicated to my homeland. No longer willing to live on the surface."

Her eyes widened. "Were you willing to do that once?"

"When I thought I was in love." Not proud of his curt reply, he strode to the door. "We should hit the road." Touching her had affected more than his body. His brain was whirling with memories that felt like they had occurred three days ago, not three years. But a lot had happened during those years. The most important, of course, was Harmony.

While Verity set her security system, Holt clamped down the emotions colliding inside him. Even if he convinced her to return to Api and Hanna changed her mind about tying with him, he and Verity had no future. He wasn't willing to open his heart again. Besides, he had made a solemn commitment to Hanna before her attorney prepared a document naming him as Harmony's sole guardian if anything happened to render Hanna incapable of raising the child who owned a huge portion of his beleaguered heart.

# *Four*

As the foursome trekked outdoors, Verity asked, "Are you sitting in front, Kirt?"

"No. I prefer to sit with Shelan."

Holt opened the passenger door. Verity slid by him, so close her essence filled his senses. He resisted the urge to touch her again. And felt guilty for the urge.

All were quiet while he drove west, but he sensed questions galloping through all their minds.

At the top of the hill near Genesee, the huge rocky mountain range loomed ahead and Shelan gushed, "Oh my. The panorama of yellow leaves interspersed among pine trees nearly takes my breath away."

Holt flashed her a grin in the rear-view mirror and Verity startled him when she said, "I've missed your dimpled grins, Holt." As though embarrassed, she turned her head and stared out the side window.

They were being followed by the same green van that had tailed Verity from the hospital. A second vehicle stayed behind the van, followed by a tan pickup truck occupied by Holt's hired detective.

He had used Arcane magic to trace the man driving the sedan and discovered he had been hired to find Verity Jane and he worked for a law firm with offices in Florida and Massachusetts. Holt didn't intend to allow him or the guy in the green van to get close to her.

During the night, he had finally managed to 'read' the van guy. For once, the dude wasn't high on crack, his thoughts not entirely jumbled. He was obsessed with Verity. Wanted to hurt her. But didn't have enough nerve to shoot her.

Because no one seemed inclined to talk, Holt asked, "Would anyone like to listen to music?"

"Yes, please," Shelan said.

Holt activated the kew's Sirius surface app.

Miles later, when they entered the Eisenhower tunnel, Kirt said, "Tunnels on the surface are quite different from Api's tunnels."

"What I remember most about your homeland are the two, long, half-day hikes Holt and I took to get there and return," Verity said. "Your tunnel is small, unlighted, unpaved, and people walk rather than ride."

"Not anymore." Kirt sounded alert. "Now, we use motor bikes that hover above the ground, so the ride is smooth and quick."

"We adore the new hoverz bikes." Shelan's eyes gleamed when Holt caught another glimpse of her in the mirror.

"The bikes sound intriguing," Verity said. "When the bikes hover above ground, they must stir up dust."

Pater chuckled, and Mater laughed. "No dust, my dear. The bikes are a joy."

After they left I-70 and cruised through Frisco and Breckenridge, Verity said, "We're approaching Hoosier Pass. It's steep and winding with sharp twists and turns."

"I know," Holt said. "I drove up here when I attended the Colorado School of Mines."

"I don't recall you telling me you graduated in Golden."

"I don't recall you asking."

She pursed her lips and stared at the scenery.

As they descended the summit, the green van pulled out as if to pass. Holt sensed the driver's intent to run them off the road seconds before he turned toward them. Stomping on the brake, Holt used his Arcane magic to lift the rental above the ground.

Instead of ramming or even sideswiping them, the van bolted across their lane, plowed off the pavement and crashed into a tree about a hundred yards away.

Holt lowered the sedan back to the ground. Verity was screaming. Shelan and Kirt uttered not a word until Holt parked on the side of the road. He cast a quick charm to calm Verity. She stopped screaming, but her face was as white as snow.

"That was an unexpected thrill," Shelan said.

"I'll say," Kirt agreed and silently conveyed, "*I cast a spell on Verity. She doesn't remember you jettisoned us ten feet above the ground.*"

As the pickup parked behind them, Mater sent a silent message. "*I spelled him. He thinks the driver was speeding and failed to pull back into our lane after he passed.*"

"Is everyone okay?" the detective asked as he reached their rental and Holt opened the door.

"Yes, but we need to check the guy who almost sideswiped us." Holt glanced at Verity, relieved to see color returning to her cheeks.

"I'll go," the detective volunteered. "I've already called nine-one-one. The police should be here soon."

"I'll go with him," the sedan driver said.

"Sorry I screamed," Verity apologized while they waited. "That dodgy driver drove at an improper speed. Are you sure you're all fine?"

"We are," Pater answered. "Don't know about the guy who drove off the road, though."

The two men returned as a police car arrived, siren blaring, lights flashing.

"The van's empty," Holt's detective reported. "The door is open. Nobody's inside. I looked around but didn't see anyone."

"Was there blood or any evidence that the driver was injured?" Verity asked.

"No. No blood inside or out. No footprints or trail to follow either."

"Guess we don't need an ambulance, but I need to write up a report," the officer said.

"I saw what happened," the detective said. "I can tell you what you need to know."

When all the excitement finally died down, Holt drove a few miles before he asked, "Are we getting close to Madeline's in-laws' cabin?"

"Yes," Verity answered. "This is Placer Valley. Turn right onto that dust road."

Holt grinned. Dust—her term for dirt and gravel. He crossed a small creek and turned.

The pickup and sedan stayed on the highway and drove on by. Holt had told his detective to get something to eat and wait for them near Fairplay.

Still looking spooked, Verity pulled a disposable phone from her shoulder bag. "I'll call Madeline and let her know we're almost there."

When she finished, she said, "Turn left at the fork in the road." Moments later, she said, "That's the lane to their cabin." She pointed ahead at a graveled driveway.

A few yards beyond a tall garage, Madeline and an elderly couple stood outside the log cabin's green door, waving, smiling and unmasked.

"Do you think we should wear masks?" Mater asked before Verity opened her door.

"No. Madeline said there haven't been any cases of Covid up here."

After introducing Betty and Phil, Madeline and VJ bumped elbows instead of their usual hug. "We haven't been together for yonks."

"A long time," VJ agreed. "We had a bit of excitement on Hoosier Pass. A bloke tried to pass us on a curve and drove into the copse."

"Was he injured?"

"We don't know. The van was empty when it was checked."

"Are you all okay?"

"Yes," everyone murmured.

"Let's go inside," Phil suggested.

"We'd prefer to sit outdoors, on your deck, if we may," Holt said. "We drove up to enjoy the aspens."

"Splendid." Betty smiled. "Sometimes the leaves turn yellow and are blown away in August. We're delighted they're lasting longer this year."

They climbed two steps and settled around a triangular table by a corner bench attached to the deck. Holt sat next to Madeline and bloxed her, but not before he read her concern about Verity's safety, which increased his determination to convince her to leave Colorado. Today's incident, along with the others that week, were churning his insides to mush.

"The aspens are a vista of yellow and gold," Shelan observed as VJ dug her old phone from her handbag and started to video them and the scenery.

"What's the name of the small creek?" Kirt asked.

"Middle Fork of the South Platte River," Phil answered.

"Are there any fish?"

Phil nodded. "The river runs through the lower part of our property."

"Some days Phil wanders down and catches trout for dinner," Betty added.

"Your pine trees look fuller, plumper than others I've seen," Shelan said.

"They're bristlecone, and they have five needles rather than two or three. Bristlecones are some of the oldest living trees on earth. They only grow in a few places. Those in Colorado are two or three thousand years old. Some in California, if the wild fires haven't destroyed them, are over five thousand."

A flock of birds flew overhead, chirping and squawking as though something had disturbed them. Then a telephone rang. "That's our land line," Betty said. "Excuse me, please."

Her eyes were bright with excitement when she returned. "Our neighbor called to say a bear is headed from her property to ours. We should go inside."

VJ continued to video as Betty motioned everyone through the prow's sliding glass doors. Nestled among pines and aspens, the log cabin had floor to ceiling windows on every wall, revealing a fantastic view of the forest and the small ribbon of river beyond.

"Let's separate." Betty suggested. "If we look out the bedroom windows, we might see the bear."

VJ and Holt followed Madeline to a corner bedroom and his parents followed Betty and Phil to another.

"There he is." Madeline pointed as a bear came hobbling down the gravel drive on all fours.

A rush of excitement scooted through VJ while she videoed the bear, and Madeline dashed away to collect the others.

All seven hurried to the back door and watched through a side window. As the bear hobbled around the cabin, they moved to the mud room, then to the kitchen, and finally back to the great room as the bear hobbled up the two deck steps. Delighted to be recording the event, VJ moved closer to the windows.

Crawling past them, the bear approached the table where they had sat moments before. Goose pimples prickled VJ's skin as the animal turned the corner and stopped in front of the glass doors, mere inches from where she videoed.

His growl made her heart lurch. She expected him to attack. Break the glass. As if something magic changed his mind, he turned his back on them, and stared at the spa cover. He crawled away. Reached the edge of the spa. Took a few more steps. And sank as the cover bent in half and slowly sagged until it hit bottom.

Phil chuckled, and the others laughed while the bear splashed around, trying to climb out, but kept sliding backwards instead. "Bet he's never been in hot water before."

"Watching him is great fun," Shelan said.

"He scares me." Madeline inched away while the others laughed, and VJ continued to video.

"I'll call the ranger station and ask someone to come rescue him," Phil said.

While they waited for the rangers, the struggling bear managed to claw his way out of the spa, gouging and mangling the cover in the process. He shook water off before he stood on his hind legs and stared at them through the glass. VJ walked forward to capture a closeup.

The bear lowered back to all fours. Hobbled closer. When he stuck his nose against the glass she jumped back. Stumbled. Started to fall.

Holt caught her halfway down to the cinnamon carpet. She blushed, her face hot. Her body heated up, too. But she continued to video the bear. He raised a paw. Scraped his claw over the glass. Growled again. Five of the seven backed away. Holt and Verity remained squatting, so close they inhaled each other's breath.

"Do you think he can break the glass?" VJ asked, trembling, videoing, and totally aware that Holt's arms were still wrapped around her.

"The glass is triple pane," Phil said, "but I'll get my rifle, just in case."

VJ's insides were shaking, her awareness spiking. "I'm fine, Holt. You may let go."

"Right." He slid his arms from her, stood and backed away.

She stood and managed to maintain a sense of equilibrium, but just barely. When she snuck a quick glance at Holt, he was watching her, not the bear. Her pounding heart reacted by pounding harder.

Rangers arrived after the bear hobbled away, shaking more water off his thick fur when he reached the front stairs—six instead of two because the cabin was built on unlevel terrain. Approaching cautiously, one ranger aimed a tranquilizer gun and stunned the bear with his shot.

"What kind of bear is he?" Madeline asked.

"Black. Only black bears live in Colorado," Phil said.

"He's brown."

"Black is the name of his species, not the color."

"What will you do with him?" VJ asked after rangers loaded him in the back of their truck and chained one paw to the guard-bar rail.

"We'll tag and drive him up the mountain, away from residential areas. If he comes down this far again, we'll try to donate him to a zoo. If we can't find one that wants him, he'll have to be euthanized."

"I sincerely hope that doesn't happen," Shelan said.

"Agreed," Madeline said.

As the rangers drove away, Betty asked, "Will you eat dinner with us?"

"We don't want to inconvenience you," Holt said. "We'll eat at Alma's Only Bar."

"Betty wouldn't have invited you if she thought you were an inconvenience," Phil said.

"Yesterday," Madeline added, "we celebrated Thanksgiving early so we have leftovers galore."

"Too much food to eat by ourselves," Betty agreed. "Please join us. We'd love one last dinner with Madeline."

VJ had a feeling it would be their last.

After dinner and the washing up, Betty and Phil followed them out to the car. "We shall miss you, Madeline, dear."

"I'll miss you, too."

"Thank you again for welcoming us into your home and sharing your food," VJ said.

"You're welcome anytime. We love your British accent."

VJ's cheeks heated. Americans were always saying that. She believed women. Didn't believe men. Most used it as a pickup line, as Freddie had.

The mere thought of him created a dizzying flashback. Or a vision. She didn't know which. He had been driving the green van. And he had tried to run them off the road. How had Holt avoided a car crash?

She saw Freddie climb out of the van, dart around trees and bushes, and hide when the two men went looking for him.

Kirt's voice brought her back to the present.

"Seeing that bear was a real thrill."

"We have bears in our forests at home, but this is the first time I've seen one up close," Shelan said. "Watching him made my heart race."

"Mine, too." Kirt winked. "A grand experience to share with our friends when we go home."

"I could send you a copy of my video on a flash drive," VJ offered.

"That would be splendid." Shelan's eyes and Kirt's were shining as they had when VJ met them three years ago. She inhaled. Smelled no illness or lingering melancholy. Knew both were healed.

As Holt pulled off the dust road onto the highway, VJ wished the day wouldn't end. Being with Holt and his parents again made her long for the kind of life they lived.

Holt checked the rear-view mirror. Two vehicles had followed them from Fairplay all the way back to Denver. As they approached Verity's apartment building, Holt caught Madeline's gaze in the mirror. "Are you planning to stay with Verity?"

"Yes. Where is your accommodation?"

"In an eight-bedroom mansion that's owned by a retired judge."

"How do you know a retired judge?" Verity asked, clearly curious.

"He and his wife live where we do. Their daughter is one of my kew sisters"

"Is she married or single?" Madeline asked, and Verity ducked her head as though embarrassed by the probing question.

"Married. To one of my kew brothers."

"How long have you and Madeline been friends?" Shelan asked.

"Since primary school, years before we emigrated to the U.S."

"That's a good long time."

"It truly is," Madeline agreed. "When I was ten, Verity's mum rescued me from a bad family situation and arranged to foster me. She treated me like one of her own daughters."

"And we feel like sisters," Verity added.

After Holt parked in front of her door, Verity blinked. All color drained from her face. He turned his head to see why and saw her empty carport.

"My car's gone," she gasped. "Someone must have stolen it."

"Someone should call the police straightaway," Madeline said.

Holt punched nine-one-one, reported the theft and gave Verity's address.

Before the police arrived, her cell phone rang.

"Hello," she answered, unwittingly hitting the speaker icon.

"Is Bob there?

"Bob who?"

"Bob Robacar."

Holt was so in tune he felt her fear. *Bob Rob-a-car.*

Yanking the phone from her ear, she severed the connection.

Silence filled the air until Holt reached for her shaky hands. "Try not to worry."

"I cannot not worry." Her voice trembled, and her eyes filled with tears.

"Perhaps we should all go inside," Shelan suggested.

"Good idea," Madeline agreed.

Verity unlocked her front door. As the others entered, she said, "I set my alarm before we left. It's been turned off."

"I'll go check the back door." Holt checked the bed and bathroom as well. Back in the living room, he reported, "There's a broken window above the kitchen sink, but the back door is still locked. I don't think anyone came inside."

"I don't sense an intrusive presence," Verity said. "My alarm must have gone off and scared away whoever tried to get in. The security company probably turned the system off when I didn't answer." She checked calls on her prepaid, saw the company had called. She hadn't heard it ring because she'd been videoing the bear with her old phone and the prepaid wasn't nearby.

"Maybe you should see if anything was stolen," Holt suggested, not particularly pleased with himself for being glad he had a reason to insist Verity and Madeline stay in the mansion with them.

Clutching the strap of the bag dangling from her shoulder, Verity checked drawers and closets with Madeline and Holt following.

"Nothing seems to be missing," she said when she finished and stared at the unsigned contract still on the table.

"Should I make tea?" Madeline asked.

"Please do."

All were sipping when the police arrived. Verity answered questions. Her companions sat in silence while the other police officer filled out forms. "You shouldn't stay here tonight," he said.

"He's right," Kirt agreed. "You best stay with us."

"We'd appreciate that," Madeline said.

Relieved he didn't have to convince them, Holt made sure both doors were locked and the security system set before he ushered everyone back out to the rental car.

~ * ~

The drive to Cherry Hills passed in a blur. VJ worried about her car, the broken kitchen window, the spooky phone call, and the near accident on Hoosier Pass. She was beyond grateful not to be spending tonight alone or in her flat.

At the mansion, a kindly middle-aged woman welcomed them with a cheery smile. "I'm Martha, the live-in housekeeper. Follow me, girls. I'll show you to your rooms. My husband, Blaine, will help Holt and Kirt carry your luggage."

They followed Martha up the grand staircase. After the men placed their bags in separate rooms, Shelan said, "Kirt and I are ready to retire."

"Perhaps we all should," Madeline suggested.

"Good idea," Holt agreed and walked away.

VJ and Madeline lingered in the hallway. Relieved to be with Holt, his parents and Madeline, VJ forced her mind off her fear. "I'm glad you'll be with me tomorrow, Madd."

"Me, too."

"Have you talked to Dwayne today?"

"No. We text more than we talk, even when I'm home."

"Why didn't he come with you to Colorado?"

"He started out with us, but on the second day, he said he had to fly home because he was needed at the office—which totally surprised me. His work load is at the end of the year, not in September, and Phil and Betty are his grandparents, not mine."

"He didn't mind you continuing your holiday without him?"

"No, but he was irritated when I decided to stay longer and rent a car to drive home instead of flying."

"He's probably worried about you driving that far alone."

"I doubt it. He complained about running out of clean shirts and underwear. I told him the washer and dryer are still in the laundry room. I was teasing but that made him angry."

"I'm really sorry he's not happy about your pregnancy."

"I was, but I'm not now." Madeline licked her lips. Looked down at the shiny marble floor. "He's having an affair with our neighbor, Carlotta. I'm convinced she's the real reason he went home. We planned this holiday months ago."

"Do you love him?"

"I've asked myself that a gazillion times. Maybe I don't. Maybe I never did. Maybe we should get a divorce. What do you think?"

"I think you should follow your bliss, not my advice."

"That's the rub. I don't have marital bliss. I married a bloke who isn't right for me."

"He loved you."

"I don't think so. I think he was infatuated, as I was. Presumably he fell for my British accent, and I fell for his glib tongue." She shook her head ruefully. "Blimey. Enough about me. I'm sorry your car got stolen, and your flat window is broken. Do you have any idea who did it?"

"Not unless Freddie had something to do with it. I suspect he wants the deed to Vincent's mansion, which brings up another point. I had a vision of him today—or rather a flashback. He's in

Colorado. He's the bloke who tried to run us off the road on our way to see you."

"What a diabolical creep! I can't believe we liked him once. That we trusted him."

"Me, either."

"Good thing I paid off his loans before I married Dwayne." Madeline frowned, reached out and held VJ's hands. "I don't want to go home."

VJ's heart went out to her. "And I don't want you to go. Our time together is never long enough."

"Righto. I could stay another day or two until you're back in your flat and feel safe. I could even stay a week or longer."

"I doubt that would please Dwayne."

"Maybe it will. Maybe he fancies more time with Carlotta."

"I really would like you to stay as long as you feel you can take time off," VJ said.

"I'm on leave. As soon as I discovered I'm expecting, I arranged for a sabbatical in case I need to stay off my feet for a while. I don't want another miscarriage." Madeline sighed. "I wish we lived closer to each other."

"I do, too."

"Maybe someday we will."

VJ summoned a cheerful smile. "That would be brilliant."

"Absolutely. Have you changed your mind about Holt's offer?"

"No."

"You're willing to push him out of your life again?"

"I don't have a choice."

"You once told me you wondered if you would ever get enough doses of him."

"I don't want to talk about Holt."

"You look zonked," Madeline sympathized. "We should go to bed."

"I agree. We're concerned about Covid, but I think it's safe to hug. I smell no disease."

Stepping closer, Madeline wrapped her arms around VJ and hugged tight. "You're the best thing that ever happened to me, Ver."

Choked up, VJ hugged her back. Madeline was truly her best friend, but Holt owned her heart. The silent admission made her eyes sting. She blinked to hold back tears.

Alone in her bedroom, VJ plunked on the queen bed and tried to unwind. Did Freddie have something to do with her missing car? Or was the car theft a random act? Would she ever see her Prius again? And why was Freddie in Colorado? To steal the deed to the mansion? He was the dodgy chap driving the green van, and she was convinced Holt had used magic to avoid an accident and somehow blocked her memory.

Unzipping her handbag, she removed the deed to the mansion and studied it. She had intended to put it in a safe deposit box but hadn't gotten around to renting one.

Mentally exhausted, she refolded the deed and stored it back in the zippered slot. Moments later, she climbed between the sheets with her handbag, the long strap wrapped around her wrist—twice.

Grateful Holt and his parents and Madeline were all sleeping under the same roof, even if only for one night, she relaxed her tense muscles. Her flat manager had texted, assuring her the broken window would be repaired tomorrow. The day after that, she had an early shift at hospital. But she had all day tomorrow plus several evenings to enjoy more time with Madeline. The unanticipated treat lulled her to sleep.

~ * ~

Holt leaned back in the bedroom recliner and let his thoughts wander. The chemistry between him and Verity was as strong as ever. When she left Api, he missed her so much he had placed his cottage on Apitcote's inventory list, packed his possessions, and gone to live on the surface, expecting to return home only for visits.

Discovering she was already living with another man had depleted the air in his lungs. Killed his optimism. He was a long time recovering. But he had accepted a position at NASA and was committed to fulfilling his agreed eighteen-month obligation.

During his first year, he learned more than anticipated. During the next six months, he learned even more. Space and the universe fascinated him.

What he learned about women exasperated him, with one exception—Hanna. She was older than he, exceptionally smart, and very brave. She would always have his unwavering respect and admiration. Harmony would always have his love. Holt had been present for her birth and had held her every day for the first five months of her life. And as often as possible after she left Api. She brought such joy into his life.

His thoughts shifted back to Verity. Images of her with another man had taken root three years ago and still thrived in his head. He couldn't keep them out. They popped up at odd times. Like today while he watched her video the bear. And again, when he kept her from falling on the cabin floor and held her in his arms. Did she respond to other men as she once responded to him? The guys she had lived with might not still be in her life, but they stood as a barrier between them. And always would.

The tap on his bedroom door didn't startle him. Nor was he surprised to see his parents after he called, "Come in." He sensed they had also overheard the hallway conversation.

Mater waved her arms and sealed the room so they wouldn't be heard.

"You look worried," Pater said. "Besides wondering who stole Verity's car, and who broke her kitchen window, do you have another problem?"

"Verity is being tailed. A man followed her to and from work all week. He has a gun, which I disabled, but he's been sleeping in his vehicle near her apartment. Today, two cars followed us. One was the van that tried to run us off the road. The other is parked down the street from here."

"She's with us," Shelan said, "so she's safe."

"For tonight," Kirt agreed, "but he's worried about the future."

"Right. Something tragic might happen if I don't convince her to go with us to Api."

Pater rubbed his whiskered chin, and Mater clasped her hands. Holt wished he hadn't confided. Both looked better than they had for months, and he didn't want to worry them. "I'll double my effort to keep Verity safe. Hire another detective to watch the people tailing her. Drive her to and from work. That should be acceptable since she no longer has a car."

"That's a good plan," Kirt agreed.

Holt knew Pater didn't believe the plan would solve Verity's problem. Neither did he.

Mater unsealed the room as Pater opened the door. "Dream only pleasant dreams, son."

"Thanks. You do the same." Alone again, Holt checked his atexts. His plans took a nose dive when he read the newest message from his kew sister, Mist.

*Closing enquays to safeguard against Covid-19. Suggest you return asap.*

If he didn't convince Verity Jane in the morning, they would have to leave without her.

He was also concerned about Madeline. She didn't want to return to Galveston. And she had several weeks off work. Would she be willing to spend part of that time in Apitcote?

Deciding to ask first thing in the morning, he closed his eyes and fell asleep in the recliner.

# Five

A vision awakened VJ. No spinning fans or dizziness this time—just a series of tiny stars circling her face. Then a yellow sunflower whose petals exploded like fireworks in a dark sky.

What she saw felt as real as breathing. She and Madeline were eating breakfast with Holt and his parents in the mansion's elegant dining room when VJ's old phone rang. She answered and a male voice said, "This is Ricardo Bentley. I'm calling to speak to Dr. Verity Jane."

She had met a man with that name in Florida when she traveled there with Vincent. "This is Dr. Verity."

"We met more than a year ago. Do you remember me?"

"Yes."

"Can you explain why we met?"

"You're the attorney who helped Vincent Jacob cancel his will, create a trust, and transfer the deed of his mansion to me."

"Excellent. I have some good news. May I schedule an appointment with you today?"

Staring at Holt, VJ whispered, "An attorney wants to see me. Is it okay to invite him here?"

"Sure."

"Do you need the address?" she asked.

"No. I'm outside." The doorbell rang.

In reality, VJ kept her secrets locked inside, but in the vision she said, "The attorney said he has good news but I might need moral support." She reached for Holt's and Madeline's hands and urged them to go with her.

Mr. Bentley greeted them with a smile. "Nice to see you, Dr. Verity Jane."

"You too, I hope."

With a black mask covering half of his face, he acknowledged Madeline and Holt with nods as VJ introduced them. Opening his briefcase, he withdrew a file and a three-ring binder. "Vincent instructed me to transfer a portion of his estate to you."

"He deeded his home to me. That's far more than I deserve."

Mr. Bentley continued. "The money Vincent gifted you was invested and has increased in value." He extended the binder. "Taxes on the gains have been paid to the IRS. I took the liberty of filing your tax return for last year. Did you complete an IRS return under your new name?"

"Yes."

"Good," he approved. "I'll have our accountant file an amended return with your new name and address. As a U.S. citizen, you are not required to pay taxes to the British Inland Revenue." He extended the file. "This contains a record of all transactions made by my firm. Vincent's gift to you was five hundred thousand dollars. Our investment department diversified your funds. You lost some money during the past year; however, you made more. Your portfolio has increased to six hundred."

"Six hundred thousand dollars?" she gasped before the vision blurred. And ended.

~ * ~

When she opened her eyes, she felt as though she had slept for hours and hours. But she was utterly disoriented.

Where was she?

Not in the bed where she had gone to sleep.

Not in the mansion either.

But she was with Holt. On a single bed, snuggled close. Both were fully dressed. Except for their feet. She heaved a quiet sigh, not knowing whether to be relieved or disappointed.

As she lay there trying to figure out how she had ended up in bed with Holt, she had a vague sensation of being inside a ski-like cage plunging at warp speed down a deep, dark shaft. Her heartbeat sped up, and her pulse raced. She still hadn't caught her breath when Holt said, "Good morning."

"Where are we?" she asked.

He looked around, his expression amused. "In my cottage."

"In Apitcote?"

"Yeah."

She had foreseen the future. She hadn't seen this. "We can't be."

"Where do you think we are?"

Miffed by his calm, she tried to leap off the bed. But her wrist was tied to Holt's, and he didn't budge. She glared at the yellow ribbon. "What is this bloody thing?" She jerked his hand with hers.

"Looks like a ribbon."

"Why is it tied around our wrists?"

He shrugged. Slowly. Nonchalantly. And didn't answer.

"Are we truly in Api?" she asked.

"Yes."

"This doesn't look like your cottage."

"I moved after you left."

"Why?"

"Various reasons."

Utterly irritated, she blasted, "You kidnapped me."

"Did I?"

"Don't try to act innocent."

"You think I'm acting?"

"Yes," she snapped, recalling her vision. She wasn't just mad. She was furious. *Mr. Bentley can't find me if I'm not in Denver.*

"I didn't kidnap you."

"What kind of spell did you cast?"

"I didn't cast a spell."

She gritted her teeth. Tried to clench both fists. But her fingers on one hand were laced with his. "What time is it? What day?"

He raised his arm, along with hers, and looked at his awatch. "Sunday. Six-fifteen p.m."

"It can't be," she wailed, unable to make her brain believe she was truly in Apitcote. "I could not possibly have slept two days and nights and missed the entire weekend." She moved her hands to swipe her hair off her face, raising Holt's hand too. "If I missed my shift at hospital without calling in, I may not have a job."

"Try not to be upset," Holt said.

Ignoring his attempt to soothe her, she jerked her emotions under control and spoke with perfect elocution. "I am furious, not upset. This is bloody ridiculous. Untie our wrists."

Holt did, so quickly he must have used magic. Instead of wadding the ribbon as she expected, he rolled it into a smooth coil and tucked it inside his shirt pocket. Only then did she notice he wore a blue shirt the color of his eyes and she wore her favorite yellow blouse and black slacks—not what she had worn to bed Friday night.

Trying to make sense of what had happened, she looked around, saw her daypack, backpack and two duffle bags, but not her handbag.

"Where's my handbag?" she choked, nearly gagging on panic.

Holt retrieved it from the nightstand on his side of the bed.

Grabbing it, she unzipped the pocket where she kept the deed. Her panic dissolved when she found it—until she discovered both phones were missing. "What happened to my phones?"

"Beats me."

"I need them. I can't stay here. I've got to go back. You must take me back."

"Leaving isn't an option."

"Don't you understand? I must leave."

"Not possible. Our enquays are closed." Rolling over, he slid off the bed in one smooth motion, stretched his arms above his head, and massaged the back of his neck. "I feel like I slept in the same position for a week. How do you feel?"

"Like I've been drugged."

He hiked his brows. "You feel sluggish?"

"No. I'm wide awake."

"I'm sorry."

"You should be," she hissed.

"You're upset. I'm sure you'll feel better after you calm down."

"I've seen little proof that things get better with the passage of time," she snapped, "and a great deal of evidence to suggest quite the opposite. This is not where I want to be. Not where I need to be." Jumping off the bed, she picked up her hiking boot and flung it at him. He ducked. Her boot missed his head by no more than an inch.

Amusement filled his eyes. "You still have a good aim."

"That isn't all I still have. You must take me back, Holt. I can't stay here," she squealed, hating the warble in her voice

"You'll have to until our enquays reopen." He strode to the door as she picked up another boot. "I'll give you some time alone to adjust."

Her other boot hit the door as he shut it behind him. Holt managed not to laugh, but he was grinning. He intended to call his parents until he saw Madeline on the couch.

Rubbing her eyes, she sat up and blinked. "Where are we?"

"In my homeland."

"Do you know where Verity is?"

Holt motioned at his bedroom door. "In there."

"Is this your home?"

"Yes."

She grinned. "Brilliant. How far are we from Texas?"

"Far, far away."

"So far my husband won't find me?"

"Yeah."

Madeline's grin expanded. "Blimey, that's flipping good news."

"Glad you approve."

"Is Verity awake?"

"Yeah. Upset, too. You might give her a few minutes to calm down."

"Okay. Mind if I explore? I need to spend a penny—locate the water closet," she translated.

"Bathroom's that way." He nodded beyond the small kitchen. "I'll step out back and call Mater and Pater. Make sure they're okay."

"Hi, Holt," Kirt answered. "Been expecting you to call."

"Hi," Shelan greeted him and explained. "We have you on speaker mode."

"How are you?" he asked.

"Fabulous. How are you?"

"I'm good."

"And the young ladies?"

"Madeline's happy. Verity Jane isn't. And I don't have to ask how we got home."

Mater's musical laughter trilled through his afone. "We haven't pulled a stunt on you since you were a child. Must admit, it was jolly good fun."

"Are you really feeling okay?" he asked.

"Yes. Great," Pater said.

"Right as midnight rain," Mater added cheerfully.

"Does bringing Verity Jane and Madeline here without their consent have anything to do with your pleasant mood?"

Pater chortled, and Mater laughed again. "Jilly's spell is gone. Our power has returned; our ability to charm restored."

"You were easy to manipulate," Kirt added. "All three of you agreed to everything we suggested."

"We tied your wrist to Verity Jane's. Does she know what tying means?"

"Not unless someone told her. I didn't. And it has no meaning without her agreement."

"Is she awake yet?"

"Yes. She's missing her phones and wants to go back to the surface. Said she needs to be there."

"Not possible until our enquays reopen." Pater sounded extremely chipper.

"We don't know when they will," Mater chimed. She sounded happy. Like her old self. Like she ought to sound. "The young lady's phones are in your living room. We plugged them in to charge."

"Thanks."

"Does Verity Jane know her phones won't work here?"

"If she doesn't, I'll remind her."

"We're under quarantine," Pater announced. "All five of us. Have you seen the notice on your front window?"

"Not yet. I'll go look now. Talk again later."

Back inside, he checked the window and read a printed message:

UNDER TEN DAY QUARANTINE
DO NOT GO OUT FRONT DOOR

In smaller print, he confirmed that all enquays were closed until further notice. For the first time in months, Holt wanted to cheer. He had ten days to convince Verity to stay in Api. Then he realized he only had nine. They had arrived last night and slept around the clock.

Standing still, he recalled the journey to Apitcote. If he'd wanted to, he could have stopped it. But he had enjoyed seeing Mater and Pater make arrangements, acting without fear, and grinning as they planned each step of their return. He had also enjoyed watching Verity and Madeline. They were as amiable as two people could be, agreeing to every suggestion and laughing at Pater's stories.

Using his Arcane magic, Holt discovered his parents had cleverly enlisted Blaine, the chauffeur/gardener, to drive back to Verity's apartment and help pack her clothes and personal possessions, after Mater used a charm to unlock the door and disarm the security system.

While eating breakfast at Denver International Airport before boarding the flight east, they had chatted with Verity and Madeline, knowing they wouldn't remember anything they said or did. Holt wasn't surprised when Mater asked Verity why she left Api three years ago, and she clammed up like a snail recoiling from danger.

Instead of traveling through one of the long tunnels denizens used for first time visitors, Mater and Pater used their fastest enquay—the cage. It was only big enough for four people, so Shelan had escorted Verity and Madeline down the steep shaft first and sent the cage back for the men and luggage. He had heard Verity and Madeline scream during their supersonic descent.

His afone beeped. Checking the screen, he saw an atext from Hanna. *Bad news. Mother's visitor tested positive. She's in the hospital, miserably sick.*

His other atexts included one from Mist. *Kew gathering in dream chamber tomorrow at ten in lieu of evening meeting. Please synk from your cottage. Your guests welcome to join us.*

Deciding morning was soon enough to catch up with his work team, he called Juhree.

"Hi, Holt. Heard you were home. No one expected you to return this soon."

"I didn't expect to, either."

"Verity Jane must have changed her mind."

"She didn't. Mater and Pater brought her. They also brought her best friend, Madeline."

"I heard that, too."

"Verity isn't happy to be here."

"We need to convince her to stay. Not only for her safety. Minalu and her sept need a tutelary. If Verity and her friend stay, they would have two. I started classes last week, so my days are full, like all our kew mates. The newcomers need someone full time. And Verity can't leave while you're under quarantine or until the enquays reopen."

"I know. Maybe the quarantine will favor us, and after she meets Minalu she will change her mind." He didn't expect that to happen but he could hope. "How is Minalu?"

"Fine. All the dwellers seem happy, but they need encouragement to venture beyond kluster fourteen. We've tried to convince them the entire realm is safe, but they've been cloistered all their lives so the thought of traveling very far from the place where they eat and sleep frightens them. They aren't even willing to go look at the cottages being built for them. Some women have volunteered to work in the community, but they're reluctant to go unless we, or someone they know, accompanies them to and from their work place. They have no idea how many denizens live here.”

“The Autumnal Fall Fest is the first Saturday in October,” Holt reminded. “If we convince the dwellers to attend, they’ll see the size of our population and, hopefully, begin to mingle and learn to trust.”

“Our kew mates agree. We’ll discuss ideas at the kew gathering in the morning.”

“Good.”

“Do you need anything?”

“Yeah. If you don’t mind conjuring.”

Juhree laughed. “I love to conjure, as you know.”

~ * ~

With Holt out of sight, VJ’s anger fled—with breathtaking speed. From her last visit, she remembered it was impossible to stay angry in Apitcote. The atmosphere was so conducive to good will, it made one want to smile continuously.

Plunking on the bed, she waited for her brain to catch up with reality, telling herself this was not a dream or a vision. She truly was in Apitcote. With Holt!

A small part of her wanted to retain anger to safeguard her heart. A bigger part wanted to rejoice. Apitcote was such a beautiful realm, she couldn’t be happier.

A gulp of regret clogged her throat as she thought about Madeline. Their plan to spend time together had been stolen by Holt’s unexpected kidnapping scheme. That should have angered VJ, but she couldn’t summon a single ounce. She would have to ask Holt to let her use his afone so she could call Madeline and apologize.

Getting off the bed, VJ looked through her daypack, backpack and duffle bags. Her clothes were neatly packed in one duffle; shoes and underclothing separated in the other; makeup and personal items in her daypack. Even the unsigned contract had been packed, unwrinkled.

A tap on the oak door startled her. "It isn't locked," she grumbled, expecting Holt and trying to sound irritated.

The door opened.

Barely daring to believe her eyes, she squealed, "Madeline!"

With a huge grin, Madeline said, "Flipping fantastic, isn't it?"

"Yes." VJ hugged her. "I'm so glad you're here. What makes you look so cheerful?"

"Holt said I'm far, far away from Texas, where Dwayne can't find me."

"Even more important is that we're together, Madd."

"Brilliant, isn't it?"

"Yes." Their shoulders shook as they laughed. Then Madeline said, "It's very quiet. I don't hear traffic or any noise outside."

"There aren't any roads. No cars, lorries, trains, buses or coaches," VJ explained, adding things she knew about Api.

"I can hardly wait to ride the moving footpaths and see hoverz boards. What do they look like?"

"Skate boards that hover above ground and have no wheels. I think they're propelled by some kind of small motor attached to the bottom."

"Amazing. Are you happy to be here?"

"Part of me is over the moon. I'm trying to ignore the nagging part that says I must leave."

When Holt knocked, Madeline opened the door with a smile.

"I had food delivered," he said. "Are you two hungry?"

"I am," Madeline said.

"Yes," VJ admitted.

Holt looked her up and down. Her stomach did uncommon flip-flops. His inspection felt like a caress. In an attempt to collect her wits, she looked away. She could not afford to let him know how much he affected her. "Couldn't we go to a constat to eat?"

"No. We're sequestered."

"What?"

"Quarantined. As are Mater and Pater."

"For how long?"

"Ten days."

"We're not sick," she protested. "I can smell disease, and we are not diseased."

"We're taking precautions just the same. Covid hasn't invaded Apitcote, but four of us spent time in a hospital where the virus was rampant. Then we spent hours on a plane with strangers. Therefore, all five will self-isolate until we make sure no one carries the virus."

"That's fine with me," Madeline said, eyes glowing.

Holt grinned. "I like good sports."

VJ crossed her arms. "The three of us are expected to live together for ten days?"

"Yeah."

"Where will we sleep?"

"You two may share the cottage. One can sleep in here, the other on the sofa bed. I'll sleep out back."

"It's too cold at night to sleep outdoors, isn't it?" VJ blurted.

"I won't be sleeping outside."

"Where will you sleep? In a tent?"

"Something like that."

Miffed at herself for exposing her concern, and mad at Holt because he had gotten her goat without even trying, VJ said, "I've never had ten days with nothing to do. I'll go stir crazy."

"There's plenty to keep busy if you're willing to get involved." His husky voice was unnerving her. His appraising eyes were worse. They made her want what she knew was impossible.

"Here's the drill," he said. "Food will be delivered at mealtimes. You may want to check the online menu and order. If not, you'll have to be content with daily specials."

"I'm going to love ordering meals." Madeline sighed. "I won't have to cook. Or shop. Plan menus. Do the washing up."

"We will have to wash dishes. Food will be delivered in re-usable containers."

"But no pots and pans." Madeline grinned, obviously delighted. "No trying to please Dwayne."

Crossing her arms, VJ said, "I need to call the hospital and explain why I'm not there."

Holt extended his afone. His orange afone. "When did you get a new phone?"

"It isn't new. It's programmed to turn black when I leave Apitcote and back to orange when I return.

"Like adjusting to automatic time zones," Madeline surmised. "How clever. I love orange. It's my favorite color."

"Mine, too." He handed his afone to Verity.

VJ made the call and frowned when blighter Flint said, "Not showing up or calling in put us in a bind. Don't bother coming back. I've already hired a temp to replace you."

Shoulders slumped, VJ ended the call. "I feel like a crumb left in the bottom of a biscuit tin."

"You're not," Madeline said cheerfully. "You're the best cookie in or out of the tin."

"You always make me feel better, Madd." Still clasping the afone, she looked at Holt. "I should call the police and let them know how to contact me."

"Tell them to call my afone or send a text to yours. Surface phones aren't set up to call Api."

"My flat rent and utilities will soon be due. How can I pay them from here?"

"Do you pay online?"

"Yes."

"You may use my afone."

"Thank you." After she called, curiosity got the best of her. "What happened to the afone you purchased for me last time I was here?"

"I gave it to someone else."

Not wanting to ask who, she did anyway. "Man? Lady? Child?"

"Woman. Her name is Hanna."

Jolts of unwanted jealousy spurted through VJ. Unwilling to satisfy more curiosity, she stiffened her upper lip and returned his afone, making sure their fingers didn't touch.

"Do you want to call your husband?" he asked Madeline.

"Not particularly. But I guess I should ring him up."

Once again, Holt extended his afone.

When Dwayne failed to answer, Madeline left a message, explaining he could only contact her by sending a text to Holt's phone number.

"Do either of you need to make any more calls?" Holt asked as Madeline returned his afone.

"Not me."

"Is it possible for us to have one of those?" VJ asked, still stiff lipped.

"Sure, if you stay beyond our quarantine. When the pandemic hit, a number of denizens returned from the surface, and most are clamoring for new afones. Our newcomers want them as well. If you decide to stay, I'll add your names to the list. In the meantime, you're welcome to use mine."

"If you live in a tent, it might be inconvenient to share yours," VJ said.

"I'll use my apad. And," he winked at Madeline, "I communicate with my kew with my mind."

Madeline's eyebrows shot skyward. "What else can you do?"

"That depends on what I want to accomplish."

"Barmy!" She stared at VJ. "You didn't tell me Holt possesses magic."

"I thought if I did, you would think I'm bonkers—ready for bedlam. Besides, he never told me that!" And she didn't believe him, anyway. Men tended to exaggerate. He was probably no different, although deep inside she knew better. Holt was one of the two men she admired. Respected. Trusted. And the only one who was still alive.

"Can you do something magic right now?" Madeline asked.

"Like what?" Holt asked.

"Conjure something from thin air?"

"I don't conjure. That's Juhree's specialty—my kew sister whose parents own the mansion."

"Verity told me about a group of people who were all born on the same day called a kew, but she didn't say you were one of them."

"I wasn't when she was last here, but I am now."

"What kind of magic do you do?"

"I read people."

"Can you read me?"

"Yeah."

"Prove it."

He touched her forehead and unbloxed her. "You don't want to see Dwayne again, and hope to stay here long enough to get a divorce. Perhaps longer."

"Good guess. What am I thinking now?"

"That you wish you and Verity Jane could live near each other for the rest of your lives."

Madeline blinked, looked at Verity. "Did you tell him?"

"No."

"Can you read her thoughts?" Madeline asked.

"No. Rene bloxed her. At my request."

Madeline's eyebrows shot skyward again. "Bloxed?"

"Blocked. People's thoughts are private. Personal. I rarely intrude unless I think someone needs help." He touched her forehead again. "You are closed. Your thoughts now belong only to you."

"What else can you do?"

"Move things. Reduce and enlarge." He snapped his fingers. The bed shrank to doll size.

"No," Verity wailed. "Put the bed back to normal."

"The same size or bigger?"

"Bigger."

Holt snapped his fingers again, enlarged the bed to king size. "How's that?"

"Too big. I'd prefer double or queen size."

He snapped his fingers. "Better?"

"Yes. Much."

He turned to the door. "I'm going to eat. Food's in the kitchen. Feel free to join me."

"I'm famished," Madeline admitted. "Can't remember when I last ate."

"Me either," VJ admitted as they followed him.

Although the kitchen would be considered tiny on the surface, the room didn't feel small. It felt right. Perfect. VJ didn't like admitting that, not even to herself, but she now remembered—everything in Apitcote was near perfect. The only imperfect thing was her life.

Holt started opening containers. The Asian food had VJ all but salivating. The delicious smells of herbs and spices stimulated her appetite. To her surprise, the food she dished onto her plate was still hot. Had Holt used magic to keep it warm?

Unwilling to admit she was pleased to be back in Apitcote, she summoned 'an attitude' and complained. "To get here, we were knocked out for forty-one hours." Her brain had automatically deducted two hours for the time change and calculated the time she had gone to bed in the mansion and awakened in Apitcote.

"Do you have a point to make?" Holt asked before chewing a bite of egg roll.

"What did you do to keep us unconscious that long?"

"Nothing that made you willing to do something you wouldn't have done if you had been fully conscious."

"If you expect me to believe that, you're a two-faced sod."

"Believe what satisfies you."

"Did someone else drug us?" Madeline asked.

"You were not drugged. You were charmed. And neither of you resisted."

VJ clamped her bottom lip beneath her upper, attempting to look disgruntled. How could she spend ten days with Holt in the confines of his small cottage and not reveal her emotions?

~ * ~

Holt helped with the washing up, put dishes away, and set the clean food containers in a basket on the front porch to be collected when breakfast was delivered in the morning. Then, he went out the back door.

Juhree and her One, Monteith, arrived within moments. Both wore klir seal bodysuits over their clothes and klir seal face shields. "Are you ready for me to conjure the bubble you requested?" Juhree asked.

"Yeah."

"How big do you want it, and what items do you want inside?"

"Big enough for a bed, a desk for my computer, apad and TV, plus a bathroom."

"Here you go." Whipping her arms in the motion of side-way figure eights, Juhree conjured exactly what he envisioned.

"Your magic amazes me."

Monteith grinned. "Amazes me, too. I get a thrill every time I watch her conjure."

"I can see the bubble," Holt said. "Can anyone else?"

"Just us and our kew mates. Do you want it to be visible?"

"Not to anyone else."

Juhree laughed.

Monteith winked.

And Holt chuckled. Knowing that his parents' melancholy was gone, and having Verity there lifted two burdens from his shoulders and made him feel ten feet tall. But height and might could not dissolve Verity's problems. If he knew why some guy wanted to harm her, he and his kew mates could help. Would she open up and confide while they were together?

# Six

"Kidnapping us was a terrible mishap," VJ complained to Madeline. "Holt Mackey should be ashamed."

"Well, as people often repeat in jolly old England, 'When in Rome...'"

"We're stuck here so we might as well go with the flow," VJ conceded, her mood improving in a blink. "No use griping about spilt milk, as Mum used to say."

"When did you last talk to her?"

"Before I left Boston."

"Did you ever tell her where you were?"

"No. I didn't tell anyone except you. Freddie knows where Mum and Lizzie and Karan live. I was afraid he might hurt them if they knew I was in Denver. Thanks for reposting all the cards and letters I sent."

"You know I'd do anything for my BFF."

VJ smiled. "I'd do the same for you."

Holt tapped the back door before he walked in and strode to the front door. "Breakfast has been delivered." After he set containers on the table, he asked, "How do you feel, Madeline?"

"Great."

"Did you have morning sickness?"

"No."

"You didn't?" VJ asked, wishing she had asked first.

"No queasiness at all. I must have slept it out."

"Did you sleep well?"

"Yes. Actually, I've slept well every night since I left Galveston."

Holt looked at VJ. "How about you?"

Her heart rate spiked. "I slept well. Thank you for asking."

"You don't have to thank me. I'm concerned about both of you."

"You should be. You brought us here against our will."

"Without your permission. Not against your will."

His afone pinged. He glanced at the screen. Concern filled his eyes.

"Bad news?" VJ asked.

"Yeah. A friend of someone on the surface has Covid, and she's hooked up to a ventilator."

"Soz—sorry," Madeline said.

"Me, too," VJ agreed. "How old is she?"

"In her seventies."

"OAPs are the most vulnerable age group."

"Not all senior citizens are old age pensioners," Holt said.

VJ's face flushed red. "Right," she conceded, wondering if she had offended him.

He nodded at the TV. "If you want to watch that, the remote is in the pocket on the side of the sofa."

"I'd like to hear local news," Madeline said. "Should we turn it on?"

"Go ahead. I've already caught up." Holt picked up his breakfast and headed for the back door. "We get surface news as well. See you later."

VJ resisted the urge to ask him to eat with them. "Let's spend today as we would have in Denver," she suggested, already missing Holt and wishing she hadn't been so snippy.

Madeline nodded. "Gabbing to our heart's content."

"Right. We shall make the most of this minor setback."

"It isn't a setback for me. Why is it for you?"

VJ explained her vision, then added, "If I have money, I hope to engage a brilliant attorney and prove I'm innocent."

"I understand that, but it won't happen for a while. I'd like to enjoy being together whilst we can."

"Sorry. We should celebrate. I shall endeavor not to act as though I have victim syndrome."

Madeline grinned. "Did someone suggest you did?"

"Me." VJ smiled. "Fate's capriciousness has planted us in a fantastic realm, and we should enjoy every moment."

"I doubt our situation could be better if we had made the plans ourselves."

"You're right, of course, poppet."

"You're in a better mood," Madeline said, opening a food container.

VJ opened another. "Indeed. Api does that to one. I had forgotten."

They discussed memories, serious and jovial ones. Their dream to leave England and live in the U.S. Madeline's job as a dietitian. VJ's lack of a job.

"Your ex-boss is a blinking arse," Madeline said.

VJ grinned. "Yes, he is."

As they finished the washing up, she said, "You should sleep in Holt's bedroom. I'll sleep on the settee."

"No, no," Madeline disagreed. "Holt is your boyfriend. You'll sleep in his bed."

"He's not my boyfriend, and you're preggers. You need to be as comfortable as possible."

"The settee is comfy and where I prefer to sleep." To prove her point, she plopped on it and reclined against cushions and pillows. "Now, tell me more about Apitcote."

"Denizens are friendly, and they treat everyone with respect. An example is using first names preceded by a title. Because you're married, you will likely be called Mrs. Madeline."

"Since I don't intend to stay married, I prefer Miss."

"Then we shall tell denizens to call you Ms. Madeline. Most call me Dr. Verity."

A while later, VJ said, "We've gabbed all morning. I wonder if Holt will join us." She looked out back but didn't see him.

"Strange he isn't around," Madeline said, joining her at the kitchen window.

"Especially after he told us we're all quarantined," VJ grumped.

"Maybe he'll show up later. Blimey. It's brilliant to be together, isn't it?"

"Surely is. I feel like I'm on holiday, except we can't go anywhere."

~ * ~

At five o'clock, Holt tapped on the front door and waited for them to open it before he entered, carrying a basket loaded with food containers. Setting it on the kitchen counter, he picked up one container and strode to the back door. "I'll leave my afone in case you want to use it." He nodded at the counter where he had set it next to the basket. "See you later."

They both hurried to the kitchen window. "Do you think he knows we're watching him?" Madeline asked when he sat on the newly mown grass.

"Probably. He's aware of more than he ought to be. Looks like he has an invisible back rest," she added after he touched his tablet, concentrated on the screen, and ate intermittently.

"How can he eat without looking to see what he forks from the container?"

"I suspect he's capable of doing far more than that."

"Do you think he slept in the garden, under the stars?"

"I don't know. I expected to see a tent. I don't even see bedding."

"Neither do I."

When two young women arrived—two young beautiful women—VJ frowned. She wasn't jealous. She wasn't. "I thought we weren't supposed to mingle with other people," she grumbled, hiding her clenched fists behind her back.

"Their masks and see-through bodysuits are much more attractive than the protective suits I saw on TV in the Wuhan lab in China months ago. Do you think one of the ladies is Holt's girlfriend?"

"Haven't a clue."

"Are you jealous?"

"Absolutely bloody not."

"I would be. They're both drop-dead gorgeous."

VJ all but stormed away.

A few moments later, Madeline followed her and grinned. "He's not in love with either one."

"How do you know?"

"Two men just showed up, dressed in the same odd jumpsuits and each woman kissed a different man's masked forehead while Holt stared at me through the window."

VJ returned to look outside. "They're gone."

Madeline arched her brows. "All five?"

"Yes. So much for quarantine," VJ muttered, unable to quell the feeling of being discarded like a forgotten toy. Last time she was there, Holt had taken her everywhere, and included her in all his activities and conversations.

With her next breath, she knew who his companions were. All four belonged to the kew. In a trice, she felt much better. But how did she know that? Had Holt somehow sent her a silent message? The idea was too preposterous to believe.

She looked out the window again. Had they made themselves invisible so she and Madeline couldn't see or hear them? Why would they do such a thing? Neither she nor Madeline had supersonic hearing. And she didn't know if Arcane magic included invisibility.

After they ate, VJ opened the back door. She didn't see Holt or anything that resembled a tent. Had he broken their quarantine?" A bit miffed, she called, "Holt? Are you here?"

He appeared, as though by magic, in the center of the grass.

She was so startled, she nearly swooned.

"What can I do for you?"

She made something up on the spot. "Check the refrigerator."

"What's wrong with it?"

"The ice cubes aren't freezing solid."

Holt strode inside, bent down and checked the small fridge that resembled the one she had grown up with in England, except Holt's looked new and much more modern. "Can't find a problem. Maybe you and Madeline are opening the door too often."

By his grin, she knew he knew she had used that as an excuse to check on him.

~ * ~

The following morning, Holt knocked again and waited for them to open the door before he entered. He retrieved a food basket from the front porch, carried it to the kitchen, selected one container and headed to the back door where he paused. "If you want to order lunch and the evening meal from the menu, you should do so at least an hour ahead. I find it convenient to order both early in the day." Staring at Verity, he added, "You remember how to use my afone to find menus and place orders, right?"

"Yes."

He nodded at the counter. "It's still there."

"We haven't used it to call anyone," Verity said. "But we checked texts and found one that stated my car has been located in Kansas City, Missouri, and will be returned when a driver becomes available. Since I may not be there when it arrives, I should decide how to deal with the problem whilst I'm roughly seventeen hundred miles from Denver."

"If you approve, I can make arrangements for your car to be delivered to the judge's mansion, and stored inside the three-car garage."

"Thanks." Her expression indicated she wanted to say more. He realized she remembered his passwords and codes and suspected she had looked through his atexts and was wondering who sent frequent photos of Harmony and texted details of her mother's health problems. If she asked, he would tell her. If not, he would keep his secret as she kept hers.

He retrieved his afone. Inside the bubble, he transferred Hanna's photos and messages to a hidden file. Copies were automatically stored on his apad, also in a hidden file.

Staying away from his guests the first night had taken a toll. Knowing Verity slept nearby had kept him awake. When he saw his bedroom light turn on in the middle of the night, he left the bubble, intending to go talk to her. He had retrieved his senses before he made a fool of himself. Back in his bubble, guilt descended like a bomb about to explode. He had almost betrayed his loyalty to Hanna. He texted to see if she was awake.

Instead of texting back, she had called and they talked for a long time. He explained his parents had brought Verity Jane and her friend to Apitcote without their permission. He also assured Hanna he had no intention of hooking up with Verity again, that he was committed to tying with her and looked forward to the joy of raising Harmony together.

~ * ~

At lunch, Holt did what he had done before. But at dinner, before he went out the back door, Madeline said, "You don't have to eat outside, Holt."

"I should give you two time to catch up."

"We'd like your company. I have a gazillion questions, and Ver can't answer all of them."

He glanced at Verity, waited for her to add her invitation. "Don't be daft," she said archly. "We would appreciate having you share your meals with us."

"Fine." Holt disguised the pleasure rolling through him. Assuming a stoic manner, he sat at his small kitchen table and opened his food container.

"So, tell us what you do outside all day," Madeline invited.

"I get caught up with what's going on throughout the realm. Then I check with my team, make decisions, allocate work."

"What do you and your team do?"

"We're in charge of security, although we all have other responsibilities as well."

"They draw blueprints to build and/or to refurbish cottages. They also keep the way-in and the way-out, what they call enquays, safe from outsiders," Verity repeated what he had told her years ago, and then she asked, "What did you use to drug us before we walked through the tunnel for half a day?"

"You weren't drugged. You were charmed."

"Can people walk, talk and think when they're charmed?" Madeline asked.

"Sure. They just don't remember afterwards."

"Is charmed like being hypnotized?"

"Not even close. Hypnotism is similar to being in a trance. Charmed is awake and functioning as you normally would."

"What's the difference?"

"Memories are swiped."

"So, how many hours did it take us to hike through the tunnel?" Verity persisted.

"How many ways are there to get to Denver?" he countered.

She wrinkled her forehead. "I'm not sure what your question means."

"You may drive or fly, ride a bus, take a train, hire a driver, right?"

"Yes."

"People enter from the north, east, west, south, or variations of different directions. Correct?"

"Of course. What are you trying to say?"

"Api has more than one tunnel, more than one way to get to the surface and back."

Verity looked rattled. He hadn't shared that before. "Did we use the same tunnel we used last time I came here?"

"No. We came via the cage."

"What kind of cage?" Madeline asked.

"It resembles an enclosed ski lift."

"Does it work the same?"

"No. It's much faster. Reduces the time to get here by ninety percent. Now, tell me what the two of you do all day."

Madeline grinned. "We faff—waste time, gab, watch TV, gab some more and ignore my husband's texts."

"If you want a change in your routine, I could arrange something to occupy part of your time."

"What would we do?"

"Meet Minalu and her sept—a group of women and children who came to live here several weeks ago. Talk to them. Get to know them. Befriend them. Help them adjust to their new environment."

"Where did they come from?"

"The other end of Apitcote."

"Is it like this?"

"The dwelling is much smaller. They have a grotto and a stream but no lake."

"Did they live in cottages? Or huts?"

"Neither. They were cave dwellers."

Madeline's eyes rounded.

Verity's did as well. "What was their life like?"

"Primitive."

"Crikey. You mentioned them. Why didn't you explain more?"

"You didn't ask, nor did you seem interested."

"Well, I am, and I'm here, so put me to work."

"Me too," Madeline said.

"Tell us more about the lady named Minalu and her sept," Verity invited.

"They are a group of women, children, and a few men," he repeated for Madeline's benefit. For the next hour, Holt explained the stumbling blocks he and the kew had encountered, emphasizing their desire to make everyone in the sept feel welcome and unafraid.

"Gotta go," he said sometime later.

"Why?" Madeline asked.

"I have kew meetings on week nights at seven."

"I thought we weren't allowed to leave your premises," Verity said.

"I don't leave."

"Then how do you attend meetings?"

"We synk. Our system is similar to zoom sessions on the surface."

"Do you need your afone?"

"No. I use my laptop or apad."

"Is an apad like an iPad or tablet?" Madeline asked.

"The same."

"It's almost seven," Verity said. "You should go. We'll do the washing up."

"Thanks." He walked to the door and stopped. "You're welcome to attend tonight's meeting. It would give you a chance to meet my kew mates."

Verity raised her eyebrows. "Are we both invited?"

"Sure."

Madeline stared at the cluttered table. "What about the washing up?"

"We'll do dishes later." Holt could use his magic, but he wanted an excuse to return. He opened the back door and waited for them to precede him.

"Why did we come outdoors?" Verity asked. "And where did you sleep last night?"

"Here. In my back yard."

"You're joshing. I looked out before I went to bed, and I didn't see you. The garden was empty."

"I stayed inside an invisible tent. Come see what it's like."

He guided them to the middle of his lawn, raised an invisible flap and ushered them inside.

"This is like being inside a gigantic balloon," Madeline said, awed.

"It's called a bubble, conjured by one of my kew mates."

Verity stared at his bed, desk, computer, electronic notebook, and lamps.

Madeline pointed at a closed door. "What's in there?"

"Bathroom. Water closet. Take a peek. Satisfy your curiosity."

Madeline opened the door. "It's small, compact, and has everything one might need."

"Why can't we see the bubble from inside the cottage?" Verity asked.

"It's camouflaged to reflect my backyard."

"How do you know where it is?"

"It isn't invisible to me."

"Why can't we see it?"

"If my friendly neighbors see me out here, they'll be tempted to come over and chat."

"You're sparing curtain twitchers from the possibility of getting exposed to Covid?"

"Yeah. But my neighbors aren't nosy. They're good people." He opened his laptop. "When we convocate or gather online, we call it synking." He touched an icon and opened the lynk. The app resembled a surface zoom session—with Mist's face in the very center. Kew mates, including him, surrounded three edges.

"We're synked early," Mist announced, smiling. "Glad you invited Verity and Madeline to join us. Welcome to Apitcote, ladies. We apologize for not welcoming you sooner. I'm Mist, in charge of communications, and tonight it's my turn to convene."

As each member introduced themselves, Verity's eyes revealed she remembered those she had met three years ago—Mist, Rene, Tess, Dane, Monteith—the five who were all born on the same June day as Drew, who had married and tied with Rene and was endowed with magic shortly thereafter. She didn't know Jordan or Juhree. Both were from the surface and shared the same August birthday as Holt, Verity, and Madeline.

Before the meeting began, Mist explained. "We nine are Apitcote's governing kew. We're heads of state—leaders of the realm. If we all go away at the same time, a kounsel of elected denizens governs during our absence. Our evening kew meetings are informal, although we do take minutes. When we meet with older denizens or elected kluster officials, we're more formal." Smiling, Mist asked, "Do you have any questions?"

"No," Madeline said.

"We're here to observe," Verity added.

Kew mates discussed the agenda items, made motions, and passed a few.

"That's all we need for the minutes," Mist announced an hour later. "I'm turning recording off. The floor is open for chatter."

Rene's face took center screen. "Drew and I examined your parents last night, Holt. They are completely recovered. The residual effects from Jilly's spirit, and the spells she cast, are gone."

"Thanks."

"Perhaps we should discuss Minalu and her sept," Tess suggested.

"Why do you want to help them?" Madeline asked.

"Because we believe pro-social giving is a major contributor to happiness—theirs and ours."

"That's true," Verity agreed. "The act of giving activates reward centers in the brain that make givers feel good."

"We know." Dane grinned, his face now center screen. "Our newcomers are shy. If we convince them to branch out and mingle with denizens, we're confident they'll get over their shyness and enjoy living here."

"Would someone explain why you want to hire me?" Verity asked. "How would I fit in?"

"The dwellers need someone devoted to them," Monteith said.

"Someone to answer questions, listen, and share their woes," Juhree added. "Someone who has time to understand and help them accept that they will have cottages to live in when the new kluster is ready to be occupied."

"Where do they live if they aren't in cottages?"

"In a cultural hall. They like living under the same roof," Holt explained.

"What they need most right now is a dietitian or a doctor to observe what they eat and encourage them to try new foods that will add nutrients to their diet without making them sick. In other words," Drew said. "Someone to teach them not to eat too much junk food and to consume sugar and dessert in moderation."

"I will," Madeline volunteered, raising her hand as kew mates had done during the meeting. "I'm a certified nutrition specialist and personal trainer at a hospital in Galveston."

Verity stared at her, a question in her eyes. "How long are you willing to stay here?"

"A good long time. To quote Shakespeare, 'I like this place and could willing waste my time in it.' I'm happy, and I haven't even seen beyond Holt's cottage."

"Marvelous." Juhree smiled. "We can hardly wait until you're out of quarantine, and we all get better acquainted."

"You look familiar," Verity said. "Have we met?"

Juhree nodded. "You were one of my nurses in Denver last January."

"I remember. You were in a bad car accident. I'm the one who told you your best friend died."

"Jilly was Holt's younger sister. I inherited her memories."

"Awesome," Madeline exclaimed. "I didn't know such a thing was possible."

"We hope you stay long enough to learn what other things are possible in Api."

"I'd like to stay indefinitely. I'm expecting a baby, but I'm separated from my husband."

"If your child is born in Apitcote, she or he will inherit long life," Dane said, "and you may live twice as long as you might on the surface."

"Really?"

All kew mates nodded.

"What smashing good news." Madeline's grin faded. "May I ask a personal question?"

"Sure," Mist said.

"Can someone tell me how to arrange to get a divorce from a distance?"

Mist nodded. "Dane, Drew and Jordan all have law degrees and not long ago they helped Jordan sever his marriage ties."

Hope filled Madeline's eyes. "Then someone will help me?"

"Certainly."

"Will I have to return to the surface?"

"Not unless you want to," Holt said. "We have people above who conduct business and handle legal matters for us."

"Thank you."

"You're welcome."

"Please tell us more about Minalu and her sept," Verity prompted.

"They are almost as new to Apitcote as you." Monteith's face moved to center screen. "We think someone who wasn't born here might be more successful than we are at helping them adjust to their new lifestyle."

"Their decision to leave the dwelling was a difficult one," Juhree added. "Before they came here, the children, who are called kidlings, practiced elocution. They are proud of the way they speak. We should treat them gently, and with respect, if we hear anyone make a mistake."

"Will do," Madeline promised.

"Whilst I'm here, I'll do my best to help," Verity added.

"Before we end tonight's gathering," Mist said, "we'd like to extend an invitation to Madeline and Verity Jane to attend our Autumnal Fall Festival."

"When is it?" Verity asked.

"The Saturday after your quarantine ends. Major holidays are held at our amphitheater and we anticipate a huge crowd. We'll reserve a table large enough to accommodate all eleven of us."

"Don't worry," Holt mumbled, sensing Verity's hesitation, "if you're not here, your space will be filled."

"I'm sure it will."

The hurt in her eyes made him wish he'd kept his mouth shut.

After he unsynked and closed his laptop, the three walked outside. "If you want to see the bubble, I can make that happen."

"Please do," Madeline said.

He snapped his fingers. Knew they could barely see the bubble, but it was visible.

Madeline cleared her throat. "I'd like to take a bath, if that's all right with you, Ver."

"Go ahead."

"I'll help with the washing up afterwards."

"We'll have the dishes done before you finish," Holt said.

"I'll hurry."

"Don't bother."

"Okay." She winked. "I'll take my time."

When they were alone, Verity spoke quietly. "You said you didn't bring us here. If you didn't, who did?"

"Not sure I should tell you."

"Why?"

"Don't want you to be upset with them."

"Your mater and pater?"

"Yeah."

"Did they charm you, too?"

He nodded.

"Is their magic greater than yours?"

"Nope."

"Not as strong?"

"Correct deduction."

"Did you know what they were doing?"

"Yeah. I allowed myself to be charmed because they were enjoying themselves—planning, making decisions, directing us, offering suggestions. They reminded me of two teenagers."

"I'm sorry I blamed you."

"Not a problem."

They wandered toward the cottage. Keeping her gaze on the ground, Verity said, "We haven't discussed what happened three years ago."

"Do you want to?"

"I don't know what there is to say."

"You didn't tell me why you needed to leave."

"You didn't ask."

"I figured if you wanted me to know, you would explain."

"I thought you didn't care."

"I wouldn't have invited you to Api if I hadn't believed you were my One."

"I didn't understand what that meant."

"Do you now?"

The question she hadn't asked when she was there before flashed. "Is a person's One the same as spouse? Wife? Husband?"

"Yes. Lifetime mate."

She sucked in a deep breath, regretting she hadn't paid more attention years ago. Finally, she said, "It wouldn't have made a difference. I still had to go back."

"Why?"

"I can't tell you, Holt. I don't deserve you. Nor do I deserve to live in Apitcote. I've made too many mistakes. Mistakes I might never overcome."

"Is that all you're going to say?"

She nodded. He sensed she was too choked up to say more. Deciding not to probe, he followed her through the back door. Inside the cozy kitchen, he said, "I'll do the dishes. You don't need to help."

She smiled. "I'll dry."

Holt winked. "That will save you from getting washer-woman fingers."

She swatted his arm. "You let me think you didn't know what that meant."

He chuckled. "Your mum told me."

After they finished the chores, Verity said, "Did you love another lady after we broke up?"

He gave her an evasive reply. "I've only loved one woman."

"The one who sends you texts and photos of her baby daughter?"

"Her name is Hanna. And I'm not interested in discussing her with you."

"Why?"

"I thought you and I meant a lot to each other once. Now, I know the feeling was one-sided. Otherwise, you would not have left me and then lived with two other men."

When she didn't comment, he said, "Are you going to satisfy my curiosity? Tell me what I did wrong? Or why you left?"

She shook her head. Then bowed it. But not before he saw a rainbow of conflicting emotions flicker through her troubled eyes. Once again, he wished he'd kept his mouth shut. "I'll say good night, then."

"Good night, Holt."

He watched her walk to his bedroom. Waited for her to enter and close the door. Then he sat on a chair by the fireplace and waited for Madeline.

When Madeline saw him, she grinned. "I've been hoping for a chance to chat with you."

Holt stretched his arm toward the bedroom door and snapped his fingers.

"What did you just do?"

"I sealed this room so Verity cannot hear our conversation."

"You want to know what's bothering her?"

"Are you willing to tell me?"

"I can't. But I can say if you are patient and give her time to resolve her problems, I think the two of you could be happy together."

"That's not going to happen."

Madeline sighed. "Ver bottles things up inside and pretends she's fine, but she isn't."

"She's fortunate to have you as her trusted friend. Can you think of anything I can do to help her?"

"Not unless you make it impossible for her to leave when our quarantine ends. Tell her the enquays are closed indefinitely."

"They are," he said.

"Good. That will give both of you time to rediscover your love."

"No. It won't." He stood, then added, "I told Verity my parents brought you to Api. If you hadn't wanted to come, they would have sensed your resistance. They manipulated but employed no force. That is not our way."

"I'm delighted to be here. I think Ver is too. She just doesn't want to admit it because she fears she can't stay."

"Perhaps there's a way to dissolve her fear."

"Maybe you're the one to help her do that."

"My kew mates and I plan to try." Snapping his fingers, he unsealed the living room. "Good night, Madeline."

"Good night and good dreams, Holt."

He glanced at his bedroom door. Wondered if Rene would be willing to remove Verity's blox. Told himself it would be bad form to ask. When the time was right, his kew mates would help her if they could. From the conversation he had overheard in the Denver mansion, he had three clues to help them—the names Freddie and Vincent and a mansion deed.

Filing regret in the back of his mind, he retrieved his afone from the kitchen counter and carried it out to the bubble where he checked his atexts and enjoyed a new video of Harmony chattering with Aleece, who looked frail and weaker than the last time he'd seen her. His mater's observation that she wouldn't live much longer might be true. Then Hanna would return to Api and they would tie.

Holt's emotions gyrated with regret. He didn't want Aleece to die. Didn't want Hanna to lose her mater. Aleece was Hanna's only living relative—except for Harmony. Soon, he would be her mate and Harmony's recognized pater. His happiness at having Harmony a permanent part of his life shouldn't be predicated on Hanna's unhappiness at losing her mater.

An image of Verity swam through his mind. If she stayed, how would she react to the lifetime commitment he had made when he thought he would never see her again?

# *Seven*

Settled in bed, VJ reviewed the kew meeting. All her life men had put her at an instant disadvantage—until she had met Holt and Vincent. And tonight, in one fleeting moment, she had learned a powerful lesson: Holt's kew mates were like him, and she had connected with each one in positive ways. A great deal of mistrust went the way of the dishwater, down the drain.

The doorbell chime pulled her from musing. Sliding off the bed, she flipped on a lamp and went to see who was calling on Holt this late.

Madeline already stood at the front door, staring down at the stoop. "Roses! Someone sent roses. Yellow roses. And orange roses."

VJ blinked at the two beautiful bouquets.

"Barmy. Who do you think sent flowers to Holt?"

"Ladies probably." Jealousy ripped through VJ as Madeline scooped them up.

"Good heavens! This card has my name on it and the other has yours. I don't know anyone who might send me flowers. And rarely have I seen orange roses. Who could possibly know orange is my favorite color?"

"Holt."

"My card isn't signed."

"Nor is mine."

"Where shall we put them?"

"Yours in the living room and mine in the bedroom?"

"Brilliant."

As VJ set her vase on top of Holt's bureau, she saw a face-down frame. Curious, she turned it over. A chill scooted down her back as she stared at a photo of a blue-eyed little girl with dimples on both cheeks.

"Do you know who she is?" Madeline asked.

"No."

"Looks like photos we saw on Holt's afone. She must be blooming special to occupy a place in his bedroom."

Dismay spiraled inside VJ. She pretended the photo didn't bother her. But it did. Doing her best to appear unaffected, she admired the roses. "They are beautiful, aren't they?"

"Yeah. I haven't had flowers sent to me for—forever. Dwayne thinks they're a waste of money."

VJ sighed. "I think they're lovely."

"And romantic."

"I can't think about romance. I'm going back to bed."

Madeline laughed. "Pleasant dreams."

"You, too, poppet."

Madeline's laughter followed her as she sashayed through Holt's bedroom door.

Receiving beautiful yellow roses made VJ feel lighthearted. Someone obviously wanted them to feel welcome. Who? Holt? His kew mates? His parents?

The instant she glanced at the framed photo again, her mood dipped. Did Holt love the little girl and her mum? He said he had only loved one woman. From checking his afone, she knew he received frequent photos of the girl. Would he explain what they meant to him? Not that she had any right to know.

~ * ~

With Verity seated on one side and Madeline on the other in his bubble, Holt synked with Minalu, as they had synked last night with his kew. He began with introductions.

"Your hair is stunning," Minalu said. "Black as midnight when moon and stars hide above clouds. Do you not agree, Mr. Holt?"

"Yes. Dr. Verity and Miss Madeline both have beautiful hair."

"My oldest son has black hair."

"Is he here?" Madeline asked.

"No. My three sons went above many moon cycles ago. I expect to see them some day. I also have a daughter, Cinnalan. Her hair is cinnamon, like mine."

"It's a pretty shade," Verity complimented.

Minalu blushed. "I like it now that Juhree gave me a potion to tame it after I shampoo."

"What else do you like?"

"Living here. My pallet is more comfortable than the flat one at the dwelling. And not having to prepare meals every day and store food for cold season is a true blessing."

"What kinds of foods did you eat at the dwelling?" Madeline asked.

"Mostly gruel made from wheat, fruit peelings and smashed vegetables. Occasionally, we had chicken and fish."

"And fresh fruit?"

"Not often." Minalu's bountiful red hair flew around her face as she shook her head. "Men use most fruit to make grog."

"Is it fermented?"

"Yes."

"Did you drink grog?"

"No. Men hoard it and drink it when they sit around fire pit and complain instead of coming to bed and warming our backs."

"Is that why you left them?" Verity asked.

"No. After much debate about our youngsters exchanging places with students in this valley, we could not agree or reach a compromise. We left to improve our lives and give kidlings opportunities to learn and experience new things. At dwelling, we worked all day. No time to play with kidlings. No time for leisure. No time to relax and enjoy other pleasures."

"Does everyone who came with you like living here?"

Minalu nodded. Once again, her hair flounced. "Very much. You will like it, too. This I know."

Eager to learn as much as possible about the newcomers so he and the kew could help them adjust, Holt stayed with Verity and Madeline for the entire discussion.

After a break for lunch, Minalu introduced two females. "This be my daughter, Cinnalan. And this be Tumela. Her parents left dwelling many moon cycles ago. Tumela be like daughter to me." With a smile, she continued, "I have invited women who do not work today to meet you." Minalu introduced each one and listened while Verity and Madeline asked questions and took notes.

"What a brilliant day," Madeline said when the afternoon session ended. "I agree that Minalu and her sept need someone to talk to and ask advice daily."

"I was hugely impressed," Verity admitted. "Minalu's sept is fortunate to have her as their leader. And as far as elocution goes, they speak hands above some of our former countrymen."

Madeline laughed. "They certainly do."

Holt reached to close his laptop. His fingers brushed Verity's. His gut clenched as awareness sidled through him. His body didn't remember he had vowed not to get involved with her again, but his brain reminded he wasn't free.

Forcing himself not to look at Verity, he lowered the computer lid and waited for her and Madeline to stand so he could. Touching Verity again would create a fire greater than the one already burning inside.

He was disgusted with his reaction. More disgusted when her arm brushed his and he ached to touch her. Draw her close. Close the space between them.

Instead, he led them from the bubble. Accompanied them to the cottage's back door. Madeline went inside. But Verity lingered. With her hair loose and flowing over her shoulders instead of knotted at the back of her head, Verity looked fantastic and he chastised himself for his thoughts.

"Are you coming in to eat dinner with us?"

"No. I'll eat in the bubble tonight. I have work to catch up on."

She looked so desirable he wanted to take her in his arms. "You should go inside," he said while he could.

"I know. But I'd like things between us to be more comfortable."

"How do you propose we do that?"

"I don't know."

He sucked in a quick, deep breath. "You want friendship, similar to what you share with Madeline?"

"Something like that."

"Do you believe that's a state we can achieve?" The trill of his afone interrupted. He read the atext. Had an excuse to leave. "Something's gone wrong with the new computer being installed at the cage station."

Back in the bubble, Holt dealt with the matter quickly and dispensed a crew to the station to fix the problem so work on the new, enlarged cage could continue.

He leaned back and reviewed the day. Verity and Madeline were naturals working with the sept. They both belonged in

Apitcote permanently. Madeline sounded willing. How could he and his kew mates convince Verity to stay?

Madeline's yell interrupted his thoughts. "Holt! Come! Now! Please! Verity's down!"

Heart pounding, he raced to his cottage. Verity lay sprawled on the living room floor. Holt dropped to his knees beside her. "What happened?"

"I don't know. We were talking and, suddenly, she went still. Like a stone statue. As though she had been pulled into some kind of trance. Her eyes glassed over. Her body swayed. And then she toppled."

He made a mental connection with his kew mate, Rene. *"Verity's out cold. Please bring your medical scanner."*

He touched his lips to Verity's forehead. Warm. Not hot. Moist though. He pressed his fourth finger against her wrist and checked her pulse. Accelerated.

Within seconds, Rene arrived, garbed in a klir seal suit and face shield. Kneeling beside Holt, she used her medical gizmo to scan Verity.

"Vitals are normal. Organs healthy. No internal problems."

"Is it safe to move her?"

"Yes."

Lifting her, Holt carried her to his bedroom and placed her on the bed.

"What happened?" Rene asked.

As Madeline explained, Verity opened her eyes—her spooked eyes.

"How do you feel?" Rene asked.

"Frightened."

"Why?"

"It's evil."

"What?"

"The stuff."

"Did you have a vision?" Holt asked, his voice raw with worry.

"I think it was more like a warning."

"What did you see?"

"Nothing. I didn't hear anything either. But I felt it. I still feel it. Does anyone else?" She shivered as she looked around the room.

"Is it like a spirit?" Rene asked.

"More like a horde."

"Breathe in slowly. Now breathe out just as slowly."

After she did a few times, Rene asked, "How do you feel now?"

"Better. It's gone. I want to sit up. See if I'm still dizzy."

Holt helped her. "Are you okay?"

"Yes. Fine."

Holt and Rene exchanged worried glances, recalling the problems his sister Jilly's spirit had inflicted months before.

"I have an idea what the evil is," Rene said. "Might be part of the reason my ancestor Clairene bequeathed her memories to me. I'll delve and let you know what I find."

~ * ~

VJ stared at the blank TV screen. She and Madeline had skimmed channels, listened to local and surface news, and turned the telly off. Madeline was studying her notes from their sessions with Minalu and her sept. VJ had already memorized hers. And she was restless.

She wandered to the kitchen and peeked out the window. Holt was visible, sitting at the desk with his computer. Whatever he had done to help her see the near-invisible bubble had increased her eyesight immensely. Whilst synked with Minalu, she had seen things in the background she wouldn't have otherwise noticed. Mattresses were spread across the cultural hall floor, dwellers' possessions neatly folded, piled beside them.

Her thoughts moved on to Holt's patience throughout the day. Although he had contributed to conversations, for the most part he had listened, occasionally nodded agreement or shaken his head if he disagreed. If she didn't already love him, she would have fallen for him today. Or tonight, after seeing the deep concern etched in his eyes after she fainted.

In spite of spending hours together, the chasm between them felt deep. Stark. Wide. And seemed to be growing. When he moved to unsynk from the session with Minalu, his hand had grazed hers. When he accompanied them back to the cottage, their arms had brushed. Both times, his mere touch ignited a spark that made her yearn for more. But he didn't even seem to notice. If his afone hadn't interrupted, she had a feeling she might have begged him to kiss her.

Restlessness drew her outside. She approached Holt's bubble with trepidation. But her feet kept moving. "Are you inside?" she called out, feeling like a blithering idiot.

In reply, Holt lifted the flap. "Want to come in?"

"Yes, please."

Entering, she stared up at him, a bit startled by the emotions flowing between them. Holt raised his hand and touched her face. Ripples of pleasure glided across her skin. His fingers felt like a micro touch, the lightness of a butterfly's wings brushing softly against her cheek. Her pulse quickened. Her knees felt weak. And the sensations intensified as he asked, his voice husky with emotion, "Did you come out to talk?"

"Yes." If only he would touch her again.

He didn't. He backed up. "Sorry. I shouldn't have touched you. Do you want to discuss your vision, or Minalu and her sept?"

"Yes. No. I came to talk about us."

"What about us?" His deep voice still sounded husky. Sexy.

"We spent all day together, and we were both a bit uncomfortable. I'd like to ease the tension."

He snapped his fingers. "Feel better now?"

She blinked. "Immensely. Like a heavy daypack has been lifted from my shoulders. How did you do that?"

Holt grinned. "Magic. You could do it too, if you tried."

"I have no magic," she staunchly disagreed.

His grin spread and his dimples deepened. "Yes, you do. If you're ever ready to accept that and learn how to use and control it, I'll volunteer to help teach you."

"That's claptrap. And we both know it."

"Don't be afraid, Verity Jane." He said her name so quietly, so softly, her body started to quiver.

"I'm not afraid. I'm sensible."

"I know. That's one reason I respect you."

Respect? She wanted more than respect. She wanted his love. Frustrated, she said, "If I were your doctor, I would insist that you take a daily dose of something to improve your disposition."

Embarrassed but unwilling to apologize, she turned and marched out, her thoughts roiling. What had she expected? For him to confess his undying love and devotion? That only happened in fairytales and movies. Never in real life.

Inside the cottage, Madeline looked up from her notes. "Did you enjoy the fresh air?"

"I guess." Plunking on a chair, she said what had been on her mind all afternoon. "Tumela is dishy—beautiful. She looks like she belongs in a bikini on a Hawaiian beach." VJ didn't know why she thought that. She'd never been to Hawaii. But she had a lively imagination.

"She is," Madeline agreed. "Like a lovely, rare, exotic creature. Almost too pretty to be human."

"Do you think Holt thinks that?"

"I can't say. Tumela kept looking at him when we were synked. I think she might have a crush on him."

VJ's mood sank lower. She had picked up on those same vibes. Noticed the covert glances Tumela sent his way. Seen the hero-like worship in her lovely eyes.

"I don't think she's your competition," Madeline said, when VJ remained quiet.

"Even if she is, I can't let that matter. But thanks for understanding."

VJ had barely climbed in bed when Madeline tapped on the door.

"Come in."

"I just discovered more flowers on the porch and they're addressed to us."

Scrambling off the bed, VJ followed her to the front door and stared down at two colorful pots—each filled with a beautiful, exotic plant. "The blossoms on each are so unusual I'm certain I have never seen them before."

"Nor I, even though your mum took us to Kew Gardens often, and we saw a collection of extremely rare species every visit."

"Time to get to the bottom of this." VJ gathered the pots in her hands, then marched through the cottage and out the back door. At the bubble, she called, "Are you decent, Holt?"

"Sure. Come on in."

"My hands are full. Would you mind opening the flap?"

"Be right there."

"Did you send these?" she asked.

"Are there cards?"

"Yes. One is addressed to Madeline and the other to me, but they don't say who they came from. You're the only person I can imagine who might have sent them. Last night, we received two dozen roses, in the event you don't recall seeing them. We love flowers, but we don't want to overwhelm the cottage space with these."

Holt snapped his fingers. Reduced the plants to miniatures—each three inches high. "Does that solve your problem?"

In spite of the warning she'd given herself not to smile, she did. "Yes. They're adorable."

"They're porcelain; no longer living plants."

"Marvelous."

"Anything else I can do?" Holt asked.

*Kiss me.* "No," she said, squelching the strong yearning bubbling inside.

He fingered a lock of her hair. "As I said before, your hair is beautiful, Verity. As are you."

She clutched the miniatures tighter. Her heartbeat ramped up. "Thank you. Good night."

Turning, she retreated to the cottage.

When Madeline spotted the miniatures, she laughed. "Blimey. They're quaint. Elegant. A better word is twee."

"I haven't heard that word for at least a decade."

Madeline nodded at the miniatures. "Holt used magic to reduce them?"

"Right."

"He's great."

"I hadn't noticed."

Madeleine laughed again. "You might succeed in telling yourself that, but you don't fool me. You're still looney about him."

"I am not. I cannot afford to be."

"Love has nothing to do with affording."

VJ extended both miniatures. "Do you want these?"

"I'll take the one addressed to me."

"I'll keep mine as a souvenir when I leave."

"You could stay, Ver. I plan to. Holt's kew mate, Drew, put me in touch with a surface attorney, and I spun the wheel into motion to divorce Dwayne."

VJ had a sudden urge to cheer. To say 'spot-on.' Instead, she said, "I cannot live here indefinitely. I must deal with my problems on the surface."

"Are you sure you can't ignore them?"

"Yes. Being suspected of murder is like a noose tightening around my throat."

"If you shared your troubles with Holt, he might have some suggestions to help resolve them."

"I care too much to involve him with my problems."

"You needn't relinquish a second chance," Madeline said quietly.

"To encourage him would be utter naff. Bad. Vulgar."

"You're both suffering. Perhaps telling him would make him feel like you trust him."

"I don't even trust myself. A moment ago, I nearly asked him to kiss me. And I'm in my nightdress. I forgot to wear a robe."

Stepping closer, Madeline hugged her. "Perhaps you should trust your instincts as I'm trusting mine."

"I can't."

Back in Holt's bedroom, VJ set her miniature on his dresser by the yellow roses, duly noting the frame with the photo was gone. Then she remembered seeing it on the desk in Holt's bubble. Turning off the light, she recalled his touch. His compliments. And she knew he had crashed through barriers and demolished the walls she had erected; removed the months and years they had been apart. She loved him. And always would.

~ * ~

Two nights later, VJ reviewed the notes she had taken during her sessions with Minalu and her sept. Having assimilated facts about each dweller, including kidlings and men, she already considered them her patients. If only they could be. She adored each and every one, including Tumela. Despite knowing she must leave, she had already invested part of her heart. She would find it difficult to go.

Her relationship with Holt was nothing like she wanted it to be. Next week, they would be out of quarantine, and she could leave as soon as an enquay reopened. She wanted them to part as friends but didn't know how to make that happen.

Getting ready for bed, she started to undress. She was in her knickers and bra when dizziness made her sway. A huge sunflower clouded her vision. She closed her eyes. Another sunflower joined the first. She staggered to the bed, using the mattress to keep from falling.

"Mad-e-line," she called as the flowers exploded and blackness consumed her.

When the vision ended, Madeline, Holt and Rene were all hovering above her. Rene removed the blood-pressure cuff from her wrist. "Your vitals are normal. How do you feel?"

"Fine. But I was dizzy. Felt like I was falling into a deep dark pit. Something surrounded me. I couldn't move. I felt paralyzed. The vision changed. I was with Mum briefly. Then you were there, Madd, but you were asleep. The place turned dark. Really dark." VJ paused and blinked. "I have no idea where we were or why we were there. I felt the stuff again. The evil." Staring at Rene, she added, "The sensations included Clairine, your ancestor. How do I know that?" Without waiting for a reply, she said, "You know what the evil is, don't you?"

Rene nodded. "It's a collection of departed human spirits. And they are truly evil."

"They want something." When VJ shivered, Holt covered her nearly nude body with a second duvet. "Do you want someone to stay with you tonight?"

"Yes. Please."

"Rene or Madeline?"

"You," Madeline said before VJ could even think. "She'll feel safer with you, Holt."

Rene laughed as she collected her medical tools. "I suppose that depends upon how one defines safe."

Following her from the room, Madeline closed the door behind them.

"You needn't stay, Holt," VJ said, feeling foolish. "I'm fine. I know I'm safe in Apitcote."

"Of course you are," he agreed. "But that doesn't mean we can't enjoy a cuddle." Kicking his shoes off, he sank on the mattress and flattened beside her.

His husky tone sent tremors spiraling across her flesh. "I think I should put on a nightdress," she mumbled, not wanting to sleep in her underwear with him so near.

"I think you should stay right where you are. However, if you think it necessary, I'll keep my eyes closed."

"Don't bother." Her mood suddenly lightened. She could have a dose of Holt. "You did say a cuddle, and we're too far apart to even touch."

Rolling closer, he wrapped one arm around her nearly bare back, the other around her blanketed waist and snuggled her head beneath his chin. "How's this?"

"Good." *Really, really good.*

"Good night, Dr. Hummel."

"Good dreams, poppet."

Holt grinned in the dark before his thoughts wandered through the past, not a habit until Verity had re-entered his life. Three years ago, he had suggested tying. She had ignored the suggestion. It wasn't until she was gone that he wondered if she hadn't understood. He had been so smitten he couldn't believe she didn't feel the same way. He forced his thoughts onward. While living on the surface, he had dated often, then less often, and finally, not at all. "Verity ruined me," he confided to Hanna one night when they shared a pizza after work. "I want no other."

That truth had been proven again when he met Juhree. As he had done with Hanna, they bonded quickly, but he soon realized Juhree's heart belonged to Monteith, just as his belonged to Verity Jane.

He didn't want to want her, but he did. Somehow, he had to convince her to stay. Apitcote needed her. Even if they never reached a point where they were comfortable being near each other, he wanted to make sure she was safe.

The tight knot inside melted as he realized it didn't gall him to know he would willingly leave his homeland to protect her. The knowledge revealed more than he had been willing to admit. He would follow Verity to the end of the earth if it meant keeping her safe. And he knew his parents and kew mates would all understand. Would Hanna understand, too? He missed her and the lengthy conversations they had once shared on a daily basis. He missed Harmony even more. A conflict between his desire to help raise Harmony and keep Verity safe lodged inside his head. Once again, he sought solace and patience, telling himself to trust the future. What should happen would, and worrying about it wouldn't change the outcome. Nor would worrying about Verity's visions of the evil spirits.

# Eight

Holt was gone when VJ awakened. But his piney scent remained. Which told her he had just left. Feeling unusually happy and lighthearted, she hummed while she bathed and dressed.

After breakfast, Holt opened his laptop, synked with the chef in kluster fourteen and said to Verity and Madeline, "Today, I want you to meet a chef."

"Hi. I'm Miss Gwen," a cheerful young lady introduced herself. "I'm one of the chefs, and I'm pleased to meet both of you."

"The pleasure is ours," Verity said.

"I understand you're a dietitian, Madeline. Our university educators are looking for one to teach classes and fill in when someone wants extra time off. Are you interested?"

"Absolutely."

"Good. I'll notify the appropriate department head."

"If we stay here," Madeline said after Holt ended the afternoon session with Minalu, "we'll work together, Ver."

Holt sensed she was tempted, but he told himself not to get his hopes up.

"Must you go?" Madeline asked.

"Yes. One should never be deterred by an arduous path."

"Tell me about that path," Holt coaxed.

The doorbell chime pulled her gaze from his. "I believe the evening meal has arrived."

When Verity opened the door, she laughed. "Tonight, we shall dine with more fresh flowers."

She and Madeline gathered the autumnal flowers while Holt carried the food basket to the table, frustrated by the untimely interruption.

"Pretty yellow and orange chrysanthemums," Madeline said, grinning. "Aren't they lovely?"

"And we don't have a clue who sent them," Verity added, frowning at the cards with their names but nothing else.

~ * ~

Holt's afone beeped as he finished sending emails to his team with the day's assignments. He glanced at the screen. Saw Hanna had initiated Facetime. Raising his afone, he answered. "Hello. How are you?"

"I'm fine, and Harmony's fine, but Mother isn't. Her friend who was in the hospital died about an hour ago."

"That was sudden. Sorry to hear the sad news. Do you need help?"

"Only if you could be with us during this difficult time. I know that isn't possible, and it isn't something you agreed to do, but having you around makes life so much easier."

"I appreciate you saying that."

"I know your enquays are all closed, and you're in quarantine, but I wanted a friend to talk to."

"I'm available whenever you need me."

"Have you watched the video of Harmony?"

"Only about twenty times."

Hanna laughed. "She's such a joy."

"That she is."

"I can't imagine not having her."

"Nor can I. Her birth brought a great deal of love into both of our lives."

"I'm so glad you agreed to share her future with me."

"I am too."

"She's patting mother's arm and telling her not to cry."

"Turn your phone," Holt said. "Let me see them."

He didn't have to strain to hear Harmony consoling Aleece. "Don't ky, Gam-ma. I wub you. Kiss me." Aiming her arms at Aleece, she added, "Hol me, Gam-ma."

"I haven't enough strength to lift her," Aleece said, so Hanna lifted Harmony onto her lap.

As the two chatted, Hanna said, "The family of mother's friend planned a small funeral service. Mom can't go because of the pandemic, which makes her friend's death more difficult to bear."

"I'm sure it does." Holt recalled the deaths and memorial service for the original Ancients who had passed away last year. Hanna and Harmony were still in Apitcote during that difficult time. "If you convince your mater to come here, her health might improve."

"I've tried, but she's dead-set on staying home and dying in her own house. Some days, I think she's actually looking forward to death."

A lump formed in the back of Holt's throat. He wasn't used to death. Still mourned the Ancients. Understood the turmoil Hanna was going through.

~ * ~

Friday morning, Holt handed VJ and Madeline wire bins. "These are for your laundry. Collect what needs to be washed and set the bins on the front porch. They will be returned this evening."

After they collected their clothes, Holt said, "I suggest we work in here today."

"There's more room," Madeline agreed.

When they synked with Minalu and her sept, Tumela said, "Before you begin today's session, may I ask a question, Mr. Holt?"

"Sure."

"Prior to your journey above, you promised to take me to a juice bar and dance with me when you returned. Will you keep your promise?"

"A promise made is a promise kept, Tumela."

Stiffening her spine, VJ told herself she was not jealous, even if Tulmela was the most gorgeous girl she ever laid eyes on.

"When?" Tumela asked, with a dazzling smile.

"When our quarantine ends."

"How long must you continue your social distancing?"

"Three days, after today."

VJ gasped. Couldn't help it. She and Madeline had started counting on Monday and forgotten they had slept all day Sunday.

"We shall meet you in person on Tuesday, Tumela."

"Yes," the young beauty enthused. "I am anxious for that day."

VJ's heart pounded. Three days. All she had left was three days. Even if she had to wait for an enquay to open, Holt would likely arrange for her and Madeline to stay somewhere else so he could have his cottage back.

While they ate their lunch, Holt said, "This afternoon you two should visit with Minalu and her sept without me. I'll work in the bubble."

"Don't you mean your man cave?" Madeline teased.

He chuckled. "I'm going to miss your sunny disposition when our quarantine ends, Maddy."

Her eyes twinkled. "And I'm going to miss seeing your dimpled grin every morning."

"If we convince Verity to stay, that doesn't have to end. The three of us could share breakfast in the constat every day."

"Could we?"

"Sure. Why not?"

Madeline turned a pleading gaze to Verity. "Your staying would make me extremely happy, Ver."

Sadness flickered through Verity's eyes. "You know I can't."

To lighten the mood, Holt nodded at the flowers delivered last night. "Would you like me to miniaturize those before they start to wilt?"

"Yes, please," Madeline said.

Aiming his magic at the chrysanthemums, Holt reduced each to a three-inch miniature.

"They're darling," Madeline gushed.

"And they add cheer to the cottage." A smile chased the sadness from Verity's eyes.

"I'll use my laptop and leave the apad for you to synk with Minalu."

"Will you need your afone?" Verity asked.

He pulled it from his pocket. "It can go back and forth between us." It would give him an excuse to return to the cottage throughout the afternoon.

When they collected food for the evening meal, the bins had been returned with clean laundry, neatly folded.

"People here apparently love what they do," Madeline observed.

"I don't know anyone who doesn't take pride in her or his work," Holt agreed.

"That's what Gwen said. It's amazing."

~ * ~

The hours flew by. Early Monday morning, Madeline reminded, "This is our last night in quarantine."

Holt nodded. "I'm taking Tumela to a juice bar tomorrow night. Would the two of you like to go with us?"

"We don't want to intrude on your date," VJ said, her back arched, posture stiff.

"It isn't a date. Tumela hasn't been inside a juice bar. She's curious, and I'm sure she would enjoy your company."

"I'm curious, too," Madeline said. "I want to go. Don't you, Verity?"

"I can't leave until the enquays reopen," she replied.

"They're all closed for a month to six weeks," Holt announced. "We're taking advantage of the downtime to inspect, modify, repair, refurbish, update. The cage will take longer. It's being enlarged and completely re-built."

VJ relaxed. Leaving wasn't an option. She had to stay at least a month—twenty more wonder-filled days in the magical kingdom of Apitcote.

Torn between two worlds—Holt's and hers—she yearned to live in his. But staying indefinitely would not solve her problems. Being wanted for a murder she didn't commit haunted her day and night, especially in her dreams.

~ * ~

Holt grinned when he saw Verity and Madeline spiffed up and ready to explore the world outside his cottage. "You both look lovely."

Verity blushed. "Are we overdressed?"

"Never in Apitcote."

"Why, what a marvelous foot path!" Madeline exclaimed as they stepped onto the colorful moving conveyance.

"Denizens used to call this the auto walk. Last February, Juhree said that's too mundane for such a beautiful convenience and called it the People Mover. The new name caught and stuck."

"Who made the decision to paint it to resemble rainbows?" Verity asked.

"The kew."

"Before or after you joined them?"

"Before."

"When did you become part of the kew?"

"In June, on Founders' Day."

As they stepped off one People Mover and strolled to another, Madeline paused and looked around. "How very lovely your homeland is, Holt."

"Yes," Verity agreed. "I had forgotten how lush and green the grass is. How beautiful the flowers. How fresh the air. How neat and tidy the thatched-roofed cottages are. How the scale of everything fits the environment. I forgot how sweet the chirping birds sound. How welcome the quiet is, devoid of traffic and blaring noise."

"Eloquently said," Madeline praised.

Holt saluted her to keep from touching her. "Your memories of Apitcote have found their way out of hiding."

Verity blushed as they resumed their trek.

In kluster fourteen, Holt took them to the constat first. "This is where denizens eat unless they want a meal in a different kluster, or decide to eat in the social kluster at a café, restaurant, juice bar or disco," he explained to Madeline. "Gwen is busy in back. I told her she would see you after lunch, but I thought you might enjoy eating breakfast here today."

"We surely will," Madeline agreed, and Verity murmured agreement.

After they studied menus, he lifted the small flag stationed on the table. "The raised flag signals servers that we're ready to order."

"Blimey. That's brilliant. I'd like a proper breakfast—a bacon sandwich and a builder's tea."

"You have a craving? Verity asked."

"Yes. But I want American bacon, not English."

Holt laughed. "A sandwich for breakfast? I shouldn't be surprised. Rene ate dill pickles and raspberries when she was expecting."

Staring at a small sign on the table, Verity read, "Serving others is a pleasure beyond measure."

"That's the weekly slogan," Holt explained. "Every Monday there's a new one in each kluster's constat. Some are inspirational. Others are comical. Most are reminders that, although we may react differently to same experiences, we share our journey through life, along with all other creatures in or on earth."

"What a lovely tradition," Madeline said. "Who comes up with the slogans?"

"Denizens take turns. Our elected officials appoint various groups—families, clubs, schools, or particular age groups. Klusters rotate the experience, a month at a time. Sometimes, the selected team sleeps in the dream chamber to come up with four or five slogans."

Verity smiled. "I remember reading a slogan during my last visit."

"What was it?" Madeline asked.

"Demeaning others precedes falling into a tar pit."

"There was a competition going on at the time," Holt said. "That slogan was a reminder that winning is not more important than the golden rule."

"The more I learn about Api, the more impressed I am."

"I appreciate your praise, Madeline."

"Probably not as much as I appreciate being here."

After breakfast, Holt guided them outside. Verity blinked when she saw small groups of children on the lawn. "Shouldn't they be in school?"

"They are."

She hiked her eyebrows. "Kidlings attend school outdoors?"

"Yes. When the weather turns cold, classes will be held in the cultural hall. The dwellers are currently living there, so we hope to have warm weather until cottages are finished in our new kluster."

"What will happen if the weather turns cold before the dwellers move?"

"Classes will be moved to a hall in a kluster where there are no school-aged children, or they may join other classes."

"You seem to have a solution or a backup for every situation," Madeline said.

"We try to look ahead, anticipate potential problems, and be prepared to nip them before they bud."

They skirted kidlings and entered the cultural hall.

Minalu met them at the door, smiling.

"Do you like living here?" Verity asked.

"Yes. Even the men. And our aged dwellers are happy to be with the Olders and Venes.

"I twig what Olders mean," Madeline said. "What's the difference between them and the Venes?"

"Twenty years," Holt said as dwellers clustered around, eager to meet Verity and Madeline in person.

Verity paid special attention to the pregnant women. "Yes, I am a doctor," she assured each one. "My specialty is women's health, and I would be honored to assist with the birth of your baby."

Holt figured she felt safe saying that because two looked like they could deliver any day.

At noon, they made their way to the constat in his kluster for lunch. While they waited for their food, Madeline said, "We convinced the dwellers to go see the new kluster where cottages are being built for them."

"Good for you."

"We also convinced them to attend the Autumnal Fall Festival on Saturday."

"Congratulations on jobs well done."

"Do your chemists have vitajoy gummies? Verity asked.

"Chemists? As in pharmacies?"

"Yes."

"If they don't, I'm sure Juhree can conjure them."

"Daily vitamins will improve the dwellers' diet."

Holt adored her accent. Her ideas. Her choice of words. He didn't want her to leave again. But if she stayed, another man would likely fall in love with her. Ask her to tie. The thought felt like a punch in the gut.

After lunch, they returned to kluster fourteen and chatted with Gwen and Minalu. As they discussed menus, a young boy dashed inside. "There's a fight at school, Mistress Minalu."

Rushing outdoors, she seized the back of each boy's collar and held them apart, facing each other. "Who started this squabble?"

"He did," one boy pointed at the other. "He said Veralane stinks."

"Did not," the other disagreed. "I said she smells bad."

VJ saw one little girl standing by herself, away from the other kidlings. Tears ran rivers down her reddened cheeks. Approaching her, VJ inhaled a rank odor she didn't recognize, and sensed the girl's elevated temperature.

"She might be ill," she announced, duly noting both boys flinch. "I think Veralane should be taken to hospital."

"Clinics serve as our hospitals," Holt said. "I'll levitate you and Veralane there and summon a kew mate to bring Veralane's mater, and Minalu."

"Good." VJ clasped Veralane's hand and his. "Let's be off then."

She wasn't prepared to be lifted in the air and knew Veralane wasn't either. The experience was one she wouldn't have wanted to miss. Veralane must have felt the same way. She squealed the whole time, gripping VJ's hand with both of hers and laughing with childish delight.

At the clinic, Dr. Lorraine guided them to a room where Holt placed Veralane on an examining trolley. VJ washed her hands. Donned surgical gloves. Checked Veralane's temperature, blood pressure, oxygen, heart rate. Before she finished, Juhree arrived with Veralane's mum, Oliv, and Minalu. "Vitals are all normal except for a slightly elevated temperature." VJ smiled to ease concern. "How do you feel, Veralane?"

"Like my feet walked in a fire pit."

"Let's take a look." Before she touched one shoe, VJ knew what was responsible for the noxious smell. "Where did the shoes come from?"

"Our ware rooms," Juhree said.

"The soles are contaminated. I recommend incinerating them asap."

"I'll see to that," Dr. Lorraine dropped each shoe in a paper bag as VJ removed them. Veralane's stockings were stuck to her feet. VJ pried them off. "Burn these, too."

Dr. Lorraine added them to the bag, and Holt used his heat to disintegrate them.

The bottoms of Veralane's feet were red, but there was no rash to indicate infection or disease. VJ inhaled deeply. The noxious smell was gone. "Your feet reacted to something in the soles of your shoes. The burning sensation should abate quickly. To speed the process, I'll apply some salve after I wash them. Is that okay with you?"

Veralane nodded.

Dr. Lorraine showed VJ where supplies were stored. As she finished applying salve, she said, "You're a brave girl to suffer without complaining."

"Why didn't you tell me your feet hurt?" Oliv asked.

"They didn't until after I put my shoes on. It started when I got to school."

"You shouldn't walk anymore today," VJ said. "I recommend you stay here overnight."

"Do I have to?" Veralane asked, her voice quivering.

"Will it be easier if your mum stays with you?"

"I guess so," she said, voice still quivering.

Dr. Lorraine winked like a co-conspirator. "Think of this as another new adventure. You can watch TV and be waited on like a princess."

"Can I see cartoons?"

"You bet. Let's move you. Then I'll show you how to use the remote to find cartoon channels."

"I never used a remote before." Her voice had lost its quiver.

"Then you're in for a new experience, aren't you?"

Veralane giggled as Dr. Lorraine wheeled her trolley to an extended-stay room.

"Would you like something to drink?" Holt asked, when she was settled. "Water, juice, milk?"

"Can I have orange juice, Mr. Holt?"

"Yes."

Dr. Lorraine punched her afone. Seconds later, a nurse entered, carrying a tray with a bottle of orange juice, a straw, and sanitizer.

Veralane pointed at the straw. "What's that?"

"A straw," Holt explained. "Use the sanitizer wipe to clean your hands before you unwrap the straw."

While she did, he sanitized his own hands and uncapped the lid. "Put the straw inside," he instructed.

"How can I drink with that in the way?"

"Place the straw between your lips and suck."

"Like this?" she asked, grinning when orange juice flowed to her mouth.

"Exactly."

"This is fun. I like straws, Mr. Holt. I liked flying, too."

He grinned. "Do your feet still hurt?"

Shaking her head, she took another sip.

~ * ~

Back at kluster fourteen, Holt and Verity found Madeline still outside with the school kidlings. Rene and her mate, Drew, showed up a few minutes later.

"We're here to take you to see more of Apitcote," Rene announced. "Thought you might like to see the amphitheater."

Enthusiasm glowed in Madeline's eyes. "Jolly good."

"I'll leave them in your care." Holt excused himself, knowing his kew mates would take turns showing them the community, and ensuring they didn't feel abandoned.

He was proud of Verity and the way she had handled Veralane and Oliv and explained to the teachers and kidlings. She truly was a gifted doctor.

~ * ~

"How was your afternoon?" Holt asked when the entire kew gathered for the evening meal in his constat.

"Very pleasant," Madeline replied. "Levitating was special. What did you think, Ver?"

"That flying is a bit less frightening than being strapped to a rocket."

Kew mates laughed. And chatted amiably while they ate.

After dessert, Holt said, "Excuse me. I'm going to fetch Tumela. Shouldn't be long. Wait for me here, ladies."

"We'll miss tonight's kew meeting," VJ said.

"We aren't having one," Rene said. "It's your first night out of isolation, and you should do something fun."

# *Nine*

Holt escorted VJ, Madeline and Tumela to the social kluster, riding People Movers through four klusters to get there. At the marble bar, he purchased juices, then found a table. "Would you like to dance?" he asked Verity.

"I'd rather not."

"I would." Cheeky Tumela grasped his arm and laughed at something Holt said as he led her to the oval dance floor.

VJ watched them gloomily. She found it impossible to purge traces of jealousy. "I've never seen anyone as pretty as she is. Current company excluded, of course."

Madeline sipped her blueberry juice. "He did ask you first."

"Probably won't ask again."

When the smiling couple returned, Tumela sat next to VJ, but Holt remained standing. "Would you like to dance, Madeline?"

"Sure." Bouncing to her feet, she grinned as he took her elbow to steer her through the crowd.

A strange chap approached their table. "Will you dance with me, Miss Tumela?"

"Yes."

As soon as Holt escorted Madeline back to their table, a pretty girl tapped him on the shoulder. "May I have the next dance, Mr. Holt?"

"Sure."

Trying not to watch them, VJ mumbled, "You looked like you had fun, Madd."

"I did. Don't know when I'll dance again. My pregnancy will likely discourage chaps from asking me."

VJ saw Tumela dancing with another bloke and Holt twirling a different girl who had boldly asked him to dance as soon as he finished with the first. She noted chaps and females were dancing by themselves, obviously enjoying the music, and people of all colors and nationalities were mingling like one big happy family.

She compared the juice bar to pub experiences. Back in England, neighborhood pubs were often occupied by families in the evening, after supper. Denizens in the juice bar were all a certain age—twenties and early thirties. From her previous visit, she recalled that young people tended to flock together in juice bars while adults favored discos.

Holt returned and sat beside her. Several men kept Tumela and Madeline on the dance floor. VJ's heart throbbed in anxious pulses when Holt refused to dance with another girl. She tried to dismantle her feelings for him. Logic didn't work. Nothing did. He was inside her, snug as a bug wrapped up inside a coiled rug.

"If you're wondering why no one has asked you to dance," he said, "it's because they assume you're with me."

"I'm not with you. You're here with Tumela. I'm just a tag along."

He leveled a chiding stare. "We need to clear the air."

"Do not," she disagreed with a stubborn tilt of her chin.

"Do too," he replied, just as mulish. "Doesn't take a genius to see you're wound up like a toy top. You've trapped frustration inside. It needs to be released. Give yourself a break. Let it out."

"Are you a psychologist now?"

"No. Just a man who cares about you."

"Oh." She couldn't think of another thing to say. She was spared the need when Madeline and Tumela returned, both out of breath from a fast-paced dance.

"I'll go order a new round of drinks." Holt excused himself as Tumela floated back to the dance floor with a different chap.

Watching Holt belly up to the bar made VJ yearn to return to his cottage, crawl in bed, and pity herself. But she didn't know how to get there without a guide.

A pretty girl carrying a tray of drinks accompanied Holt back to their table. After she unloaded the tray, he gave her what VJ considered an over-the-top tip. "We should pay for our own drinks," she said.

"Tonight's my round," Holt replied, reminding her of England and the differences between their language.

Sitting beside her again, Holt alternated between glancing at the dancers and watching her. She felt like he was studying her as though she were a bug stuck under a microscope. And it made her nervous.

"She's a friend," Holt said, watching her watch Tumela.

"She's beautiful."

"Yes. She is."

VJ stared into his mesmerizing gaze. Wished her heart wasn't breaking in pieces again. Wished she could give him what she yearned to give. Wished he wanted her as much as she wanted him.

She bit her bottom lip. Swallowed hard. Sipped her orange squash—a favorite soda since childhood.

Holt picked up his drink, took a hefty swallow.

"What are you drinking?" she asked to make conversation.

"A concoction of oranges and bananas, blended with coconut milk and ice. Would you like a taste?"

"Yes." After one tasty swallow, she said, "It's delicious."

"Should I order one for you?"

She stared at her half full glass. "If you don't mind."

He raised the small flag to summon a server. "You're a remarkable woman, Verity Jane."

She bit her bottom lip to keep from saying, *And you're a remarkable man.*

The silence no longer felt uncomfortable. The only thing that could have made it more pleasant was his hand holding hers.

An image of them cuddled on Holt's settee opposite his fireplace flashed. The image felt so real it gave her pause. A memory from her previous visit? A vision of their future? Or just a fantasy she wished to be real?

VJ kept quiet when they accompanied Tumela back to kluster fourteen. She and Madeline laughed and talked about how much they had enjoyed dancing with different chaps.

"Except Vane," Madeline said. "He made me uneasy."

"Vane is a visitor, not a denizen," Holt said. "What did he do?"

"The wanker held me too close and made insulting suggestions."

"Did he bother you, Tumela?"

"No. I was spared his attention."

After leaving Tumela at the cultural hall, they headed for Holt's cottage. "You didn't dance, but did you enjoy the music, Ver?"

"Sure."

Madeline's next attempt at conversation fell on deaf ears.

At his cottage, Madeline scooped up two vases of roses.

"Would you like me to miniaturize those?" Holt asked.

"I'd like to keep them fresh for a few days, until the petals open." She carried them inside, shut the door, and dimmed the outdoor light—programmed to turn on at dusk and off at dawn.

Not sure he appreciated Madeline's clever thoughtfulness, Holt asked, "Are you planning to leave when the enquay's open, Verity?"

She nodded.

"Would you stay if you could?"

"Yes. I don't want to leave you again, Holt. It was brutally painful last time, and I fear it might be worse now."

"Wow," he said, totally surprised.

"And I'm concerned about Madeline," she continued. "I'd like to be around when she has the miscarriage. I might be able to help. Plus, I enjoy working with the sept dwellers. I know them individually, as if each one is my patient. They've shared their secrets, their desires, their hopes."

"When are you going to share those things with me?"

"I'm not going to break their confidence."

"Not what I'm asking. You know I want to share your problems."

"Not going to happen," she announced.

"What we resist persists," he said, still reeling from her quiet admission.

"I don't know how to resolve the issues connected to my life."

"Tell me about them."

"I've already said more than I think prudent."

Choosing a different tack, he said, "You weren't safe on the surface."

She jerked her startled eyes back to his. "How do you know that?"

"The guy who attempted to mow me down in the hospital parking lot is the same guy who tried to run us off the road on Hoosier Pass. He followed you to and from work all week. At night, he slept in a van as close to your apartment as he could find a parking space. He had a gun, Verity."

"I wasn't aware I was being followed... except for—a couple of days," she stuttered.

"The day we drove up to see the aspens, another vehicle joined the van. Two men were tailing you. The second guy slept in his car the night we stayed at the mansion. That's one of the reasons Mater and Pater brought you here. They were worried about your safety. Just as I am. If you go back, you could be in danger again."

"I think one vehicle might have been driven by someone who wasn't dangerous."

"But you can't be sure, can you?"

"No. I don't want to leave, Holt, but I will when it becomes necessary."

"What will make it necessary?"

VJ didn't know how to reply. Just being near him completely dismantled each and every objection. "Let's not talk about this anymore tonight, okay? Can't we just enjoy whatever time we have to be together?"

"Fine. Let's call another truce."

She extended her hand.

Holt took it between his. "Done."

VJ's pulse throbbed at the hollow of her throat, and her heartbeat sped up. How could a mere touch put her in such a dither? She felt like a besotted ninny. Also, at a distinct disadvantage with him staring so intently. Memories rolled in like waves from the sea. At times, his eyes were as blue as the sky on a sunny day. At others, they were as dark as the ocean during a thundering downpour. Tonight, they were a mixture, combined with questions she didn't have the bravery to answer. "I guess it's time to say good night," she said through her constricted throat.

He raised his hand and waved. "Good night."

~ * ~

Juhree arrived at Holt's cottage as the trio returned from breakfast. She didn't ring the bell. Merely tapped on the screen before she walked in. With an impish grin, she announced, "I'm here to help you prepare for the Autumnal Fall Fest."

"What must we do?" VJ asked, not wanting to take time away from the dwellers.

"Allow me to kit you out."

Grinning at her British expression, Madeline quipped, "My wardrobe is somewhat limited."

"That's why I'm here."

Holt sauntered to the back door. "I'll leave you to your fun. Juhree's skill is fantastic. I think you'll be impressed."

"Do you want to see what clothes we have?" Madeline asked after Holt meandered outside.

"No need. You deserve something new. Pretend I'm your fairy godmother, and I will conjure whatever you fancy."

~ * ~

"The amphitheater is totally huge," VJ said when they arrived at the Fall Fest. "Larger than it looked when Rene and Drew brought us here a few days ago."

"Righto," Madeline agreed. "Even with thousands of people, it doesn't feel crowded."

Feeling Holt's gaze on her, VJ turned hers to him.

"This is where I was inducted and welcomed into the kew." His warm smile sent pleasurable thrills bouncing through her.

"Your parents are approaching." Madeline's statement pulled their attention off each other.

"Everything looks beautiful," VJ said.

"I'm quite astounded by the transformation," Madeline added.

Pride glowed in Shelan's eyes. "Kirt and I were on the planning committee, and we helped decorate. Instead of tablecloths that might rustle in the breeze, we opted for the simplicity of colorful autumnal tables. Yours is in the center. The dwellers' surround yours."

"The committee seated you and the newcomers in the place of honor," Pater said.

Plentiful food, covered and ready to be eaten family style, tempted appetites. As denizens filled their plates, Elden, son of original Ancients, hovered above the crowd, moving between tables to smile a welcome to all.

"Holy cow," Madeline said, "The old bloke's flying."

"How old is he?" VJ asked.

"A hundred and sixty-five."

"When was his last birthday?"

"August sixth."

Madeline's mouth rounded in a surprised 'O.'

"That's our birthdays, too," VJ explained, unnerved as well.

"We know," Holt said.

"And yours." Dates of birth had always held a special meaning to VJ, especially after she met Madeline and discovered they were born on the same day and year.

Her attention was drawn to Minalu sitting nearby. As they stared, VJ sensed the sept leader possessed some kind of magic. Did it take someone who had magic to recognize that in another? Was Holt right? Did she possess magic? If so, could he teach her how find, use and control it?

*"Good things will happen today."*

Startled by the silent message, VJ stared at Holt. Saw him talking to Madeline. She glanced at Minalu. Knew the message had come from her.

VJ concentrated; tried sending one back. *"Communicating this way is good."*

*"Convenient, too."*

Holt nudged her arm. "You're not eating. Is something wrong?"

"No. Everything's fine."

After denizens ate their fill, most kew mates went to dance. Even Madeline danced—with chaps she had met at the juice bar. Only VJ, Holt, Juhree and Monteith remained at their round table.

"I see Grandee and Grama Care," Juhree announced. "I'm going to go chat. Want to come with me?"

Monteith smiled. "I'll join you in a few."

With a warm smile, she floated away, levitating above the crowd.

"How can she fly in a dress and still look prim and proper—like Mary Poppins without a brolly?" Verity asked.

Monteith grinned. "Juhree is one of the most capable humans I know."

"And you adore her," Holt said.

Monteith's grin faded, his expression serious. "Don't think I could live without her." He looked so grave it made VJ want to hear their story.

"I've been wanting to talk to you, Verity." Monteith surprised her.

"What about?"

"Your vision of Apitcote, and the influx of people who will attempt to get inside."

VJ glanced at Holt, then back at Monteith. "My visions have always come true, but I'm never absolutely positive the next one will."

"We want to be prepared in any case. Please tell me exactly what you saw. Every detail you remember."

"Okay."

When she finished, Monteith nodded. "Holt said you didn't know we had more than one enquay until recently."

"How many do you have?"

"Eight."

VJ gulped but managed to ask, "Are they all secure?"

"Seven are. The eighth doesn't have much, other than what Mater Nature provides—rocks and sagebrush, and a simple computer system." Monteith glanced at Holt. "We got around to checking and installing while you were on the surface."

"Did Falo give you any trouble?"

"He wasn't happy to see us, but he didn't thwart us. He was curious. Even went with us. I think he hoped to see his sons nearby and encourage them to return."

"Who is Falo?" VJ asked.

"Minalu's pallet mate, although they no longer share one."

The discussion ended as Tumela approached. "Would you dance with me, Mr. Holt?"

"Sure." Glancing at VJ, he said, "Will you excuse me?"

"Of course." But once again, she felt left out.

Juhree returned as Holt and Tumela strolled away. Sensing she wanted to dance with Monteith, VJ said, "I'm going to explore the trinket booths."

Before she reached the first one, Madeline caught up, and they explored together.

As they headed back to their table sometime later, a chap approached and tapped Madeline's shoulder.

"Will you dance with me?"

"Yes. Thank you."

VJ sat next to Monteith who was watching kidlings and children mingle and play.

"Does it bother you to see Holt and Juhree chatting as though they're the only two people in the world?" VJ asked, trying not to look at them.

Monteith shook his head, just once. "They love each other as brother and sister."

"That's what Juhree said. But are you sure?"

"Yes, although Holt and I were kind of rivals when Juhree first came to Api. Holt invited her to Mist and Jordan's tying ceremony before I even thought about it. We both danced with her, but I claimed the most. Must have irritated him until he accepted that she's my One. Not his."

"Is there still rivalry between you?"

"Not at all. Holt is part of Juhree's heart. I'm a larger part, and her soul is connected to mine."

"You're very secure in your love."

"We are now," he agreed. "Do you love Holt?"

"Do I look or act like I love him?"

"If you did, I wouldn't have asked. You're both good at concealing your feelings."

A distant memory drifted through VJ and she used it to change the subject. "I remember asking Mum once what my feelings were."

Monteith laughed.

"I have another question."

"What?"

"What did you mean when you said tying ceremony?"

"Holt hasn't told you what tying means?"

"No." She almost blurted that their wrists had been tied once, but she didn't.

"Tying is what marriage is on the surface."

Unable to conceal her surprise, VJ merely nodded.

A commotion nearby drew her attention. As she turned her head, Minalu tapped her shoulder. "Dilane is on the verge of delivering her babe. We should return to our kluster."

"She'll be better off at the clinic." Monteith didn't ask which woman was Dilane. He simply cradled the flush-faced very pregnant woman in his arms and levitated away."

Holt scooped VJ's hand in his and followed Monteith.

The baby girl arrived twenty minutes later.

"That's one of the fastest accouchements I've ever seen," VJ said, when she joined Holt and Monteith in the waiting room.

She was nearly startled out of her sterilized shoes when Juhree arrived, levitating Tinna. "You have another patient, Dr. Verity."

VJ touched Tinna's wrist, inhaled and knew the baby would soon be born. After she scrubbed again, she examined Tinna and explained, "Your baby is ready, however not quite in the hurry Dilane's was."

"I asked for assistance as soon as I felt cramps. Dilane waited until she couldn't conceal them." Tinna cringed as another contraction began.

"Thanks for bringing her here, Juhree." VJ motioned for a medic to roll the trolley to the delivery room.

Within the hour, VJ delivered the second baby, a boy.

When she entered the waiting room, Minalu and Madeline were there, along with all of Holt's kew mates. Men stood behind their Ones, Holt stood behind Minalu and Madeline, who had apparently been levitated there.

He smiled, and in that instant, VJ realized her bond with him and his kew mates had grown.

She checked her four patients again before she removed her surgical garb.

"The Fest is still underway," Holt said before he and his kew mates levitated everyone back to the amphitheater.

Monteith grinned as they trundled back to solid ground. "We arrived in time to watch the Wacky Waddle Regatta."

VJ scanned the arena. "There's no water. How can one have a regatta without a river or a lake?"

"With bottomless boats," Holt explained.

"Never have a I seen or heard of a bottomless boat race."

"Then you're about to witness your first. Teams of denizens race across the amphitheater, carrying long, bottomless boats around their waists, with their legs poking out beneath. It started as a joke about fifty years ago. Now, it's part of the Fest's annual event. Every year the race attracts hundreds of participants."

"Is there a reward for the team that finishes first?" Madeline asked.

Humor filled Holt's blue eyes and his dimples winked when he grinned. "The winning team will fly around the arena with kew members. Tonight is our first time to be involved."

"Winners consider levitating with the kew to be an honor," Dane explained. "Prior to last year, the winning team received a banner to display in their constat. Rene was the only one who levitated back then, with the exception of our original Ancients. Denizens respect all magical gifts and are reluctant to ask anyone to share theirs. This year, we volunteered to be the prize."

As the race began, laughter and clapping filled the arena. VJ thought she and Madeline laughed harder than anyone else.

"That was indeed wacky, wobbly and funny," Madeline said after the last team crossed the finish line. Denizens were clapping and cheering so loud she had to shout to be heard.

"An experience I wouldn't have wanted to miss," VJ yelled.

Just as the noise began to subside it started up again, increasing in volume until it reached a thunderous roar. Denizens turned back to where the race had begun. VJ recognized Holt in front of his four kew mates, legs sticking beneath a bottomless boat as the blokes charged across the field at break-neck speed.

"We're the losing team," Holt shouted after they crossed the finish line.

Teams from the actual race, winners first, lined up to shake losing team's hands while the crowd continued to laugh and cheer.

"What jolly good sports," someone yelled.

"Hoo-ray for our kew," someone else shouted.

"Are kew sisters planning to entertain us?" another roared.

Rene waved the men away. As soon as they moved, she, Tess, Mist and Juhree stepped inside their boat.

"Mist should not run." Jordan reached out to snatch her from the boat. "She's too far along."

But Mist levitated away with her kew sisters, straight above, taking the boat with them.

"Don't fret," Rene called. "We don't plan to run." Winking at the crowd, she added, "Watch and witness the first ever airborne wacky regatta."

Spreading their arms as though they were wings, kew sisters flew around the arena in mid-air, circling above the crowd.

The orchestra struck up a snappy tune as the flying boat and its occupants moved up and down, swaying to the music while the crowd sang:

"Twinkle, twinkle, little stars
How we wonder that you are
Up above our heads so high
Pretty diamonds in our sky.

~ * ~

"It's after midnight," VJ said, startled time had passed so quickly. Only she, Madeline and kew mates remained at the amphitheater.

"The arena is completely cleared of rubbish," Madeline said, her eyes wide with astonishment. "When did that happen? Who did all the work?"

"My grandma Care," Juhree answered with a gamine grin, "cleaned the easy way,"

"How?"

"Juhree and Care not only conjure," Holt explained, "they also make things vanish or return to where they originated."

Madeline sighed. "Apitcote truly is magical."

"I think the people make it so," VJ said. Delivering two newborns had put her in her element. The day could not have been more perfect—unless she didn't have to worry about leaving.

"You look happy," Madeline said as they followed Holt's kew mates to the People Mover.

"I am. I feel as though I've graduated from university, and medical school, and moved on to the other side of the door to life."

"Can't improve on a feeling like that," Holt commented, joining them.

*I could if I could find a way to prove my innocence and reclaim what you and I once shared.* As she had done before, VJ dashed the thoughts away. This was not a night for a glum mood. She had enjoyed a marvelous Apitcote holiday and delivered two babies to boot.

Two pots of flowers greeted them when they reached Holt's cottage. There were two small boxes as well. One addressed to VJ. The other to Madeline. Inside were identical silver bracelets, each with two hearts entwined.

"They're lovely! Absolutely blinding!" Madeline exclaimed, admiring hers.

VJ stared at Holt. "Did you send these?"

"I've been with you all day."

"You could have arranged for them to be delivered or used magic."

"True."

"That doesn't answer my question."

"You don't answer mine."

VJ let her frustration show. And grow.

Holt gave her chin a gentle tap with one finger. "Can't have everything you ask for unless you're willing to give in return."

"Excuse me." Madeline clutched her flowers and bracelet. "I'll shuttle these inside." With both hands full, she used her pinky to open the screen latch.

"Would you like to have the flowers and pots miniaturized first?" Holt asked.

Madeline grinned. "Sure. I love seeing you do that."

He snapped his fingers.

"Whooping brilliant," Madeline beamed.

"You and Verity are more fantastic than magic," he countered.

Every ounce of VJ's frustration dissolved. Reaching for his hand, she lifted and kissed his fingers, startled by her own bold, flirty display.

Holt tipped an imaginary hat and whistled as he strolled away. *Good night, ladies, good night gentlemen.*

"Today was totally fun," Madeline said as VJ shut the door behind them. "I don't ever want to leave. Everyone treats me like a dear friend."

"You are their dear friend, and you shouldn't feel obligated to leave just because I do."

"You don't have to go. People have choices."

"Not me."

"Will you come back? At least to visit?"

"That depends on a number of things. But we'll find a way to keep in touch, Madd." VJ lifted her heart bracelet from its bed of white velvet. She had a feeling these were meant to keep her linked with Madeline. "Let's wish these on each other and vow never to remove them."

"Brilliant."

When they finished, Madeline said, "I don't want to sound greedy, but I wish we had phones like Holt's.

"They're called afones, spelled with an 'f'. I wish we had one, too."

# *Ten*

Breakfast was on the table when the threesome arrived at the chateau to talk with Rene and Dane about Verity's visions and Rene's memories inherited from her grandmater.

"I delved deeper and found more information about the evil you sensed, Verity."

When she shuddered, Holt touched her arm. "Are you okay?"

She nodded and turned her gaze back to Rene. "Do you know what the evil is?"

"Hundreds of departed spirits. Clairene used magic to rid them from this section of our realm by sealing them in a far-away tunnel. But she had doubts they would always remain there. Hopefully, your vision has given us time to prepare for their return."

"What do you think they will do?" Drew asked.

"I'm not sure, but I suspect they intend to inflict some kind of harm."

Holt cleared his throat. "I think they want what Jilly's spirit wanted—to inhabit bodies so they can live again."

"How awful," Madeline exclaimed.

"How can we prevent that?" Verity asked, clearly upset.

"You and I have both seen parts of the future, but neither of us fully understands what we've seen," Rene said. "We need to unravel the puzzle. I suggest discussing possibilities in our kew meetings. Do you have any objections?"

"No. Actually I think that's the best way to proceed."

"We'll start tonight."

"Tonight cannot come soon enough," Verity mumbled just before she blinked and her body went rigid. Holt reached out and caught her before she hit the floor.

Rene touched her forehead. "She isn't ill, but her vitals are elevated. I think she's having a vision. We should take her up to the dream chamber. That environment will aid her."

Holt carried her up the spiral staircase. The other three climbed behind.

Verity was out a full three minutes. When she finally opened her eyes, she looked from Holt to Madeline, then at Rene and Drew.

"Are you okay?" Holt asked.

"Yes. However, stars are still spinning around my face." She raised her hand and tried to swat something invisible to Holt, away. Apparently failing, she closed her eyes and breathed in and out, slowly, then more slowly.

"Are you still in the vision?" he asked quietly.

"No. I'm perfectly fine, or I will be as soon as my heart rate slows."

The other four looked from her to each other and kept quiet until she spoke again.

"The spirits are demon furies who hear but cannot see. Somehow, they will unite with ugly horrid creatures. Some only have one eye."

"Trolls," Madeline predicted.

Holt hiked an eyebrow. "Trolls?"

"Yes. I've read about trolls. Most have one eye. Some have none. They don't like anyone or anything. They're mean. Selfish. Stingy. They live alone or in small families. But they don't like each other. I can't imagine why they were created."

"I've never believed they were," Verity said. "I thought they existed only in Norwegian folklore, and the tales were used to scare children into being good."

"Can you tell us what we need to do to protect Apitcote?" Drew asked.

"Afraid not," Verity said. "That's something we'll have to figure out."

"At least we have a heads-up warning," Rene concluded.

"I have no idea when my vision will happen. Could be soon. Could be years from now." Still feeling strange and disoriented, she sat up, and looked around the oversized room, trying to get her bearings. The entire floor was covered with a thick mattress, similar to wall-to-wall carpeting.

"This is the dream chamber," Rene explained.

VJ had heard about the room but hadn't been there. "I think it helped me navigate through the horrific vision."

"Are your visions like nightmares?" Drew asked.

"No. Every vision is quite different. And they don't always begin with the same warning."

"What warned you today?"

"Stars circled my face. Spun around me like a mild whirlwind." She blinked. "Some bits are still spinning at the edges of my eyes." Raising her hand, she flicked them away.

"What else can you tell us about the vision?" Rene asked.

"It was quite disturbing. Covid will not come to Apitcote, but a sleeping sickness will."

"Do you know how many denizens will fall asleep?"

"Hundreds. And I don't know what to do to protect them. I fear deep sleep might be a prelude to the spirit demon furies taking over bodies."

"That is disturbing," Madeline said, and VJ had a sudden flash. Madeline would be intricately involved, which meant the spirits would infiltrate Apitcote within her lifetime.

~ * ~

Hanna's atext took Holt by surprise. He hadn't heard from her for several days and hadn't atexted her because he knew she would text when she had time.

*Mother is fine—no Covid. I have someone set up to stay with her so Harmony and I can travel to Api. If an enquay is open, will the Thanksgiving week work?*

He read the atext with conflicting emotions. Made a swift decision. Atexted back.

*Trax enquays will be open. I'll reserve a cottage when you send exact dates.*

~ * ~

VJ kept so busy she barely believed how fast each day passed, how quickly time blended between meals and bedtime. If only she could add more hours to each day.

At kew meetings, Holt's presence was both a soothing balm and a source of physical awareness. As he taught her and Madeline which People Movers to navigate through the community, their relationship changed. She couldn't decide whether that was better or worse. He acted distracted. She felt more attracted.

One night after Madeline returned to kluster fourteen to tell folklore stories, VJ hurried out to the bubble. Tired of waiting for Holt to make an overture, she had decided to take the initiative.

"Are you ever going to kiss me?" she blurted as soon as he lifted the flap.

"Hadn't planned to," he said, obviously quite startled.

"Why? Because you don't love me?"

When he didn't answer, she asked, "Are we tied?" She was tempted to reach out and run her fingers down his shirted chest, wishing she had caught him shirtless.

"We are not tied. Denizens aren't tied just because someone ties them. Couples both have to agree to join their lives."

"If you didn't use your magic to tie our wrists, who did?"

"Mater and Pater. Who told you what tying means?"

"Monteith. I'd rather have heard it from you."

"When did he tell you?"

"At the Fall Fest. Did you suggest tying when I was here before?"

"Yes."

"It went right over my head. Why didn't you explain?"

"Stupidity on my part." The tenderness in his gaze made her heart do tiny little flip flops.

"Well, are you going to kiss me? Or not?"

"Not."

Her heart fell. "Why?"

"You're leaving, and I am not free to pursue or kiss you."

"What do you mean you're not free?" Dread crept up her spine. "You're not tied to someone else, are you?"

"Not yet."

"Not yet?" she echoed, pain ratcheting through her along with deep devastation. "Are you planning to tie with Tumela."

"No."

"Someone else."

"Yes."

"Who?"

"Someone I met after you abandoned me."

She fled before she burst into tears. In his bedroom, she shut the door, and cried until her tear ducts were as empty as her heart.

~ * ~

On Halloween, most denizens worked during the day, but at dusk they donned costumes and joined in revelry at the social kluster.

Perched on stools in a juice bar, Juhree grinned at VJ and Madeline. "There are lots of activities outdoors. Let's go have a different kind of fun."

VJ forced a smile when Juhree hooked her elbows with theirs. Outside, the threesome bobbed for apples while Holt, Monteith and another chap watched.

"Want to participate in some team games?" Juhree asked as they dried their faces with warm fluffy towels.

"Yes. Where?" Madeline asked.

"In the meadow." Juhree grabbed Monteith and Holt's hands. "Come along. We'll need partners."

"Mind if I join you?" the chap who had watched Madeline asked.

"Please do," Juhree invited with a gamine grin.

The first relay was passing a candy lifesaver from a toothpick held between one's teeth to the toothpick held by the next person in line. VJ was paired with Holt. They stood so close she inhaled his piney cologne, which made her nerves quiver.

Holt looked as relieved as VJ felt when the game ended before their turn.

"Our team lost," Monteith said.

"Only by seconds," Juhree said, clapping and cheering for the winning team.

Wishing she had stayed home, VJ clapped too, but her heart wasn't in it. Being near Holt was painful. They had avoided each other since the night he told her he intended to tie with someone else.

The second relay was exchanging an orange beneath their chins with their hands clasped behind their backs. All six team mates laughed when a partner on the other team dropped the orange, and the couple had to start over at the head of the line.

When it was their turn, Holt tried to transfer the orange from his neck to VJ's, keeping so much distance between them, he couldn't manage such a simple task.

She was tempted to complain, but Madeline did it for her. "One last push, if you please, poppet."

Holt burst out laughing. The orange dropped on VJ's feet.

Juhree laughed. "Our team's going to lose again."

"But we're good sports," Monteith added, also laughing.

VJ looked at Holt. He looked at her. Neither moved. Or said a word. The look in his eyes sent a mixed message. Surely, he didn't want to kiss her, did he?

Madeline nudged her elbow, pointed at the sky. "Look."

Denizens began to ooh with awe as mannequin ghosts sailed through the air, dipping and swaying, attached to poles with bungee cords while spooky music filled the night.

"What jolly good fun," Madeline said after they found a spot to sit and watch fireworks.

"Can't remember when I last frolicked with such unrestrained abandon."

"Me either," Juhree said. "Never have I been carried away by such disport."

"History will remember all three of you." Holt sounded serious. He looked only at VJ.

Her heart pounded. Ached. Yearned.

At the conclusion of the fiery display, Monteith announced, "It's past midnight."

"May I escort you and Madeline back to my cottage?" Holt asked. "I have a surprise."

"You do?" VJ asked, startled. He had barely spoken to her during the last week.

"He already gave me mine," Madeline said. "Minalu's waving. Must have something to tell me. See you later, Ver."

At his cottage, Holt guided her out back to his bubble. She hadn't been inside since that awful night when the cracks in her heart felt like they bled raw while tears ran down her cheeks.

He extended a Halloween gift bag. It was heavier than it looked. She almost dropped it, but he caught and set the bag on his bed.

Separating sheets of yellow tissue, VJ withdrew a flat yellow object. "Is it an iPad or a tablet?"

"Apad. iPads and surface tablets don't work in Apitcote."

"Thank you. I'm sure it will be an enormous aid."

She offered her hand. He shook it, his gaze unwavering as they stared. Couldn't he feel the magic chemistry? She felt it even when they weren't touching.

He released her hand before he said, "I regret missing the opportunity to share our futures."

"May I ask a question?"

"You may."

"What's her name?"

"Hanna. She has a child, a daughter named Harmony."

"The little girl in the photos?"

"Yes."

"Did you agree to tie before or after you approached me in Denver?"

"I made the suggestion before Harmony was born. Again afterwards. And several times after that. I never retracted my offer. Hanna agreed a few weeks ago."

"Have you told anyone else you plan to tie?"

"No."

"Thank you for satisfying my curiosity." But he hadn't answered her question, she realized, as s

he turned and strolled away.

A sudden chill warped through VJ as a vision of Vane and the girl he left the juice bar with flashed. They were in the bank, trying to get inside the vault.

"Holt," she called, as she reached the cottage door. "Vane and his companion are trying to rob the bank."

He rejoined her in a flash. Taking her elbow, he levitated them above rooftops to the business kluster. As they landed, Rene sent a silent message. *Juhree and I both just had a flish. Vane and Jin are at the bank. Meet us there.*

*Verity had a vision. We're already here*, he sent back. *We'll wait for you before we enter.*

Seconds later, kew mates arrived.

"Should we discuss our plan before we confront them?" Jordan asked.

"The plan is to boot them both out of the realm," Dane said, his tone curt.

"Jin used to work at the bank, so she thinks she knows how to open the vault after hours. What she doesn't know is the locks are time sensitive and can't be opened when the bank is closed."

"Or that we beefed up security after she stopped working here," Rene said. "The vault isn't locked to keep denizens out. It's locked to protect our treasury from unsavory characters. Seems Jin's guest, Vane, is one, even though he cleared security to get here."

"Are we ready?" Monteith asked.

Everyone nodded.

Even though there were surveillance cameras, Mist started recording as they walked inside. The would-be thieves stopped fiddling with the vault lock. Both looked shocked at being caught.

"Stealing is unacceptable, Jin," Dane said, in a deceptively calm tone.

"Did you really think you would succeed?" Rene asked.

Jin's face turned red, but she didn't reply.

"You have disgraced yourself," Monteith said. "Stealing is ugly. Demeaning. Disgusting."

Jin puffed up her shoulders as though self-defiance would save her. "What are you going to do?"

"You know the consequences."

"I'm to be banished. Condemned to a life on the surface. What if I won't go? I'm a denizen. You can't make me leave."

"If you stay, no one will serve you at any constat, or wait on you where food is available or sell groceries to you. You could starve."

"I have friends. I will not be shunned."

Vane made an attempt to rush through the line kew men had formed. When Dane, Drew and Monteith held hands to stop him, he started punching and cursing.

With one snap of his fingers, Holt flung Vane across the room. When he landed on the floor, moaning and groaning, Holt didn't have a single regret. He had avenged Madeline, and the demeaning manner Vane had inflicted on her.

"You've hurt him," Jin squealed, running to Vane. "There's no need for violence."

"What do you call what he started if that wasn't violent?" Tess asked.

"The wanker is leaving Apitcote," Dane announced. "And you're going with him, Jin."

"We can't leave." She raised her head defiantly. "All the enquays are closed."

"There are ways to send undesirables out," Dane said. "You'll be escorted to the end of the trax. After that, you will hike through the tunnel."

Once again, Jin squared her shoulders. "We'll use hoverz bikes."

"No," Dane disagreed. "Bikes and boards are no longer available for you. Once you are beyond the trax, our security system will ensure Vane never returns."

"What about me?" Jin said. "Will I ever be allowed to come back?"

"That isn't up to us. It's up to Mater Nature. I suspect you didn't plan to return, anyway."

"We'll need someone to meet us and drive us to an airport," she said with a haughty toss of her head.

"When you reach Atope, you can call someone to pick you up. If no one shows, I suggest using your feet."

"I'm a denizen, and I have a right to certain privileges."

"Not any longer. You'll get little help and no sympathy when denizens see what you attempted," Monteith said.

Jin suddenly looked horror-stricken. "You mustn't show this on TV."

"We won't. Newscasters will."

Jin's eyes popped wide open as Tess nodded at the security cameras before Dane lifted her and Vane into the air and levitated them out of the bank.

Vane and Jin looked as though they had shrunk inside their skin as they walked away.

"Are they leaving Api now?" Verity asked.

"Yes," Rene said. "As soon as they collect their possessions, they will be sped through the trax tunnel. Staying would prolong their misery and upset denizens."

~ * ~

Sipping afternoon tea at the constat, Madeline said, "We're still getting flowers--every week—and gifts sometimes—like the afones. I've been trying to figure out who's responsible. Do you have any ideas yet?"

VJ shook her head, her shoulders slumped.

"What's got you so down in the dumps? You've been moping for days."

Holt's news had inflicted so much pain, VJ felt like her heart was half dead. Lethargy and apathy were constant nighttime companions. "Holt's getting tied to a woman he met after I left."

"I can't believe that. He loves you."

"I barely believe it myself. I had a vision of us together in the future. Two actually." She shrugged, still trying to resign herself to fact, and erase the visions of snuggling together in his cottage by the fireplace. "Maybe they were just pipe dreams. Not visions."

"You two belong together. I'm sure you'll work things out."

"We can't. He's an honorable man. He proposed. Hanna accepted. He will not withdraw the offer."

"Don't be too sure," Madeline said as Holt entered the constat and strode toward them.

VJ's heart began to pound. It was painful to see him. Even more painful when she didn't. She knew he avoided her whenever he could. "What's wrong?" she asked, certain something was by the look on his face.

"One of Minalu's sons is here. All three have been gone for years. Two returned a few days ago. The oldest, Dominic, said his brother, Nando, is ill and at the dwelling. Falo wants Minalu to return."

"Has she agreed to go?"

"No. She wants to talk to you." Holt nodded at the yellow afone he had given Verity while they were quarantined. "Perhaps you should call or synk."

"I'll use this." Grabbing her new apad, VJ synked with Minalu. "Holt said your son is here."

"Yes. I am happy to see Dom." Minalu's eyes filled with sorrow. "He asked me to return to the dwelling. I cannot. I am sad my Nando is ill. However, if I leave, the women will feel I have abandoned them."

"What about Falo? Don't you want to see him?"

"Of course I do. However, he was invited to live here. He refused. Nando will recover without me. If I return to dwelling, Falo will do his best to keep me there. I cannot be parted from women and kidlings. Nor from Cinnalan. And she does not want to leave and miss school."

"We could send a medic to the dwelling and bring Nando here to heal," Holt said.

"That is good suggestion. Will you make request for me?"

"Of course."

Instead of calling a medic, Holt connected with Rene and Drew. After he explained, Rene said, "Of course we'll go. Will you ask Verity to accompany us?"

"No need to ask. I want to go with you."

The knot in Holt's stomach softened when he realized Verity had tuned in and heard the silent conversation. When had she had discovered she had the gift?

Moments later, the small group gathered at the end of the southernmost People Mover. Madeline, Minalu and Tumela were there to bid them goodbye. Holt sensed Verity's reluctance to leave Madeline. It would be the first time they had been apart since their arrival.

He glanced at Madeline. Her gaze was locked with Dom's. Both looked dazed, as though they had been struck by the same star. Everyone else noticed. Went quiet. And watched the mesmerized couple.

Finally, Madeline spoke. "I feel as though I should know you."

"I feel the same."

"I'm Madeline."

"I'm Dominic. Family and friends call me Dom. I'd like to get better acquainted."

"I'd like that as well."

"We'll see each other again," he promised. "I need to go."

With an elegant nod, Madeline agreed. "Yes. Your brother needs you."

"May I go with you?" Tumela asked.

Minalu shook her head. "Tumela is needed here." Minalu's eyes said more. *She thinks she loves Dominic. Last week, she thought she loved you. She does not love either of you. Infatuation is what consumes her.*

Surprised by the silent message, Holt stared at Minalu. *I do not communicate with others this way. Only with you and Dr. Verity. Thank you for bringing her and Miss Madeline to us.*

Tumela tapped him on the shoulder. "Can you persuade Mistress Minalu to change her mind, Mr. Holt? I promise I will not be a burden."

Minalu frowned at Tumela. "You cannot levitate; therefore, you will be a burden."

To break the awkward situation, Holt reached for Verity's hand. "Drew will levitate Dom. I'll levitate you."

Holt caught Dominic's relieved expression as Minalu guided Tumela back to the People Mover, and the team levitated above tree tops.

# *Eleven*

At the grotto, Falo looked grim.

While Rene and Drew examined Nando and checked his vitals, VJ whipped up a brew with ingredients from her medical satchel. "He's dehydrated and needs liquid. This contains herbs and should help him begin to heal."

Rene nodded approval as Verity slipped a straw in the potion, captured liquid and used the straw to drip liquid between Nando's parched lips.

As it dribbled into his mouth, VJ announced, "He's in a trance."

"Do you know why?" Drew asked.

"Not yet, but I'm working on it." A heretofore unknown power surged through VJ as she saw what Nando was reliving—he and Dom on the surface, making their way back to the place of their birth.

"We shouldn't go home without Zeg. Leaving him behind will make Amma and Papa grieve."

"Zeg is working," Dom replied. "He likes his job. We could not convince him to leave the surface."

The vision showed the two brothers hiking across a wide field, climbing a mountain range, stumbling around trees, brushes, sagebrush. They carried only small backpacks containing water and bits of food.

Opening her eyes, she announced. "Your sons were hungry. Nando ate something he shouldn't have."

"What?" Falo asked.

"A poisonous plant. He will recover," VJ added, "but it will take time. He is not diseased and has not been exposed to Covid-19."

"He will live?" Falo asked.

"With proper care and medication. We should take him to Apitcote."

"He stays here!"

It took a full hour to convince Falo the team wouldn't leave without Nando. Finally, Dom intervened. "He must go, Papa. We will return when Nando recovers."

The magic power to see the past without being there lived inside VJ. The flashback was a marvelous, wonderous gift. She sought Holt's gaze. Almost lost herself in warmth and depth as he levitated them back to Apitcote. He startled her when he squeezed her hand and sent a silent message. *What do you make of Madeline and Dominic?*

*That she may have met her match but might not be willing to let a relationship flourish.*

*That's my take, too. When did you discover you could communicate silently?*

*At the Fall Fest. Minalu sent me a message. At first, I thought it came from you.*

Back in Api, Drew flew Nando directly to the clinic where Drs. Lorraine and Val took over his care.

"We'll feed and keep him hydrated with intravenous drips," Dr. Lorraine promised.

"We'll fetch Minalu," Holt said. "She's anxious to see him."

~ * ~

Nando recovered quickly and joined Dom and Minalu at the cultural hall. Tumela frowned every time she saw Madeline with the brothers, sharing meals at the constat and enjoying some lengthy conversations.

One day, when Madeline and VJ met them for lunch, she said, "I suggest we invite Tumela to eat with us. Does anyone object?"

Dom shook his head and Nando grinned. "Do you know where she is?"

Madeline winked at VJ. "I suspect you can answer that question."

VJ winked back. "She's on her way here."

Moments later, Tumela rushed through the door. She stopped short when she saw the four of them together, watching her.

"Will you join us for lunch?" Madeline invited.

Tumela looked at each one's face before she answered. "I do not wish to be in the way."

"We would be happy to have you eat with us," VJ said.

"Yes," Nando agreed.

"We've been waiting for you," VJ added, pleased to see Tumela's smile instead of her usual pout when she looked at Madeline.

"Thank you." Tumela sat beside Dom and ignored Nando. Didn't even ask how he felt.

As Madeline and VJ returned to the cultural hall, VJ said, "Lunch was enlightening. I learned three things: Tumela fancies Dominic. He fancies you. And Nando fancies Tumela. How does it feel to be part of a love quartet, Madeline?"

"Not good. Dom may like me, but he doesn't know I'm expecting a baby, or that I'm married and have filed for a divorce. I'm not free to encourage him, and I'm not sure I want to even when I am."

"Well, you need not decide for a while. Dom promised Falo they would return to the dwelling. They're leaving tomorrow. Perhaps time and distance will help you figure out what you want your future to include."

~ * ~

Expecting to fall asleep quickly, VJ closed her eyes. A sunflower appeared. The dark center blinked and grew in size as yellow petals swung one way, then the other. When the vision finally came, it was a repeat of the one she'd had of being in the big Denver mansion with the attorney, Ricardo Bentley.

When the vision ended, she felt haunted. Sad. Lonely. Even with Madeline in the other room. *I have to leave, but I don't want to.*

Tears threatened. Seeped from her eyes. Her problems felt insurmountable.

Out in the bubble, Holt sensed Verity's mood. Springing to his feet, he stalked to the cottage. When Madeline opened the back door, he said, "Verity's in 'a mood.'"

"I sensed she's troubled. I didn't know what to say or do to cheer her."

"I'll give it a try." He tapped on his bedroom door.

"Come in."

He stepped inside. Saw her surprise. Knew she had expected Madeline. "You're in a strange mood." He closed the space between them.

"My mood has improved."

He sat on the bed. Drew her into his arms.

"I seem to need this," she said.

Holt knew he was digging a deep hole by being there. "I need it, too."

She looked up at him. "This is a dream, isn't it?"

"One come true."

She fell asleep in his arms.

Spooning her close, he fought desire. Sensed her jumbled dreams and more. Knew she would be gone before the weekend.

~ * ~

Convinced she had only dreamed about Holt sensing her despair and holding her in his beloved arms with exquisite tenderness, VJ tried to cheer herself by looking at the photos on her cell phone. Having kept her old phone charged, she scrolled through photos of Mum, sisters, and their families. A gush of emotion swelled inside. She hadn't seen them for more than two years when Vincent encouraged her to take a holiday and gave her first-class round-trip airfare from Boston to Heathrow.

Deciding to look at videos, she watched the one she'd taken of the bear in Placer Valley. Quite by accident, she found a video she hadn't realized she had.

Her last conversation with Freddie had been recorded!

How had it happened? Barely able to believe her eyes, she watched the video again. She had a near confession from Freddie stored on her phone! They were standing in the hall in Vincent's huge mansion, outside her room where Freddie had abruptly announced, "Vincent is dead."

"I need to see him." She had tried to brush past him, but Freddie grabbed her arm, squeezed hard and twisted it behind her back.

"No, you don't."

"Are you sure he's dead?"

"Yes."

"How did he die?"

"From an overdose."

"How do you know?" She saw the truth written on Freddie's face that night. And it was there now, in the video. "You killed him."

Freddie's smirk made her want to pummel him until he bled. Fear had kept her still, aided by his twisted arm lock.

"But you'll get the blame, smart tart," he taunted, "because you're his doctor. His paid caregiver. And he treats you much better than an employee deserves to be treated. Take my advice. Leave Boston, and don't ever come back."

"Why are you doing this, Freddie? Why do you hate me so?"

"Yours is but to go or die," he snarled, "not to know the reason why."

In the video, VJ was shaking. Now, she was shaking too. She closed her eyes to quell the turmoil swirling inside. She had proof, at least semi-proof, of her innocence. She had to return to Boston and clear her name. Had to prove she hadn't murdered Vincent.

Jumping to her feet, she dashed out to the bubble. "I need to talk to you, Holt."

"Come in."

She started blathering before she even saw him. "I've got to go to the surface."

"Why?"

"There are important things I must do."

When he didn't comment, she summoned anger to fortify her decision. "I'm going back!"

Holt still didn't say a word. Just stared at her.

She stomped her foot, prepared to battle.

His gaze urged her to calm down.

But she was too upset. "I know the cage enquay is functioning. If you won't take me there, I'll find someone who will." Dashing back to the cottage, she started packing.

Dizziness struck while she stuffed her second duffle. She plunked on the bed and closed her eyes. Bright stars spun through a dark, black void, moving closer, backing away, looming close again, backing up.

She fell sideways. What she saw was as vivid as it was unnerving.

When it ended, tears filled her eyes and emotion clogged her throat. In addition to the mob searching for Apitcote and the fountain of youth, the horrific evil would put people in a deep sleep and try to control their bodies and brains. The evil had a name—vire-- and it would join trolls and wage a battle against any who stood in their way and attempt to destroy Apitcote.

She hadn't recovered from the dual shocks when Holt appeared at the bedroom door. "I've made arrangements for someone to take you to the surface."

Keeping her face averted, she slid off the bed and resumed packing. "When can we leave?"

"Farrel is manning the cage station tonight. He'll be there when you arrive." Holt extended a sheet of paper. "Here's a list of People Movers that will take you there."

Snatching the directions, she mumbled, "Thanks." All at once her decision faltered. Her heart dipped to a new low. What should she do about the vision? And would she ever see Holt again?

She couldn't ask because he had left the bedroom.

Deciding to stop and tell Rene about the awful vision, VJ finished packing and scurried to the living room.

"Holt said you're leaving," Madeline said.

"I am." She hugged her best friend. "I have proof that I didn't kill Vincent and I have to go."

"I'll miss you."

"I'll miss you, too. But I'll stay in touch." Her backpack and handbag were clutched in her fists. Both duffle bags hung on her shoulders, bumping against her back as she scurried to the nearest People Mover.

"Are you really going to let her go?" Madeline asked, breathless from running out to Holt's bubble. "Go after her. Or go with her. She might need help and she needs your love."

Staring at his afone and Hanna's atext, Holt marveled at what he had just read. He had intended to atext Hanna and tell her Verity was leaving, and he intended to follow her. But there was no need to send one. Hanna's atext freed him.

Madeline saying the word 'love' turned his frown upside down. "I have no intention of letting Verity go without me." Plans already made, he called Farrel. "Verity Jane is on her way."

"I know. She called. Said she's taking time to say goodbye to your parents and Rene and Minalu before she leaves."

"I'll be there directly."

Holt levitated to the station. And beat Verity by a good twenty minutes.

When she arrived, she frowned. "I thought we already said goodbye."

"You did. I didn't."

"Then say it." She didn't wait, just brushed by him.

"No."

She spun around. "If you're not going to say goodbye, why are you here?"

"I'm going to the surface."

"Why?"

"I have my reasons."

She stuck her nose in the air. "Don't tell me then."

"Didn't plan to."

Inside the newly enlarged cage, she stared at the stools as though they were her enemy. Finally, she sat on one, and buckled herself in.

Holt stayed on his feet. He liked air spinning around him and was still getting used to his amazing ability to levitate. And tonight, he felt capable of flying to the moon—the one above the surface, not the much smaller one in Apitcote.

As the ascent began, he sensed Verity wanted to glare at him, but the cage was moving so fast she couldn't catch her breath. She clung to her seat as though her life depended on it. In spite of the speed, Holt levitated closer, balanced his feet on the cage floor and patted her shoulder to charm her.

He felt some of her fear recede. But she wouldn't look at him. Not that he would complain. He had the rest of his life to smile into her fantastic eyes. And he intended to do exactly that.

When the cage slowed twenty-five minutes later, she blurted, "The speed is tremendous and unnerving."

"The ride will soon be over." He took her hand and calmed her with another charm, although he doubted she knew what he had done. The speed had unnerved her far more than she had anticipated. He suspected what she faced on the surface might unnerve her even more.

Prepared for whatever she did, he kept her hand in his. From that moment on, he did not intend to let her out of his sight.

As the cage door slid open, Holt unbuckled Verity's seat belt.

She stumbled out. Leaned against the safety gate. "Crikey. That was gawd-awful."

"I enjoyed the ride."

"We should act our age, not our shoe size."

Holt adored her witty retort. "I would like to have known you when you were seven."

"How do you know my shoe size?"

"Men don't tell all their secrets."

She frowned. "Where are you going?"

"Where are you?"

"I hate when you answer my question with a question."

"I'm going with you... therefore, I need to know your destination before I know mine."

"Oh." That silenced her but not for long. "Why?"

"Because I love you."

Once again all she said was, "Oh."

To help her out of her stupor, he said, "A friend named Waren agreed to meet us at the rim of the cave to drive us to the nearest airport."

"My legs are wobbly. I need to sit still for a moment or two."

Guiding her to the lone bench in the dark cave, Holt sat beside her. There was only one light pole. He snapped his fingers, brightened the bulb, then patted her back as he patted Harmony's when she needed comforting. "Are you okay?"

"I don't know. This—you—that is, I didn't expect you to follow me or say…"

"I love you," he supplied.

She stared up at him, her eyes raw with emotion. His heart reacted by pounding. To calm her as well as himself, he drew her close and held her, giving them both time to adjust their breathing back to semi-normal.

Inhaling her unique carnation fragrance, he spoke quietly. "I made a decision to follow you when you left before Hanna told me she does not want to tie. I am free to love you. Free to follow you. Free to do whatever we wish—as long as it's together."

When Verity didn't reply, he added, "I don't know what your problems are, but I'm determined to help. Until you accept and learn to use it, my magic is stronger than yours, so you won't be able to stop me. From this moment on, I'm going to be with you day and night. If you try to ditch me, I'll chain your wrist to mine, and you won't be able to escape. That could be awkward. For both of us. I don't want to exert force, nor make your decisions. They should and will be yours. However, I am not willing to negotiate this one area. I can be as stubborn as you. I won't budge."

Sensing she wanted to pull away, he drew in a worried breath and loosened his arms.

Verity sighed. Looked up. Reached for his hand. Clutched it tight. But didn't speak.

He knew she was wrestling with her thoughts and decisions. "Did you truly believe I would stand by and do nothing to help you?"

"I don't want my problems to be yours."

"They are. Always will be."

She went quiet again. He wanted to kiss her. Instead, he gave her time to think.

Finally, she said, "I've reached a long-awaited conclusion."

Holt didn't dare relax, but he controlled his voice, and quietly asked, "Have you?"

"Yes. It's time to explain my—a—sordid past, and the mistakes I've made."

"Talking about them might expel them from your mind."

"I doubt that very much."

He slid his free arm around her slender shoulders, thinking she needed more time to collect her thoughts. But she spoke immediately. "Being near you makes me feel as though I've swallowed a dose of truth serum. I don't know how I managed not to tell you before. Perhaps because you've been patient and didn't make me feel pressured. Perhaps because I'm so relieved you love me and are free to touch me at last."

"I'd like to kiss you."

"Please do."

Leaning closer, he kissed her gently. Tenderly. And with all the love blooming in his happy heart. When the kiss finally ended, he said, "I'll do my best not to interfere with your decisions."

"I know." She treated him with a tremulous smile. "I'm not sure where to begin, so I'll start way back when I was a child. Pap didn't like me. I don't know why. He liked my sisters, but he resented me. He played with Lizzy and Karan and brought surprises. For them. Never for me. He hit me. Almost every day. Sometimes he beat me."

"Why didn't you tell your mater?"

"He said if I did, next time he'd hit me harder. Sometimes he did anyway. He never touched me when Mum or sisters were around and I found ways to avoid being alone with him when I could. I didn't know how truly horrid he was until the night before my ninth birthday."

Verity shuddered, as though the mere memory frightened her. "That night he crept into the bedroom I shared with my sisters and stuffed a scarf in my mouth before I was fully awake. Then he carried me to the loo—and told me to undress. I didn't, so he ripped my nightdress and knickers off. By then, I had come out of my stupor, and I was so mad I started kicking and punching. I kicked him so hard in the groin, he doubled over in pain. I raced back to the bedroom and hid in the wardrobe. I should have run to Mum and told her what he did. I guess I was too gobsmacked to think rationally."

Her words gushed out like they'd been dammed up too long and finally pushed a hole through the dike. "The next day Mum had a smashing 'do'—a fantastic birthday party for me. By nighttime I was so tired I fell asleep as soon as I hit the bed. Mum's screams woke me up. I dashed to their bedroom. She and Pap were on the floor. He was straddling and punching her. Yelling that she spent too much money on my 'do.' I ran close and bit his neck. He reacted by slamming me against the wall."

She paused, sucked in another breath. "My lip was bleeding and my shoulder hurt something awful, but I ran to the neighbors for help. The husband went with me to rescue Mum, and his wife called the police. They came, handcuffed Pap, and had me and Mum taken to hospital. The couple took care of Lizzy and Karan. Mum and I were gone three days. We had a kind, compassionate female doctor. That's when I decided I wanted to be one.

"When we went home, Mum had the locks changed and a restraining order issued to keep Pap off the property. She had to go to court to get it. When he got out of jail, he wasn't allowed in the house. He told Mum he wanted to spend time with my sisters. Eventually, she agreed but she never let him get close to the house or to me. When he came to collect Lizzy and Karan,

Mum walked them down the pavement. He always met them at the car.

"I didn't know Mum and Pap hadn't divorced until I was fifteen. That's when I discovered there was no money for me to attend university. Mum worked and Pap gave her money but not enough to save more than a few quid. During the next year, Madeline and I saved every pence we could and arranged to emigrate to the U.S. We skipped A levels because I wanted an ocean between me and Pap—Castor—and Madeline and I wanted to stay together.

"Shortly after we arrived, we met a bloke named Freddie. He was nice. Took us out to eat and to parties and cinemas. Bought us treats and gifts. Made me believe he was in love with me and wanted to marry me. I turned him down. Explained I wanted to go to university and medical school and become a doctor. He said borrowing money from him would be smarter than trying to get student loans. I was elated, and I worked and studied hard. Whilst I was in medical school, he started treating me poorly. As soon as my residency began and I had a bit of money, Freddie started hounding and haranguing. He wanted me to repay the loans. He wanted me to do favors. He wanted a lot of things I don't care to repeat. He doubled the interest rate. Said our contracts had clauses that allowed him to do so.

"Mum had an accident, and I returned to England to take care of her. Then I met you. My world changed, and I believed I had a chance for a happy future. I was ecstatic when you invited me to your homeland and introduced me to your friends and parents. Mist patched my phone so I could receive texts from the surface. Freddie sent some every day. I got one that said he knew where Mum and Lizzy and Karan lived, and he threatened to harm them if I didn't return and to do his bidding."

"What did he want?"

"First, he made me take care of a friend. Probably the only one he had. The bloke was a druggy. I did what I could to help him, but one night he overdosed and died. Freddie said his uncle had cancer and needed a caretaker. He didn't expect him to live very long, and he wanted me to be the one who cared for him during the last months of his life. He said if I did, he would consider that as payment for my loans. I agreed. Didn't think I had a choice. Cancer has a smell, and I smelled it the instant I met Vincent. He looked old. Haggard. Unutterably miserable. And he was only seventeen years older than I. Life seemed so unfair. He was kind and genteel, as I envision royalty ought to be." She paused again, had difficulty going on. Her voice shook when she did.

"Vincent was wealthy. He owned a huge mansion, bigger than Juhree's parents'. Older too but kept in top notch condition. I was with Vincent two months when the treatments started to work. For a year and a half, he was in remission. He felt so good he planned a holiday, and we flew to Miami. I hadn't been to Florida, and I enjoyed the skyscrapers, the sun-drenched beaches, everything. Vincent introduced me to his new attorney. Explained he had decided to sell his assets, convert them to cash, and give money to people he deemed worthy. I still don't know what that meant. Just before we left Miami, Vincent gave me a gift. A huge one."

"What?" Holt asked.

"His mansion. His attorney arranged to have it deeded to me. When we returned to Boston, Freddie had moved in. Vincent insisted that he move out. But Freddie wouldn't budge. Vince was in the process of having Freddie evicted when he died. I wanted to see him, to confirm he was dead. But Freddie wouldn't let me. He said Vince was stiff as a board, and he had already called the morgue. When I asked how he died, Freddie said Vincent had swallowed an overdose. Committed suicide. I said he couldn't have killed himself because I kept all meds under lock and key. Freddie laughed, waved a key, and called me a smart tart. And if I stayed smart, I'd hightail it out of Boston and never return. If I didn't, he would sic the law on me. Tell them I killed Vincent."

Once again, her voice shook. "Freddie pulled a gun and reminded me I had lived in the luxurious mansion for two years, and he didn't intend to reduce my loans by a cent. In fact, he intended to double the interest again. Using the gun, he motioned me back into my room and watched me pack. Made sure I didn't take anything that didn't belong to me, including the portable safe containing the meds prescribed for Vincent."

Hating what she had suffered through, Holt said, "I'm sorry Vincent died. You must have loved him."

"I did, but not as I love you." She stared into his eyes. In her depths, he saw the love he had wanted to see for days, weeks, years.

"Vince was a dear friend and mentor. He taught me about men. And love. And life. I think I'm more capable of loving you than I was before I met him."

"I love you," Holt said again.

"I'm so glad. I love you, too."

He kissed her. She kissed him back. He sensed she was shaken. Delighted. Elevated to a new realm.

"I was certain I couldn't prove my innocence," she continued. "Therefore, I ran away as Freddie suggested. But tonight, I found a video of him on my old phone. It's like a miracle. I didn't know I had it until after I watched the video of the bear in Placer Valley. I must have hit record on my phone when Freddie banged on my door and dragged me into the hall to announce Vincent was dead. By his cunning gleam, I was certain Freddie had broken into my medical safe and stolen drugs to give Vincent the overdose. Now, I think I can prove it. At least I want to try. And I might have money to hire an attorney and have Freddie charged with murder."

"You do."

"Before I woke up with you in Apitcote, I had a vision of Vincent's attorney, who said Vince had gifted five hundred thousand dollars to me. If that's true, I can pay off Freddie's loans and have him put behind bars."

"That's a good plan."

"I have to do this.

"Of course you do. What you don't need to do is try to convince me. Together, we'll see that you are cleared, and justice is served." Holt knew he would remember the love in her eyes for the rest of his life. He was so choked up he had to clear his throat before he could speak. "So where should we start?"

She looked relieved. He felt victorious. Gathering her close, he held her for a long, unhurried time before he kissed her again—this time arousing passion and a promise of much more.

Eventually, he said, "Where do you want to start?"

She squared her shoulders. "First thing is to go see Ricardo Bentley."

"How do we find him?'"

"His main office is in Miami. I looked him up on my afone. He hasn't moved."

~ * ~

"I'm surprised the flight to Miami is fully booked," VJ said as she fastened her seat belt in first-class.

"Me, too," Holt agreed. "With Covid-19 on the uptick again, international flights are limited, and the U.K. has prohibited flights from the U.S. for the second time. I expected more people to stay put."

"I suppose they're tired of being cooped up." 'VJ adjusted her face mask. "Api spoiled me. I used to wear masks for twelve-hour hospital shifts. Now I don't even want to keep one on for the duration of this flight."

"We don't have a choice."

"I know."

In spite of the crowded plane, she relaxed, and soon nodded off. When she awakened, her head was resting against Holt's shoulder.

"We're on final descent," he said before he kissed her forehead.

She reached for his hand. "Thank you for coming with me."

"Thank you for sharing your secrets."

"I want to return to Api. I had another vision of the evil before I left. If we don't do something, it will seize denizens' bodies, take over their minds, engage with trolls and try to destroy the realm. I told Rene, but I want to be there to help."

"I'm sure you will."

"I'm glad you're sure. I'm not sure of anything, except that I love you."

~ * ~

Ricardo Bentley smiled when he greeted VJ and Holt in his office lobby. "Follow me," he invited, and led them down the long hallway.

In his office, the information he shared was a repeat of VJ's visions. Even so, she was still surprised when he said, "Vincent gifted you five hundred thousand dollars that has increased to six hundred thousand."

Thinking the consultation was over after Ricardo extended the file and binder she'd seen in her visions, VJ started to stand. "We don't want to take up too much of your time."

"I have more to tell you, Dr. Verity."

Perching on the edge of the chair, she set the binder and folder back on his desk and folded her hands on her lap. "What?"

"From what you've said, I suspect what I say next will come as a surprise."

"Don't keep me in suspense."

He looked from her to Holt. "She may go into shock. Are you prepared to catch her if she passes out?"

"Yes."

Turning his gaze back to her, he said, "Vincent isn't dead."

Her mind froze in disbelief. Her body tilted forward. Just before her mind went completely blank, Holt's strong arms caught her.

It took a few moments before she opened her eyes; a few more before she could ask, "Did he say what I think?"

"Yes," Holt said, his tender gaze locked with hers.

Ricardo cleared his throat. She jerked her gaze to his.

"Vince is alive and still in remission."

VJ's pounding heart felt like it had gushed halfway up her throat. She doubted she could utter another word until it calmed. Inhaling slowly and exhaling just as slowly, she realized Holt must have removed her mask because it was gone.

"Would you like something to drink?" Ricardo asked. "Water? Coffee? Tea?"

"Water," she gasped. "Please." She drew more air into her lungs while Ricardo fetched a bottle of water and twisted the cap off.

She took one small sip. Then another.

When Holt tightened his hold, she realized she was cradled in his arms. She summoned a smile. "I'm fine now, Holt. You needn't hold me any longer."

He released his arm beneath her knees. Allowed her feet to slide to the floor. Made sure she was steady before he let go. Then he clasped her hand and focused on Ricardo.

"Where is Vincent?"

"In Boston, in the mansion he deeded to Dr. Verity."

Heart pounding, she said, "I can hardly wait to see him."

Ricardo's smile broadened. "I'm sure he feels the same about you."

"Do you know if the mansion's property taxes have been paid?" she thought to ask.

"Yes. Vince made arrangements to have our office pay them every year."

"Where to now?" Holt asked as they left the law firm.

"Boston," VJ said. "To see Vincent."

Holt winked. "I'm looking forward to meeting the other man in your life." He kissed her before he added, "We should call. Make sure he's home. Let him know we're on our way."

"I'm sure he would appreciate a warning."

"Do you want me to do the calling?"

"Yes. Please. I'm still so stunned I probably won't be able to choke out the words I should say."

"You'll do fine, poppet."

# *Twelve*

They donned new masks as they had done on both flights and at the law office before they rang the immense mansion's doorbell. Expecting cook-housekeeper, Lois, to open the door, VJ was startled when Vincent opened it himself. A broad smile gleamed in his eyes. In the past, they had enjoyed a doctor-patient relationship with minimal physical contact but she was so happy to see him she latched her arms around him, hugged tight, and gushed, "I'm so glad you're alive."

Vincent hugged her back. "I'm happy as well, my dear Verity Jane."

She inhaled. Confirmed his cancer was still in remission.

Stepping back, she introduced Holt and studied Vincent while the two men measured each other. Her former patient no longer looked haggard. He teemed with good health. Like a man in his prime. Fit as a fiddle. With the exception of a few silver hair bits tinging his temples, he looked handsome and years younger.

Vince grinned. "You don't need masks indoors. Please take them off.

As soon as they did, he announced, "There's someone in the library waiting to see you, Verity."

Fearing it might be Freddie, she gripped Holt's hand as they followed Vincent through the living room and down the long familiar hall.

Utterly surprised by the woman in the middle of the room, VJ dashed across the carpet, launched herself into her arms and clung. "Mum. What in heaven's name are you doing here?"

"I live here," Beryl said.

VJ's voice wobbled like an unstable cable car as she asked, "Wh-at? Wh-en? How did it happen?"

"I'll answer all of your questions after you introduce your companion to Vince."

"She already has," Holt said.

Beryl smiled. Holt and Vincent were smiling as well. "Shall we sit?" He motioned at four chairs in the middle of the library.

Happier than she'd ever been, VJ beamed as Holt settled beside her. "When did you come to the U.S., Mum?"

"Last year. When you went missing. Before Covid. Before travel restrictions."

"You sent letters to me through Madeline," VJ gasped. "But you never told me you were here. Why?"

"We wanted to surprise you."

"Well, you bloody well did. How? I mean when did you meet Vincent?"

"Before you were born."

More shock waves riveted through her as Mum leaned forward and clasped her hand. "I never thought this day would come, although I'm over the moon that it finally has." Beryl paused to catch her breath. "When I was a teenager, I lived in the states for a few years. One rainy day, Vincent and I met in a public library."

"That day was one of the best of my life." Vincent took Beryl's free hand. "We fell in love immediately."

Beryl's bottom lip trembled. "The first time we kissed my heart stopped beating."

VJ had never seen her mother look so alive. Or animated. She positively glowed. "Our parents tried to convince us it was just a teenage crush and we'd get over each other." Beryl looked at Vince again and they shared an intimate smile.

"So, we eloped. Hours later our furious parents snatched us apart and had the marriage annulled. Mine took me directly back to England and kept me in a Croyden flat. I wasn't locked in, but there were few cell phones back then, and they wouldn't let me use the land line. Transatlantic calls cost a bomb. Racked up minutes quickly. And I had no coins to use a public telephone booth. In any event, Mum and Dad wouldn't allow me to go out alone. They watched me like twin hawks. With no way to communicate outside, I was one very brassed-off girl.

Mum looked too emotional to go on, and Vince continued. "My parents prevented me from following Beryl. I managed to get their phone number and called a few times. Beryl never answered, and her parents always hung up on me. The day I turned eighteen, I called again. And discovered she was married. I didn't have enough money to fly to England, anyway. By the time I did, she had a child.

"I finished college and refused to work for Dad. He owned a financial consulting service and spouted that I would never amount to anything without him. I proved him wrong by dedicating my life to making money. As the years passed, I checked occasionally to see if Beryl was still married. She was, so I left her alone. Then one day, with the advent of computers and the world wide web, I decided to expand and deepen my research. That's when I discovered you ... your age. I dug deep enough and made enough enquiries to assume that you were my daughter."

"Your daughter?" VJ squeaked, her heart thumping so loud she thought everyone heard it.

"Yes. And you are."

VJ flung herself into Vincent's open arms. Her happiness tripled when Mum embraced them. And she was beyond happy when Mum beckoned Holt to join them.

After a while, VJ breathed out, "Somehow, I must have known."

"How?" Vincent asked, curiosity evident.

"I loved you. I felt close to you. Our months together were some of the happiest of my life. You taught me that all men aren't mean. Cruel. Despicable."

"I never loved anyone else." Pain filled Vincent's eyes. "I believe your mother has more to say."

Beryl nodded. "After a few months back in England, I realized I was pregnant. Mum and Dad were furious all over again. They acted like I had deliberately brought disgrace upon them. I was only sixteen, and they refused to let me contact Vince. Insisted that I marry Castor—a bloke they knew but was a stranger to me." Tears filled Beryl's eyes. "When you were born, I named you Verity Jane, using Vincent's initials. They were all I could give you of him."

VJ swallowed the lump in her throat. "Thanks for telling me."

"So how did Freddie get in the picture?" Holt asked, sounding as emotional as they did.

Vince answered. "My unmarried cousin needed a place to live. I agreed to let her and her son, Freddie, move in with me. He was obnoxious. Snooped through everything, including my file cabinets. Hacked my computer and discovered what I had— that I had a daughter, also that you had moved to the U.S. He looked you up, introduced himself. You know the rest."

"I guess we should be grateful he got us together," VJ said.

"I knew who you were the instant I saw you. I had collected the few photos of you posted online. You have my eyes and your mother's beautiful smile." Vincent paused before he continued. "Freddie thought I was on my deathbed. Probably hired you as a sadistic joke. He expected to inherit most of my wealth. When I went into remission, he thought it was only temporary. I believed the same. The longer I remained in remission, the more agitated Freddie became. He moved back in here when you and I were in Miami. I made the mistake of telling him we went to Florida to meet with my new attorney. I also explained I had canceled my will and set up a trust that included you. I shouldn't have told him anything, including the fact that I deeded the mansion to you."

Vince grimaced before he continued. "Freddie threw a tantrum. Went berserk. Wanted to kill me. I thwarted his attempt to force an overdose down my throat or allow him to jab me with a needle. Then I had Simmons toss him out the front door without his possessions, including his computer and briefcase. I had all the locks changed so he could never get back in. We have not communicated since."

Vince paused, leaned back in his chair. "Your disappearance baffled me. I didn't know Freddie loaned you money—my money—to get through college and medical school until I hacked his computer and went through his briefcase. Had I known, I would have found a way to pay for your education and none of the events that transpired would have unfolded as they did." With a mischievous wink, he added, "I have your contracts, Verity Jane. Thought we might burn them together, tonight, in one of the fireplaces."

VJ's heart was pumping fast. "I'd like that. But I have to ask. Why didn't you tell me I'm your daughter?"

"I knew nothing about the state of Beryl's marriage, and I didn't want to tell you something she might not want you to know."

"So how did you two get back together?" Holt asked.

Beryl replied, "When Verity went missing, Vince called me. His attorney hired a detective to search for you, poppet. It took months, but the chap finally found you in Colorado and summoned Ricardo Bently. Then you disappeared again."

"Verity had a man stalking her," Holt said. "After I arrived in Denver, another started tailing her. At the time, I wondered if Freddie might have hired him. But today, I discovered it was Ricardo Bentley."

Vince nodded. "Ricardo followed you to the mountains. I instructed him to stay near you until Beryl and I could get there. We made airline reservations as soon as he texted a photo to us confirming you were the one we were searching for. Needless to say, we were devastated when we arrived and discovered you had disappeared again—in the middle of the night."

"I'm responsible for that," Holt said. "I knew Verity was in danger, and I told my parents. They took her and Madeline and me to my homeland."

Beryl smiled. "I'm happy Madeline is still in your life, poppet." Curiosity sparkled in Beryl's eyes as she focused on Holt. "I enjoyed meeting you in England whilst Verity Jane was helping me recover from the accident that rendered me quite helpless. She later told me you broke up." Tears misted her eyes as she looked at Verity. "My dear daughter, it is so very wonderful to see you with your young man."

"He isn't mine."

"Yes, I am," Holt disagreed. "I know your secrets." But she didn't know his.

He was grateful Beryl continued. "In any event, I'm happy to see you together again. Verity Jane didn't have much use for boys whilst growing up. I always thought her experiences with Castor were responsible."

Verity aimed her thumb at the vaulted ceiling. "Spot on, Mum."

"I'm truly chuffed—delighted—to see you and your real father together also, my darling." Beryl glanced back and forth between them. "You're both tall and lanky and beautiful."

"You have the same golden-brown eyes," Holt added.

Verity stared at him, her gaze laced with love. "Thank you again for coming with me."

"No need for thanks. I love you." He buzzed her cheek with his lips. He had to tell her about his commitment to Harmony.

"Will you forgive me for not telling you Castor isn't your father, poppet?"

"There's nothing to forgive. I'm so happy he isn't. When I was little, I was afraid of him. Afraid he might sneak up and kill me. Later, I felt he blamed me for losing you. That's why I left England. I thought your life would be more pleasant if you didn't have to worry about me. Do you know why Castor hates me?"

Beryl's pain-filled eyes reflected so many emotions Holt wanted to take her in his arms and comfort her. He knew Vince felt the same way when he wound his arm around her shoulders.

"Castor knew I loved your father. I tried to be a good wife, but Vincent had claimed my heart, and Castor was a controlling bloke—much like my father. He was always grilling me, demanding to know if I was in contact with Vincent, unwilling to believe I wasn't, unwilling to believe I was faithful. After a while, I perceived he resented you; however, I didn't realize how much until the night of your ninth birthday. When he slammed you against the wall and broke your collarbone, I knew we couldn't live with him any longer."

"Are you still married to him?"

"No."

"Actually, your mother agreed to be my wife. Again." Vince smiled and gave Beryl's shoulder a gentle squeeze.

"Are you married?" Verity asked.

"Yes."

Giddy with happiness as she watched her parents, VJ couldn't stop smiling. Nor could they. She glanced at Holt. He wasn't smiling. He was in 'think mode.' She assumed it had to do with Freddie. Focusing on Beryl, she asked, "When did you divorce Castor?"

"When you went missing. I decided to cross the pond and didn't know if I would return. Just hearing Vincent's voice was reason enough to leave jolly old England."

"Castor is such a blighter. Why did you stay married to him all those years?"

"It had to do with his position at work. After he got out of jail, he was convinced a divorce would spoil his chances for advancement. I suspected that was rubbish; however, he promised to pay child support. He kept his word. Deposited money in my account on the same day every month without fail. I suspect he did so in order to spend time with Lizzy and Karan. In his odd way, I believe he loves them."

"I hope he does." But VJ wondered if he was capable of loving anyone.

"So, what are we going to do about Freddie?" Holt asked.

Beryl shivered. "He sounds like a horrid human."

"He is," VJ agreed. "I have a video I think you should see."

They moved close together and watched the video stored on her old phone.

"No wonder you left without saying goodbye. Freddie shoved a gun against your head and forced you to leave believing you were responsible for my death."

"I am outraged," Beryl said. "I haven't even met the bloody bloke and I'd like to put his head in a permanent chokehold."

Vince cleared his throat. "I didn't pay much attention to Freddie while he was growing up, but I gave him a decent allowance and agreed to finance his loan scheme to help friends through college. My former attorney wrote and approved the contracts, and I believed they were fair for both parties. I had cancer before I discovered Freddie was taking advantage of the situation.

"I'd like to know if Verity's loans have been canceled," Holt said. "If not, we'll take care of that now."

Vince winced. "Of course, her loans are canceled.

"But Freddie deserves to be punished. Do you have any suggestions?"

"There's no need. A couple of weeks ago, Freddie got arrested for attempting to rob a department store and holding employees and customers as hostages. He's facing numerous charges and will likely be tied up in court for years. I refused to pay his bail, so he's still in jail."

"Thankfully we can put Freddie behind us," Beryl said, and then asked, "You're staying here tonight, aren't you? You have no other plans?"

"No. None. We came in such a hurry, we didn't have time," Verity admitted.

"Of course, you will sleep here," Vince said. "This is your home."

She blushed. "I still don't think you should have deeded it to me."

"Why not? You would have owned it someday."

"I'm concerned about your future, Dad. Did you dispose of your wealth?"

Vince smiled. "I appreciate your concern. I gifted money to a few people—my loyal household staff—your staff as well—who stood by me when they believed cancer would kill me, and they might be out of work. However, I retained the bulk of my estate. Your mother and I are younger than most retirees, but we have decided to retire. We have enough income from various investments to live comfortably, travel if we choose, or do whatever we want."

"You're welcome to live here," Verity said. "It's really your home, not mine."

"We own an organic farm in Kansas," Vince said. "We've talked about living there part of each year."

"Yes," Beryl said. "The farm has hot water springs below ground."

Verity's eyes jolted to Holt's. A silent question flowed between them. The mythical Fountain of Youth?

Verity wrinkled her forehead. "Where is the farm? How far from medical facilities?"

"Feels like it's in the boonies, but there's a small town a few miles away, a big city about thirty miles from the house, and tenants live on the property, so it isn't isolated."

"You might be better suited to living in Api," Holt said. "Our atmosphere is conducive to good health and long life."

Verity stuck her hands on her hips. "You've invited Mum and Dad to live in Api, but you haven't asked me."

"I asked in September, remember?" Kneeling on one knee, Holt took her hand in his. "Now I have another question. Will you be my One? Tie with me? Share your life with mine? Pledge to live together for the remainder of our lives, Verity Jane?"

Dropping to her knees, she flung her arms around him as his arms circled her. "Yes! To all four questions."

Withdrawing a small box from his shirt pocket, Holt opened the lid and lifted a sparkling ring. "May I?" he asked.

In reply, she raised her left hand. He slid the ring onto her fourth finger. "I promise to love and cherish you with every breath I breathe."

Verity stared at him, then at the intense yellow stone. "The ring is beyond gorgeous, Holt. It's magnificent. Like you."

"What kind of gem is it?" Beryl asked.

"A Canary Diamond."

"Where did you get it?" Vince asked.

"I saw the stone in a jewelry shop in Api and had our artisans craft the ring for your daughter."

"It's truly beautiful," Verity said.

"Not nearly as beautiful as you."

He pulled a yellow ribbon from another pocket. "Shall we tie?"

She nodded once, and he understood she was too choked up to speak. Gathering her back into his arms, he kissed her tears away before he kissed her lips, sealing their promise with more than the fancy vivid yellow ring.

Mesmerized by the love glowing in her eyes, he almost forgot they weren't alone until Beryl cleared her throat. "I'm curious. What does tying mean?"

Holt stood and lifted Verity gracefully to her feet. "Same as marriage. But more convenient. Less hassle. No clergy or someone licensed by the state necessary to perform a ceremony." He smiled at Verity, then at Beryl and Vince. "Couples in my homeland often ask people they love to tie their wrists together when they're ready to pledge." Extending the ribbon, he asked, "Will you two perform the honor for us?"

"With pleasure." Beryl smiled, and Vince's face broke into another broad grin before laughter echoed through the library.

After everyone stopped laughing, Vince said, "I knew before you walked through the front door that some unusual events would occur today, but this certainly wasn't one of them."

Holt clasped Verity's hand. "I apologize for interrupting the flow of events, but I need to tell Verity something before we tie. Will you excuse us for a few minutes?"

"Sure. We'll go tell Lois to plan a special dinner for us."

When they were alone, Verity watched him with wary eyes. "What's wrong?"

"Nothing. From my viewpoint, something is right. Very right. I need you to know what it is before we tie."

"What?"

"When we were apart, I made a commitment. One that involves my future and yours as well, if we tie."

She hiked one eyebrow. "If?"

"I want us to tie, but I'll understand if you don't after I tell you what I committed to do."

"Tell me."

"I agreed to help raise Harmony."

"And? What else?"

"Isn't that enough?"

"I guess I don't fully understand. Where is she?"

"In Philadelphia. She was born in Apitcote. She'll return when she turns five, perhaps before."

"How old is she?"

"Fifteen months, and she already talks."

"Why did she leave Apitcote?"

"Her grandmater has cancer. Aleece is also an invalid, confined to a wheelchair. Harmony's mater, Hanna, left to take care of her."

"Why didn't you tell me before now?"

He licked his dry lips and gave her a level stare. "Because I didn't know if you would agree to share my life."

"How did you meet Hanna?"

"We worked together at NASA."

"You worked at NASA?"

"Yes. After you left Api, I missed you so much I decided to move to the surface so we could be together."

"Why didn't you tell me back then?"

"Because you were living with another man. I had already applied at NASA and been offered a job. To fulfill my obligation. I worked there a year and a half. Then you were with Vincent, so I went home."

"I wish I had known."

"I should have called."

"Why didn't you?"

"I was jealous of Vince, and the other guy you lived with."

"Did it never occur to you that I might have been their doctor—caretaker?"

"No."

"Back to Harmony. She's the little girl in the frame I saw in your bedroom and out in the bubble, isn't she?"

"Yes."

When Verity went quiet, Holt decided to explain more. "In Api, some people don't tie or find their One until the women are beyond their childbearing years. If a woman or a man wants a child before they find their One, they select someone they admire and ask them to help create a baby. I didn't do that with Hanna, however, when she told me she planned to be a single parent and asked if I would help raise Harmony, I agreed because I wanted a child to be in my life. My commitment lies within the parameters I grew up with." He had fudged the truth, but he had promised Hanna he would never explain all the details without her permission.

"What does your commitment to help raise Harmony entail?"

"So that you understand my full future responsibility, Hanna had me legally appointed as Harmony's guardian if something happens to her."

"Your commitment would not likely have happened had we not split up; therefore, I will happily share your responsibility. I've always wanted a daughter. I'll do my best to help Harmony feel loved and to earn her love in return."

Holt drew her between his arms. "I have never loved you more than I love you at this moment. From what my kew mates say, my love will grow with every day we share."

"I like how that sounds. I love you too, Holt. Now, let's go make use of that yellow ribbon."

"Nothing would give me greater pleasure."

Verity laughed. "I can think of something that might."

He laughed, too. "I'm sure you can." He angled his head and she angled hers. Their eager kisses were filled with passion and promises for a happy future.

# Thirteen

After the foursome parted for the night, Holt said, "I have an idea. If you don't like it, say so. I'll understand."

"What?"

"Let's make our tying night one we'll never forget. An event that will stand out and live in our memories for all the years to come."

"How?"

"More than three years ago, we made plans to camp out in Api's woods. The anticipated event didn't happen. Do you remember?"

Verity nodded. "It was something I really wanted to do."

"We can sleep in a bed anytime. Tonight, let's camp out in your mansion."

"Where?"

"On the carpet, downstairs in front of the fireplace where we watched Freddie's contracts burn to ashes."

She flung her arms around him. "Flipping brilliant. Let's do it."

Pleased with her enthusiasm, Holt had to kiss her again. And again. And again.

Both were out of breath as they gathered pillows and duvets off two beds, and crept back down the stairs, trying not to disturb her parents or quiet Lois and stoic Simmons.

After Holt used magic to rekindle the fire, they planted themselves on the soft, plush carpet in front of new flames.

"The library seems a fitting place to spend our first night together," Verity said.

"Because we met in a library, I think sleeping in one will make our tying night more special."

"When we were apart, I forgot how good your memory is. And how romantic and thoughtful you are."

"You remember now. That's what's important."

"I didn't know life could be so swimmingly fabulous," Verity breathed between kisses.

"I expect it will be even better now that you've agreed to live in Api with me."

She caressed his cheek. "During our years apart, I didn't think you loved me."

"I should have made sure you did. I have a confession." He paused, his gaze serious. "On second thought, maybe I should wait a few days. I don't want to upset you on our first night together as life mates."

"I won't be upset."

"You might be."

"I'm so happy right now I can easily promise not to get angry." She crossed her heart with her right hand. "Today has been the best day of my life, Holt. I'm not suspected of murder. Vince is alive. He's also my father. Mum is here, and I think they'll agree to visit us in Api. But most important is that you and I are tied. I love you so much, I'll forgive anything you say."

Taking her left hand, he kissed her ring finger. "In the process of sorting through Api's problems, I made a very difficult decision."

"What?"

"I decided to follow you to the end of the earth even if it meant never seeing Harmony again. I asked Juhree and Monteith to assume guardianship in the event something happens to Hanna and I'm not around to do so."

"But you will be around."

"Yes. I thank you from the bottom of my heart."

She caressed his cheeks and smiled. "See how easy it is for me to keep my promise not to get upset. I love you, Holt. I'm proud of you. I'm awed by your unselfishness. Welcome back into my heart."

"It's where I plan to stay."

"I certainly hope so."

They kissed again, soaring to a place they hadn't soared before.

Neither got much sleep as they loved and snuggled through their very special tying night.

# *Fourteen*

As Holt, Verity, Vince and Beryl approached the cage to Apitcote, Verity whispered, "I'm prepared for the speed, but Dad and Mum aren't. Can you slow the descent or cast a charm so they won't be frightened?"

"Sure." Holt snapped his fingers. "Our descent will feel like we're on the Soaring ride at Disney World."

"Excellent."

Later, as they unbuckled and left the cage, Beryl said, "That was wonderful."

"I enjoyed the ride as well," Vince said.

"How about you?" Holt asked Verity.

She smiled. "Easy peasy."

As the foursome exited the station, Verity grinned. Denizens had gathered to greet them—Shelan, Kirt, kew mates, Minalu and her sept, including the two new babies. Everyone except

Madeline. All welcomed Beryl and Vince as though they were family and congratulated Verity and Holt for tying.

Shelan beamed. "Kirt and I are so happy to have you as part of the family."

"We feel the same way," Vince replied with a wide grin.

"Does anyone know where Madeline is?" Verity asked, still scouring the crowd. Her worried expression filled Holt with concern.

"She's at our cottage," his mater said, her eyes solemn. "When I visited her in her new cottage she was hemorrhaging and feared she might lose the baby. I took her directly to the clinic. Madeline miscarried last night. We invited her to stay with us. We didn't want her to be alone."

Holt didn't wait for Verity to ask how to find Mater and Pater's cottage. Taking her hand, he levitated her there.

Madeline looked tired, but happy to see them. "I hoped Holt would bring you back, Ver."

"I intended to return if I possibly could. I'm so sorry I wasn't here for you."

"It's okay. Holt's parents have been marvelous, and I have so many friends I feel quite properly at home." She dabbed her eyes as tears formed. "Shelan said you tied while you were on the surface."

"We did."

"Congratulations. I want to hear everything that happened."

"I'll tell you all about it. First, I need to know how you're feeling."

"Weepy. A bit slumped—bits of low energy. Otherwise, okay."

"We're both sorry for your loss." Holt gave Madeline's shoulder a sympathetic pat.

"I didn't want another miscarriage. I wanted a baby." She grimaced. "I'm still cramping. Is that normal?"

"Yes. Your uterus is contracting. Do you want me to scrub and examine you?"

"I don't think that's necessary. Dr. Lorraine took good care of me. She performed a D&C, and said I should have a quick recovery."

"Do you want to go home with us?"

"Shelan and Kirt invited me to stay here until I feel well enough to be on my own. I want to put my name on the cottage list in the new kluster so I can live near the dwellers when they move. Is that possible?"

"You're already on the list," Holt said. "And you're welcome to live with us."

"Newlyweds need time by themselves. I know. I've been one." When she dabbed at her tears again, VJ offered a clean tissue.

"I'll give you two some privacy and time to get caught up," Holt said, excusing himself.

When they were alone, Madeline said, "Dwayne texted the night before I miscarried and asked me to call. The attorney Drew connected me with sent a letter along with my petition for a divorce. Dwayne is furious. Said he'll fight me tooth and nail to make sure I don't get a single item, not even my clothes. He accused me of abandoning him. Go figure. He sleeps with Carlotta, and I get the blame for our divorce. I don't want to see him ever again."

"You don't have to."

Madeline sighed. "Every time we talk, he harps about not having clean clothes."

"How do you respond?"

"I don't, although I'm tempted to suggest that Carlotta do his dirty laundry. Or he could take it out. He said the house needs cleaning, dishes are piled up. Bed needs changing. He must think that's all I'm good for."

"If you get a divorce, he'll be the loser."

"You think?"

"Yes."

"He claimed he doesn't want one. Lowered himself enough to beg me to return. I'm not going to. He's an unfaithful lout. Even if he ends the affair with Carlotta, there will be others. He flirted with waitresses on our honeymoon. I tried to ignore it, but now I realize we weren't meant to be together. He isn't willing to sell the house or split the profit. I don't care. All I want is my freedom. He can have everything. I've been gone more than two months, and I haven't missed him or a single item. He said he wouldn't pay child support either."

"Do you want me to call and tell him about the miscarriage?"

She nodded, dabbing more tears. "Would you?"

"Of course. If he shouts, I'll hang up."

Madeline smiled through her tears, squeezed VJ's hands and looked at their twin heart bracelets. "These are quite unique."

VJ touched her twin silver hearts to Madeline's. "They will keep us close, always."

"I think so, too. You're the best, Ver."

"So are you. Are you sure you want to stay with Shelan and Kirt?"

"Only until tomorrow. They need privacy. You won't be far away and now that you're back, we'll be able to see each other as often as we want."

"You bet we will," VJ agreed, knowing Madeline had needed to vent. "Holt said cottages in the new kluster will be ready to move into during the Thanksgiving weekend, and he put us on the list when he added your name."

"That's wonderful." Madeline spread her arms and hugged VJ.

"If we tell the dwellers we're moving there, maybe Minalu's sept will look forward to the move."

"Bob's your uncle," Madeline said, grinning. "Everything is okay."

VJ waved at all the colorful vases scattered round the room. "You have a lot of flowers. Many people love you." She smiled while Madeline sniffed and dried the last of her tears. "We're both going to have a wonderful future, Madd. I had a vision of yours. You'll have choices, and I'm confident the one you choose will make you happy."

"Thanks for telling me. I have more to look forward to now. I want a baby. Maybe more than one. And I'm an optimist, looking forward to new adventures."

A tap on the door sounded. "I wonder who could that be," Madeline said.

Sensing kew mates had brought her parents, VJ said, "Shelan and Kirt as well as someone you haven't seen for a long time, and someone you only met once."

"You're making me curious. Who?"

"I haven't told you all my good news. Close your eyes, Madd, and prepare yourself for a lovely surprise."

Madeline did as asked. VJ opened the bedroom door, motioned Beryl and Vince inside. "Say hello, Mum."

"My dear Madeline, I am so very sorry to hear you lost another baby."

Madeline blinked. "Beryl? Are you truly here? Or am I hallucinating?"

"I am here, my dear girl, and I am extremely pleased to introduce you to my husband, Vincent Jacobs—Verity Jane's biological father."

Madeline's eyes popped wide open. "What?"

"They eloped when they were teenagers," VJ explained. "Their parents had the marriage annulled, and Mum's took her back to England."

"Castor isn't your real father?" Madeline asked, dumbfounded.

"No. Isn't it great? I was born shortly after Mum married him."

"Do not cry for us," Beryl said as tears filled Madeline's eyes again. "We are happy now. I expect you shall soon be as well."

Madeline smiled through her tears. "My emotions are really wonky at the moment."

"For very good reasons," VJ soothed. "Your hormones are readjusting."

"Right, poppet," Beryl agreed. "We should leave straightaway and give you time to heal. Soon I would enjoy a lengthy chat to catch up."

"I'd like that, Beryl."

"My darling girl. I once wished you were one of my daughters. When you moved in with us, I felt as though you were." Bending, Beryl embraced her. "Have a good rest, poppet. I shall look forward to hearing all about the dwellers. Verity said they adore you."

"If she said that, she must know more than I," Madeline said.

"Her visions have helped us both, my dear. I expect that shall continue."

VJ gulped as a sunflower spun before her eyes. "Holt," she breathed, her legs wobbling as she staggered toward him.

"I'm here," he soothed, gathering her close as the vision consumed her.

It was about Madeline's choices—one included magic that depicted so many possibilities VJ wanted to cry. The other so vague it gave her chills. Either choice would take Madeline away to a place where VJ could no longer see her. Unless she accepted the invitation and went with Madeline. But if she did, she would never see Holt again.

# *Fifteen*

"Are you ill?" Beryl asked when Verity opened her eyes.

"No."

Holt knew the vision had upset Verity. Still clinging to him, she forced a smile as she focused on Madeline. "I saw us together. We were wearing the twin heart bracelets someone gave us."

"Brilliant," Madeline said. "I suspected they were gifted for a reason."

Vince looked totally perplexed. "What just happened?"

"Our daughter had a vision," Beryl explained.

"Do you have visions often?"

"Not until recently."

"Did you have visions when you lived with me?"

"Occasionally."

Holt knew he had to get her out of there. She was shaking. Having trouble breathing. He sent a silent message to his parents.

With a slight nod, Mater claimed attention. "Kirt and I would take great pleasure in showing you and Vince to your cottage, Beryl. It's newly refurbished and three doors from ours."

"And," Kirt clasped Shelan's hand, "We would be honored to have you join us for the evening meal at our shared constat."

"That would be lovely." Beryl flicked a glance at Holt, indicating she agreed he should take Verity home without delay.

He tightened his arms as she slumped against him. "We'll see everyone later." With a nod at Madeline, he lifted Verity, carried her outside, and levitated home.

"You're still trembling," he said after he blew the door shut behind them. "Are you cold?"

"A-huh," she mumbled, lips quivering.

"Should I light a fire?"

"Yes, please."

Placing her gently on the sofa, he summoned two fluffy duvets and wrapped them around her before he snapped his fingers at the fireplace and created fuel-less flames. Then he sat beside her, scooped her onto his lap and held her until she stopped shivering.

"Do you want to talk about it?"

"Always, with you."

"What did you see?"

"The three of us—Madeline and you and I—in a dark, bone-cold place. The only light came from our two miners' helmets. Madeline was flat on the ground, asleep. We couldn't awaken her. Beyond her head was a huge boulder and something else I couldn't see. You couldn't miniaturize it because it was invisible and without shape or form. It was mentally communicating with Madeline. It wasn't human but it wanted to be. It was the vire—evil spirit demon furies—attempting to steal her body and take control of her mind. She was fighting it, and there was nothing we could do except watch her silent struggle. A strange light appeared above our heads—small at first, then expanding, sending brilliant beams in all directions. One beam touched Madeline and offered sanctuary. If she chooses that path, we may never see her again."

Verity shivered, and Holt tightened his hold. "I don't know what to say or do to comfort you."

"Just hold me and keep me warm."

"I will."

When the doorbell rang, he said, "That's Juhree and Monteith, delivering our tow sacks and luggage from the cage station."

"We should invite them in."

"Come in," he called.

Their two kew mates levitated tow sacks and duffle bags inside before Juhree stared at Verity, still on Holt's lap. "Are you all right?"

"I'm good now. Thanks for asking."

Turning her gaze to Holt, Juhree said, "I collapsed your bubble this morning, disposed of the furniture and moved your possessions back inside the cottage." She motioned at the kitchen table where she had left his laptop, apad, and folded clothing.

"Thanks," Holt said.

"You are always welcome." Juhree walked to the door. "We'll leave you now."

"See you tomorrow," Monteith said before he followed her outside.

When they were alone again, Verity exhaled. "We should unpack."

"Do you feel up to it?"

"Yes. It will help take my mind off the vision."

"We could unpack without moving."

"How?"

"First think. Then visualize. After that, do what feels right to make it happen."

"Can you give me a demonstration?"

"Sure." Snapping his fingers, he sent his stacked clothes flying off the kitchen table to the bedroom. With a grin he announced, "My shirts and trousers are hanging in the closet. Underwear and socks are in the top dresser drawer. The other three drawers are empty, waiting for your things."

VJ concentrated and visualized. Raising her hands she wiggled her fingers at her daypack. She was so startled when her magic worked, she lost concentration, and everything fell on the floor in an untidy mess.

Holt chuckled. "It almost worked. Want to try again?"

"Yes. Quite." Scooting off his lap she stood, visualized and wiggled her fingers again. To her utter astonishment, her attempt worked exactly as she envisioned. Soon everything she had taken to the surface was unpacked and stored where she wanted each item to be.

"That was fun," she said, lightheaded with wonder. "Your prediction about me having magic is true. How did you know?"

"The instant I met you I knew. You are a very special person, Dr. Verity Jane Mackey."

"So are you, Arcane Holt." Caressing his cheek, she added, "You told me you are an Arcane, but I have no idea what that means."

"Arcane magic means different things to different people. Mine gives me the ability to zero in and locate a person, place or thing. In addition, Arcane magic allows me to compel. That kind of magic is very powerful. I rarely use it."

"Why?"

"Compelling has consequences."

"What kind?"

"Severe ones."

"Give me an example."

"I'll give you three. The loss of other magical skills. The loss of sensibilities. The loss of the ability to love."

"How do you know?"

"I used it once. Afterwards I could not love my sister, Jilly. I wanted to, but it was impossible. I could not even like her. I think she sensed how I felt. I will always regret that."

Verity didn't ask what he had done, and he didn't know if he would ever tell her. Some things were best left unsaid. It had taken years to forgive himself. Years to believe he was strong enough to resist the compelling temptation and worthy to be a member of the kew.

Plopping on the sofa again, Verity snuggled close. After he pulled the duvets around them, she said, "It's a relief to be home."

"I feel the same."

"I feel free."

"Good." Bending his head, he kissed her, long and leisurely.

Much later, he asked, "Is your vision still bothering you?"

"A bit, but it has faded."

"Is there anything else you want to tell me?"

She sucked in her bottom lip, then nodded. "In the vision, I had a chance—to go with Madeline. Away from Api. Away from you. I don't know if I had a choice—the chance to stay with you."

Holt gulped; his Adam's apple bobbed. "Thank you for telling me. I believe you belong with me, and I'll do my best to keep you." He cleared his throat and suggested, "If we talk about something else, perhaps the unpleasantness will recede."

"I hope so."

"I'd like to clear up concerns you may have about the surface."

"Go ahead."

"If you agree, we will cancel your apartment lease and have your possessions moved to storage."

"The furniture should be donated to charity."

"Blaine picked up your Prius from the police and drove it to Juhree's parents' mansion. It's stored in their garage as I promised."

"It should probably be sold or donated. I don't think I'll be needing it again."

"If left where it is, we or other visitors who stay in the mansion could use it."

"That's a good suggestion."

"Do you any have other concerns that need attention?"

"No. As you said early on, you are very thorough. Thank you, poppet."

Chuckling, he tickled her where he knew she was most ticklish—on the arches of her feet.

She laughed, struggling to get away, and they slid off the sofa in a tangle of duvets, arms and legs.

"This is what I call a kerfluffle." She giggled even though Holt had stopped tickling.

"It's cooler down here." He untangled duvets and smoothed them across their laps as they watched the dancing flames.

"Thank you, Holt."

"What for?"

"For knowing what I needed after that weird vision and giving it to me."

"Would you like to discuss the vision again?"

"Yes. It ended with a flashback of the vision I saw of people gathering to search for the fountain of youth."

"Anything new?"

"No, but it reminded me of the farm Dad owns in Kansas. Maybe that will come in handy when the mob gathers."

"Do you think he would be willing to sell?"

"We should discuss the idea with our kew mates before we ask."

"Our thoughts are in tune."

"What I'd like us to do now is to enjoy our homecoming. I'm so happy to be here with you, free from worrying about Freddie and knowing I'm not wanted for murder, I feel as though I could fly."

"Someday soon you will."

"Really?"

"When you're ready. Your surface problems are behind us. Let's concentrate on the present."

"We already are." She turned serious. "I have a confession."

"I'm eager to hear it."

"I'm afraid I'll never get enough doses of you."

The tenderness in his gaze earned him another confession. "I've never felt like this before—in love and free. It's quite bloody fantastic." Verity kissed him and the rest of the night they floated in a cocoon of pleasure and joy.

~ * ~

Concerned about Verity's visions, Holt sent an early message to kew mates. At eight a.m. they gathered in the dream chamber to hear details. She concluded by saying, "The throngs hunting for the fountain of youth will search caves and caverns in three states. Our concern is for those who scour Kansas."

"There are no caves or mountains near our eighth enquay," Dane said. "It's a hole in the ground surrounded by sagebrush, boulders and concealed by Mater Nature and protected by our newest computerized system."

"Might be advisable to add additional security," Holt said.

"We've already decided to," Dane said. "We'll just do it sooner than planned."

"Like this week," Monteith added.

"How will we deal with the hordes of people?" Mist asked.

"We built Atope," Rene reminded. "We could build a village with a fountain and call it the Fountain of Youth."

"Denizens have formed a team to replace those working in Atope," Drew said. "We can form another to manage the new community."

"Great!" Jordan enthused. "A community with a fountain might keep the crowd from looking for our enquay. If we build it far away, they won't even stumble close."

"I have a suggestion," Verity said.

"What?" Drew asked.

"Dad owns a farm in Kansas that has an underground hot spring. There's a cavern nearby. Perhaps we could pipe hot water from the spring to the cavern and call it the FOY."

"What a splendid suggestion," Rene said. "If we use the farm, we could add whatever we deem necessary to attract the seekers. Perhaps provide housing."

"It's an organic farm. If seekers need jobs, they could work there."

"How big is it?"

"A bit over a hundred acres."

"Where is it located?"

"In Harvey County—south-central Kansas—half a mile from a paved road and thirty miles from a good-sized town."

"Is your pater willing to sell?"

"I haven't asked.

"Perhaps that's the first thing we should do," Monteith said.

"I'll go talk to him now."

~ * ~

"We don't want to sell," Vincent said. "The farm is an income-producing investment." He smiled at Beryl. "Kansas isn't a community property state, so I instructed Ricardo to have the deed changed to joint ownership. I have no objection to allowing the kew to use the hot springs in order to protect this special place. What do you think?"

Beryl smiled. "I am in total agreement."

"Is there any unused land that could be used for campers? We want to keep seekers away from Api's enquay."

"Some acreage at the west end isn't under cultivation. You should discuss the possibility with our farm manager. He's a good man. We trust his opinions."

Wanting to talk to Madeline when she left her parents, VJ found her new cottage and rang the bell. Madeline opened the door.

"How delightful to see you. Come in."

VJ's grin faded. "You stopped attending kew meetings. Why?"

"I don't belong there anymore. You're all couples now and I'm an outsider."

"Nonsense."

"There's a time and place for everything, Ver. Yours is with Holt and his kew mates. Mine is nearby, but living my own life. Doing my own thing."

"I don't want you to feel left out."

"I don't. Whilst you were gone, Gwen took Tumela and me to a disco. We had a wonderful time and we plan to do that again when you attend kew meetings."

"Was it awkward spending time with Tumela?"

"Not particularly. Dom and Nando are still with Falo."

"Are you and I losing our closeness?"

"Never." Madeline fingered the twin hearts on her bracelet. "This feels like a connection to you."

VJ raised her wrist and touched her bracelet to Madeline's. "Mine feels the same. I think whoever gifted them filled them with some sort of magic to help us feel close whether we're together or apart."

"I have a similar feeling." Madeline sucked in her bottom lip as though contemplating what she wanted to say next. "I've always thought there was a reason I was mistreated by my family and taken in by your mum.

"I believe our destinies are linked, as connected as our friendship. Maybe the reason we met when we were so young has something to do with being here."

"I agree, and I think something big is going to happen. Something monumental. And the two of us—you and I—will be involved."

"I know, Madd. And I'm afraid whatever it is won't be pleasant."

"Or easy. I have no magic, but you do. Your magic might help us, Ver."

"Are you talking about my visions?"

"More than that. You don't have headaches. You don't get cramps before your periods every month. You're never sick. When I am, your touch always makes me better. Last night you hugged me, and today, I feel quite back to normal. Your touches made your mum and sisters better whenever they were ill. I believe you have the ability to heal, Ver."

"You observed all those things and never said a word about them to me."

"Didn't think I needed to. I thought you knew you possess magic."

"I always felt like the odd one out, except with you and Mum, but having magic never entered my mind."

~ * ~

At the evening kew meeting, VJ reported, "Dad and Mum don't want to sell the farm, but they're willing to let us use the hot spring and vacant land if their property manager has no objections."

"It's winter and cold, especially at night," Drew reminded. "If seekers camp out or live in tents, there could be problems and health issues."

"Yeah," Jordan agreed. "How can we help people find decent places to live if they squat miles from civilization?"

"I could conjure housing," Juhree offered.

"Smashing!" VJ envisioned the circular row houses in Bath, England. "Twin, double decker row houses would provide homes for a mass of people without taking up much land."

"We could build a new community," Rene said.

Always the cautious one, Dane said, "Someone should go look at the farm and see if it suits our purposes."

"Verity and I volunteer," Holt said.

"If you go tomorrow, Monteith and I could go with you," Juhree offered. "I don't have classes during the weekend."

~ * ~

"We'll stay here," Vince said when Verity asked if he and Beryl wanted to accompany them. "We visited the farm in July. Our manager is a fine young family man. I'll call and tell him to expect you."

"The farm is lovely," Beryl added. "Our visit was smashing. We stayed in one of the cabins. It was clean and newly refurbished. The property is quiet and peaceful."

"Might not be if a mass of seekers shows up."

"Invading the farm will be better than invading Apitcote," Vince said.

Holt nodded. "Glad we agree."

~ * ~

To avoid Falo, Minalu's former pallet mate, the foursome left during the night.

Arrived at the farm early in the morning.

Met the managers, Zeg and Pilare, a husband and wife who had a baby boy named Fallon.

VJ swallowed a gulp of excitement. "I know who you are."

Zeg blinked. "I don't recall meeting you."

"I know your brothers."

"What are their names?" Zeg asked, his gaze skeptical.

"Dominic and Nando. You are Minalu and Falo's youngest son."

Zeg's eyes widened in shock. "How do you know these things?"

"Your brothers returned to the dwelling. On their way, Nando ate something poisonous. He was ill for a while but he has recovered."

"Amma and Papa—how are they?"

"Your mum is fine. I'm not sure about your papa. They are no longer together."

Zeg's brows shot skyward. "What happened?"

When VJ shrugged, Monteith said, "I can explain. Last summer, Juhree and I and another couple went to see the karst—your sept calls it the stone garden. We had a map showing an enquay on the other side beyond two mountains and we decided to find it. Instead, we met your mater. And Cinnalan, your sister, who was born after you left. We also met your pater. We invited them to visit our realm, a fair distance away, and they did. One of our mates suggested a student exchange. The women in your sept loved the idea. The men did not. They left the women's pallets. Then the women left the cave and came to live with us."

"Wow!" Zeg looked stunned. "What an unusual coincidence."

"I don't think so," VJ said. "I suspect Mother Nature is helping some of her favorite humans connect."

Pilare's eyes grew round. "I don't understand."

"Verity has visions," Holt explained. "She has seen parts of the past and future. Before the end of the year, someone will spread a rumor about a fountain of youth. Crowds will come to Kansas looking for it. We plan to divert their attention away from the enquay and provide a place for those who linger—in case they decide to live there."

"That's why Mr. Jacobs called. He said you are on a mission to protect a very special place."

"Your homeland and ours," Holt agreed.

"Verity and I weren't born there," Juhree said. "But Api is our home now."

"Mr. Jacobs is my father," Verity added. "He's willing to let seekers camp on the farm if you have no objections."

"He's the owner. We do what he wants."

"Baby Fallon is beginning to fuss. Does he need a nap?" Verity asked.

Pilare passed the noisy baby to Zeg. "Give him a bottle while I show our visitors to their cabin."

Inside the cabin, Pilare glanced at their daypacks. "Did you bring food? If not, Zeg and I would enjoy having you eat dinner with us."

"Eat with us instead," Juhree invited.

Pilare's eyes twinkled. "That would be a rare treat. We don't get many chances to eat out. Especially since the pandemic."

"It's decided then."

Pilare nodded and smiled. "I'll go relieve Zeg so he can show you around the farm."

Zeg gave them a full tour. At the cavern, they hiked below ground. "Piping hot water here should be a simple matter," Holt said.

"Right," Monteith agreed.

*I can do that in a matter of minutes*, Juhree silently conveyed.

Back in the sunshine, Holt eyed the acreage. "There's enough empty land to build the twin double decker row houses you described, Verity."

"Do you have any objections to adding row houses for people to rent?" she asked Zeg.

"No, but I doubt you'll get the farm rezoned. The previous owner tried to increase the size of the RV park but failed to obtain approval from the county. Change is never an easy process."

"That could be a problem."

"There's land beyond the farm for sale. I don't know how it's zoned, but it might be residential."

"I saw the sign that said, 'for sale by owner,' VJ said. "Let's call and ask." Closing her eyes, she used memory recall for the phone number, punched digits into her afone, and turned on the speaker.

The owner sounded eager. "My grandparents left the land to me and my sister. We petitioned to have it rezoned for residential use and obtained approval. My sister and I were working with a construction company to build a community with residential and commercial areas, but our plans ended when the pandemic hit. If we don't sell the property in a few months, we'll list with a realtor. We've moved on in different directions, and are no longer interested in developing the land."

"Is there water on the property?"

"Yes. A replenishing aquafer. Electricity, too."

"We're interested in buying. Can we see the land today?"

"Are you serious?"

"Yes. And we'll pay cash."

~ * ~

The sale went through without a hitch.

Holt and Monteith applied for building permits online.

Juhree conjured dinner for the six adults. Baby Fallon alternated between sucking his dummy—pacifier—and playing with it while the couples ate.

Kew mates slept three hours, then headed home, avoiding Falo again by traveling in the dark.

On Sunday, they slept in, catching up on sleep. After brunch, VJ and Holt hurried to kluster fourteen and found Minalu in the cultural hall, rocking Tinna's baby.

"We have some exciting news," VJ announced.

Minalu stopped rocking. "I am listening."

"Yesterday we met your youngest son, Zeg. He's managing a farm my father owns. He's married and has a baby boy. His wife's name is Pilare, and the baby is Fallon."

"Named after his grandpapa."

"I know this isn't any of our business, but if Zeg brings his family to visit, they'll likely see Falo first. He might try to keep them there."

"I do not doubt that. He keeps Dominic and Nando beyond their desire." She set the rocker in motion again, her gaze wandering to the baby sleeping in her arms.

"Would you like to visit them?"

"No." The stubborn tilt of her head confirmed her earlier decision. "This is my home. This is where I stay."

"What about Zeg and his family?"

"If my youngest son wishes me to meet his family, he will bring them here."

VJ stifled a frown. Although they had avoided Falo, she sensed a confrontation coming—soon.

# Sixteen

At the kew meeting, Holt concluded, "We should be prepared to travel back to the surface as soon as the mob starts looking for the fountain of youth."

"How long will it take you and Monteith to draw blueprints?"

"Less than an hour," Holt said.

"If we wait until the mob seeking the fountain arrives, what will we do with them?" Verity asked. "We can't have a mass of people watching us use magic."

"Tess and I will cast charms to put the seekers to sleep," Rene said.

"Can we keep them charmed—unconscious for days? I'm concerned about their health."

"'Course you are," Holt agreed. "But they won't be unconscious. They'll be in a state of hibernation, their body functions slowed to a snail's pace."

"How will we know each seeker's needs? Will we have to 'read' each individual?"

"Yes. But that won't take long," Dane said. "Supplementals sense people's needs without consuming a lot of time."

"I'm excited. I hope our plan works," Verity said.

"We're all excited," Rene said. "And everyone in Api is indebted to you and your parents."

~ * ~

Minalu was chatting with VJ when Holt landed at her side. "The kew needs us."

He waited until he levitated them out of earshot before he explained. "News about a fountain of youth is spreading online. People are already pouring into Kansas, looking for the magic fountain. Several groups are camped fifty miles from our eighth enquay."

"How do you know?"

"Rene and Tess both see them."

"Seekers should be searching for a cave or cavern near the mountains."

"They might be following Zeg and his family. He put a tenant couple in charge of the farm and he and Pilare are on their way to see Falo and Minalu. They're camped in an open field, afraid to travel closer because they don't want to lead anyone near the enquay."

"Which means we're going to the surface now."

"Correct."

At their cottage while they packed necessities, VJ said, "Mist's due date is less than a month away. Do you think it's safe for her to go with us?"

"Rene flew home from Alaska a few hours before Rance was born, so I doubt Mist will consider staying behind. And, if she happens to go into premature labor, she'll have an excellent OB/GYN nearby."

VJ grabbed her medical satchel. "Good thing I always take this along."

As they were about to leave, Holt's afone dinged. "It's Hanna." The disappointment in his eyes tugged at VJ's heartstrings. "We won't be here when they arrive tomorrow." He punched his speaker icon so VJ could hear the conversation. "Hello."

"Hi Holt. I've canceled our trip. Mother tested positive for Covid. Her doctor wants her in the hospital, but I can't convince her to go."

"Sorry to hear the bad news," Holt said. "Is there anything we can do to help?"

"Just be patient about seeing Harmony. She's over her crankiness. Content to sit near Mom, even when she sleeps. She seems to know how to comfort her better than I do."

"Take care of yourself, Hanna. You've been exposed to Covid twice. Maybe you should insist on taking Aleece to the hospital."

"Good advice. I'll try to take it. I'll call or text if the situation changes."

Sticking his afone back in his pocket, he took hold of VJ's hand.

"I'm sorry about Hanna's news, Holt. How long has it been since you've seen Harmony?"

"Too long. Not since August. Three months—ninety-four days."

*He counts the days.*

"We need to go," he said.

Gear collected, they set off for the south forest where kew mates had agreed to meet. As they flew above cottages and People Movers, VJ said, "I wish you didn't have to levitate me. I'm the only one who can't fly."

"You have the ability."

"I do?" she asked.

"Yeah. Rene conveyed the power for me to endow you with the gift at dawn."

She blinked. "Did you endow anything else?"

"Don't think I need to. You have your own magic." He levitated down to the ground.

"Why did we stop?"

"You said you want to levitate."

"I do. But I don't know how."

"Close your eyes and think it. Then do it."

Closing her eyes, she spread her arms and thought about flying. Before she knew it, her body was lifted off the ground. "I'm flying," she squealed.

"Course you are, poppet." Joining her in the air, he grinned, and they levitated to the end of the last People Mover.

A bit breathless from her first levitating experience, VJ watched Rene and Juhree create klir seal suits for everyone.

"Time for lift off," Holt announced.

When they reached the dwelling, VJ swept her gaze around the barren grotto. Bitter cold had replaced the mild days of autumn and dead leaves littered the frozen ground, along with remnants of leftover food from more than a few meals.

Falo didn't just frown when he saw them, he yelled. "Stop. You no welcome." His speech had deteriorated along with his elocution. Bulky clothes covered him from ankles to chin, and burlap encased his feet. He had lost both front teeth and he looked years older.

"Why you here?" he demanded, eyes fierce, tone angry.

"We're on our way to the surface," Jordan said, his voice deliberately quiet.

"No give permission to use tunnel. Go! Git! Return to own land."

"There's a problem above that concerns you as much as it concerns us," Dane said. "Groups of people are looking for the entrance."

Falo blanched. "How many?"

"We estimate two or three hundred and we expect more. Some have weapons, and they are not afraid to use them."

Falo's eyes widened in shock. "What they want?"

"They heard a rumor that there's a fountain of youth below the ground, and they want to enjoy its benefits."

"There no fountain."

"You know that, and we know that, but they don't," Holt said.

"One person above is your third son, Zeg," VJ said.

Falo's belligerence faded, his bloodshot eyes filled with hope. "How you know?"

"We met him on the surface more than a week ago. He manages a farm my father owns."

"She's a visionary," Holt injected. "She sees him as plain as day."

Awe filled Falo's eyes, and he uttered no further objections. "You go. I go, too."

"Would you like someone to levitate you?" VJ asked as they entered the wide mouth of the dark funnel shaped tunnel.

"No. I walk."

"The others will reach the surface long before us if we walk."

"You no walk. You go." He flapped his elbows like wings. "You fly."

"Not unless you fly with us. We have miners' helmets to light the way. You don't even have a fire torch."

Dom and Nando came running. "Where are you going, Papa?"

"Above. You come, too."

Kew mates didn't wait for more jabber. Although they were already levitating thirteen denizens to manage the new community, those levitating only one clasped Falo's, Dom's and Nando's elbows and scooped them off their feet. VJ grinned as she levitated to catch up.

The cone-shaped tunnel slanted from the wide bottom to a small top. Only one person could exit at a time. By the time everyone did, Holt and Monteith had checked Mater Nature's veil and installed a new robotic computer that would 'read' future entrants.

Dusk had fallen when kew mates levitated west toward the seeking campers. Fires burned where sage brush had been cleared. The strong smell wasn't pleasant, but VJ was impressed that the crowds had used the sage to brew tea.

"Where they come from?" Falo asked.

"All directions."

"How we keep them from dwelling?"

"The new security system will handle that, and we plan to swipe their memories and plant new ones so they believe they have found the fountain of youth."

"Why you not make them go away?"

"Most have no place to go. They've lost or given up their homes. We'll cast a charm to keep them asleep while we create a community where they can live and thrive."

"What means community?"

"It's similar to your dwelling and the realm where we live. Watch and observe."

Falo, Dom and Nando's eyes widened in surprised awe as kew mates levitated above the huge fields and cast charms that put seekers to sleep.

Tess and Rene swiped memories and planted new ones as they flew. Behind them, Mist and Jordan videoed. Monteith and Juhree doused campfires to ensure they didn't spread.

VJ helped Holt levitate Falo and his sons to the bubble Juhree had conjured around Zeg, Pilare and baby Fallon.

Staring at the sleeping family, Falo mumbled, "Youngest son give me grandchild." His dour expression softened as he watched the baby wiggle and sigh. "What wrong with you?" he asked Dom and Nando. "Why you no mate? No give me grand kidlings?"

Nando replied. "I want to go to the other end of our realm and find a mate."

"I wish to live there as well," Dom admitted and VJ read longing inside him. A quick flashback revealed he had a daughter and was contemplating going to see her while he was on the surface.

VJ sent a silent message to Holt, filling him in, before she delved any deeper. But Dom was now blocked. And he had sensed her probe.

He glanced at Holt before he met her gaze. Cleared his throat. "You know?"

"Yes. We both do," she whispered.

Holt snapped his fingers. Falo and Nando closed their eyes. "We can talk. They won't hear us."

"Where is your daughter?" Verity asked.

"With her amma. I discerned their presence as we flew over one group. Orlane is hungry. Hasn't eaten since yesterday morning. I need to get to her. She's whimpering in her sleep."

"Do you want us to take you?" Holt asked.

"I would very much appreciate that."

Holt took Dom's elbow and the threesome levitated above the crowds.

Dom pointed at one large group. "She's down there."

When they landed, Dom bent and gathered her in his arms. "You're safe now, dumpling," he said when she whimpered. "Dada will take care of you."

"She needs food. Let's get her some." Holt took hold of Dom's elbow again.

"May I levitate Orlane?" Verity asked.

Sensing Dom's reluctance to let her go, Holt said, "Dr. Verity's healing touch will be good for your daughter."

"She's been through an ordeal," Dom said as he placed Orlane carefully in Verity's arms.

~ * ~

The kew's plan worked smoothly. Seamlessly. As though it had been rehearsed. They finished a day earlier than anticipated.

Seekers awakened, disorientated at first, as though unable to believe what they saw, then delighted to be in a community that appeared to be as new as it was. Checking their phones, they read Mist's text, and laughed as they wandered from their new stacked homes to the gap between and squabbled over who was in charge of what at the farmers' market.

The management team gave them time to sort things out and grinned when people eventually calmed, introduced themselves and muddled through the chaos.

"Where's Dom?" VJ asked when kew mates were ready to leave.

"I'm here," Dom announced, carrying Orlane who was sound asleep. "I've decided to keep her."

Holt had 'read' Ilma, knew she slept with a man, and didn't even know Orlane was gone.

"I sent a text, so she'll know Orlane is with me," Dom said.

"Good. Let's go."

In the tunnel, kew mates levitated Falo and his family back to the dwelling.

As soon as they landed, Falo nodded at Orlane. "She daughter?"

"Yes."

"Why you not bring before?"

"The reasons are many and complicated."

"What you call her?"

"Orlane."

Pilare stepped closer, smiling as Orlane opened her eyes. "I am your aunt Pilare. I hope we will be friends."

Sticking her two middle fingers in her mouth, Orlane leaned her head against Dom's chest. Falo stalked away, kept his back to them.

The dwelling looked even less welcoming.

"On behalf of all who dwell in our realm," Holt said, "we extend an invitation for you to live with us, where life is more hospitable in the winter months than it is here."

Falo turned and snarled. "You want take sons away as you took pallet mate."

"We didn't take Minalu," Monteith corrected. "She left of her own accord. If you change your mind and decide to join her, you will always be welcome, as are all who dwell here. If your sons wish to live in our realm, they will make that decision, not us."

As kew mates levitated over the first mountain, VJ said, "I sense Dom and Nando want to go with us, but Zeg feels obligated to stay."

"I sense the same. We'll stop and wait, give Dom and Nando time to walk through the tunnel."

# Seventeen

When Dom and Nando joined them, VJ asked, "Are we going to leave Pilare there, alone with the men?"

"Don't think we have a choice." Holt looked at the brothers. "Do you want us to levitate you?"

"Yes, please."

As they flew over the second mountain, a huge sunflower claimed VJ's vision. Struck by sudden dizziness, she called, "Holt?"

He levitated closer. "Are you having a vision?"

"Yes. My hand. Please hold my hand."

He complied. "Should we land?"

"Yes. I need stability. Levitating requires concentration, as do visions."

Holt sent a silent message to kew mates, urging them to continue, and he, Dom and Verity would catch up. Moments later, they landed on the limestone karst floor. "Are you okay?"

VJ didn't answer. She couldn't because the sunflower surged close. Sucked her inside the black center. She felt like she was tumbling after Alice, down the hole to Wonderland. Suddenly, she couldn't move. Could barely breathe. The air in her lungs seemed to vanish. She was enclosed in something thick. Dense. Hard, like stone.

Fear catapulted through as evil clawed at her from all directions, trying to enter her mind. Steal her body. And her soul.

Her life flashed before her eyes. Determination followed. She had survived Castor's abuse. Freddie's awful manipulations. Graduated from med school. Delivered babies. She could survive this. With a surge of absolute terror, she summoned an image of Holt. And exhaled. Blew the evil from within her.

Tears pooled in her eyes as she dragged air back into her lungs. She was certain death or evil had very nearly claimed her.

"Verity," she heard Holt say as though from far away. He squeezed her hand.

Fortified by his touch, her brain clicked. Stupor vanished. Numbness fled. "Hurry. We must leave straightaway."

Seizing Dom's elbow, Holt followed as she shot up through the air, clinging to his other hand.

Kew mates had turned back and were levitating toward them. *Stop*, VJ silently ordered without realizing she even knew how to do such a thing until her mates reversed direction and silently asked, *Why?*

She inhaled and almost choked before she replied. "The evil is down there with some horrid creatures."

Rene levitated close. "Did the evil tell you anything?"

VJ shook her head, as much to clear it as to answer. "It told me nothing."

They flew in silence the rest of the way to Apitcote. When they reached the end of the forest, all levitated down and stopped near the first People Mover.

"You had a difficult vision," Rene observed. "What did you see?"

"Nothing. I only felt."

"What did you feel?"

"The vire. Bloody, awful evil." Chills made her shake. She swallowed. Unclenched her fists. "I felt imprisoned inside stone. The vire stole my air. My sight. Tried to steal all of me. I don't know how I managed to escape."

"Do you know if the vire sensed the rest of us?"

"No. Logic insisted I get away as soon as possible."

"We know where it is," Rene said with a calm VJ envied. "That will help when the time comes to do something."

VJ glanced at Dom, Orlane and Nando, whose eyes were glazed. She knew Holt had charmed them so they wouldn't hear about the threat looming ahead until he thought it necessary. "Clairine sealed the evil there fifty years ago. We have time," she added, without knowing how she sounded so confident. "If we didn't, I would know. Please believe me."

"We do believe you," Rene soothed. "And we won't meddle. We know you'll tell us when the time is right."

Verity let out a relieved sigh. Holt heard the silent message she sent only to him. *We must develop an antidote for the sleeping sickness the vire will thrust upon denizens.*

*I believe you will succeed*, he sent back. He believed the kew could and would overcome anything that threatened their realm. Snapping his fingers, he released Dom, Nando and Orlane from his charm.

"Would you like to clean up a bit before you go see your mater?" Rene asked.

"Yes," Dom replied for all three.

"You may do so at the chateau."

"I'll conjure new clothes," Juhree volunteered.

Gratitude laced Nando's eyes. "We appreciate your generosity."

~ * ~

Minalu met VJ and Holt the moment they entered kluster fourteen. Without so much as a greeting, she blurted, "Kidlings are unwell."

"All of them?" VJ asked.

Minalu shook her head of heavy hair. "Twelve."

"Including Cinnalan?"

"No. Sicklings are inside. On their pallets. Doubled over in pain."

"How long have they been ill?"

"Since last night."

"Have any up-swallowed?"

At Minalu's puzzled expression, she clarified, "Vomited? Upchucked?"

"No."

Still garbed in her klir seal suit, VJ hurried to the cultural hall, found the nearest water closet, scrubbed, donned new surgical gloves and rushed to examine a brother and sister who were both writhing in pain on their shared mattress.

"Tell me where you hurt most," VJ urged, coaxing Tad to lie flat on his back so she could examine him.

"My stomach. It feels like it wants to kill me, Dr. Verity."

"Where are you most tender?" she asked, gently pushing spots on a stomach that looked as if it harbored a sixth-month fetus.

"Everywhere." Tad groaned, lifting his hips off the mattress.

"Tell me what you've eaten during the last two days."

The long list confirmed VJ's suspicion.

After examining his sister, Mita, VJ checked the remaining ten kidlings. All had eaten too much food and consumed several tempting desserts.

VJ swallowed a lump of guilt. She and Madeline had been tasked with teaching the dwellers the value of good nutrition, to introduce new foods slowly, and to eat balanced diets. Kidlings hadn't learned. Twelve had overdosed.

"I feel derelict of duty. Madeline has been teaching classes at university for a professor who took the week off. I should have been here with the sept at meal times."

"You are not derelict," Holt disagreed. "You were exactly where you needed to be."

Still feeling guilty, she opened her medical satchel and administered medicine to aid digestive problems and reduce pain. Afterwards, she faced anxious Minalu and the kidlings' worried mums.

"Time will cure what ails them—indigestion. Your kidlings gorged. Added too many new foods at one time and their bodies are rebelling. I gave them medication to ease pain and help heal the internal problem."

"We should not have allowed them to eat at a table by themselves," one mum said.

"They have learned a valuable lesson," Minalu disagreed.

"Give them only water and Jell-o until the evening meal. Then they may eat soup. I'll ask Miss Gwen to have Jell-o and liquids sent to the cultural hall throughout the day. By tomorrow afternoon, they should be ready to go outside and resume normal activities."

"Will it be safe to rise from their pallets so soon?" Minalu asked.

"Moving around will be good as long as they stay hydrated. Exercise should speed their recovery. All they need is a good dose of TLC."

"What means TLC?" one mum asked.

"Tender loving care." VJ put her medical tools away before she said, "Zeg and his family returned with us, Minalu. They're with Falo. Mist patched Zeg's phone so he can call or atext when they're ready to travel here. Holt and I agreed to levitate to the dwelling and bring them."

Pure joy radiated in Minalu's eyes. "You are most kind."

"Dom and Nando came with us." Holt nodded at Dom as he approached, once again carrying Orlane on his shoulders.

Minalu smiled. "I sensed you would bring your daughter to us, Dom." Spreading her arms, she welcomed Orlane into her life. "You are sweet as an angel, little one."

Orlane reached for Minalu's hair. But she didn't yank or pull. Just fingered Minalu's silky locks. Then she stuck two fingers in her mouth and sucked. But she kept hold of Minalu's strands.

While Dom answered Minalu's questions, Tumela rushed inside and greeted Dom with a brilliant smile. "I am very happy to see you again, Dominic."

"It's good to see you, Tumela." He waved at Nando as he joined them. "Nice duds, brother."

"Yours, too." Keeping his eyes off Tumela, Nando embraced Minalu. "I have missed you, Amma."

"I missed you as well. How is your papa?"

"Ornery as ever." Nando said, still ignoring Tumela. "But he is pleased to have Zeg and his family nearby."

"Papa's not just ornery," Dom said. "He has aged prematurely."

"You should bring him here," Tumela said.

"We'd have to use force," Nando grumbled.

"Perhaps not, if I go with you," she disagreed, turning her attention to him. And looking startled before she asked, "Now that you have returned, will you eat meals with us?"

"Of course they will," Minalu said.

"Not me," Nando said, holding Tumela's rapt attention.

"Why?" she asked.

"Juhree and Monteith invited me to eat in their constat. They offered to introduce me to some young ladies, and I'm looking forward to dancing with them."

"You dance?" Tumela asked, flirting with her eyes.

"Sure."

"Will you take me dancing?"

"Maybe."

"Tonight?"

"No. I already have plans."

"When then?"

"When you grow up."

"I am grown."

He looked her up and down. "I hadn't noticed."

Minalu's expression went from curious to amusement as she watched them.

Turning to Dom, Tumela asked, "Will you take me dancing, Dominic?"

"No. I have a daughter to look after."

"Cinnalan can mind her."

"In time, perhaps. But you are much too young for me, Tumela."

Clearly disappointed, Tumela turned to VJ and Holt. "I would like to return to the dwelling and convince Falo to come and live here. Can you tell me how to get there?"

"You can't convince him," Nando said flatly.

"I would like to try."

"Dr. Verity and I will be happy to levitate you," Holt offered.

"Thank you, Mr. Holt. Will you be available the day after the Thanksgiving feast?"

"Your sept will be moving into their new cottages that weekend," VJ said. "Would you mind waiting until next week?"

"No. I will go when it's convenient for you."

"I should go with you," Nando said.

"I would welcome your company." Tumela said, winking at VJ.

After they strolled away, VJ said, "I think what just happened was Tumela's intention all along."

Holt chuckled. "My gut says she's going to let Nando chase her until she catches him."

"I agree. Do you think her interest in Dom was feigned?"

"I haven't a clue."

VJ leaned against his chest, taking comfort in the circle of his arms as he closed them around her. "I have some sad news. Falo will be gone before Christmas day."

"Sorry to hear that. Should we go tomorrow? Thanksgiving isn't until the day after."

"Tomorrow is too soon. Falo is angry. He and Nando both need a few days before they see each other again. Plus, Zeg and his family may want to return with us. They should have some time with Falo before they leave the dwelling. And I doubt very much that Tumela will convince him to leave the grotto."

As they strolled to the People Mover, VJ saw Dom watching Madeline as she hurried toward them.

"I missed you," she gushed, "How did things go above?"

VJ grinned. "Exactly as planned."

Madeline clapped her hands gleefully, her eyes sparkling. "I have news! Good news. I'm free. No longer married. The judge granted a quick divorce after he heard I had already deserted the nest."

"Let's share the evening meal," Holt suggested. "Give you two a chance to catch up and me the opportunity to listen to two of my favorite women."

Madeline glanced at Dom before they stepped on the People Mover. "Who is that kidling Minalu is carrying? I don't recall seeing her before."

"Dom brought her back from the surface."

"Do you know why?"

"He said there were some complicated, and extenuating circumstances."

VJ resisted the urge to invite Dom and Orlane to eat the evening meal with them. She hadn't seen details in her vision of Madeline's future, just possibilities. Did one include Dom's 'ready-made' family? Or was that wishful thinking on her part?

"Living here is fantastic," Madeline gushed as she raised the small flag to summon a server. "I never knew life could be so exciting. Or that I could be so happy. After a failed marriage and two miscarriages, I thought happiness was for other people."

"What makes you so happy?" Holt asked.

"Life. Apitcote. Denizens. Dwellers. Teaching classes. Being near the two of you. Seeing Verity's mum again. Hearing Vincent is her father. Discovering Castor isn't." Madeline grinned. "Not necessarily in that order. Every morning, I wake up excited to be alive. The feeling is quite unique. I have fewer possession than I had on the surface, yet I feel as though I have more."

"I feel the same way," VJ said, duly noting Madeline hadn't mentioned Dom or even looked at him since she asked about Orlane.

After a server took their orders, Holt asked, "Are the dwellers ready to move?"

"Some are. Others adore living in the cultural hall. They tell me that every day. They haven't lost their fear of being separated."

"You could explain the hall is needed by the denizens who welcomed them into their kluster, invited them to share their loos, and explain they are taking advantage of their wecome?"

"Excellent advice," VJ said. "You could also tell them the hall should be available for denizens to resume monthly socials."

"Good advice."

Their food arrived as Minalu entered the constat with her family. Dom glanced around and stopped looking when he saw Madeline. She pretended not to notice. But VJ felt the vibes dancing between them. She bit her bottom lip to keep from making a comment. Newly divorced, would Madeline be receptive to another chance at romance? If so, how would she feel about being Orlane's stepmum?

~ * ~

The visual assault began as VJ strolled toward the fourteenth kluster. Multiple stars, fans and sunflowers swarmed before her eyes, spinning close, gyrating away, making her lightheaded. Sensing more than one vision, she plunked on the cold ground and closed her eyes. Vision after vision sped by, so numerous she wondered if she would remember them all.

Holt was working with his crew when he sensed Verity experiencing something unusual. Suspecting it might be a vision, he used his Arcane sight to zero in to her location.

"I have to go." Leaving his crew staring at him, he levitated to kluster twelve. Found Verity lying on the cold ground between People Movers. Her cloak, spread across the dry winter grass, barely covered her.

Plucking her gently into his arms, he felt her trembling. Using magic to shuck his parka, he tucked it around her while he waited for the vision to end.

When she finally opened her eyes, she looked all in—as though she didn't have an ounce of strength left.

"You were having a vision?"

"Multiples."

"Do you want to share?"

"Definitely."

"Here or at home?"

"Home, please."

He levitated them there. Removed his parka from her shoulders. Adjusted her cloak. Covered her with a TV throw, then asked, "Would you like a cuppa?"

Teeth chattering, she gave him a bleak smile. "A spot of cream tea would be nice."

Holt snapped his fingers. Twice. His first snap created flames in the fireplace. His second boiled water in the teapot and levitated the tea tray to the living room. While the tea steeped, he sat beside Verity and willed his heat to warm her.

After a few sips, her violent shivering stopped. "The visions were brain-popping, Holt."

He wound his arm around her shoulders. And listened.

"We will be parents. We shall have more than one child."

"Boys? Girls?"

"One of each. Your parents will dote on them. Mine will be over the moon."

Holt grinned. "What else did you see?"

"Minalu will hold Dom's son two years from next spring. He will be born on Rance and our child's birthday, April sixteenth."

"I've seen no indication that Madeline and Dom are still attracted to one another."

"I have, although I don't know if Madeline will be the boy's mum. His birth is more than two years away, and she has many paths to choose from."

Holt nodded thoughtfully.

"Mist and Jordan will have twins. One, two days hence, earlier than anticipated. The other later, on Christmas night."

"That's highly unusual."

"But not impossible."

"Are you going to tell them?"

"I prefer not to. Dr. Lorraine hears only one heartbeat and has advised them to be prepared for the possibility that one twin might be stillborn."

"Will both live?"

"I believe so, but fate can be fickle, life uncertain."

"Did you see more?"

"Yes, although I'm not explaining my visions in sequence. Someday the kew will decide to divide responsibilities. Each couple will assume care for two or more klusters, rather than everyone feeling responsible for the entire Apitcote realm twenty-four/seven."

Holt nodded again, amazed at her ability to keep each vision separate.

"Juhree and Monteith will have a child next year. On Christmas day. Very early in the morning. Juhree will continue her studies and become a fantastic doctor."

"Sounds like a lot of babies."

"Right. And all will levitate before they learn to walk."

"Flipping hallelujah!" Holt cheered, then frowned. "How about Rance and Abee? Will they levitate as well?"

"Yes. Sometime after the new year. Their parents do not yet know."

"Will you tell them?"

"If there's a time when it feels appropriate." Verity touched his cheek. "Thank you for always listening. And hearing me out."

"You know I'd be unhappy if you didn't want to share."

She nodded. "The births are the good visions. I had bad ones, too. Shall I move on?"

"Please do."

"On the surface, Covid vaccinations will be available before the end of next year, contrary to what news media will report. Many people will get the jab. Others will resist. The coronavirus is mutating. New strains will be discovered. People will unmask and then be told to wear masks again, especially indoors and with crowds. Within two years, eight and a half million people will be behind in rents. Four million will be evicted. In addition, masses of people will enter the U S and other countries illegally."

"You saw more, didn't you?"

"Yes. The vire will invade Apitcote and put people to sleep. I have an idea how we might combat that problem. I expect the new medics shall be a great help."

"You still don't know exactly what the vire is?"

"As Rene said, it is departed evil spirits from the distant past."

"Should we gather the kew and discuss the evil?"

"I prefer to wait until tonight's kew meeting. Much of what I saw came in flashes. I need time to sort through the information.

And Madeline is at the constat helping Gwen and Harlan prepare tomorrow's Thanksgiving feast. I should spend the day with the dwellers."

"They and all of Apitcote's denizens are fortunate to have you and Madeline here."

"I believe Madd and I are the fortunate ones." VJ watched the flames dance in the fireplace, then looked back at him. "There was an eighth vision, Holt."

He hiked his dark brows. "About?"

"Hanna's mother. Aleece refuses to go to hospital. She needs a ventilator. Without one, she will die. Hanna and Harmony may soon be free to return to Apitcote."

"I don't know whether to be sad about Aleece or happy about Harmony's return."

"I sense you are already mourning and rejoicing. I shall do my best to comfort your sorrow and share your joy."

Embracing her, Holt held her close for a long, unhurried time while they mulled the visions that would surely change their lives and others'.

~ * ~

Dread clutched VJ when it was her turn to speak at the evening kew meeting. "Please seal the dream chamber before I begin."

Holt snapped his fingers. "Done."

VJ had decided to keep the multiple visions to herself and Holt. More than three years would pass before all the babies were born, and she thought everyone should discover their personal news themselves. But she explained what she had seen about the vire.

"When Rene's ancestor, Clairene, could not destroy the evil spirits, she sealed them inside a boulder in a cavern near the karst. The spirits have substance but no form. However, they are growing as microbes mutate and grow, intent on combining their evil into a mighty powerful force. Although the factions don't always agree, they plan to spread a sleeping illness throughout the land that will allow them to take over denizens' bodies, minds and the realm."

"What can we do to stop the evil?" Dane asked.

"I'm hoping the resident medics who graduate in December will help create a cure or an antidote for the sleeping illness."

"That's an excellent idea," Tess said.

"The evil spirits are cunning and have learned much during their years of imprisonment. They relish the idea of fooling humans without us even knowing they are out and about."

"I'm confident," Rene said, "that we can, and will, devise a plan to combat the vire and keep it from harming a single denizen."

Grateful for Rene's verbal support, VJ listened to her mates talk. She was nervous about the evil spirits and trolls. Would she and the resident medics find the combinations to create the serum she hoped to create?

The throbbing in her heart eased a bit as she realized her kew mates were confident they would succeed. But a heavy weight pressed down on her shoulders. She couldn't shake the thought that she might be separated from Holt. Or the visions of Madeline's future. They shared most meals and worked in the same kluster and saw each other daily. VJ cherished those moments because she feared her best female friend might go away and they would not grow old together as they had always hoped. She tried not to think about being parted from Holt. That was much too fearful.

A quick flashback threw her into a tailspin. Would she get trapped by the vire and not see Holt or Madeline again? That vision was the worst ever. Not one she dared mention. She told herself she was not superstitious, but feared discussing it might make it come true. Burying it deep, she plastered a smile on her face and followed Holt down the spiral staircase. As Charles Dickens had written, 'This was the best of times. The worst of times.' A time that both inspired and despaired her soul.

~ * ~

"Your plan for kew parents to eat Thanksgiving dinner with dwellers and then move to a different table to share dessert with their own families worked well," Shelan complimented as Holt took his first bite of pumpkin pie.

"This is a lovely way to spend Thanksgiving after so many years across the pond where Thanksgiving isn't celebrated," Beryl said.

"We appreciate being included in your effort to help the dwellers feel as welcome as everyone has made us feel," Vince added.

Holt grinned. "How are you feeling?"

"Great. You were right about the atmosphere here. It is special. I wake up feeling as young as I did the day Beryl and I eloped more than thirty years ago."

"Have you told your parents you're no longer single?" Verity asked.

Holt knew she had suggested he call them before and after his cancer was in remission, but he hadn't.

"Yes. I explained that Beryl and I are married again. Also that we have a grown daughter who is a doctor. Dad said Mother nearly fainted with the news. Then she grabbed the phone and asked me to forgive them for interfering years ago. She wants to know when they can see Beryl and meet Verity."

"What did you say?"

"I told her we'd call when we're back in the country, also that we have no idea when that might be."

"Did you ever tell them about your cancer?" Verity asked.

"No. We're not that close."

"You didn't see them when I lived with you. That must have been difficult for all of you."

"Not as difficult as you might assume. My parents belong to a country club. Keeping up with their friends has always been more important than spending time with me."

How sad, Holt thought and knew Verity felt the same way when she nudged his knee with hers, and empathy filled her eyes.

"Holt," Kirt said, interrupting his thoughts, "is the friend you worked with at NASA coming to visit at Christmas time?"

"I don't know."

"What's his name?" Beryl asked.

Holt glanced at Verity. "She's referring to Hanna." To his parents, he said. "Hanna hasn't shared her plans for the holidays. Aleece has Covid-19, and she's very ill."

"Perhaps you should send Hanna an atext," Kirt suggested.

"I will." But Holt had no idea what to send. A warning. Condolences. He glanced at Verity again and received a silent suggestion. *Just hearing from you might cheer her during what must be a very difficult time.*

He sent a silent thank you.

She responded by reaching for his hand and squeezing gently.

"Hanna has a little girl named Harmony," Pater explained to Beryl and Vince.

"Has she been here?"

"Harmony was born here. We saw her often until Hanna went back to the surface to take care of her sick mater."

"How old is Harmony?" Madeline asked.

"Fifteen and a half months. She was born on Holt's birthday," Mater said.

The sudden stiffness in Verity's fingers alerted Holt that she was upset because he hadn't told her. He hadn't deliberately not told her. He just hadn't pointed it out.

Feeling guilty because Verity had opened so fully with him, he pushed his other problem ahead. Someday, he would ask Hanna's permission to tell Verity everything. But not while Hanna was consumed with worry for Aleece.

# Eighteen

Jordan's atext summoned them before breakfast. *Mist is in labor. Please meet us at the clinic.*

VJ grabbed her satchel and levitated beside Holt. He stayed with kew mates and Mist's parents, while VJ and Dr. Lorraine encouraged Mist to bear down in the delivery room.

The early birthing was neither difficult nor prolonged. It seemed the first baby wanted to protect the one left behind. VJ was concerned about Mist, though. She started to cry before VJ cut the baby boy's umbilical cord.

"Is he alive?"

"Yes." She smiled when the baby made noise. "He sounds healthy. Dr. Lorraine will examine him to make sure."

"My contractions have stopped. When will the second baby be born?"

"We have to rely on nature for that answer," VJ replied.

Dr. Lorraine finished examining and cleaning the newborn. Wrapped him in a warm blue blanket. Placed him in Mist's arms and smiled. "You have a healthy son."

After monitoring Mist for an hour, VJ said, "Your second baby isn't ready. The twin's birth dates won't match."

Jordan looked thunderstruck. "I've never heard of twins not being born on the same day."

"Such events don't often occur; however, your baby seems to want more time inside before joining you."

"Why?" Jordan asked.

"Mist has two uteruses," Dr. Lorraine reminded. "The babies may have been conceived at different times, which would explain why I didn't hear both heartbeats on the same day months ago."

"Double uteruses are rare," VJ added. "Only one in about two thousand women have two, which means there's a one in fifty million chance of twins being born several weeks apart."

Jordan hiked his brows. "Are you telling us the baby might not be born for weeks?"

"I'm saying it's possible."

"Right," Dr. Lorraine agreed, having had the discussion previously with VJ.

"You kept telling us the babies were different in size," Mist said. "Is the second baby still alive?"

"Yes." VJ smiled. "Enjoy your son and get used to being parents."

"Thanks for being here," Jordan said when kew mates entered Mist's room.

"Any idea when the other baby will be born?" Jordan asked VJ.

"If I were to speculate, I'd say you have about a month."

"That's a long time," Jordan said.

"Is there a test to determine if he or she will live?" Mist asked.

"Dr. Lorraine has already ordered another ultrasound. We should know this afternoon."

The text Jordan sent that evening was only five words. *Baby girl has strong heartbeat.*

~ * ~

"Have Mist and Jordan decided on a name for their son?" Madeline asked at breakfast.

"Joel. A combination of Jordan's name and his mother's, Ellen."

"How clever. I wonder if they've picked a name for their daughter."

VJ smiled. "If not, they have a few weeks to decide."

"You saw that in a vision?"

"I did."

"Anything else I ought to know?"

VJ nodded. "Dwayne's having regrets about your divorce. He's going to initiate a reconciliation before Christmas."

"Not sure I wanted to hear that." Madeline chewed her toast before she spoke again. "You know I moved yesterday while you were with Mist and Jordan."

"Yeah," Holt said. "The cottage on one side of yours is reserved for us."

"My other neighbors are Minalu and Cinnalan. Dom and Orlane share the cottage next to Minalu's, but Nando has requested a cottage in a different kluster. He thinks that will encourage other dwellers to spread out."

"I'm sure it will."

"When do you plan to move?" Madeline asked.

"We could start today. Is it possible to levitate furniture?"

Holt chuckled. "Actually, it is. Should we?"

"I'd love to."

~ * ~

A few days later, Holt and Verity levitated Nando and Tumela to the far side of the karst where the couples parted.

While Tumela and Nando hiked through the tunnel to see Falo, VJ and Holt looked down at the karst. Creepy sensations tainted the pleasure of overlooking the beauty of one of nature's beautiful, unusual formations.

Verity didn't realize she was frowning until Holt touched her wrinkled forehead. "What do you think you will gain from that furrowed brow?"

"Not much."

"You're worried about your visions, aren't you?"

"I'm trying not to be." Shivers crawled down her spine, but she managed a smile. "Worrying makes one suffer more than one ought to."

"Worrying won't change the outcome."

"I know overthinking is overrated, however sometimes my brain won't stop spitting out thoughts or churning potential scenarios."

"Tell me what they are."

"The vire thinks it knows me. It's wrong. My vision indicated it will go after Madeline. Hope tells me it won't be able to control her or me."

"How certain are you that it won't capture you again?"

"I am not certain of anything. I wasn't prepared last time, but I am now. I hope my inner guard will warn me." She twisted the ring on her finger. "I also hope these will help keep me grounded and safe." She patted the hearts on her bracelet, then touched his cheeks. "I want you to be safe, too."

"I'll be on guard."

She wrapped her arms around him. Closed her eyes. And saw creatures as ugly as they were mean. "They're down there."

"What? The evil?"

"And trolls. It's a bloody shame this beautiful place harbors such ugly creatures and evil spirits and the potential destruction of Apitcote, isn't it?"

"Your visions have forewarned us. We will defend Apitcote and defeat whatever we must."

"I love your confidence."

"And I love you."

"I have a nagging feeling we should enjoy each and every day."

Holt caressed her back. "We already are."

In spite of enjoying the quiet time alone with Holt and the unusual beauty surrounding them, an avalanche of relief trooped through VJ when Tumela and Nando returned.

"Papa won't budge," Nando reported.

"We could kidnap him," Tumela said.

"But we won't," Holt disagreed, "however tempting that might be." His tone signaled no room for debate.

Without further discussion, they hooked elbows and levitated home.

Kew mates and Minalu listened while Nando reported, "Papa would not relent. Although Tumela soothed and coaxed, he refused to come here."

Minalu sighed. "I did not expect otherwise."

"He does not look good," Tumela said, sadly. "He is unhappy. Zeg and Pilare are doing their best to cheer him. The only thing that seems to help is baby Fallon."

"If I were to go to him," Minalu said, "he would not welcome me. He thinks I betrayed him by leaving."

"Zeg promised to call if he thinks we should return."

"I am proud that Zeg and his family stay with him."

"Papa wants me and Dom there."

"Then go. With my blessing," Minalu urged.

Nando looked at Dom, a question in his eyes. "He would be pleased to see Orlane."

"We will return," Dom agreed.

~ * ~

Snow ushered in the month of December. Youngsters ran out to play, licking fat fluffy flakes off their lips as they twirled in lighthearted abandon, rolled huge snowballs to build snowmen, made snow angels and engaged in snowball fights. Even adults joined the fun and frolic.

Good will prevailed throughout the realm. People greeted each other with cheerful smiles, happy hearts, and, as they did every holiday season, denizens below wished for world peace above. 'Merry Christmas' and 'Happy Holidays' were often accompanied by, 'and Peace on Earth for all.'

One night, Holt pulled his afone from his pocket and checked his messages. "Got an atext from Hanna."

"How is she?"

He extended his afone. "She sent a photo of Harmony."

Verity admired the photo and read the brief atext. *Thanks for your concern. Harmony is fine.* "Hanna didn't mention herself or her mum. Have you tried calling her again?"

"Yeah. Her afone rings but doesn't go to voice mail. I have a feeling something's wrong."

Verity caressed his cheek. "Her mum is ill. She's likely very worried."

"Yeah. She's alone. Doesn't have any family except her mater and Harmony." He wrapped his arms around Verity, taking the comfort she offered by holding him close. "Hanna was a good friend when I needed one. If she needs one now, I'd like to help."

"You could send a text and offer to."

"I'll do that."

But days sped by and Hanna didn't reply.

Shoppers rushed home to wrap gifts. Denizens decorated trees and cottages, both inside and out. Klusters vied to depict the prettiest decorations, the most lights, the cleverest panoramas. Millions of lights twinkled throughout the realm and families strolled around after dark to enjoy displays, often stopping to visit and share hot drinks.

"I almost feel like a child again," Madeline said as they sipped tea in the new constat one afternoon. "I don't want any Christmas gifts. Being here is enough."

"I agree, although I feel special—because I have Holt and his love."

"I'm so happy for you, Ver."

"I'm happy we're both here, that our dream to live close has come true."

"Me, too." Madeline sipped more tea. "Dwayne sent a text last night. Your vision of him wanting to reconcile happened."

"Did you reply to his text?"

"Yes. I decided it would be cruel not to. Told him I'm not returning. I'm so glad Shelan and Kirt brought us here."

As Madeline topped their tea, she said, "I'm still getting flowers every week."

VJ laughed. "Mine haven't stopped either. Every Friday a new bouquet is delivered to replace the one that's ready for the dustbin, I mean the compost plot."

"Righto." Madeline's laughter joined VJ's. "Occasionally, I get gifts. I've added a miniature crystal teapot and a tiny silver Aladdin's lamp to the curio cabinet you and Holt gave me as a house warming gift. A few months ago, life was terribly dull. Now, we live extraordinary lives where magic reigns. This is exactly where I want to be."

"I feel the same."

"Thousands of denizens live here. I don't know all their names, but someday I hope to."

"You know the most important name."

Madeline sighed. "Dom. Just saying his name makes me quiver. I've never felt like this about a man. I love him, but I'm afraid to trust what I feel."

"If he's right for you, you'll know when the time comes."

"I love Orlane, too."

"I know. Your eyes glowed when you were together."

"Dom has called every night since he and Nando returned to the dwelling. He said Orlane cried for her mum only once. That's kind of sad, isn't it?"

VJ nodded. "Dom was right to bring her with him. Does he say how Falo is?"

"Not good. Orlane and baby Fallon are the only ones who please him." Madeline pursed her lips. "Let's talk about something happy. I never dreamed we would have so many of the same friends. I love them all."

"Do you enjoy working with Gwen and Harley, planning menus for the dwellers?"

"Yes. They suggested asking Dom to work here when he returns. He said he dreamed about me. That's why he went to the surface long ago—to find me. When he met Ilma, he thought she was the girl he dreamed about. He was disappointed when he realized she wasn't. And when he saw me here, he was bowled over."

"Sounds like you're getting serious."

"It's way too soon for that. But I am looking forward to seeing him when he returns. Orlane is a special bonus."

"You miss them."

"I do, but they need to be with Falo."

VJ nodded but said nothing. She knew Falo's days were numbered.

# *Nineteen*

At the evening kew meeting, Holt gave an updated report on the new surface community. "The seekers have selected a name for their new home. POE—Paradise on Earth. Our cameras count the number of new seekers arriving each day. Good news is there aren't as many as we anticipated."

"Our team is dealing with them, so there's no need for a trip to the surface," Monteith concluded.

"Someone should go to the dwelling," VJ said. "Falo is ill, and we should provide food if the men need some."

"Who's free to go?" Holt asked.

"I am," Verity said.

"Monteith and I are," Juhree added.

"Us, too," Drew said.

"And us," Dane added.

The eight left early the next day.

At the dwelling, Falo's lifetime friend, Yoka, greeted them; his expression looked grave. "Falo is unconscious."

"We should take him to Minalu," Juhree said.

As the oldest son, Dom spoke for the family. "We agree."

"Can you conjure a proper stretcher to airlift him?" VJ asked Juhree.

"Certainly."

Dane and Drew levitated Falo onto the conjured stretcher and buckled him inside fluffy duvets. Other kew mates clasped Dom, Nando, Zeg and Pilare's elbows. Rene took baby Fallon in her arms. Dom kept Orlane in his.

Yoka and the men all looked as though they had lost their dearest friend.

"The invitation to live in our village remains open," Holt said. "Your pallet mates, kidlings, and our denizens will welcome you with open arms."

"We will discuss this," Yoka said, his gaze solemn. "We appreciate all the food you have provided, and your concern for us and Falo."

~ * ~

In Minalu's cottage, Falo stirred, opened his bloodshot eyes and stared at her. At Cinnalan. At each of his sons. Too delirious to speak, he closed his eyes. And slept again.

VJ and Holt guided Zeg's family to a nearby cottage. "This is where you may live."

Pilare's eyes brightened. "It's lovelier than I hoped to imagine."

"Are you planning to stay?" VJ asked.

"Probably," Zeg said. "We enjoyed managing the farm but missed being near family."

"Where are your relatives, Pilare?"

"Scattered around the country. We hope to visit them occasionally, but we think this is where we would like to live."

"If we do," Zeg said, "I'll talk to your father and recommend the tenant couple we left in charge to take over managing the farm."

"I'm sure Dad will appreciate your advice."

~ * ~

Falo died four days later.

Without his leadership, sept men left the dwelling and trudged to the valley, carrying their possessions on their backs. Their loads were light, worldly goods few.

Sensing their arrival, Holt alerted kew mates and they met the new arrivals at the edge of the south forest where the dwellers had stopped to stare at the first People Mover.

"You have arrived in time for Falo's funeral," Holt said. "Also, to celebrate Winter Solstice, and to enjoy Christmas, reunited with your sept."

"That is good," Yoka said as men pointed at the rainbow-colored People Mover. "What is that?" he asked.

"We call it a People Mover," Holt explained. "Apitcote has several magic conveyances. Come, let us teach you how to use this one."

Slack-jawed, the men tromped close. A few managed to step on without stumbling. Others were too hesitant to try. Sensing their trepidation, Holt sent a charm to calm them. After that, they grinned and walked on, heads held high. By the time they reached kluster twenty-four, all were preening.

Sept women, kidlings and the eight men all welcomed them to their new homes.

~ * ~

"Seeing the sept reunion was a sight I wouldn't have wanted to miss," Verity said as she sat beside Holt in their cottage that evening.

"Nor I," he agreed.

"They reminded you of Harmony, didn't they?"

Holt nodded. "Hanna sent an atext. Aleece isn't expected to live much longer."

"Is she still at home?"

He nodded. "Hanna's college friend is staying with them to help take care of Harmony so Hanna has more time with Aleece."

"Do you want to bring Harmony here?"

Holt wanted that desperately, but he said, "Having a child around is a full-time responsibility. One of us would have to quit..."

Verity touched his lips with one finger. "Neither of us would have to stop doing what we enjoy. Apitcote has abundant caretakers and caregivers, as you well know. Venes adore watching preschool children, and denizens all help each other, especially our kew mates. Every denizen will not only be willing to help, they will want to."

Having Harmony with them was a deep-seated desire. But until they dealt with the vire, Holt thought she would be safer on the surface. "If we bring Harmony here now, she would live with us. Sleep in our cottage every night. We would have to ensure that she eats, sleeps, and dresses properly. We would be responsible for another life. That's a lot to have thrust upon a newly tied couple."

"I agree. But you love Harmony, and together we can, and will, do whatever is necessary."

"Have you had a vision about Hanna?"

"No. However, the doctor part of me is concerned about her health. She could get Covid. We must be prepared for the possibility that Harmony might live with us before she turns five."

Holt blinked. "I never meant to imply that Harmony will live with us. In Api, if a couple isn't tied, women raise their daughters and men raise their sons."

"So that's how it works. I wondered why there aren't any disputes if parents aren't tied."

Holt smiled. "You could have asked."

Verity grinned. "Blimey. You're right. I should have."

~ * ~

"Falo's funeral was sad," VJ said after dwellers paid tribute to the man who had slept at Minalu's side for so many years.

"Papa's death placed a pall over our lives," Dom said. "We plan to encourage everyone to put grief behind, celebrate his life, and be thankful for the years we shared."

"That's a healthy attitude," Holt said.

"The men look good in their new clothes," Madeline observed. "And the women and kidlings are delighted to have them here. Our new kluster social committee is planning a 'Do'—a party to introduce the men to the joy of monthly holidays."

"Do you think the committee will teach the men to sing and dance and play as they taught the women and kidlings?" Holt asked.

"That's part of their plan."

"Will they succeed?"

VJ grinned. She hadn't had a vision, but she didn't have a single doubt. "Absolutely."

"When is the 'Do?'"

"Saturday. In the new cultural hall. Dwellers are looking forward to sharing it with the newly arrived sept men.

As Holt talked with men from the dwelling, VJ scanned the cultural hall where dwellers and denizens had gathered after Falo's service. All had shed tears. Cinnalan still had some in her eyes. VJ walked to her. "Are you all right, Cinnalan?"

"Yes, but I love Papa, and now I will never see him again."

"It's very difficult to lose people we love," VJ consoled.

Cinnalan wiped her tears. "Isn't it wonderful that we have baby Fallon and Orlane to help us during this sad time?"

"It surely is," VJ agreed.

"What's bothering you?" Holt asked, joining her when she stood alone, staring out a window.

VJ touched the hearts on her bracelet. "Not a lot. However, I was wondering when, or if, I'll ever see my sisters again. I missed both of their weddings and haven't met my nieces or nephews."

"Someday, we'll travel to England, and you will spend as much time as you desire with them," Holt promised.

VJ summoned a smile, hoping that was a promise he could keep.

~ * ~

"The 'Do' was hugely successful," Madeline said as she strolled home with VJ, Holt, Dom and Olane in the crisp cold night air. "Everyone enjoyed the games and had scads of fun."

"The soiree added cheer to the season," VJ agreed.

"What did you like best?" Madeline asked Orlane.

"Jingle bells, jingle bells," Orlane sang. "I liked singing."

Dom swung Orlane from his shoulders to his arms. "Did you have fun tonight, dumpling?"

Orlane nodded with the most enthusiasm VJ had seen from the frail little girl. Raising her hand, Orlane twirled her candy cane. "Treat. Sweet. Yum. Yum."

Other than singing, those were the most words VJ had heard her say. "Has her appetite improved?"

"Most of the time she picks at her food," Dom said. "But she does eat one decent meal each day."

"Have you considered giving her chewable vitamins?"

"Yeah. She likes those. Calls them yum-yums."

A siren blasted through the dark night air.

"There's a fire in the Venes kluster," Holt announced, staring at his afone.

"We're needed," VJ said. "Let's go."

~ * ~

At home, hours later, Verity observed, "Doctors and medics worked together very well, taking care of burns and smoke inhalation patients. And kew mates knew exactly what to do so there was no confusion. It was like a miracle."

Holt squeezed her hand. "Good magic is a miracle."

"I'm still learning that. And Juhree's ability to repair damaged cottages and property was no less miraculous."

He grinned. "Her Grandmater Care was a great help."

"Yes. We are all fortunate they have such magical gifts. Do you know what caused the fire?"

"A few children from a nearby kluster started a bonfire to make s'mores. They added too many logs. Let the flames burn out of control."

"That's a relief. I was afraid it might have been caused by the vire."

Knowing she rarely stopped worrying, Holt drew her close to comfort her and cast a charm to help her sleep.

~ * ~

Monday night, six denizens wearing yellow lab coats gathered around VJ and Holt as they shared the evening meal with Madeline.

"May we introduce ourselves?" one man asked.

"Please do," VJ invited.

"We're the newly graduated medical students," one said. "I'm Judy."

"I'm Jim, her One. We tied while you were in quarantine."

"Congratulations."

"Thanks."

The other four—Kathy, Paul, Dan and Kaye—took turns introducing themselves. "We call ourselves Rezees," Kathy explained. "Our lab coats tell denizens we're in the final stage of our training."

"We're all looking forward to working in the lab with you, Dr. Verity."

"I'm sure the pleasure will be mine."

"Will I have to schedule an appointment to see you?" Holt asked, after they left.

"Never," VJ promised.

"The 'Do' put me in the Christmas spirit," Madeline said as they strolled home. "This will be my happiest ever."

"Mine, too," Holt agreed.

"Our first of many," VJ added, constantly worried about the vire. To push the evil spirits from her mind, she said, "Tell us how Christmas day is celebrated here, Holt."

"Same as Christians celebrate on the surface. We don't work on the special day. Meals are prepared ahead and available for pick-up Christmas Eve to take home after kluster parties. For those who miss parties, kew mates use magic to door dash food. We enjoy a leisurely day, visit relatives and friends, exchange gifts, discuss the past year and consider the year ahead."

"Are there any denizens who don't celebrate Christmas?" VJ asked.

"Yes. Some gather and celebrate in their own fashion. Others spend the day alone, but all tend to enjoy the day off."

Madeline smiled. "I plan to deliver my gifts to every dweller early. I'd like to spend most of the day with you, if that fits your plans."

"It does."

Madeline's eyes sparkled. "I hope Orlane enjoys the day."

"I'm sure she will."

At home, VJ shivered, and rubbed her hands together to warm them.

"What's wrong?" Holt asked.

"Winter Solstice is Monday. The official start of winter. I'm concerned because Celtic traditions and Germanic lore include the belief that Solstice is a time for troublesome spirits to walk the earth, and Zorostrian reflections warn that Solstice is a long night full of evil spirits. Do you think the evil will invade Apitcote that night?"

"Winter solstice is considered a turning point in the year in many cultures," Holt said. "I've been told that years ago, our ancestors celebrated as pagans did. Took a live tree inside so wood spirits had a place to keep warm during the cold winter months. Food and treats were hung on branches for the spirits to eat. That tradition ceased many decades before I was born. We treat Solstice as a festival of light spreading from dark, and denizens light candles in every kluster and have a sing-song, along with hot drinks.”

“Good.” The apprehension stealing through VJ melted. “We won’t think about doom and gloom. That’s why our kew mates are confident we will overcome the vire.”

“Exactly.” Holt tapped her chin gently. “No need to worry more than once, remember?”

“Yes.” No longer shivering, she added, “I shall not need to endeavor to enjoy this happy season. I already am, made more joyful because I am with you. Ta and cheers and every other word that means thank you, Holt.”

He responded by gathering her close and loving her all through the night.

~ * ~

Christmas morning Holt awakened with a smile. As Verity stirred, he said, “Merry Christmas, Dr. Mackay.”

“Same to you, Arcane Holt,” she murmured, grinning. “What should we do first?”

“Open presents.”

“Right, man of my heart.”

When she opened Holt’s last gift, she squealed in delight. “A new medical satchel. Smells like leather.”

“Do you like it?”

“Of course. I love it. Not as much as I love you, though.” Opening the bag, she exclaimed, “It contains all of Apitcote’s medical gizmos. How wonderful. Thank you.”

“You’re welcome.”

She nodded at the small pine tree they had decorated with orange lights, yellow ornaments and shimmering gold tinsel. “I love our tree. I don't want to undecorate when the Christmas season ends."

"Should I miniaturize the tree before the needles fall off?"

"Yes. In a few days. That way we can enjoy it all year."

His grin expanded. "Every year."

Her last gift for him was a gold wedding band. "Will you wear it?"

"Sure. Why wouldn't I?"

Verity shrugged. "I don't know, but you gave me a ring, so I wanted you to have one. And," she winked, "I want to brand you as mine."

"You branded me and my heart the first time I saw you."

She swiped the moisture at the corners of her eyes. "I'm so happy I might cry."

He pulled her close. "I have a better idea. Let's kiss instead."

They were still in each other's arms when the doorbell chimed.

Hand in hand they strolled to open it.

"Merry Christmas," Minalu and her family, including Tumela and Madeline, trilled.

"We promised to show Orlane Christmas trees today," Cinnalan announced. "May we show her yours, Dr. Verity and Mr. Holt?"

"Certainly. Do come through." All ten trooped in. The small cottage didn't feel small. Or the space confined. It felt cozy. Perfect, Holt decided, like his One.

Orlane pointed at their tree. "Pretty."

"Wow," Cinnalan added. "It is. Really pretty. And different."

"Quite unlike any other anywhere in the world," Madeline surmised.

"We brought presents." Cinnalan's eyes glowed as she extended two.

Verity looked a bit overwhelmed when the others extended gifts. "You shouldn't have."

"This is our first Christmas to have the opportunity to give gifts," Cinnalan said, still grinning. "And we had so much fun buying and wrapping them."

Madeline laughed when Verity glanced at her. "Yes. I helped them decide what to buy. It was quite the most fun I've ever had shopping."

"We enjoyed our shopping spree." Holt motioned beneath their tree, winking at Cinnalan. "Will you help me distribute our gifts, poppet?"

"Oh, yes, Mr. Holt."

"You bought one for all of us," she said after she handed three to Zeg and Pilare.

As they opened gifts, Holt watched Nando and Tumela, holding hands, smiling at each other, squeezing fingers. Oblivious to the others, the couple didn't seem to care who saw them embrace. Perhaps because they had grown up in such close confines where there was little or no privacy except at night when the cave was pitch black.

Nando looked up, saw Holt's stare and announced, "We have agreed to mate. Will you celebrate our joining with us?"

"Sure," Holt replied.

"When?" Verity asked.

"To honor Falo," Tumela said, "We will wait ten moon cycles before we choose a date."

Holt glanced at Minalu and read approval in her dark eyes.

When they left, Madeline whispered, "I'll be back soon."

"Do you think she'll return alone?"

Verity shook her head. "I doubt Orlane and Dom will let her out of their sight today. All three look smitten when they're together."

"Tumela seems to be over her fixation on Dominic."

"And her crush on you."

Holt chuckled. "Tumela is sweet, but not shy."

Verity swatted him playfully. "How would you describe me?"

"There are not enough words to describe you, so I will use only one. Perfect." Bending his head, he kissed her, long and leisurely.

On Christmas night when they were back home by themselves, after visiting parents and kew mates with Madeline, Dom and Orlane, Hanna called. She had set up Facetime and Holt saw Aleece sitting in her wheelchair near the Christmas tree. Harmony stood beside her. Love swept through him. Seeing Harmony always thrilled him.

"Merry Christmas," Hanna said.

"Merry Christmas to you. How is everyone?"

"We're all good, including Mom. Say 'hello' and wave."

Aleece looked shrunken and frail. Her tired eyes indicated she would soon be gone. Verity squeezed Holt's wrist, letting him know she sensed his thought.

"Harmony wants to show you what Santa brought." Hanna's screen captured Harmony up close, holding a doll.

"San-ta brought me ba-bee siz-ter." She thrust the doll in front of her face. "See. Pret-tee, lit-tel baby siz-ter. She sweeps a-lot. See." Harmony cradled the doll whose eyes closed. "She wikes me. I wike her."

"I like you," Holt said, pleased with Harmony's reaction to his gift.

Her grin deepened her twin dimples. "I wike you. I wub you. I wanna see you."

"You can see me on the phone, can't you."

"Yez." Harmony set her doll down and pulled Hanna's phone closer. "Mer-ree Chriz-maz, Miz-ter Holt." Spying Verity, she added, "Mer-ree Chriz-mas pri-tee waidey."

"The pretty lady's name is Doctor Verity," Holt said.

"Dok-ter Bera-tee," Harmony repeated. "Dok-ter Bera-tee. I wike Dok-ter Bera-tee."

"And I like you," Verity said.

"I kiss you." Harmony kissed Hanna's phone. "Kiss me."

Verity dutifully kissed Holt's afone.

"Have you had a nice day?" Hanna asked, when she retrieved her afone.

"One of our best," Holt said. "How about you?"

"One of our best as well. And probably Mom's last Christmas."

"Do you want us to come to the surface?" Holt asked.

"No. Covid is still rampant. Stay where you are and be safe."

"You do the same," was all he could think to say.

"I need to get Mom's inhaler," Hanna said when Aleece began to cough. "Happy New Year."

"Same to you."

"You handled the conversation very well," Verity said.

"I felt choked up."

"I could tell."

"Harmony's talking a blue streak."

Verity smiled. "Most toddlers don't start talking that well until they're nearly two."

"Yeah. She's special."

"Right, and I adore her. We're going to be fine, Holt. I promise."

"How can I thank you?"

"You already did when you pledged your troth on our tying day."

"I pledged my heart before our tying day."

"Me too, actually. We're soul mates, Holt. The future is ours."

He smiled, a tender smile. "I do love you more each day."

"Diddo, Miz-ter Holt."

His burst of laughter echoed through the cottage. "Merry Christmas, pri-tee waidey."

Sitting beside Holt on the settee while he dozed, VJ waited to hear from Jordan and Mist.

When her afone rang, she pulled it to her ear and answered quietly. "Hello."

"Jordan here. Mist's water broke and she's having contractions."

"Meet us at the clinic," she said.

"Will do."

"What time is it?" Holt asked groggily.

"Ten forty-five."

"Can't be. It's still dark outside."

VJ grinned as he rubbed his eyes. "You only slept a few minutes. That was Jordan. Mist is in labor."

Holt came fully awake. "You did say the baby would be born tonight."

"She has more than an hour to deliver her Christmas baby. Should be plenty of time. Mist's first delivery was easier than most."

The baby girl arrived at eleven-thirty.

Another hour passed before VJ joined Holt in the waiting room.

"Was it a difficult birth?" he asked.

"No. But the afterbirth took longer than I anticipated."

"Is Mist okay?"

"She's fine. As is the baby. They decided to name her N-o-e-l."

"Goes with the season, and rhymes with her brother, Joel."

"Joel has one syllable. Noel has two. And according to Jordan, they are going to be super-duper kidlings."

"And spoiled?

Verity grinned. "Probably."

# Twenty

"The week between Christmas and New Year is always a favorite," Holt said as he and Verity waited for Madeline to join them for breakfast.

"I love the slowed down pace."

"Kind of like the lull before the storm?"

Verity nodded. "I'm concerned about my visions. Sometimes I feel like we're flogging a dead horse—trying to find a solution that's unsolvable. I've wracked my brain but can't think of anything we can do to keep the vire away."

Holt swallowed his reply as Madeline arrived. "Today is Boxing Day in England."

"Do you have plans?"

"Yes. Dom and I organized a kayaking day for children."

Minalu approached, her expression grave. "I apologize for interrupting, but I need to speak to Dr. Verity."

"Is something wrong?" Verity asked.

"Cinnalan had an experience she wishes to share. May we schedule an appointment? Today, if possible. If not, tomorrow."

"How about tonight?" Holt suggested.

"What time?"

"Seven."

"Tonight is good. We would like kew mates and Madeline there as well."

"We'll tell them," VJ said.

Minalu attempted a smile, but her eyes were worry filled.

"She's upset," Holt said as Minalu ambled away. "I couldn't read her. Never have been able to. Think she's still mourning for Falo?"

"I think she regrets his death but something else troubles her at the moment."

"She didn't sound panicked, but I sensed immediacy."

"I sensed the same. The kew could meet now."

"I'll catch Minalu and ask if she prefers earlier. If so, I'll communicate with our kew."

Moments later, Holt returned. "Everyone has agreed to meet at the chateau in fifteen minutes."

~ * ~

Minalu sat beside Cinnalan on the wall-to-wall mattress, facing kew mates who leaned on cushions stacked against one wall, trying to look relaxed, hoping to make their guests feel welcome. Rance and Abee were downstairs, being minded by Rene's parents. Baby Joel lay cuddled in Jordan's arms. Baby Noel slept in Mist's.

Questions rattled through kew mates' minds, but no one had answers to silently share. As usual, Minalu's mind was closed. Holt hadn't been able to 'read' Cinnalan or 'delve' either. She was also closed. He sensed she wasn't just nervous. She was frightened.

He started the gathering by saying, "We're here to listen to Cinnalan."

She adjusted her position, sat up straighter. "Can you fix this room so no one can hear us?"

"Of course." Holt snapped his fingers, and sealed the chamber.

Cinnalan drew in a long breath. "A huge bird that cannot fly came to the valley last night. He told me something evil will put people to sleep and steal babies." She stared at Jordan and Mist. "I fear they might steal yours, and I am scared for them. They will be taken to a dark place that has no light."

Minalu patted Cinnalan's back while Jordan and Mist snuggled their infants closer.

"They must never be alone," Verity said.

"Right." Holt gentled his tone. "Did you talk to the bird, Cinnalan?"

"Silently. He talks but didn't want to out loud because the evil might hear. He doesn't want to help steal babies, but he will because he says he must. You have to keep your babies safe." She stared at Jordan and Mist again. "In the awful dark place, they will cry and no one will be there to feed or comfort them before they finally go to sleep."

"Did anyone else see the bird?" Verity asked.

Cinnalan shook her head. "He is invisible, but I could see him. His name is Shadow."

Chills dashed down Holt's spine. "Do you know what else might happen in the dark place?"

"Madeline will find the babies, but I fear they will not wake up until the evil can control them."

"Do you know when they will be taken away?"

"Shadow said when the ground is warm like summer. I think he gave me the warning so we could be prepared."

Concern filled all kew mates' eyes as each pondered what Cinnalan had said.

Verity broke the eerie silence. "The bird is a cassowary. I see him in a dark cavern—on the north side of the karst." She turned her gaze to Madeline. "Holt and I will find you."

"I am scared," Cinnalan said.

"You're not the only one." Mist's voice quivered before she kissed baby Noel's cheek.

"May I speak?" Minalu asked.

"Of course.

"I have what some call magic. I see what others do not see. I call myself a seer. You call it a visionary—as Dr. Verity and Rene are. My sept is a matriarchal society. I accepted leadership soon after Cinnalan was born. Falo anticipated I would be much older and did not like when my Amma stepped aside, and I arose from birthing pallet early to assume responsibility. Falo did not like my magic. He said it made me too powerful. I have always felt it to be a burden. You may want to know what I do. I make fire with a twist of my wrist. I make calm when calm is needed. I know when someone in my sept is ailing. When any dweller needs companionship. When one needs help. Or cheering. I see harm before it happens. I see bad. I see good also. Like kew sisters, I see extraordinary events."

Minalu paused, waited for questions.

"Can you tell us anything about the sleeping illness that will come?" Verity asked while Holt was still forming the question. "Will it be curable?"

Minalu's gaze lingered on each individual before she answered. "I do not know. However, I do know baby Fallon may be a threat to all who live in this village."

There were no gasps of surprise. Everyone, including Madeline, knew there was already a threat in the realm.

"Baby Fallon does not have the coronavirus," Minalu added. "However, a rash has attached to his feet and may spread to others."

Once again, complete silence filled the dream chamber.

"There is more," Minalu said. "Pilare will get the rash next. Zeg will suffer with the rash as well."

"When?" Verity asked.

"On first day of new year."

Holt riveted his eyes on Rene. "You and Drew are healers. Can you help them?"

"We'll try. I have a cream that should ease discomfort."

"I love my family," Minalu continued, "and I will give my life for baby Fallon. My greatest fear is that others will be infected, and my sept will be blamed. Is there a way to pull the rash from baby Fallon and insert it into my body if it requires a host?"

Verity shook her head. "I haven't heard of that happening, although I believe anything is possible."

"If not, I shall take Fallon to the dwelling. Perhaps distance will keep the rash from spreading here. Zeg and Pilare will go as well. They have already agreed."

"No one will want you to leave," Rene said. "We're Sensitives and Adepts. We read Pilare and Zeg prior to traveling through the veil. They are good humans."

"And I smell disease," Verity added. "They were not diseased when they entered the realm."

"If my body can hold the rash instead of Fallon," Minalu said, "I am willing to forfeit my life."

"Death is not a solution," Verity said before anyone could voice the questions spiking through their minds. "Baby Fallon must not die. If he did, the rash could explode and expand. Contaminate the air we breathe."

Stunned expressions covered everyone's faces.

"We should share this news with denizens," Mist said.

"I prefer not," Minalu said. "We do not want them to resent us."

"They will not resent you, Zeg, Pilare or baby Fallon. All will be concerned and offer to help."

"Rene is right," Tess said. "No one will blame anyone."

"We don't keep secrets from the public," Dane added. "Being informed is what makes our realm function smoothly."

Rene nodded. "Perhaps we could delay the news until Friday, when the holiday season ends and allow everyone to enjoy what remains of this special time of year."

"Good suggestion," Drew agreed. "January first is soon enough. In the meantime, we'll work with Zeg and Pilare and try to contain the contagion."

"Will you announce who the carrier is?" asked Madeline.

Holt nodded. "There's no need to keep it a secret. Knowledge is often a weapon against the enemy."

"I agree," Monteith said. "All denizens have the right to know something could attack or attach."

A squeak escaped Verity's throat before she said, "I know what causes the rash."

"What?"

"Slime." She looked as surprised as everyone else as she added, "It attached last night when Pilare and Zeg took Fallon for a midnight walk." She looked at Minalu. "The slime attached here. In the valley. Not on the surface. It could have attached to anyone."

Holt knew she had seen that in a vision. "Illness has found its way to Apitcote."

"Not illness," Verity disagreed. "Slime. The evil spirits are slime."

Dread spun through Holt as she added, "The slime is invisible, and it's spreading and clinging to Zeg's and Pilare's possessions."

"We should burn everything," Dane said.

"Right," Rene agreed. "Dane and Holt have heat. They can incinerate."

"Do you think Zeg and Pilare would object to me examining baby Fallon?" Verity asked.

"I know they will not," Minalu replied.

"I'll go with you," Holt said. "We should wear klir seal suits and mask up."

"Might be wiser to go by myself."

"We're partners. You risk, I risk."

"We're kew mates," Dane added. "And all on the same team."

"Right," Tess agreed. "One risks, we all risk. When I was enslaved in Brazil, the entire kew risked their lives to free me, and bring me home."

"Time to suit up," Rene announced, opening windows to collect elements from Mater Nature.

After everyone donned klir seal suits with hooded masks, they levitated to kluster twenty-four.

Baby Fallon was asleep when they arrived. Awake before VJ inhaled and confirmed he did not carry coronavirus bacterium or any other disease. But she smelled a familiar scent. "There's a noxious odor, similar to the one attached to Veralane's shoes weeks ago. The rash on Fallon's feet is unfamiliar. I'll draw a prick of blood and have it analyzed." Squaring her shoulders, VJ continued. "We think your possessions should be burned, Pilare. Please don't fret," she added, at her crestfallen expression. "Juhree offered to conjure everything we destroy."

As Zeg and Pilare collected clothes and oddments, Dane and Holt used heat to disintegrate their belongings.

"What do you do when you have rubbish?" VJ asked when she saw no ashes or dust.

"We have zero waste," Holt replied. "We incinerate, recycle or repurpose."

"Do you need magic to do that?"

"Yes," Dane answered, "and technology."

Juhree conjured a solution, and kew mates sanitized every inch of the cottage. Then she conjured again, replacing old clothes with new, along with cherished oddments, while Minalu held and cooed to baby Fallon as he fussed and grabbed at the soles of his red feet.

VJ pulled a jar from her satchel and applied salve Rene had given her.

"Thank you," Pilare said when Fallon stopped fussing.

"My pleasure," VJ said. "I smell no internal problem. No disease."

"I scanned baby Fallon," Rene added. "As Dr. Verity said, something attached to his feet that caused the rash. Drew and I would like to scan both of you to determine if you have any evidence of disease or the anticipated rash."

"Please do," Zeg invited.

Rene and Drew used small oblong instruments to scan the couple from the tops of their heads to the tips of their toes. "I found nothing," Drew announced when he finished with Zeg.

"Nor did I," Rene said as she finished with Pilare.

VJ inhaled, and silently agreed.

Zeg and Pilare withdrew to shower before donning the new clothes Juhree conjured.

"Perhaps it's time to implement the DGP—Disaster Guide Plan," Rene said. "For those who don't know what it is—at the turn of the century, the Ancients who governed Apitcote foresaw events that could transpire after they were gone and wrote a Disaster Guide Plan for us to follow. I suggest we be the team to implement their plan."

"I agree," Dane said.

"As do I," Holt added, having re-read the DGP twice after VJ's disturbing visions. "Apitcote has twenty-one residential klusters. I suggest each of us assumes the responsibility for two or more. Responsibility is the wrong word. Our jobs are to be the go-to person for anyone who has questions. We'll share concerns, provide information, report back to each other, and so on."

"How will we decide who assumes leadership for klusters?" VJ asked.

"We all know which are right for us," Rene said. "The kluster with the chateau is mine. As is the Ancients' kluster." She nodded at Drew. "Yours?"

"Klusters six and seven. Having them side by side will be convenient for denizens as well as for me."

"I'll take klusters twelve and thirteen," Tess said.

After each kew mate named their klusters, Cinnalan said, "That was very logical. You all chose klusters you live in or where you visit the most."

Holt smiled fondly. "That's right, poppet."

"No one chose ours."

Kew mates communicated silently, agreed to ask Madeline, and wanted VJ to do the asking.

She turned to Madeline. "We want you to take on the task of leading kluster twenty-four."

"I haven't been here long enough to be a kluster advisor. I'm not capable."

"Of course you are," VJ disagreed.

"I have no leadership experience whatsoever."

"You have what you need."

"I feel inept and overwhelmed."

"Because you are logical."

Madeline managed a weak smile.

VJ reached for her hands. "Are you frightened, Madd?"

"Yes."

"You're not alone. We all are, but we will be nearby to help." VJ allowed a smile to swim across her face. "So, will you accept the additional job of being a kluster go-to?"

Madeline swallowed, still looking a bit dumbfounded. "I suppose I could give it a go."

"Thank you."

"Denizens are taught the DGP in school, and teachers review the guide every year," Tess explained for those who hadn't grown up in Api. "I suggest asking teachers to start a refresher class immediately. A crash course should be taught in kluster twenty-four for those who are not familiar with the plan."

"Good suggestion," VJ agreed. "I'll attend that course."

"Me, too," Madeline said, looking a bit less stunned.

"Great," Jordan said. "Juhree, Drew, and I need to learn the plan as well."

"I'll publish the class schedule," Mist said, "and have it announced on TV. I'll also post it online."

"If the rash turns into a pandemic, denizens should be prepared to self-isolate and reduce or cease travel between klusters," Dane said. "The slime must be contained."

"The slime is invisible," Monteith reminded. "We've already stopped most travel to and from the surface. Should we cease travel between klusters as well?"

"What do you think?" Tess asked VJ.

"I don't think that's necessary yet; however, we meet daily so we can make decisions as needed."

"Right," Jordan said. "Mist needs time to prepare what to report on TV. I suggest someone call or visit school teachers today."

"Communicating is my job," Mist reminded, embracing Noel protectively, "although I have so many thoughts spinning through my head, I'm not quite sure where to begin."

"You'll sort them out," Rene said, "you always do, and if Verity agrees, she and I will go with you."

"Thank you," Mist said.

Pilare and Zeg returned from showering, garbed in new clothes.

"We hope to halt the contagion before it spreads," Dane said. "But we don't know how to combat an invisible slime."

"We're willing to do anything to help," Zeg said.

Verity gave a slight nod. "Tell us where you were last night."

"Fallon woke up in a playful mood a few hours after he went to sleep. We put him in the pram and took him for a walk, hoping that would make him sleepy again."

"Did you use People Movers?" VJ asked to confirm her vision.

"Yes. We rode them from one end of the valley to the other."

"Did you keep Fallon in the pram the entire time?"

"No. We stopped once and stood him on his feet near the last People Mover by the forest."

"Did you see anyone whilst you were out and about?"

"No."

VJ cleared her throat. "You may help by staying inside until either I or another doctor or medic gives permission for you to go out again."

"We will," Zeg promised.

"Do not allow visitors inside your cottage. Minalu can explain how to order meals and have them delivered to your stoop." She glanced around at everyone. "Do we all agree to wait until New Year's day to share the news with the populace?"

"Yes," Holt said, and VJ saw approval in Minalu's eyes.

"It's bound to be a gloomy holiday," Juhree surmised.

VJ sent a silent message to Holt. *"I saw the sleeping illness. I did not foresee the rash."*

*"You can't foresee and predict everything."*

*"I think they are connected."*

*"I don't know whether to be relieved or more disturbed."*

*"Let's try not to worry about the sleeping illness. We need to get through the rash problem first."*

"Right. Deal with one problem at a time."

~ * ~

At dusk on the first day of the new year, the merry tune 'Twinkle, Twinkle Little Star" played throughout the realm as Verity and Holt walked home after the evening meal.

"Outdoor music is lovely," Verity said.

"That tune is our kew's designated song," Holt explained. "We use music to alert denizens that Mist is about to deliver a message from the kew on TV."

Inside their cottage, he turned on the telly, and watched Mist report the news about the invisible slime and anticipated rash.

Denizens accepted the news with equanimity. There were no murmurs of fear. Merely acceptance of facts and concern for Pilare, Zeg and baby Fallon.

When Zeg called, VJ was prepared. "Pilare has the rash. Her cheeks are so red she looks like she's been slapped."

"I'll be there in a jiffy." Suited and masked, VJ dashed to the cottage a few hundred meters away.

Zeg opened the door before she rang the bell. "Pilare is so miserable she can barely lift her head. I told her to stop trying."

"Where is she?"

"In bed."

VJ hurried to the bedroom. Pilare's eyes were closed. VJ uncovered her and lifted her night dress. Red welts and splotches covered most of her body. Despite believing the rash was caused by invisible slime, the list of rashes ran through VJ's analytical mind—Measles. Chicken pox. Roseola. Hand-foot-mouth disease. Fifth disease. Scarlet fever.

Pilare's eyes fluttered open. "Do you know what ails me?"

"It looks like it's a cousin to Fifth disease—parovirus B19. The common name is Slapped Cheeks. Are your joints sore?"

"Everything hurts."

"Are you having difficulty breathing?"

"Yes." Her eyes drifted closed. "I'm very tired."

Wondering if she might have an illness combined with the rash, VJ inhaled. Pilare was not diseased. She did not have Covid-19 nor a virus. Even so, VJ gave her a thorough examination. When she finished, she asked, "How much contact have you had with Fallon's feet?"

"I kissed them the night we took him for the long walk. That's when I discovered the bumps on his soles."

"Rest. Sleep will be good for you."

"I doze but can't seem to stay asleep."

"Do you want a sedative?"

"That would be helpful."

VJ gave her an injection to calm her quickly and help her sleep.

When she left the bedroom, Zeg asked, "Did you give her something to make her feel better?"

"A jab—an injection. Her temperature is slightly elevated. Keep her hydrated."

"Will do."

VJ removed items from her satchel. "Here's more of Rene's cream for the rash. Surgical gloves to wear when applying. Burn them after each use. The tablets are for pain and will make her groggy."

Glancing at baby Fallon, wiggling and kicking on a blanket spread on the floor, she asked, "Do you mind if I look at him?"

"Please do."

VJ checked the soles of his feet. His skin was still bumpy, the rash bright red. "Has he been cranky?"

"Somewhat."

"You may apply the milder cream every four hours." VJ withdrew packets. "These are relaxing powders. They will help if Fallon has trouble sleeping. Use them sparingly."

Closing her satchel, she asked, "Do you need help with him?"

"No. How much do we owe you?"

"Nothing."

Surprise filled Zeg's eyes. "Medical care is expensive on the surface, even if people have insurance. And house calls are practically unheard of."

"Apitcote differs from the surface in many ways."

"We're learning that. Thank you for coming so quickly."

"Call if you need me."

~ * ~

Happy to find Holt home, she talked as she removed her klir suit. "What ails Pilare and Fallon isn't related to the coronavirus. I'm relieved about that. If we knew exactly where the slime is located, we might be able to isolate it."

"Can you think of a way to find it?"

"Not without examining the entire karst. Even then, I doubt Api has what's needed to prevent the slime from spreading. It's already here in the valley."

When Holt spread his arms, she walked between them and leaned her head against his shoulder. "I talked with kew mates yesterday and told them Apitcote is overpaying me. They know I want to work without compensation, but they didn't agree. I feel strongly about this, Holt. Do you think you could persuade them to change their minds?"

"Rene relayed your conversation to me. She suggested we revisit the discussion next year. For now, I suggest saving the money for our trip to England, and for our children's education."

"Capital suggestion." With a warm smile, she nudged closer. "Being alone with you is the best part of every day."

"Right." He kissed her—more than once. Until she gasped, "Rene just sent a silent message. We both had the same thought about finding the slime and isolating it. She and Drew are on their way to scan People Movers."

"Can we help?"

"Yes. If the slime has an odor, I will smell it."

# *Twenty-one*

The obvious starting place was the People Mover at the south end of the valley where Pilare had taken baby Fallon out of his pram and stood him on his bare feet. It took hours to inspect and scan, inch by slow inch.

Daybreak dawned as Rene said, "My scanner just detected something." She stared at the light blinking on her device.

"Mine also detected something strange," Drew announced.

"I smell it," Verity added. "Only at this end, though. Since the steps revolve, perhaps we should inspect the entire contraption again."

"Right," Drew agreed, already bending down.

"The scent is faint, but it's here," Verity said before Rene's and Drew's scanners blinked. "I see slime." Verity lifted her gloved hand to inspect the substance.

"It's stronger here," Rene said.

"We should close this People Mover now," Drew announced.

"Should I summon Juhree to conjure a shield?" Holt asked.

"Yes."

While they waited for Juhree, Drew said, "We should inspect every People Mover."

"It will be long and tedious," Rene agreed, "but worth the effort. Especially if it helps stop the contagion."

"The slime smells like the dank odor that clung to Veralane's shoes weeks ago."

"She didn't have a rash," Rene reminded.

"The soles of her feet were red, but I suspect the slime hadn't made strong contact with her flesh even though her stockings were stuck to her feet."

"You don't think we can contain the slime, do you?"

"I hope closing this conveyance and inspecting the others will help. Tomorrow Zeg will be ill by nightfall. I wonder how many others will follow and how soon."

"Only time will tell," Holt said, grateful when Juhree and Monteith arrived, and she conjured a long protective bubble to cover every inch of the half-mile People Mover.

~ * ~

Dark clouds covered the entire sky, hovering above thatched rooftops as VJ, Holt and Madeline strolled to the constat for breakfast.

"Ten adults have the rash," VJ announced after they ordered.

"As predicted, no one blames the newcomers," Madeline said.

"Right. But everyone is concerned. Denizens aren't used to sickness or ill-health."

"This must seem like a rude awakening after and a long and beautiful dream."

"It is," Holt agreed.

"I wish I could say things will get better, but my visions indicate they will get worse."

Madeline pursed her lips as she studied VJ. "That white lab coat looks good on you. Are you ready to work with the new medical residents?"

"Excited and eager. I'm hoping they help find a cure for the awful rash." *And the coming sleeping sickness.*

At the medical laboratory a short time later, the six residents greeted VJ with warm smiles. All wore yellow lab coats, and each one grinned. "It's brilliant to see all of you again."

Judy, the pretty long-haired blonde spoke first. "We're pleased to see you, Dr. Verity."

Kathy smiled. "As we mentioned before, we'd like you to call us rezees—the name we chose to use while we're resident doctors."

"Jolly good," VJ agreed. "I understand your schedule is to spend three hours each morning with me here in the lab, two hours with Apitcote's doctors in clinics and three hours researching. Evenings and weekends will be devoted to circulating among the dwellers to get better acquainted and teach the new residents about medical procedures, should they be required."

Jim nodded. "That's the plan. We'll rotate sleeping at clinics when we're on call. How does that sound?"

"Busy. Before we discuss our first project, I would like each of you to tell me something about yourself."

"Jim and I attended university and medical school together," Judy said."

VJ noted they both still had the sparkle of newlyweds, and wondered if people thought that about her and Holt. A group of denizens and dwellers at a nearby table had clapped and whistled when she had kissed him after breakfast before they went their separate ways.

"Paul and I have an eight-year-old daughter named Tanzy," Kathy said.

"We've always been interested in the medical field," Paul added, "so a few years ago we changed vocations and went back to university together."

"Dan and I are not a couple," Kaye announced without glancing at him.

"We are friends." He avoided looking at her, too.

VJ knew they had competed in medical school, vying for top exam scores. With tests no longer an issue, she suspected romance had a chance to blossom and would.

"Let's begin today's session with a discussion about the rash. Doctors, medics, and I have ruled out a variety of disorders and concluded the strain is unknown to mankind."

No one gasped, indicating all residents kept updated with daily news.

"Our job is to find a way to combat the rash, which I believe is caused by slime. Our first adult patient, Pilare, admitted to kissing baby Fallon's feet prior to discovering the rash, therefore, it appears to be highly contagious."

"What has been prescribed?" Paul asked.

"Rene created a cream that provides more relief than oft-used ointments, but it does not cure."

Ideas and suggestions were tossed and floated about, creating a sense of unity. "We're combating an invisible enemy," Kathy concluded.

"I suspect the slime contains microbes so tiny they might have slipped through some tests," VJ said.

"Should we try different testing procedures?"

"That's my first suggestion."

"Do you have others?"

"Yes." VJ smiled, anxious to begin her experiment, but willing herself to slow down. The rezees needed groundwork before pursuing her idea.

For the next few days, the rezees researched potential cures, compared notes, shared knowledge. VJ worked right along with them and consulted with Apitcote's doctors and medics daily. While they treated rash patients, other denizens went on about their business. Most were unaffected by a potential pandemic until fifty denizens in two more klusters came down with the rash.

One morning, only five rezees arrived at the lab. "Kaye woke up with the rash," Dan explained. "We were both on call. I suggested she go home and stay."

"You did good," VJ approved.

~ * ~

At the combined kew and Disaster Guide Plan meeting, she reported, "Our scientists and doctors are confused. No one understands how the slime found its way from kluster twenty-four to kluster seven. How it skipped seventeen klusters. There's no pattern to the spread."

"Kaye is our newest victim. Did she ride People Movers?" Tess asked.

"Yes. Perhaps it's time to close them," Rene said.

"Do you know who Kaye came in contact with that the other rezees haven't?"

"Yes," VJ answered, frustrated. "We've asked every question we could think of to make logical assumptions."

"We should be grateful the illness hasn't affected the Venes or Benes or Ancients," Drew observed.

"I find that rather curious," Tess said. "Don't you, Verity?"

"Yes. Older denizens must have some kind of immunity. No one the age of my parents and older have contracted the rash. I wonder why."

"Could it be age related?" Holt asked.

Before VJ could reply, a familiar sunflower blocked her sight. Closing her eyes, she leaned against Holt. When the vision finally ended, she announced, "The rash doesn't affect those above forty-five. It concentrates on younger people."

"Do you know why?"

"Not yet, but I hope to find out."

During their walk home, Holt's afone beeped. He read the atext. "It's from Hanna. Aleece died last night, and Hanna is in the hospital. She has Covid."

"That's terrible," VJ sympathized. "Do you need to go to the surface and get Harmony?"

"No. Hanna's college friend is taking care of her, and Hanna wants Harmony there when she goes home." Holt waited a few moments before he added, "There will be no funeral for Aleece."

"That's sad," VJ sympathized. "I wish we could do something to help."

"I wish the same."

VJ put her arms around him and held him close for a long unhurried time.

~ * ~

Shortly after the medical students gathered in the lab, VJ's afone beeped, along with all the others.

"It's an atext from Mist," Kathy announced.

"An alert," Paul added as everyone checked afones. "The rash has spread to more than half of our klusters." He looked from one rezee to the other. "Doctors and medics have confirmed more than two hundred cases."

"The Disaster Guide Plan is in full effect," Jim said. "Travel between klusters ceased more than a week ago."

"I'm glad we have a plan," Judy said. "Denizens will now social-distance and mask up if they find it necessary to go out. Most will order meals online and eat at home."

"Schools will close. Social activities will cease," VJ agreed, deciding to begin their research in the field she wanted to pursue. "I have an idea related to research during my last year at university. At the time, it was being considered as a cure for cancer. I haven't heard about follow-up, but I think we might use the idea to isolate and kill the rash."

"Explain more," Jim encouraged.

"I heard the information whilst attending the University of Utah. I hope to use it to develop an antidote for the rash and the upcoming sleeping illness. I think the slime is responsible for both, and we should pursue the possibility with all due haste."

"Tell us more."

"Utah researchers created a serum to inject people using properties created by bees. The serum forms a quarter-size beehive in layers of skin. Mixed with residual cell cultures, the beehive draws cancer cells from all parts of the body, isolates, contains and destroys. If we develop the correct serum, I'm confident the beehives will draw the rash inside, isolate and destroy it."

"Pure genius," Dan said, enthused. "Divide and conquer. That's how wars are won."

"Thanks," VJ said, also enthused.

Judy nodded. "Scientists have known since ancient times that bees play an important role in healing the human body."

"Right," Jim agreed. "Intricate beehive systems include living quarters, food storage bins, nurseries for young larvae, and every area gets constant maintenance. If we use the substances bees produce to repair and maintain their hives and combine them with the proper compounds, we could create a serum that works."

"Excellent," Paul said. "Where do we start?"

"By collecting information," VJ replied.

"I have a good feeling about this," Kathy said.

"I atexted Dr. Lorraine and asked her to share all information collected by Api's researchers who have studied bees. She sent the link to information and data previous researchers collected. Does anyone want to download tonight and report on their findings tomorrow?"

All five hands shot in the air.

"Brilliant. I look forward to a lively discussion in the morning."

~ * ~

Rezees were eager to share what they had read. "Honey has natural preservative properties and contains so little moisture it's difficult for bacteria and microorganisms to survive," Kathy reported.

"Because it's thick, only small amounts of oxygen can penetrate, which is a barrier to bacteria's growth," Paul added.

"It's extremely acidic," Jim continued, "due to a special enzyme in bee stomachs called glucose oxidase. When mixed with nectar to create honey, the enzyme produces gluconic acid and hydrogen peroxide, byproducts that lower the sweetener's pH level and kills bacteria."

"I didn't realize honey can be stored for years if it's in a sealed container," Judy said.

"Neither did I," Dan agreed. "Stored properly, honey never expires. It has an endless shelf life, proven by archaeologists who unsealed King Tut's tomb in 1923 and found containers of honey. Researchers performed a not-so-scientific taste test and reported the three-thousand-year-old honey still tasted sweet."

Clearing her throat, VJ announced, "It's time to begin our project."

"We're ready," the team chorused.

~ * ~

By the end of the week, they had created a serum that formed a circle in the shape of a beehive on skin cultures.

"But we haven't found the right compounds to kill the rash," Dan said, having tested numerous varieties.

"Mixing venom with other bee properties has been done. We just need to discover the right combinations," VJ reiterated.

"An Australian researcher used the compound in bees' venom called melittin. It destroyed breast cancer cells within an hour without causing harm to other cells," Jim said.

"That could be what the researchers in Utah discovered," VJ observed.

"Might be the ingredient we've been missing," Judy said.

For two more days, VJ and the rezees worked overtime, testing, refining, defining.

When they were confidant the vaccine would work, Dan said, "Kaye volunteered to be our first patient."

"Good. Who wants to administer the first sharp?

"Sharp?" Kathy asked, eyebrows hiked.

"That's what Brits call a syringe," VJ explained.

"We should all go," Dan said. "Kaye misses being part of the team."

"And we miss her." VJ grabbed her satchel.

The rezees exuded so much pent-up energy, VJ sent a silent message to Holt asking him to join them and cast a charm to calm her team.

Which he did—without telling them.

At Kaye's cottage, she asked, "Where will you inject the serum, Dr. Verity?"

"On the fleshy part of your calf. Far from your heart and other vital organs."

Kaye summoned a halfhearted smile. "I really hope this works."

"We all hope it works." Holt's dimples winked when he grinned.

"Are you ready for the first jab?"

"Certainly, Dr. Verity."

~ * ~

"Within a few hours Kaye was out of bed, walking around, asking for food," VJ reported at the evening kew meeting. "I shall examine her again in the morning."

When she did, Kaye said, "I feel great. Fully recovered." This time her smile looked genuine. "I think we should offer the jab to everyone who has the rash."

"We should probably test it on a few more patients first."

"I don't think that's necessary," Rene said, having accompanied VJ. "Kaye's recovery is remarkable. Our visions agree, Verity. You and the rezees have found a cure."

With warp speed, rezees produced the serum.

A few hours after injections, the beehive formed on patients' skin and trapped the rash inside.

Rashes disappeared almost overnight.

Denizens recovered. The beehive vaccinations didn't disappear, but they shrank from the size of a lumpy quarter to a smooth dime.

"Will the vaccines leave side effects?" Jordan asked one night.

"Just a small scar that will continue to protect denizens who got the jab." VJ smiled. "We made a pretty good fist of it."

"We certainly did." Tess grinned. "We should celebrate."

"Discontinuing self-isolation, and re-opening constats, schools, warerooms, businesses and travel between klusters will be a good start," Holt said.

"It surely will," Tess agreed.

~ * ~

The remaining days of January passed without illness of any kind. The gloomy dark clouds disappeared. Blue skies reappeared. Sunshine filled denizens' hearts and souls as everyone rejoiced at the lifted restrictions. Anxious to resume monthly holidays, social groups made plans to celebrate both February holidays—Valentine's Day and Secret Pal weekend. Committees worked hastily to make up for lost time.

All seemed to be well in paradise below the surface.

But Holt and Verity knew differently, and despite agreeing that worrying wouldn't help, they worried together, plagued by nightly questions they discussed again and again. When would the sleeping illness arrive? How serious would it be? Would the beehive jabs conquer it as it had the rash? And when would Shadow the cassowary return and attempt to abduct babies?

Would he wait until summer when the ground was warm? Or come sooner? Would he take both Joel and Noel? And how many other babies would be stolen?

~ * ~

The rezees stockpiled beehive serum which gave birth to another idea.

At the kew meeting, VJ said, "The rezees created enough serum to vaccinate all denizens. We think doing so will provide immunization for the coming sleeping illness."

"Including babies?" Tess asked. "Are they too small to be inoculated?"

"Vaccines will not be necessary if we protect them from being abducted."

"Do you have an age group in mind?" Drew asked.

"I motion that we jab—inoculate—everyone between the ages of eight and forty-five, excluding only those who prefer not to be included."

"I second the motion," Holt said.

"Any discussion?" Jordan asked. Hearing none, he called for the vote, which passed unanimously.

Tess made the announcement on TV that evening ending with, "Injections will be available for all of those who choose to take advantage of recommended vaccinations at clinics beginning tomorrow at eight a.m."

No one was surprised to see the long lines in the morning, including kew mates.

At lunch with Holt, VJ said, "I've been thinking about the cassowary. Cinnalan said it will steal babies when the ground is summer warm, but I wonder if there's a way to force the abductors to act sooner. Catch them off guard before they are fully prepared."

"Genius. You're an absolute genius!"

"Thanks." Jumping to her feet, VJ plopped a kiss on top of his head. And laughed when onlookers clapped and cheered.

"What do you have in mind?" he asked as they left the constat.

"The evil spirits disturb us. We disturb them."

"That doesn't explain what you intend to do."

"We shall simply go to the karst and perturb. Agitate."

"When?"

"Tonight."

"Who?"

"I for one. You for another, I hope, along with any kew mates who volunteer."

Everyone did—except Jordan and Mist. All agreed they should stay home, protect Joel and Noel, and keep them far away from the karst and the vire.

Kew mates left at dusk. Boosted their levitating to full speed. Soon the karst loomed ahead. Cold. Dark. Forbidding. VJ shivered as they slowed and levitated down to the limestone floor. As they approached the tunnel with the noxious odor, she said, "Tonight our job is to roust and harass. Make the evil believe we know more about them than we actually do."

"This should be fun. We get to brew mischief," Tess said.

"What are those ugly devils?" Drew motioned sideways at a horde of the ugliest animals VJ had ever seen. Not even horror film creators made such repulsive, hideous beasts.

"Trolls," she said, recognizing the monsters from a vision. "The creatures who will help the cassowary steal babies unless we find a way to stop them."

"Are they evil?"

"Yes. But not the evil that wants babies. The trolls are in cahoots with the vire because they are mean, cruel monsters who thrive by harming others."

Changing directions, VJ aimed her helmet light at the trolls and flew toward the horde. The creatures squealed and squawked as kew mates joined her pursuit. Trolls who had eyes pointed at them before they started to run. Other trolls followed, tramping around pillars and ridges, dodging towers, bumping into fissures. When they reached a sinkhole, they changed directions, still squawking and making awful ungodly noise.

The trolls found an opening in the karst wall and scurried inside.

"Are we going to follow them?" Dane asked.

"No. But we are going to hang around for a bit. Ensure they know we're still here."

VJ spied a large dolomite crystal. Found a flat spot to land nearby. A place for all eight to perch. After inhaling, she said, "I don't think many humans have been in this part of the karst."

"I still hear the trolls. We disturbed them," Juhree said.

"Exactly. And if I am not mistaken, they will communicate our presence to the evil spirits and they will know they are no longer alone in this part of the valley."

Holt winked and repeated her earlier words. "They disturb us. We disturb them."

"What more can we do?" Dane asked.

"Trolls hate loud noise," VJ said.

"Let's sing," Tess suggested. "At the top of our lungs. The trolls and evil might hear us and wonder what we're doing. Why we're here. And how long we intend to stay."

"Good idea," Holt approved.

Everyone suggested songs—old and new—and kew mates sang. On tune. Off tune. And with voices blending like a practiced choir. They sang for over an hour before Juhree said, "I'm cold. Anyone mind if we build a fire?"

"I've been trying to think of something to spook them," Drew said. "Fire is a mighty fine idea."

"We need a snack. Let's make s'mores," Rene suggested.

"Fantastic," Dane said as Juhree conjured graham crackers, Hershey bars, marshmallows and stiff wires to toast them.

"This is fun," Tess said, "and we're not even brewing mischief."

"I'm thirsty. Could you conjure hot chocolate, Juhree?" Monteith asked.

"Sure."

As they enjoyed the snacks, mates shared troll stories they had heard as children. The tales were very dissimilar to the trolls who inhabited the karst.

"I've never heard stories of trolls who didn't have eyes and were so mean they fed off their own misery," Drew said.

"I didn't get a good look," Dane said. "Can someone describe what these trolls look like?"

"They're short, fat ugly buggers and their brains are only about the size of a walnut." VJ said. "Even small children can trick them."

"The sun turns trolls to stone," Rene said.

"If one makes them frustrated enough, they burst apart," Tess added.

"They're easily distracted."

"Some are watching us." VJ nodded at the tunnel entrance where the trolls had taken refuge. All kew mates turned and shouted, "Boo!"

The trolls jumped, turned and fled.

Holt laughed. "I think we've done our job."

VJ laughed, too. "I think you are right, man of my heart. Let's go home."

# Twenty-two

Madeline called early. "I feel peculiar. Wonder if I'm lurgy—ill and possibly contagious."

"Tell me your symptoms." VJ said.

"I itch something fierce. Like tiny microbes are gnawing flesh at the end of my nose and between the toes of my left foot. It's totally weird."

"I'll be there in a jiffy."

VJ suited, masked up and hurried next door. As was often the case early in the morning, Holt was at her side, also masked and suited, prepared to assist any way he could.

After examining Madeline and paying extra attention to her nose and feet, VJ said, "I detect nothing. And I smell no disease."

"I feel feverish."

"Not surprising. Your temperature is a hundred and one."

"Did you bring the beehive vax?"

"Yes, but you already have one."

"I'd like two. I have a feeling both will help me in future."

VJ didn't argue. Unusual times called for unusual decisions. She pulled a sharps from her satchel. The hypodermic felt heavy in her hands as Madeline pulled her legging up to her knee, exposing her unvaccinated calf.

VJ also pulled a Q-tip. "I'm going to swab your nose and have the lab analyze."

By afternoon, the rezees lab report indicated nothing remarkable detected.

The next morning, Madeline called again. "I'm recovered, but I need to talk to you, Ver. In private."

Moments later, VJ sat with Madeline at her small kitchen table.

"Last night I saw Shadow, the invisible bird Cinnalan described. He was here, in front of my cottage when I opened the door to retrieve my evening meal. He silently conveyed that I should follow when he kidnaps the babies."

"I know," VJ said.

Madeline set her teacup down, her forehead wrinkled. "You had a vision of us?"

"Yes. I promised that Holt and I will find you. We must defeat or demolish the evil. That's the reason we're here. We must save Apitcote. I can't say what will happen if the vire wins."

"What shall we do?" Madeline asked, tears threatening.

"I don't yet know, but when the time comes, we'll do what must be done. It's part of our destiny. If we fail, it will be up to my kew mates to destroy the evil. But they are dedicated to good deeds, not hate and violence. You and I may have to kill the evil to get rid of it. Doing so may cost us the men we love."

"That's why I backed away from Dom."

"I want to be prepared, but I have no idea what for. I think we should tell Holt and Dom."

Madeline shook her head. "There is nothing they or anyone else can do to stop what will happen."

"Forewarned is knowledge."

"It may also be a death sentence. I fear I have already told you more than I should. And for that I may pay a price."

"Thanks for taking the risk." VJ blinked. More than once.

"Is something wrong?"

"The bird is huge," VJ announced as though in a trance. "His body is covered with dense black feathers. From a distance, they look like black hair.

"You see the bird?"

"Yes, Madd."

"Do you see anything else?"

"Cinnalan. Communicating with the bird. He is telling her the evil lives inside a huge boulder in the dark cavern where the babies will be taken."

"Why does the vire want babies?"

Shivers raced through VJ. The evil wanted what it had failed to get from her when she was trapped inside the stone. Her voice shook as she answered. "It wants their bodies. It craves their youth. Their lack of knowledge. They think babies are too young to discern between good and evil and will be easy to manipulate and overtake."

~ * ~

VJ waffled between telling Holt and keeping Madeline's secret. Too concerned to concentrate, she struggled to make a decision during her three hours with the rezees. In the end, she knew she must tell Holt. She could not withhold information that might be vital to survival. Hoping she wouldn't alienate Madeline, she levitated home, and called Holt. "I need to see you as soon as possible. At home."

Holt arrived five minutes later. She had another vision before he got there.

"What's troubling you."

"I have information to share."

"What?"

Needing time to decipher her latest vision, she said, "Would you hold me before I explain?"

"Of course." Spreading his arms, he folded her close. "This is always a pleasure." He kissed her forehead, each cheek, her chin.

She inhaled. Gathered her courage. "I guess I'm ready."

"Should I start a fire?"

"That would be lovely."

When they were seated on the settee, she said, "Madeline shared something that concerns everyone in Apitcote. She doesn't want me to tell you, but I think it's too important not to." She gave him a bleak smile. "According to Madeline, she and I must protect Apitcote from the evil that's coming. You and your kew grew up without violence in your lives. Madeline and I didn't. And we might use violence against the evil. Even then, I don't know if we can destroy the vire."

Holt tightened his arms around her. "I'm relieved you told me. When the time comes, we'll use force if it's needed. Supplementals not only attempt to resolve problems and disagreements without resorting to violence, we're dedicated to keeping our realm safe. If violence is required to fight evil, so be it."

"I had another vision after I asked you to come home."

"Do you want to share?"

"I saw trolls. The ugly, horrid creatures. They won't steal babies because parents have been warned. Instead, they will steal small children—kidlings—toddlers."

"We should tell our kew mates and have Mist televise the possibility. Parents and denizens should all be warned. Told to guard toddlers as well as babies."

"Should we tell Madeline's secret to Dom?" Holt asked.

"Madeline doesn't want him to know."

"She won't be doing the telling."

"You have a devious mind, Holt. I didn't know that."

"Men stick together to protect those we love."

"Let's ponder the idea for a while. The time doesn't feel right yet."

"Fine. I'll ponder. However, I doubt pondering will change my mind."

~ * ~

Back home after the kew meeting, Holt snuggled Verity close as they sat by the fireplace.

"I have a feeling the vire won't wait until summer."

"Is there anything we can do to be prepared?"

"I can think of one thing."

"What?"

"Inoculate toddlers with the bee serum. If the vire steals toddlers and they are vaccinated, the serum will draw the vire slime inside the beehives and isolate it."

"Do you know that for certain?"

"Yes. I have seen it. I also know Mist's and Jordan's twins will not be taken, but Orlane will. Even though she will never be alone, the vire will succeed in its attempt to abduct her. If jabbed—inoculated—she'll survive."

"We should administer the vaccinations soon."

"Before daybreak," VJ agreed.

Holt sent a silent communication to their kew mates.

All atexted back immediately. "We agree. Do it."

Holt atexted again. "The rezees are on it."

Verity closed her eyes. When she opened them again, she smiled. "Every time I look at you, love comes flooding in. It's a wonderful feeling, Holt. You are the greatest joy in my life."

He swallowed hard. Never had he felt more humbled. "Nothing can be more perfect than our union," he said, and bent his head. The kiss was perfect. Like his One.

~ * ~

Sleep did not come easily. VJ tossed and turned. Dozed. Slept fitfully. Saw the cassowary steal Orlane and put Minalu to sleep, along with other parents while trolls kidnapped toddlers.

More tossing and turning followed the vision. A weird dream of Madeline wandering deep into the forest woke VJ up.

Clearing fog from her brain, she listened to the steady rhythm of Holt's quiet breathing. She was still separating the dream from the vision when the doorbell chimed. She grabbed a dressing gown and raced to the front door. Holt was right behind her, shoving his arms through the sleeves of his robe.

Standing below the stoop, Drew said, "A dark shadow passed over the realm last night. Rene and I weren't the only ones who saw it."

Fear sizzled through VJ as Holt asked, "Did anything happen to cause concern?"

"Cinnalan is gone. Minalu is asleep and won't wake up. Some parents have fallen under a sleeping spell and cannot be awakened."

"Have you notified the kew?"

"Yeah." Drew ran a hand through his messy hair. "I'm telling you in person because we didn't get a response to our messages or atexts. Can you meet us at the chateau asap?"

"Absolutely."

"My afone isn't where I left it," Holt said as they dressed.

"Nor is mine." VJ tapped the side of her head after a vision flashed. "They're outside. On the ground. The trolls who abducted the toddlers didn't know how to disable or turn them off so the dark shadow—the vire who hovered above our cottage—blocked the messages Rene sent."

Three minutes later, they joined kew mates at the chateau. Mist and Jordan each cuddled a baby. Their vigilance after Cinnalan's warning had worked. Joel and Noel were safe.

Rapid footsteps pounded on the spiral staircase seconds before Dom burst into the dream chamber. "Orlane is missing."

"So is Madeline," VJ announced, relieved she'd the vision and learned more about the evil vire slime and the trolls.

"A bird who can't fly managed to abduct Orlane, Cinnalan, and Madeline?" Dane asked.

"The cassowary took Orlane," VJ clarified. "Cinnalan sensed Orlane being taken and followed. Madeline sensed the kidnapping and followed as well." She paused before telling them what they did not yet know.

Dom dashed a hand through his thick, black hair. "We have to find them."

"We will. But more than those three are missing. A dozen toddlers were kidnapped by trolls. They will soon be with Madeline, Cinnalan and Orlane."

All six rezees ran up the spiral steps and rushed into the dream chamber.

"A bunch of denizens won't wake up," Jim announced.

"How many?" Drew asked.

"More than a hundred in three different klusters."

"We think the dark cloud put them to sleep."

"It did," VJ agreed, pulling the knowledge from her most recent vision. "The dark cloud was made up of vire—the demonic fury spirits Rene saw in her ancestors' memories. They have lain dormant for fifty years, but they were mutating and growing. They have regained some of their power and are working with the trolls to take over Apitcote. As I mentioned before, some of the vire has no substance, but it is no longer lighter than air. It has the ability to form shadows and clouds. Some vire occupies the slime that caused the rash and sleeping illness. Other vire attached to the cassowary and is forcing him to do their bidding."

"What do they want with innocent children?" Jordan asked.

"Everything," VJ reiterated. "Their bodies. Their brains. Their lives. They stole the toddlers because they couldn't get babies, and they believe toddlers are too young to resist what they plan."

"How can we find them?"

"We'll have to trust my instincts. And Rene's."

"Do you know where they are?"

"In the bowels of the karst."

A loud horn blared outside. Emergency alert music followed.

Everyone dashed downstairs. Rene turned the telly on with a flick of her pinky. The music outside stopped. A newscaster announced, "This is an emergency broadcast alert. Some kind of spell has apparently put denizens into a deep sleep from which they cannot be awakened. A toddler has been kidnapped. An eight-year-old girl and an adult woman are also missing. Parents are cautioned to keep children home, close by. Not to panic. Do not go anywhere alone. Wait. More calls are coming in." Seconds later, the broadcaster added, "Parents are reporting missing children. How many? Six. Eight. No, ten."

As soon as the broadcast ended, VJ announced, "I'm going to go find them."

"We're all going," Rene said.

"Joel and Noel will be safer here," Mist said.

"Right," Holt agreed "You and Jordan must stay with them."

"Good," Jordan said. "We'll keep in touch."

"I want to go," Dom said. "Nando and Tumela will take care of Amma."

"I'll levitate you," Holt offered.

"Should we collect supplies?"

"No. I'll conjure whatever we need," Juhree said.

"Atext Nando," Verity admonished. "Tell him we're leaving now."

Without wasting another second, Holt took Dom's hand, and kew mates shot to the sky, flying across the valley, above rooftops, light poles and trees at near lightning speed.

When they entered the forest, VJ projected her voice for everyone to hear. "I see trolls and the toddlers they carried through a dark tunnel to the cavern. Madeline and Cinnelan are also inside, hibernating on the cold ground."

"Do you see anything else?" Holt asked.

"Flowers surround them—not dead flowers. Pretty ones. Colorful, too. Insects or fairies or tiny baby angels are flying around and above."

"Elementals, not angels," Holt breathed out, astonishment mingling with relief and gratitude, and so many other emotions he couldn't name them all.

"What are elementals?" Verity asked.

"Tiny blue insects, bumblebees, honeybees, fireflies, butterflies, moths, candle flies. All are luminescent and possess healing power and protection."

"Good." She motioned with her hand to alter their direction before she spoke again. "The cassowary agreed to help the vire because it separated him from his mate and won't release him unless he does what they order. Cassowaries mate for life, and he is miserable."

"Do you know anything new about the trolls?" Rene asked, also projecting her voice.

"No. Only that they are beastly ugly buggers, none look alike, and they are mean devils."

As they landed on the karst floor, VJ said, "From this point on, we must whisper or communicate silently."

"There's a pile of rocks blocking the main channel of the tunnel," Rene conveyed as they approached the noxious smelling cave.

"How will we get through the blockage?" Dom asked.

"Won't be necessary," VJ said. "The cavern is located in a side arm before the blockade, and we'll be there soon. I'm communicating with Madeline. She feels us getting closer."

"That's good news," Holt whispered.

VJ motioned right. "The tunnel is there. Levitate low, but don't touch the ground," she cautioned.

"Why?" Dom asked.

"The slimy vire slithers on the ground."

"Thanks."

"Years ago, Dane and Rene's ancestor sealed the evil spirits inside a boulder in the cavern. They have escaped, and some move about in slimy sludge or via the cassowary and trolls. The vire is what put denizens to sleep."

"Appreciate the explanation." Dom floated an arm's length from Holt toward a rocky-edged wall. "It's shiny—like coal," he whispered. His helmet light blinked and went out.

"The vire senses you," VJ said as he floated backwards until he bumped into Holt. "It made your light go off."

"I'll fix that," Juhree said. And did.

"I don't see the tunnel arm," Dom said.

VJ waved at the spot where his light had blinked off. "It's there, near the ground. We shouldn't crawl. We'll have to levitate through. Try not to touch the contaminated ground or sides or ceiling."

"Who should go first?" Monteith asked.

"Me. Then Rene. If we deem it safe to continue, Holt will levitate Dom through and follow him. Drew next. Then Tess, Dane, Juhree. You will levitate last, Monteith."

After everyone cleared the crawl space, VJ said, "Madeline is feeding information. We should not touch the slimy ground when we reach the cavern. Continue to levitate until Juhree sanitizes and covers the ground with aluminium."

"Never heard of ahl-u-minium," Dom said. "What is it?"

"Sorry. Americans call it aluminum foil. Can you conjure extra strong foil or canvas or something to protect our boots, Juhree? The klir seal suits protect our bodies, but we don't want to risk contaminating our feet."

"I'll conjure a covering similar to our klir seal suits," Juhree said.

"Perfect."

"Has the vire invaded the youngsters' bodies, or Cinnalan and Madeline?" Holt asked.

"They're trying but the elementals and Mater Nature are repelling them."

"How long have you known that?" Holt asked.

"Since we left the forest. Madeline relayed the information."

"Do you know where the vire is?" Holt asked.

"Some are in our valley keeping the sleeping denizens under their evil spell. Most are inside the boulder in the cavern. A few are outside the boulder, spread across rocks and stones and the cavern floor."

As they flew, VJ sent another silent message. *The evil has sensed us. And I am no longer connected to Madeline.*

Holt's heart was pumping double time. He sensed Verity's was as well. The smaller tunnel channel looked to go on indefinitely, but Verity stopped before they could see the end. "We've reached the cavern. Please hover until Juhree conjures a proper ground cover." Moving aside, she motioned Juhree to precede them.

While Juhree conjured, kew mates' miners' helmets glowed brighter. Holt sensed Juhree was responsible. The increased light allowed everyone to see inside the cavern where Cinnalan, Madeline, Orlane and eleven other toddlers lay flat on their backs without a ground cover to protect them from the slime and cold draft seeping along the ground. The trolls were not visible.

*The vire does not see, but it hears and feels vibrations,* Verity conveyed, mouthing her words for Dom to read. *From now on, no more whispering. I apologize, Dom, but the kew must communicate silently.*

*I think I can tune in,* he surprised everyone silently. *All I need is permission.*

You have *it,* Rene approved, drawing a grateful nod from him and her kew mates.

Glancing at the abductees once again, Holt swallowed. If Harmony had been in Apitcote, she might be one of them. The lump in his throat tightened to a hard knot. For the first time since Hanna had taken Harmony to the surface, he felt grateful, although he regretted that Hanna had tested positive for Covid again.

VJ floated inside, leaving the others behind. She inhaled. Smelled no decay or death, but the noxious smell was so strong she feared it might overpower them if they breathed in too much. *Juhree*, she silently communicated. *Can you create nose guards or do something to mitigate the bloody rank stench?*

"We can." Rene and Tess floated through the entry, aimed their hands at the flowers surrounding the captives and snapped their fingers. The scent of roses, carnations and other lovely flowery smells replaced the noxious odor.

VJ was pleased, even more so when Rene said, *Our klir seal suits have in-built nose guards. Activate them by inhaling deeply and exhaling slowly—for as long as possible.*

*Thanks*, VJ said as Juhree covered the cavern floor with klir seal suit material. *Should I put the cover beneath the abductees and conjure blankets?*

*Yes. Please.*

While Juhree conjured, VJ levitated above Madeline and hovered. Inhaled. Found no disease. She touched Madeline's forehead. Checked her pulse. When she looked up, Rene was examining Cinnalan, who held Orlane clamped against her chest.

*No fevers here*, Rene conveyed. *Strong heartbeats. How is Madeline?*

*About the same. Temp below normal by two degrees. That's not unusual."*

*How is Orlane?* Dom asked.

Fine, Rene answered.

*What about the other toddlers?* Holt asked.

*They're fine*, Verity conveyed. *I inhaled and checked everyone. All except two were inoculated last night and will soon have beehive rings to draw the vire inside.* Moving away, Verity helped kew mates examine each toddler.

*Their beehives are not fully formed*, Drew said, inspecting one toddler's leg.

They should be soon, VJ said, hoping vaccines had not been jabbed too late.

*Are you synked with Madeline?* Holt asked when they finished examining.

*No. She sleeps deeply, as though compelled.* Taking Madeline's hand, VJ sat beside her friend, then reached for Holt's hand. His warm clasp confirmed her thoughts. He was part of her strength. She sent him a silent message. *Please stay nearby. Your strength adds to mine.*

*Count on it*, he messaged back.

VJ moved the duvet aside to study the beehives on Madeline's calves. The serum had drawn poisonous vire inside. But not destroyed it. Tiny, miniscule red dots beneath her skin were moving around, attempting to escape the beehive rings.

The twin heart bracelet on Madeline's wrist glittered beneath the glow of VJ's helmet light. She touched the hearts on her bracelet to Madeline's, hoping the gesture might synk them. The pleasant aroma of pine needles and clear, clean air filled her senses and a sudden burst of brilliant light enveloped Madeline. VJ knew it was Mater Nature. And the quiet words she spoke were heard only by her.

*When the confrontation with the vire begins, the flowers, elementals and I shall protect Madeline, Cinnalan and the toddlers, allowing you and your mates to conquer the evil spirits.*

Comforted by the words, VJ drew the duvet back over Madeline before Juhree tapped her shoulder. *I covered most of the cavern floor. However, I left the other end untouched. There's something there that doesn't want to be disturbed.*

*Is it evil?* Holt asked.

*Not that I could tell. It seems like a cornered animal.*

*It is,* VJ confirmed. *Shadow—the invisible cassowary Cinnalan told us about.*

Do you think the vire kept its promise and reunited him with his mate?

*No. I sense only one cassowary. Does anyone else sense the animal?*

*I do,* Rene said. *He's hungry and thirsty.*

*Should I conjure food and water? Cassowaries eat over two hundred varieties of fruits and plants. They prefer fallen, over-ripened fruit. I'm willing to take food to him.*

*Don't carry it,* VJ warned. *Cassowaries are capable of inflicting disastrous harm. I suggest levitating water and food, and leave him be until he knows we don't intend to hurt him.*

As Juhree conjured overripe fruit, Monteith asked, *Do you know where the trolls are, Verity?*

*No. However, I suspect they're not far away.*

When Juhree levitated fruit and water across the cavern, VJ re-checked Madeline's pulse.

*What do we do now?* Dom asked.

*I would like to pick everyone up and take them home, but any attempt to do so will not only fail, it could result in serious injury or put us in the same coma-like trance the captives are in.*

*Is it worth a try?*

*No. We cannot risk losing anyone else to the vire's evil spell. It senses we're here but not how many we are. Our klir seal suits will protect us, but we must be very careful. Give the vire as little information as possible. Continue to communicate silently. For the time being, all we can do is wait. Madeline will tell us what to do when she can. At this moment, she's unable to. Perhaps if we sit around them and join hands, she will sense us and synk with me again.*

*Where should I sit?* Dom asked.

*Where would you like to?*

*Near Cinnalan and Madeline.*

*Go ahead.*

Dom squatted between his sister and Madeline. Kew couples settled on the klir tarp, forming a circle around the abductees. Dom patted Orlane and Cinnalan.. But he didn't touch Madeline.

Squeezing Holt's fingers, VJ silently said, *I saw elementals before we arrived, but they're gone. Do you know where they are?*

*I sense them*, he answered. *Nearby*. A brief grin flashed across his face. *They're in the tunnel razzing the trolls. Forcing them to run out into the sunshine where they will be turned to stone.*

*How awesome*, VJ said. *Please convey that information to the others.*

*They already know.*

VJ heard a rumble. Then a terrible chorus of thunderous roars. The sound of heavy feet pounded the tunnel floor. Hideous creatures, some with eyes, others without, ran past the cavern opening. Behind the monsters flew a huge swarm of elementals. Numbering in the thousands, the tiny insects forced the horrific beasts from their dark shelter.

*Someone should follow them*, Drew said, *so we know what happens.*

*Tess and I will*, Dane volunteered.

VJ refrained from telling anyone, except Holt, that she could see the action. In a flash, she knew he and Rene saw what was happening as well.

The pounding footfalls, rumbling grunts and awful noise faded as the trolls ran farther away. Squeezed through the crawl space. Ducked in and out of small chambers, trying to hide from the elementals, but failing. Each time they attempted to turn back, the elementals descended in hordes and forced them onward toward the mouth of the tunnel, out to the sunshine and their extinction.

*The trolls are stones,* Dane reported as soon as he and Tess returned.

*Ugly, distorted stones,* Tess confirmed. *I always believed trolls were only mythical creatures. If I hadn't seen them, I wouldn't believe they exist.*

*The trolls helped the vire for only one reason,* VJ conveyed. *They don't like humans. They envy us because we have the ability to love and they don't.*

*Must live a sad existence.*

*Not anymore. They're stone,* Rene reminded.

*One less problem for us to handle,* Drew said, looking relieved.

*We videoed everything,* Tess said, *and sent it to Mist so she can share it with denizens.*

*We knew you would,* Monteith approved.

*I have an idea.* VJ yanked her afone from the pocket inside her klir seal suit and sent an atext to Mist, sharing the communication with her team. *Ask denizens to save hair strands from combs and brushes and shaving odd-bits from men's razors.*

Mist atexted back immediately. *How will I get them to you?*

*Send them with the rezees. I'll atext and ask them to join us.*

*Hoverz bikes can speed them here,* Holt added, drawing a wink from VJ.

*We'll need to levitate them through the crawl space.*

*I'll handle that,* Rene volunteered.

Kew mates sat in silence, waiting for something to happen. Nothing did. Every thirty minutes, Verity, Rene and Drew checked the sleepers' vitals and beehive vaccinations. Holt mouthed a sigh of relief when Verity announced, *Temperatures and blood pressures are back to normal. The duvets Juhree conjured apparently took away the chill, and the vaccines are serving their purpose. I'm grateful they're working so soon.*

*I'm grateful there are no spiders or bugs or creepy crawlies in here,* Juhree said.

*My ancestor, Clairene, made sure of that,* Rene supplied. *She didn't want the vire to have any help when it escaped from the boulder.*

*Where do you think the trolls came from?*

Rene's gaze turned somber. *Many years ago, trolls disappeared from the old country. Most found their way below ground and traveled through a series of tunnels and caves beneath ocean floors. Some found their way to Australia, New Zealand and islands. Others traveled to this continent. A few denizens have reported seeing odd creatures in our woods at night, but no one ever got close enough to determine what they were."*

# Twenty-three

When conversation lulled, Juhree asked, *Is anyone hungry?*

*I am*, Monteith said.

Juhree smiled. *I'll conjure lunch.*

In the afternoon, she conjured biscuits and tea.

She conjured again at supper time.

When it was late, she conjured duvets and pillows.

*Are we going to turn our helmet lights off?* Dom asked.

*If we do, I can conjure flashlights*, Juhree offered.

*I'd like to have some light, not pitch black*, Tess said.

*Me too*, VJ admitted, grateful for the small torches—flashlights—Juhree conjured, along with backpacks and other items each mate requested.

The team slept off and on, disturbed once by a faint howling that echoed through the cavern like a lost lovelorn soul.

In the morning, VJ checked beehives on the captives' calves. Both of Madeline's looked darker. Fuller. More rigid. She suspected more vire had been drawn inside and were trying to escape but couldn't. Cinnalan's and toddlers' beehives were fully formed and collecting foreign particles, too.

*Yes,* she mouthed when she read the questions in her kew mates eyes. *Madeline and Cinnalan are still under the vire's spell, but they are fighting, and controlling it.*

*Can you tell us anything about the toddlers?* Dom asked.

*The vaccines are protecting them. They are asleep, but they are okay.*

Communication ceased as air around the cassowary swirled like a dustless dust devil. *Guess we should feed Shadow,* Juhree said, and conjured water and overripe fruit.

*I just saw the area at the end of this tunnel arm,* VJ shared. *It's similar to the grotto where the dwellers lived and is inhabited by pairs of cassowaries. They don't live in groups, but they communicate by loud booming. The noise that disturbed us during the night came from Shadow's mate.*

A sudden loud, thunderous noise boomed through the cavern. Everyone jerked. Only the toddlers, Cinnalan and Madeline remained still. *That was Shadow,* VJ said. *He's talking to his mate. She's in the grotto.*

*The vire is cruel to keep them apart.*

*That it is.*

VJ moved, hovered above the boulder. *I sense evil but see nothing.*

*My sensors tell me a battle was waged here,* Holt said, joining her. *The dried slime lost and is near extinction. The wet slime is mulling over it, attempting to steal and absorb whatever power might remain.*

*Awesome sensors,* Drew complimented. *Mine sense the same.*

*I'm grateful for your sensors,* VJ said. *I have none.*

*Yes, you do,* Rene disagreed. *Holt and I both sense them.*

*Teach me how to use them.*

*They require intense concentration. Focus, then tell us what you sense.*

VJ's heart began to pound. *I sense the evil vire. It leaves the boulder through a ten-inch exit on the ground.*

*Where?* Holt asked.

VJ pointed at a spot about a foot from Madeline's head. *I used my special vision to see it under the klir seal tarp.*

*I did the same,* Holt said. *Now, it's plain as day.*

*Knowing where it is might help us free Madeline and the others from the spell,* VJ mouthed.

We'll keep that in mind, Holt said.

VJ had also sensed Mater Nature again. And she knew the vire didn't know Mater Nature had joined them.

~ * ~

No one complained about the wait. Everyone kept busy levitating about, inspecting the cavern, checking the captives. Except Dom. He kept a tight grip on his daughter's and sister's hands. When Verity asked why he didn't touch Madeline, he said, *I'm waiting for a signal. She's connected to you. She isn't connected to me.*

As Holt rotated his shoulders to roll tension away, Tess said, *Has anyone noticed that the flowers haven't wilted? They look as fresh today as they did yesterday.*

*I noticed,* Rene said.

*Any idea who's responsible for them?* Drew asked.

Rene, Juhree, Tess and Verity nodded. *We think we know, but we're not entirely certain. Who would you guess?*

The elementals? Drew asked.

No, VJ said.

*The evil?*

*Certainly not.*

*Who then?*

*Mater Nature.*

Holt hiked his dark eyebrows. *You think Mater Nature is responsible?*

*Yes,* VJ said. *Quite certain.* Before anyone could comment, she raised her palm to halt conversation. *Madeline has synked with me.*

*"The vire is angry that you found us. The conglomeration of evil spirits who refused to leave the world when they died is pooling its combined evil to make itself strong. They think they are stronger than they really are. They have been arguing amongst themselves, battling for control. Their goal to overtake human bodies is how they perceive they will live again and not only regain the power they once had, but increase it. Let's hope they have acted too soon, before they are truly strong enough to fatally harm."*

VJ's blood chilled as she silently relayed Madeline's information to her team and Mist and Jordan back in the valley.

*Do you think Madeline will mind if I hold her hand?* Dom mouthed.

*No.* Verity mouthed back. *If she feels your touch, it might help sustain her.*

*I want her to feel my love.*

*I believe she already does.*

*Are you still synked with her?*

*Yes. She said the vire is moving around inside the boulder.*

*We should examine the boulder again,* Holt said. *See if there's another escape route.*

Verity nodded. *Right.*

Everyone except Dom re-examined the boulder. No one found another escape trail—only the small ten-inch opening VJ had first seen.

A loud boom made everyone jump. Tess jumped higher than anyone else. *Shadow is trying to move closer.*

*He can't,* VJ said. *The vire will not allow him on this side of the cavern.*

*Do you know if the vire can fly?* Juhree asked. *Does it crawl or slither around?*

*I doubt anyone knows,* VJ said.

*What if we fail?* Dom asked. *What if March comes and goes and we're still here?*

*We won't fail,* VJ said and her kew mates bolstered each other with silent agreement.

VJ knew Drew and Rene missed Rance just as Tess and Dane missed baby Abee. Feeling a bit down, she told herself it was the vire attempting to infiltrate her mind. *What if we fail? We will not fail. But what happens if we do?"*

She kept her doubts to herself, but sensed Holt knew she had them. *How long would they continue to be inactive? How long before they could deal with the vile vire and go home?*

Holt touched her cheek gently and silently communicated. *You saw the future. You believe your vision. The rest of us believe it, too. No one will die. Apitcote will remain a secret place beneath the surface where denizens prosper and live together in peace and tranquility for many years to come.*

The weariness that had threatened to overcome her vanished. She blinked. Blinked again. Sat up straighter. *We will not spend another night in the cavern. Today will be a day like no other. It's time for the men to shave, and for the women to collect strands of hair.*

Relieved to have something different to do, teammates dug razors, combs and hairbrushes from Juhree's conjured tow sacks. Men shaved, saving odd-bits in containers Juhree also conjured, and women collected their hair strands.

*What do you plan to do with the hair?* Drew asked.

*This.* VJ spread hair bits on the ground at the edge of the boulder where the vire slime exited through the ten-inch space. *Next time vire ventures out, the slime will mix with our odd-bits. Our DNA is not very strong in hair bits, but it will infiltrate their spirits and weaken their power.*

*Brilliant!* Holt flashed a grin. *You are absolutely brilliant.* He gave her cheek a smacking kiss. *Mixing good genes with bad will dilute their evil!*

*I wish we had more hair-bits.*

*You sent for more,* Rene reminded. *Mist has been collecting them and the rezees will soon whizz them here. Drew and I will levitate them through the crawl space.*

*You're brilliant.* Drew kissed Rene.

*Absolutely brilliant,* Dom agreed.

Caught up in the excitement, Tess added, *The more hair-bits we collect from different people, the better Verity's plan will work. Varying DNA will confuse the vire, if not to extinction, then perhaps it will reduce their wicked evilness.*

Rene agreed. *I've messaged Jordan and asked him to speed the collection. Even if we fail to destroy the vire, its power and hatred will be weakened, its desire to harm reduced.*

*The vire won't know what we've done,* Holt said. *It will expect to be superior. And that will aid in its destruction.*

*Spot on,* VJ cheered silently, aiming her thumb at the dark cavern ceiling.

*Should we look around the boulder again and make sure there's only one vire entry and exit?* Monteith asked.

*Yes. Be sure to keep your full masks in place. We don't want to give the vire a chance to attach to any part of our bodies. We shall either defeat or outsmart or destroy. There is no other way.*

As they had done before, Kew mates levitated around and above the huge boulder, inspecting, sensing, inhaling. Finally, Holt concluded, *There's only the one entry you found early on, Verity.*

VJ nodded. *Madeline just said the vire wants me to open so it can attach and communicate. It will want the same from each of you. Take care to keep yourselves closed. Bloxed. As I mentioned earlier, the vire hears but cannot see. It depends on sound and vibrations to get where it wants to go. When differing factions argue and disagree, the vire separates and loses some of its power. When we strike, we should do so when it is at its most vulnerable.*

*How will we destroy the vire if we can't see it?* Juhree asked.

*Do you have a suggestion?* VJ prompted.

*We could seal it inside the boulder, cover it with klir seal suit substance, pour cement over and around the klir seal, and repeat the process. Will that be strong enough to contain it?*

*I'm certain it will, and I was hoping you would volunteer. Is that something you can do?*

*Absolutely.*

*Good plan,* Monteith approved.

*How long will the klir seal and cement last?* Holt asked.

*Thousands of years. After that, it will be up to new generations to face the problem we now face."*

Madeline squeezed VJ's hand. She closed her eyes and listened. *"Cinnalan is communicating with Shadow. The vire didn't keep its promise to reunite him with his mate. Shadow is terribly upset and wants to destroy the vire."*

*"What can he do?"*

*"Less than the nine of you. They're using his anger to fuel their power."*

*"Can we do something to ease Shadow's distress?"*

*"Cinnalan said he would like someone to touch him."*

*"I'll tell my kew mates."*

*"Will you give Dom a message?"*

*"You know I will."*

*"Thank him for coming with you. Tell him I love him."*

VJ relayed the conversation. Patted Dom's arm when he smiled. Able to see Shadow now, she walked to the other end of cavern, and petted him with her gloved hands. *I see the cassowary. You can see him, too.*

Tension in the thick dank air relaxed as the team watched her gently stroke the huge bird no one had encountered before. *Shadow's mate is wailing. Do you hear her?*

Each kew mate nodded as faraway wails echoed through the tunnel and into the cavern. It was a reminder that they were all far from their families and people they loved. Suddenly VJ felt isolated. Nine against the vire, plus Madeline and Cinnalan, who slept, and twelve toddlers, two of whom had not been reported missing, and were not inoculated, and none who had so much as twitched a muscle, weren't very good odds against an enemy no one could see.

Madeline conveyed more information. *The vire left the valley some time ago and is returning, crawling in here, slithering beneath the klir seal Juhree provided. Apitcote's denizens numbered in the hundreds when the vire spirits were locked inside the boulder many years ago. Denizens now number in the thousands. The vire is not prepared to face so many humans, although they think they are. Be careful. They want your magic. If they seize you, they will try to turn your magic on you, Verity."*

*Check this out.* Holt extended his afone.

VJ glanced at the small screen. *Troops of denizens on hoverz bikes are heading this way.*

*Dozens,* he agreed.

Rene said, *Mist is videoing and sending her live feed to the TV station for broadcasting. She and Jordan left Joel and Noel with her parents. They'll be joining us.*

*Amma is awake, and she's driving a hoverz bike with the rezees,* Dom conveyed.

*Team leaders in every kluster have gathered their teams and joined the army of denizens,* Drew added.

*They're whizzing through the forest. Kampers and Komads have joined them.*

*Who are they?* Dom asked.

*People who live and thrive in our forests. The trolls stole two of their children,* Rene reported. *The two who are not inoculated and weren't reported missing in the valley. I messaged Mist and Jordan that everyone will have to be levitated through the crawl space. They agreed to do it.*

VJ raised her hand, palm out to stem further conversation. *Madeline is sharing info.*

*"A ginormous discussion in going on inside the boulder. The vire has divided itself into three factions. Apart, they are not nearly as strong as they are when they agree and act as one. They know there's a mass migration of denizens heading here. They are angrier and more frustrated than I even perceived. United or divided, they won't give up without a fight."*

*"What will they do?"*

*"That information has been kept from me. If all else fails, I fear they will kill me and Cinnalan to prove their power. So far, they haven't succeeded in snatching a single body or controlling one mind. They are blaming each other for their massive failure. We can only hope they acted too soon, before they were strong enough to cause serious harm."*

*"You're not alone, are you, Madeline?"*

*"No. I am not."* Her lips curved in the sweetest smile VJ had ever seen.

*"Will you do me a favor, Madeline?"*

*"I'll try."*

*"Thank Mater Nature for being with you."*

*"That I can do."*

*"Do you see her?"*

*"I do. However, I cannot see you, Verity. Nor can I feel you. Are you still you holding my hand?*

*"Yes."* VJ squeezed. *"Did you feel that?"*

*"I feel nothing—except light—bright shining light. It's coming from Mater Nature. Do you see the light?*

*"No. But I sense it."*

*"The elementals are returning."*

VJ tore her concerned gaze from Madeline. A collection of colorful luminescent insects she had seen in her vision were fluttering through the entry, lighting the cavern as the swarm grew and circled the ceiling.

A tiny light bubbled from Madeline's lips. Floated in slow motion toward the cavern ceiling, as though borne by tiny fairy's wings. The light expanded filling the cavern with light brighter than the midday sun. From the ceiling, a single beam shot down to Madeline.

Dozens of beams fell, each one sparkling with a brightness, the likeness of which VJ had never seen. Or even imagined. The beams spread, landing on kew mates, Cinnalan, Dom, Orlane and the other eleven toddlers. It was like witnessing a miracle in full, animated, color motion.

The swarm of elementals descended to the sleeping victims, forming a protective shield as they fluttered and hovered.

Then Mater Nature spoke. *You have the gifts and power to bury the evil vire that escaped the boulder. Do what you must to rid it from this realm. We shall contain it within this chamber.*

"Madeline's beehives are shrinking," Rene announced. "Do you know what that means, Verity?"

"Cinnalan's is shrinking too. The serum is doing its job. Collecting and destroying the vire." Something silenced VJ. Paralyzed her. Trapped her. Sucked her inside the boulder. She didn't have to guess what it was. She had been there before.

She tried to communicate. Didn't know if it worked. So she shouted: "I'm inside the boulder. Surrounded by stone. It's pitch black. Confining. Stifling. I can barely breathe. The vire is sucking air out of my lungs."

"Don't let it!" Rene shouted back.

Suddenly, everything went quiet. VJ felt woozy. She was outside her body. But still felt cold.

Was she dead? She saw Holt kneeling beside her—as still as an ice sculpture—his expression frozen in shock and fear as he stared at her, his fingers caressing the ring on her left hand.

Then she heard Madeline. *"I'm in here with you, Verity. Mater Nature can pull us from the boulder, but you will no longer be mortal if that is what you choose. If you wish to stay alive, you must summon the strength to free yourself."*

Although she was not inside her body, VJ felt sick to her stomach as she recalled her vision of having to make a choice between Holt and Madeline.

A glimpse of Holt holding her in his loving arms flashed. She didn't want to die. Didn't want to leave Holt. If she accepted Mater Nature's offer, she would lose him.

She had lost him once. Determined not to lose him again, she summoned a glimpse of her tying ring and the bracelet with twin entwined hearts, believing they could help her navigate through the chaos. Sure enough, they filled her sight, and spun and spun.

"Help" she screamed, wondering if Holt could hear her. "Please," she begged, "please help me, Holt. I am trapped with the vire."

He blew at the boulder.

VJ felt air squiggle through the thick, solid stone. She sucked it in, kept staring at the whirling ring and heart bracelet.

He blew again. She sucked again. Greedily. She knew her body was outside the boulder. Still, she felt faint. Woozy.

With the greatest effort she had ever known, she blew. And flew. Right through the cold dense stone. She landed on top of the boulder. Stared down at Holt's head. Her body no longer lay on the ground.

"Holt."

He looked up. Spread his arms. She slid into them like a well-greased nail. They clung while Kew mates clapped and cheered. Thrills as strong as a powerful orgasm raced through her and she knew Holt felt the same conjoining thrills. Raising her left hand, she placed her yellow Canary diamond ring against his gold band. Golden electric sparks glittered from both rings. She interpreted that as a sign of victory. Also, a defining moment that would forever be relived and remembered.

She inhaled deeply, sucking in needed air with great gulps.

Happy to be free, she had a sudden urge to weep. Had she lost Madeline? Left her inside the boulder to fight alone? Or to be pulled by Mater Nature, and no longer mortal?

Knowing they would both fight to do what each deemed right, VJ gasped, "We need to contain the vire."

"Righto." Juhree conjured a huge klir seal sheet. Monteith helped her fling it over the boulder.

Frightened she might be drawn back inside the boulder, VJ clung to Holt's strong arms until his afone beeped. All the others beeped too. Dane sent a silent message. *Check your afones. A broadcaster is announcing that all the sleepers in the valley are awake and—*

"We haven't the time." VJ leapt from Holt's sheltering arms and sprang into action.

"We've come to help," a group of tall strangers announced, ducking under the low cavern entry.

"Who are you?" Dom asked.

"Komads and kampers. Evil spirits stole two of our young uns."

# Twenty-four

A loud noise drew attention. The cassowary was visible. He tried to move. But his feet were frozen to the ground.

*Free him. Send him to his mate.*

Holt didn't know whether he heard the words or merely thought them as Cinnalan awakened, passed Orlane to Dom, and shot across the cavern chamber. Her feet didn't touch ground, not even when she petted Shadow.

"You shouldn't touch the cassowary without gloves or protection," Dom shouted.

"It's all right," Cinnalan shouted back. "All the vire left him and united inside the boulder.'

The huge bird lowered his head to her shoulder. She patted his head, then guided him toward the exit.

"This is it!" Verity's shout echoed through the cavern.

Shadow jumped at the boulder, using his secret weapon, lethal five-inch dagger claws. The boulder cracked. Started to split.

"Hair bits," Verity shouted. "Need hair bits. Stat!"

Rene levitated what they had left. Verity tossed them at the splitting boulder. "Need more. Scissors. Juhree. Please conjure scissors."

As soon as she did, Verity whacked off strands of her long black hair and threw them at the splitting boulder. Kew mates, komads and kampers did the same as Shadow jumped again. The boulder broke apart, tumbled in opposite directions. The klir cover followed one half.

Shadow attacked the other half in a frenzy. Teammates tossed more shorn locks at the split boulder. Turning to the other half boulder, the cassowary kicked again and again, its lethal claws pounding while mates cut and tossed more hair.

The electric mood intensified as Mist, Jordan and rezees whizzed through the entry, carrying tow sacks filled with hair-bits. Kew mates grabbed the sacks. Scattered bits. Covered every inch of the split boulder.

Vire surged from the rubble. Its slime formed a smoky cloud. Billowed and heaved toward VJ. Holt threw more hair bits. Kew mates did the same, momentarily obliterating their own vision. The cloud lunged at Holt. Trapped him inside.

VJ held her breath, willing Holt to hear her. "Breathe in the filtered air from your klir seal suit. Use your nose. Do not breathe through your mouth. Do not taste or inhale the vire essence."

Watching him struggle made her feel faint. Her knees turned weak. She swayed. Saw Holt touch his ring before he curled his knees to his chest. She felt him gather a spurt of inhuman strength. Straighten his body. Hiss the breath from his lungs with one mighty blow.

The surrounding vire fell away from Holt. Surged toward Madeline's body only to be thwarted after mixing with airborne hair-bits and Holt's outstretched arms that magically forced the vire back toward the boulder.

As though drugged, the cloud weaved back and forth, suspended in mid-air.

"Heat," VJ gasped. "Use your heat, Holt."

He aimed his fingers at the cloud. Dane aimed his, too.

Their combined heat was not enough, VJ realized. Turning her wrist, she aimed her ring and bracelet at the cloud. A jolt of lightning speared from her ring and the twin hearts. Struck the cloud, creating a bright fire. Flames circled the mass and burned—a brilliant mixture of blue, yellow and orange.

VJ sent another lightning bolt. The fiery cloud swayed drunkenly toward the boulder. Kew mates threw more hair bits. The mass sucked them in, greedily.

In unison, kew mates blew, separating the fiery mass into thin wisps that exploded into a blizzard of tiny ash shards. They tossed more bits at the shards.

Fire and flames flared and then disappeared, along with the smoke as the airborne vire died, its black ashes dropping on the separated boulder.

"Now, Juhree!" VJ shouted. "Now!"

Whipping her arms, Juhree conjured another huge klir seal cover. VJ and Holt slammed it over and all around the dual mounds. Sensing vire attempting to escape at the bottom, VJ reached for another sack of hair. But Dom was already dumping massive hair bits.

She sucked in a deep filtered breath as she and Holt secured the klir seal cover at the base and tightened it across the ten-inch escape hatch, duly noting the small amount of living vire clinging to mortal hair bits.

Juhree conjured buckets of cement. Kew mates poured the thick mixture over the mounds, forming another layer on top of the trapped dead ashes and what remained of the live vire slime.

Holt and Dane sent heat to partially dry the cement, knowing it would take months, possibly years, to cure in the cold, dank cavern.

Juhree conjured another klir seal sheet. All kew mates helped settle it on top of the hardening cement.

Minalu and denizens had arrived. VJ didn't know when. Her thoughts were on Madeline as she directed mates and helped finish what still needed to be done.

Juhree conjured more batches of cement. The team worked tirelessly, alternating klir seal covers and cement until there were ten layers of each.

Shadow turned toward the cavern exit.

Denizens and kew mates backed away to give the huge bird room. The cassowary opened his wide mouth and spit at the cement mound before he trotted through the exit, like a proud, prancing horse. With one loud bellow, he galloped down the tunnel toward the grotto to join his mate.

Mater Nature's light brightened. *Well done, my friends.* Her light began to dim as though signaling the elementals to withdraw. With one dip that looked like a salute to all those in the crowded cavern, the magic insects flew away in tandem, back through the entry above denizens' heads, their gentle musical humming gone when the last tiny light disappeared.

The flowers that had guarded the captives shimmered in the sparse cavern light as they fluttered through the air, landed on the boulder and planted their stems in moist cement.

Looking awed and relieved, denizens, komads and kampers carried kidlings from the cavern, out into the tunnel.

Toddlers awakened.

But Madeline did not.

Staring up at the cavern ceiling, VJ watched Mater Nature's light make a slow trail back to Madeline where it rested at the seam of her lips.

VJ's heart stopped. For one frozen moment, she thought she saw Madeline's spirt take hold of the beam and float up to where it hovered, high above. The beam blinked off.

Only a few helmet lights lit the cavern that smelled of wet cement and fresh flowers. Kew mates were out of breath, but full of great satisfaction as denizens chanted, swelling in song after they heard Mist announce, "The evil vire is gone. It will harm us no more."

Dropping to her knees, VJ took hold of Madeline's hand. Cold and stiff. Her fingers were the opposite. Limp and warm. Her face was cool to the touch. Her expression at peace. Puzzled by the odd combination, she inhaled. Knew Madeline had escaped the boulder. And was still alive. But where? In their world? Or another?

VJ looked at up her kew mates. Then at Dom. Cinnalan. Minalu.

Their silent question matched hers.

*Will she wake up?*

VJ found an answer. "If Madeline chooses life, she will awaken when she finishes talking with Mater Nature." VJ reached for Holt's hand. But he wasn't where he had been moments before.

Frantic, she swiveled her gaze, searched the cavern. "Where is Holt?"

Everyone turned their heads, looking for him. "He must have stepped outside," Monteith said.

Jumping to her feet, VJ leapt through the entry.

Holt was walking away in the direction the cassowary had gone.

"Holt," she called. "Stop please."

He did. When she reached him, he touched her cheek gently, tenderly. "I love you."

"And I love you. I can't live without you. You mustn't leave me."

He bent his head. Kissed her, tenderly. Then he smiled. "I couldn't leave you, regardless of how hard I might try."

"Why are you out here?"

"I wanted to thank the elementals for protecting the children. And I did."

"Thank you. I love you more than the whole world. Don't ever scare me like that again or I'll—I'll—"

He cut off her stammer with another kiss.

"Thanks for ending my tirade," she said. "I don't know what I'd do if you left me."

"I know what you would do."

"What?"

"Track me down and kidnap me."

She laughed. "Exactly."

Taking his hand, she urged him back inside the cavern.

Madeline was still asleep. VJ sensed she had entered a different dimension. Wondered if she would ever talk to her friend again.

"Please tell me Madeline will awaken," Dom beseeched, his eyes flooded with emotion.

"I can't. I have a feeling she is being given a choice between living and going somewhere that's different than dying, but no longer in our realm."

"The denizens are departing," Rene said quietly as more left the crowded tunnel. Crawled through the short crawl space. Began their trek back to the valley.

Those who stayed behind waited for Madeline to stir, concern evident by their grave expressions.

VJ lifted Madeline's limp arm. Touched her entwined heart bracelet to Madeline's. Both silver bracelets glittered in VJ's helmet light. The entwined hearts turned to gold.

Madeline's cheek twitched. Then her eyelids fluttered.

"I think she's waking up," Dom said, holding her other hand.

"She is," VJ agreed, relieved Madeline had decided to come back and knowing her friend would be changed by what she had experienced.

"Hello," Dom said when she opened her eyes.

Instead of replying, Madeline smiled at him, then at each team member who had spent hours guarding her and the others.

"Thank you for coming to our aid," she said, her voice as light as a whisper. "I could not always communicate, although I knew all of you were with me in spirit."

Her gaze settled on VJ, and she sent a silent communication. *I've never felt like I did much good in the world, and I don't understand how I am so fortunate to have you in my life. You've always been there when I needed you. I could not have survived the vire without you. I owe you more than I may ever be capable of repaying.*

VJ was too choked up to reply. And she knew Madeline understood.

Turning her gaze to Holt, Madeline said, "I have missed doing the washing up with you and Verity Jane. Those days and nights in your cottage will always be cherished memories."

When she looked at Dom, all she said was, "I would like to go home."

"Do you want something to eat or drink first?" Holt asked.

"No. I am neither hungry nor thirsty. I am replete."

A somber lot levitated Minalu, her family, and Madeline back to kluster twenty-four.

"I don't want to be alone," Madeline said after Holt placed her gently on her bed.

"I'll stay with you," Dom offered, "unless you prefer Verity."

"I prefer you." Again, her voice was a mere whisper.

"If you want something to eat, Juhree conjured soup, tea and Jell-o," VJ said.

"You will thank her for me?"

"You know I will. Rest and get well, Madeline. I'm not the only one who needs you."

~ * ~

Verity, Holt and Dom waited patiently for Madeline to tell them about her time with Mater Nature, hoping she would share when she was ready. Madeline didn't look different, and yet, she did. Her demeanor had changed as well. Quiet. Serene. Very soft spoken. Between Dom and his family, she was never by herself.

One evening, when the two couples sat together in her cottage, she said, "We did the full monty, Ver. We pursued the evil spirits to the absolute limit, and prevented them from harming humans."

"Yes," Verity agreed.

"I'm ready to explain what happened whilst I was in the cavern."

"What?" Verity asked, and Holt sensed she knew he and Dom wanted to hear but were reluctant to pry.

"I am one of them."

"Them?"

"Mater Nature's helpers. Like you, I am capable of magic." She looked from Verity to Holt and then at Dom. "I can grow your hair back to what it was before you sheared your locks to help defeat the vire." Raising her hands, she touched each one, and restored hair length and thickness.

Verity merely stared.

"That isn't the most important thing I learned from Mater Nature."

"What is?" Dom asked.

"Love." Madeline turned her gaze to Verity. "Love saved you, too."

She nodded. "Love pulled me from the boulder more than once."

"You communed with Mater Nature?" Dom asked, his gaze tender.

"We did not commune. We talked, face to face. She taught me much. So very, very much."

"What does she look like?"

"An ethereal nymph. More beautiful than anyone or anything I've ever seen. Kinder than kind. Gentler than gentle.

Wiser than wise. Too amazing to be real. That is why we don't see her. She is too perfect for our world."

~ * ~

Another week passed before VJ managed to speak with Madeline alone.

"It seems years since we've had a good chinwag."

"It certainly does," Madeline agreed. "Silent communication isn't nearly as good as a long gab."

"Should I make tea?"

"I already have." Madeline summoned her teapot with a gentle fling of her wrist, and filled two teacups. "Dom and his family have spoiled me. I have done nothing beyond being waited on. Don't get me wrong, mind you. I adore them and everything they have done, but I don't feel as though I deserve such attention."

"Why not, you braver-than-brave lady?"

"Because I am me, not a princess nor a heroine."

"You are a heroine in every sense of the word. You saved Apitcote from evil. Because of you, the sleeping sickness and vire are gone."

"I'm not the one who saved Apticote. There isn't a denizen who didn't play a part in ridding the realm of the vire, whether they went to the cavern or stayed behind."

"You are the one who held it off."

"I couldn't have done so without you."

"Have you made a decision about Dom?"

"Not yet. I cannot encourage him because we aren't 'there.' I need time. I cannot commit until I have adjusted to my new way of thinking."

"I knew you would be changed."

"I'm not sure I want to be. It's rather frightening. I may always be alone. Loving Dom may never be enough for me to form a lifetime commitment."

Setting her cup and saucer down, VJ reached for Madeline's hands. "I'm here whenever you need me or want to talk."

"I know." Madeline smiled. "I have a request."

"I know." VJ extended her arm, the one with the twin heart bracelet and touched her hearts to Madeline's. "Mater Nature turned them to gold."

Madeline nodded. "Yes. And at last, I feel whole again."

Tears fogged VJ's vision.

"I sense you would like to hear more about Mater Nature."

"I am curious," VJ admitted.

"Her hair is spun of both gold and silver threads. And she is tall. Taller than the bristlecone pines in Placer Valley. Taller than the ceiling in the cavern. She knelt to fit in. She is more beautiful than all the beauty in the galaxy. Wiser than any human. She is you and me and all women who cherish love and peace."

"Do you regret not going with her?"

"You knew I had a choice?"

"I knew."

"I could not go without you, Verity. You summoned her to me. You're the reason she offered to take me away from mortal cares. The one who convinced Apitcote's denizens that the rash and sleeping illness didn't come from Minalu's sept."

"Actually, I did very little."

"Not true. You helped the rezees create serum for the vaccines. You directed the action of every kew mate in the cavern. You worked as fast as humanly possible and somehow managed to keep the vire away from Cinnalan and me and the toddlers."

"Mater Nature and flowers and elementals kept the vire away, not me."

"You were responsible for them being there."

"Was I?"

"We both know you were. And now, I'm ready to discuss what most disturbs me. I killed," she said sadly. "I drew as much of the vire as possible into the beehives and destroyed it. If I had it to do again, I would."

"You didn't kill. The vire wasn't human. It was spirits—evil spirits. And a lot of things helped destroy the vire."

"I will always feel as though I killed, and I would not like that information to leave my cottage."

"Your secrets are safe with me."

"You know my other as well?"

"Yes."

"Does it show?"

"To me. I see a part of Mater Nature glowing in your eyes. She would not want you to feel it is a burden or keep you from finding happiness with a mate."

"I know. I will adjust. And I shall never leave Apitcote. Not even for a moment. You and Holt and Mater Nature are my family. At one time, the thought of never returning to England saddened me. Now, it is a relief not to feel I must return to see Mum. Mater Nature arranged a visit between us whilst I hibernated. Mum divorced Paw after you and I left England. She lives with her sister by the sea in Bournemouth. None of my brothers have married. They still live with Paw and spend a great deal of time at the local. They do not cook. They live on pub grub and ale. They are a sorry lot. They do not miss me or Mum. And we do not miss them."

"That part of your life is behind."

"And has been for a long time."

"The future is ahead. Unknown."

"True, although I know I will be invited to join your kew. I shall refuse. Minalu's family is a kew unto themselves. Someday, if my love is truly enough for Dom and for me, I could be part of their family. We will not levitate but we will all have magic."

"You are magic, Madd."

Madeline's smile encompassed her entire face. "I would love to be Orlane's step-mum. I would also like a child of my own. I am not sure I would like another husband. I do not wish to fail again."

"In Apitcote, it isn't unusual for singles to parent a child without a live-in mate."

"I know. However, that won't work for Dom or for me. We are both too traditional to rob a child of living with two parents."

"There's no reason you can't both love Orlane and help raise another child, is there?"

Madeline's eyes glowed. "Thank you for reminding me that the future is open to all possibilities."

"Please do remember one thing, Madeline. Sometimes, in the American game of baseball, batters often strike twice before one scores a home run."

"I shall keep that in mind." Madeline smiled again. "You need no permission to share this conversation with Holt. I give it anyway. There should no secrets between those who love as you do."

"I love you, Madd."

"And you know I love you, Verity Jane."

Back home, VJ smiled at Holt who had arrived at the cottage moments before. "I'd like to 'open' and allow you to 'read' my conversation with Madeline."

"There's no need."

"I know, but I want you to know because I want no secrets to divide us."

Holt smiled. "Mind if we cuddle by a fire while I 'read' you?"

"That would be lovely."

He sent his heat and started a fire, then sat beside her and wrapped her between his arms.

When he finished 'reading' her, VJ said, "When we were in Denver and you offered me a job last September, I didn't understand why you mentioned researching departed spirits. You had an Arcane premonition, didn't you?"

"Yeah. After the kew discovered Apitcote had two more enquays, I sensed the evil. It was similar to what I experienced when Jilly's spirit invaded."

"I apologize for not taking your comment seriously. There will always be evil in the world."

"And there will always be people like us who do their best to overcome evil so we and those we love may live in peace."

"Do you resent my friendship with Madeline?" she asked.

"No. Do you resent mine with Juhree?" he countered,

"I almost did when I first met her, but Monteith set me straight. She's like the sister you always wanted Jilly to be."

"And Madeline is your sister."

"True. But you are my greatest love."

"As you are mine."

# Twenty-five

The call from Philadelphia came a week later, after tranquil days and passionate love-filled nights.

Holt grinned as he answered. "Hello, Hanna. How are you?"

"At the moment I'm fine, but it's time for you to see Harmony. Can you come to the surface?"

"Is tomorrow too soon?"

"Tomorrow is good."

Verity didn't say much when he told her they were going. Holt had a feeling she was nervous about meeting Hanna, but beyond eager to see Harmony.

As soon as they reached the surface, he asked, "Would you mind if we go see Hanna and Harmony before we check into our hotel?"

"Of course not. I'm as anxious as you are."

Hanna's college friend opened the front door. Like them, Francine wore a mask, but her coverall was stark white and cumbersome looking, quite unlike their form fitting klir seal suits.

"Glad you're here," Francine said as Harmony rushed forward and wrapped her little arms around Holt when he knelt in front of her.

"You look fun-nee."

"These outfits protect us from your mater's illness," Holt explained.

"Out-fit. Me wanna outfit."

"Maybe that can be arranged." Scooping her up, he hugged her tight. Looked around. "Where's Hanna?"

"In her room."

Holt wasn't prepared to see Hanna in bed. Not even when Verity shot a silent message. *She hasn't recovered from Covid. And she didn't tell you.*

Hanna looked frail. Far worse than he could have imagined. When she spoke, her voice sounded weak. Strained. "I'm ready for Harmony to be with you. I want you to take her home. I am dying."

Holt's heart felt like it weighed a ton. "We should take you to Api, Hanna."

"We've been over that." She coughed until she was worn out, too weak to open her eyes.

*I understand why she refused,* VJ silently communicated. *She doesn't want to take the chance of spreading Covid.*

"She would be better off in my homeland."

"Perhaps. Perhaps not. The virus is wicked, Holt. In Denver, I saw patients in hospital who returned a few months after they healed from Covid. Some had heart conditions. Others had respiratory problems. A few had both. Doctors feared internal organs were permanently damaged. I don't suppose the medical profession will know the truth for a long time."

"Have you had a vision of her?"

"No."

Holt turned his gaze back to Hanna. "She's resting."

"I'm not resting. I'm gathering my thoughts. I want to talk to Verity. Alone."

Still holding Harmony, Holt carried her from the room. VJ saw him dry the tears running down Harmony's dimpled cheeks.

After Holt shut the door, Hanna said, "Please sit. What I have to say will take more than a moment."

VJ perched on the chair beside the bed.

"I could not die until I saw you."

VJ didn't correct her. Hanna was diseased. Very near death's door. "I have looked forward to meeting you. We'll take good care of Harmony."

"I know you will. That is not why I waited for you." She closed her eyes. Inhaled slowly. Weakly.

The physician part of VJ wanted to help. Knew there was nothing she could do. She touched Hanna's bony wrists, anyway, hoping her gift to heal might work. "Can I do anything for you?"

"Only listen. And not judge. Or fault Holt."

"I shan't."

"That will make my passing easier. I want to unburden my conscience. One night in a weak moment when I was down in the dumps, I answered a question Holt occasionally asked, which I continually ignored. I agreed to tie with him. I regretted my decision immediately and would have withdrawn my 'yes' had he not told me you were back in his life, but resistant to staying in Api. I thought if you both believed he wasn't free to tie with you, that you would desire each other more so I strung him along, knowing you were both suffering, but growing closer, nonetheless. You are his One."

"I believe that."

Hanna closed her weary eyes. "I have more to tell." Her voice sounded a bit stronger, but there were still tremors. "Please listen with an open heart and try not to judge me too harshly."

"I'm not a judge."

"But you are the woman Holt loves; therefore, you deserve to know that Holt is Harmony's father."

VJ's heart nearly stopped. Shock numbed her brain. But visions of Holt and Hanna together in bed swam before her eyes. Raw, gut-wrenching pain swirled, deep down. She felt like the 'other' woman who had no right to be there. And betrayed by the knowledge Holt had withheld.

"You are upset."

"I am fine," she forced herself to say.

"I'll give you a few moments to calm yourself."

How does one calm oneself when one hears such news? Why hadn't he told her?

Painful thoughts tumbled inside. Holt and Hanna had made a baby together! Why had he let her believe he and Hanna were merely co-workers? Friends? That he had done a good deed by agreeing to be Harmony's guardian if anything happened to Hanna?

VJ inhaled, and summoned the capacity to rationalize. Holt had turned to Hanna after she left Apitcote, so she shouldn't resent their relationship. He didn't expect to see her again. He loved Harmony because he was her father. Had they lived together as a family in Api before Hanna returned to the surface to care for her mum?

Hanna coughed. Motioned at a white plastic bottle on the night stand. VJ helped her sip dry mouth solution and spit it into a clean basin.

"It wasn't as you may assume," Hanna said. "You are smart, but you haven't realized the truth. Holt promised not to tell anyone. Ever. Except his parents. But I want you to know. Holt and I did not sleep together. We were never intimate. Harmony was created in a petri dish. I had in vitro-fertilization. Holt was the donor."

VJ's brain struggled to register Hanna's confession as she continued. "I had my eggs harvested when I was in college. A fertility doctor told me eggs are most healthy when one is young. I knew I would never marry. My cousins took turns raping me when I was a teenager. After those horrible experiences, I couldn't stand the idea of intimacy, and I vowed never to be mauled again. The mere idea makes me vomit. Because I'm so squeamish, I insisted my doctor, my female doctor, put me to sleep for in vitro fertilization."

"Thank you for telling me."

"I don't want Harmony to suffer for my actions."

"She won't."

Hanna managed a feeble smile. "I thought I would feel better if people believed the donor was anonymous. Holt agreed to keep my secret. He isn't just a good man. He's the best of the best. I knew when I met him that he was the man I wanted to father my child. It took months to convince him. He finally did, but only after I agreed to live in Api and, if we had had a son, he would assume all of the responsibility for raising him. I would share as much of his life as possible. If we had a daughter, I would be responsible. That is the Api way. We were both eager to be parents, but neither wanted intimacy. Holt didn't betray you. His love for you is honest, true, unfaltering. He is a faithful man. Your One and Only."

Hanna's words had slowed. Her voice had lost its strength. She closed her eyes briefly. "Did you and Madeline enjoy the flowers?"

"Flowers?" VJ asked, puzzled. Then she knew. "You're the one who sends them?"

"Holt sent the first few—the roses, exotic potted plants, chrysanthemums. I made arrangements with the florist for weekly deliveries after Holt told me you had returned. I wanted you to feel welcome. To stay. To be with him. To be Harmony's other mother and help us raise her. I didn't know until Covid struck the second time that we wouldn't share."

"And the gifts? Did you arrange for those?"

"No. Holt must have. The flowers will stop when I'm gone. Will you explain why to your friend, Madeline?"

"Yes. But I agree with Holt. We should take you to Api."

"It's too late. Even if I had gone there after Mother passed away, I don't believe Api could have saved me. I already had Covid. When I stopped texting, I was in the hospital, too sick to lift my afone. It's an awful disease."

As though the conversation had exhausted her, Hanna's eyelids fluttered shut. When she spoke, her voice sounded even weaker than moments before. "I have arranged to be cremated, but if I were to have a headstone I wouldn't mind if it read, 'Here lies a great manipulator.' Hanna smiled, a truly beautiful smile, and VJ thought the manipulator looked like an angel, or exactly how one ought to look.

"I knew Holt would be a truly good father, and I am absolutely right. Harmony inherited all of his good qualities, including his magic and, hopefully, none of my bad."

Too weak to move more than her eyes, she stared at VJ. "Please summon the others."

VJ opened the door, motioned Holt, Harmony and Francine in.

"I wanted to see you one last time and say goodbye. This is my last day. My trek to the stars."

VJ took her limp hand and squeezed gently. Hanna whispered only four more words. "Take care of Har-man-nee."

"We will," Holt promised, still holding Harmony and tightening his arms when she started to cry.

Hanna stared unseeingly at the ceiling. VJ knew she was gone before she checked her pulse. Collecting her emotions, she closed Hanna's unseeing eyes, crossed her hands on her chest.

"We should call hospice. Or nine-one-one. Someone needs to declare her dead."

"I'll call hospice," Francine murmured. "They will facilitate her transport to a mortuary."

"Did she sign a 'do not resuscitate' document?" VJ asked, as a doctor ought.

"Yes. It's on the dining room table, along with instructions. She made arrangements to be cremated. No funeral. No service."

After she left the room, VJ said, "I've seen a number of people die. I've never seen anyone as brave as Hanna."

"She was a remarkable lady," Holt said.

Wanting comfort, VJ leaned close, inhaling his essence as he embraced her with his free arm.

"Mommie gone," Harmony said, tears rolling down her cheeks.

"She went to be with her mum," VJ said. "She knows we love you, Harmony, and will give you the best care we are capable of giving."

Holt pulled them both closer. "How are you?" he asked.

"Good."

"Are you sure?"

"Yes." Her voice quivered and tears formed.

"Did she tell you I'm Harmony's biological father?"

"Yes."

"I wanted to, but I had given my word."

"I know."

VJ looked at Harmony again. "Do you know you're going to live with us?"

She nodded. "Mommy said I will live with Pater and my new mummy."

More tears flooded Verity's eyes. One fell, landed on her ring. Another landed on her heart bracelet. "You gave me a ring and twin heart bracelets to me and Madeline. They're what brought her back and helped me escape from the stone. How did you know?"

"I forged them to protect you both."

"I thought Mater Nature turned the hearts to gold, but it was you, wasn't it?"

"I charged them with protection charms, but I did not use magic to change silver to gold. That must have been Mater Nature. And I am pleased you both wear them every day."

VJ leaned her head against his shoulder. "I'm so grateful for you. For your love. Your strength. Your magic.

"No more grateful than I am for you." Holt kissed her tenderly.

"I wan kiss," Harmony said.

After each kissed one of her cheeks, Holt said, "Your mater was very brave, Harmony. A wonderful mum. Part of her will live on in you."

"Yes," Harmony agreed with a nod. "Down. I wan down."

Lowering her to the floor, Holt laced his fingers with VJ's as Harmony tugged them from Hanna's room to hers. Letting go, she picked up a photo collage and pointed at Hanna. "Mommy." Next, she pointed at Holt. "Pater." Tapping her thumb on Verity's photo, she said, "Mummy. Doctor Beratee." Last, she pointed at herself. "Harmony. Daughter."

"I think Hanna did her best to make the transition for Harmony as easy as possible," Holt said as Harmony plopped on the floor and gazed at the photos.

"I agree."

"Are we going to be okay?" Holt asked.

Verity smiled through her tears. "We already are."

"Do you resent Harmony?"

"No. I love her. And if I hadn't left three and a half years ago, you probably wouldn't have fathered her. I wouldn't know Vincent is my father, and he wouldn't have married Mum. Our lives unfolded as they should. We are together now."

"You're right. Again. Which doesn't surprise me. That's only one of the many reasons I love you."

Verity turned her smile on Harmony. "Your new mummy would like to hold you. May I?"

Harmony jumped up. Raised eager arms. VJ lifted and hugged her.

Two fat tears escaped Holt's eyes as he realized there was no gap between the two females he loved with all his heart. No need to bond. They already had.

Harmony reached out and patted his cheek. "Don't ky, Pater."

He wrapped his arms around her and Verity again.

Harmony clapped her small hands, her cheeks dimpled with childish delight. "We fam-lee."

Holt could only marvel and rejoice as he held his two most precious gifts close. Hanna had knitted them together before she died. Her gift would grow, as would love and devotion.

Verity's eyes filled with love and compassion as she mopped his tears. "Are you okay?"

"Yes," he said, his voice husky with emotion.

VJ kissed him, basking in the glory of their love.

"Kiss me," Harmony said. Once again, they each obliged.

Then Holt said, "You had a vision about the future, didn't you?"

"Yes. I'd like to share it with you. And with our kew mates as well."

"Tell me now."

"In a few years, we will invite two more people to join the kew. They will claim to be time travelers. I don't know whether they will accept our invitation, but I do know they will love Apitcote as we do and be tempted to live there."

"Another adventure to look forward to," Holt said, smiling.

"I wan a-vent-ure," Harmony said.

Verity caressed her cheek. "You will have many, sweetheart."

"I magic. See." With a quick jerk, Harmony flew out of their arms and levitated around her bedroom.

"Did you know she inherited your magic?" VJ asked.

"Yeah. That's one reason she started talking so soon."

Not knowing what else to say or do, she asked, "Is there anything I can do to help you now?"

Holt shook his head. "I have but one need."

"And what might that be, dear husband?"

"Daily doses of thee, Dr. Berratee."

Harmony flew back into their arms. "I wan dose of Dr. Berratee, too."

"You shall have all the doses you want," VJ promised before she kissed Harmony's dimpled cheek. "And quite possibly just as many from your doting pater."

Clasping VJ's cheeks, Harmony smacked her lips against VJ's. "I wub new Mummie."

"I love you too, my darling poppet." VJ glanced at Holt. His tears were gone, but his body trembled against hers. Death had claimed Hanna today, but VJ had never felt so loved.

# Meet Peggy P. Parsons

Peggy worked as a secretary, an office manager and eventually owned her own consulting business. She has always had stories in her head and wrote her first full length novel when she lived in Croydon, England with her husband who was seconded to the U.K. Back in the U.S. she joined RWA and learned how to cut and edit. She retired from the business world and golfed, taught friends to play mahjong, and joined a dance club. A current member and former President of the Sun City Poms, she enjoys dancing, marching and practicing (four hours three times/week). During the last year the Poms performed in 70 events, including shows at retirement centers, charity events, high school assemblies/pep rallies, and marching in parades. She loves writing fantasy romance and hopes everyone has a little bit of magic and a lot of love in their lives.

# Other Works From The Pen Of
## Peggy P. Parsons

***Glimpse of Eternity*** – Transported back to the 1850's, Kacy meets the man she has loved and lost in other lives, but he refuses to believe the preposterous tales she spins.

***Glimpse of Forever*** – Hurtled back in time by an evil wizard, Jennifer meets her deceased husband only to face losing him again.

***Glimpse of Never-Ending Love*** – After traveling to the future, a stalker threatens Catharine, forcing her to turn to Tyler for help, but old fears make it difficult to trust him.

***One Stolen Night*** – Having broken up with her high school sweetheart, Pamela Tate follows her dream of attending the University of Hawaii where she meets the legendary Robin who steals more than her bruised heart.

***Yours Till Niagara Falls*** – Embarrassed by her attempts to warn Jade about a conniving college classmate, Kia flees to her beloved camp in the Adirondacks to mourn the recent loss of her family. When Jade shows up uninvited, she agrees to let him stay. She's attracted and wants to trust him, but his association with an unscrupulous man makes her wonder if he might be there for a sinister reason.

***Paper Marriage*** – Having grown up as next door neighbors in Provo, Utah, Analyn and Chandler were once best friends. Although he's now a cynic and claims he doesn't believe in love, he insists on marrying her temporarily to protect her from another man. Analyn fights her love, unaware that Chandler's secret is the reason he claims he'll never love her.

***Yesterday's Secrets*** – Running away to escape her cruel stepmother, Janlou embarks on a bus journey from east to west. Along the way she meets Kree, who asks her to be his pretend fiancee. When she discovers her father and stepmother have been charged with her murder, Kree returns with her to prove she's still alive. At the courthouse she meets her real family who announce she was kidnapped when she was very young.

***Apitcote, Book One – The Supplementals*** - After healing Drew when he falls over a cliff, Rene goes home. Returning to the surface a few years later, she loses her memories. She finds work at his law firm but doesn't remember him. Determined not to let her disappear again, Drew convinces her to move in with him. When her parents show up, they travel to Apitcote, where Drew discovers Rene is expected to help save her homeland. He shuts her out, convinced she will leave him. When she does, Drew embarks on an adventure that changes his life in unusual ways.

***Apitcote, Book Two – The Conjurer*** – Juhree trusts her instincts to find her way through dark tunnels to deliver Jilly's ashes to her homeland beneath the surface of the earth. When the Supplementals welcome Juhree and her magic, she feels she has found the place where she belongs. She falls in love, but to her dismay Jilly's spirit terrorizes her and Apitcote–her objective is to take over Juhree's body, steal her magic, the man she loves, and rule Apitcote.

# Dear reader,

I hope you've enjoyed reading this tale of a wondrous place where everyone lives in peace and harmony... well, almost.

Your opinion is valuable to other readers like you, who may be looking for books like mine.

Please consider taking a few minutes to post a review, however brief, on the site where you purchased this book on the Wings ePress web page.

You may also want to visit my author page at the Wings' website where you can find the rest of the books I've written as well as the others in the Apitcote series.

Thank you!

Peggy P. Parsons

# Visit Our Website

*For The Full Inventory*
*Of Quality Books:*

### **<u>Wings ePress, Inc</u>**

*Quality trade paperbacks and downloads*
*in multiple formats,*
*in genres ranging from light romantic comedy to general*
*fiction and horror.*
*Wings has something for every reader's taste.*
*Visit the website, then bookmark it.*
**We add new titles each month!**

*Wings ePress, Inc.*
*3000 N. Rock Road*
*Newton, KS 67114*